As a journalist, historian and documerthon has long been fascinated by the secrecies, deceits and ambitions of the state. His previous books are *Allies at War* and *Warlords* (with Joanna Potts). *Woman of State* is his first novel.

WOMAN
OF
STATE

SIMON BERTHON

ONE PLACE. MANY STORIES

This novel is entirely a work of fiction. The names, characters and incidents portrayed in it are the work of the author's imagination. Any resemblance to actual persons, living or dead, events or localities is entirely coincidental.

HQ
An imprint of HarperCollinsPublishers Ltd.
1 London Bridge Street
London SE1 9GF

This edition 2017

1
First published in Great Britain by
HQ, an imprint of HarperCollinsPublishers Ltd. 2017

ISBN: HB: 978-000821436-4
TPB: 978-000821437-1

Printed and bound by
CPI Group (UK) Ltd, Croydon, CR0 4YY

Our policy is to use papers that are natural, renewable and recyclable products and made from wood grown in sustainable forests. The logging and manufacturing processes conform to the legal environmental regulations of the country of origin.

For Penelope,
and for Helena and Olivia

CHAPTER 1

July 1991

'The movement needs your help.' She's lying next to him in Falls Park, the summer of 1991. A-levels are over, the sun shines, university beckons. A scholarship at Trinity College, Dublin, is in the offing and, in the case of clever Maire Anne McCartney, the teachers are confident.

'Whaddya mean, Joseph?' she asks, propping herself on an elbow and looking down into his eyes.

'You're committed, aren't you,' he says. It's a statement – a confirmation – not a question.

'Course,' she replies. 'Politically, anyway. Freedom, equality.'

'Politics won't get us there. It's the struggle that matters.'

'I'd never stand in your way, Joseph, you know that. It's just not the way for me.' She leans down and gives him a peck on the forehead.

The brightness of the day illuminates him, the chiselled chin, full lips, straight nose, the sparkle in his azure eyes. She expects him to put his arms round her, pull her on to him and roll in the grass till they laugh themselves to a halt. Last night they made love three times; she can still feel him inside her.

He turns away, avoiding her. She detects a tightening in his eyes, a clenching of the cheeks she's never quite seen before.

'You know I love you, don't you, Maire?'

'Course I do. And I love you too, Joseph. Don't I always say it?'

'You do. But just this once I need you too,' he says, turning back to her. 'I mean the movement needs you.'

A quiver of alarm. 'I dunno what you mean.' He shifts away again. 'You better tell me,' she urges.

His eyes swivel and engage hers with a ferocious intensity. 'There's a Brit peeler over here – name of Halliburton – Special Branch. On some kind of loan. We've been tracking him. He gets lonely at night, drinks in the Europa, eyes up the bar girls. But doesn't follow through. Around eleven, he's in his car, heading back to Castlereagh. They're either housing him in the station or somewhere near; we're not sure. We wanna speak with him.'

'Speak with him, Joseph? Whaddya mean, speak with him?'

'Interrogate him. Find out what he's doing. Get some intelligence.'

'And then what? When you've interrogated him.'

'Just scare him. Let him know we're onto him. Suggest it's time he leaves.'

'What'd be the point of that?'

'Propaganda. How we ran a Brit SB man out of our island. It'll read well.'

'And that's all?'

'Aye, that's all.'

She rolls over and sits up straight – he raises himself alongside her.

'Does Martin know 'bout this?' she asks.

'Course he knows.'

'And 'bout you speaking to me.'

'He would, wouldn't he? But it couldn't come from him, could it? Not brother to sister. Wouldn't be right.'

'But he knows.'

'Well, he would.'

She stands up, the warmth of the sun heating her back through her light-red jumper. It's not enough in itself to create the sweat that's prickling her. He springs up and ranges alongside.

'We just need you to attract him. Your quick wits, quick tongue, it'll be easy. Just a chat-up in the bar, you're a student wanting a free drink. You take him to a flat. We got one ready in the university area.'

He outlines the plan. All she's doing is picking up a bloke over a drink. Happens every night, hundreds of times over. She's listening hard – he cranks it up. 'Look, Maire, there are moments when you can't just stand by and look on. Be a passive observer. At some point, everyone has to do their bit. Look at the leadership now, the politicians. Do you think all they ever did was talk?'

'I've just finished A-levels, Joseph.' Her first instinct is to repel him but right now, at this moment, she doesn't want to show weakness that could invite his disapproval.

'Aye, you've done well. But you're eighteen now, grown up. An adult. You've responsibilities.'

'What about responsibilities to myself?'

'That's just selfishness. It's not just the struggle, it's your friends, your family, your community.'

She halts abruptly. Divis mountain ahead, so often a dour, brooding darkness, seems almost radiant, a mass of green light.

'I've never got involved in that way.'

'Aye, but this isn't like that.'

'You promise me it's just to interrogate him?'

'Aye.'

'No violence. No beating. Just propaganda. Just to show you can do it.'

'Aye.'

'I need to hear you promise me, Joseph.'

'That's fine. I promise.'

'You give me your word.'

'Aye.'

'And Martin approves?'

'Aye, he would, that's for sure. No doubt 'bout that.'

She thinks in silence. She remembers the hunger strikers dying when she's still a girl and the hatred for the British oppressor. Three years later, she shares her big brother's pleasure when the IRA blows up Mrs Thatcher's hotel in Brighton. She knows the cause is just but, for her, school, good results, getting to university become the priority. The British state is still hateful, but her belief in the 'armed struggle' deflates like a slow puncture.

Yet Joseph has touched a nerve, a lightning rod brushed by lingering guilt. Maybe he's right and she's been selfish. She copped out when others didn't. If what they're planning is for propaganda, not violence, perhaps it's just another act of cowardice to keep on avoiding it.

She flicks a glance at him. What if he's lying? Just talking shite? When did they last let a peeler walk free? She looks away. He's never lied to her before. Not that she knows, anyway.

Momentarily, a cloud obscures the sun, turning the mountain-side an unyielding brown. He's saying nothing, the quiet oppresses her. Time seems to freeze – the flapping of a bird's wing high above reduced to the slowest of motions.

His expression has retreated to that beautiful poet's dolefulness when she's about to disappoint him. Like those early months after the first full kiss when she wouldn't go the whole way. Until she did. If she says no to this plea – a plea he's made with such passion – will he ever forgive her? Might she even lose him? She thinks of asking – but doesn't want to hear his answer.

She turns. It's visceral – she just can't displease him. 'OK, I'll do it. Just this once. For you.' It's as if the words have tumbled out of her mouth before she even made a decision. A sudden consolation – maybe she'll still be able to get out of it. She chides herself for even thinking it. Her rational self re-engages. 'And there'll be no violence?'

'Yes, there'll be no violence.'

She's told her mother she'll be in for tea that evening. Rosa has cooked cottage pie and peas, one of Maire's favourite dishes. She plays with her food, even forgetting to splash it with ketchup, and speaks little.

'What's up with you, Maire?' asks Rosa.

'Aye, girl, you need to eat,' chips in her father. Rosa casts him a warning glare to keep out of it.

'Sorry, Mum,' she says. 'Just not feeling hungry. Dunno why.'

Rosa, who's come to realize that Maire must be sleeping regularly with Joseph, betrays a sudden alarm. 'Not feeling sick, are you, love?'

Maire looks up with a wan smile. 'It's OK, Mum, I'm not feeling sick.'

'Well that's all right, then, love.' At any other time, Maire would hug her mother out of sheer love for her maternal priorities. On this evening she feels only emptiness in the pit of her stomach.

As they're clearing plates, the front door clangs opens and Martin breezes in, bestowing smiles and kisses all round. Maire suddenly wonders what her parents think of him; whether they even know his prominence in the movement. Politics in general are sometimes discussed at home, but the rights and wrongs of violence are no-go. It's only, and infrequently, mentioned when she's alone with her brother. They must suspect – they'd be blind not to – but have decided it's best to keep out.

'Hey, little sister, you're looking gorgeous as ever,' Martin declares, not a care in the world.

Maire attempts a show of response but recoils. Surely he must know about Joseph's conversation with her today and her acquiescence. She wonders at his bravado, and the masking of his double life as happy-go-lucky son and IRA commander.

He notices her listlessness. 'What's up, kid?' How can he even contemplate such a question? She searches for a hint.

'It's nothing,' she says, 'just a chat I was having with Joseph.'

'So how's the world's greatest revolutionary doing?' There's an edge of condescension in her brother's tone. Again she flinches at his duplicitousness.

'Full of schemes, as always,' she replies.

'Aye, that he is,' says Martin. 'That he certainly is.'

He's giving her nothing. Literally nothing. No comfort, no support, not a hint of empathy. Perhaps that's the way it has to be.

They decide to try it the next Saturday night. More people milling, more cover, guards more likely to be down.

She prepares. She's cut her hair, taking three inches off the long auburn tresses, and used straighteners to remove the waves and curls. Instead of the hint of side parting, she brushes the hairs straight back, revealing the fullness of her face and half-moon of her forehead. She examines the slight kink in her small, roman-shaped nose. As always, she dislikes it. She applies mauve mascara and brighter, thicker lipstick to her cupid lips. She wears a black leather skirt, above the knee but not blatantly short, and a bright-pink, buttoned blouse that doesn't quite meet it in the middle. The gap exposes a minuscule fold of belly. She pinches the flesh angrily. Through the blouse, a skimpy black lace-patterned bra, exposing the top of her firm small breasts, is visible. The overall effect is not a disguise, just a redesign. While it doesn't make her look cheap or a tart, she's unmistakably a girl out for a good time.

She's steeled herself, told herself it's just a job. Clock on, clock off three hours later. Thoughts of how to pull out have besieged her every minute since she said yes – even though she instantly knew she couldn't. But once she's done it, that'll be it. Never again.

She's kidding herself. Once you're in, they've a hold over you – you're complicit. She thinks of her brother – did he recruit Joseph? How did they get their hold over him? She remembers that tightness in his face. Did they ever need to?

She arrives just after 8.30 p.m.

As agreed, she finds a bar table with two chairs, sits down and appears to be waiting for her date to arrive. A waiter comes – she orders a vodka and Coke.

He's already there, sitting at the bar. The description, both of him and his clothing, is accurate. Late thirties, sandy hair retreating at the sides, a ten pence sized bald spot on top covered by straggles of hair that offer an easy mark of recognition from the rear. On the way in, she's been able to catch more; the beginnings of a potbelly edging over fawn-belted, light-brown trousers. Brown loafers and light coloured socks, dark-brown leather jacket. Perhaps the brown is an off-duty discard of the policeman's blue. On his upper lip, a pale, neatly trimmed moustache. Brown-rimmed, narrow spectacles sitting on the bridge of a hook nose. Somewhat incongruously, pale blue eyes. From those first glimpses, he seems a nicer-looking man than she expected. A relief, given one part of the task that lies ahead. But ugliness becomes a victim more easily.

They say he usually drinks one or two before chatting up the bar girls and waitresses. Around 9.15, when she's been waiting three-quarters of an hour for her elusive date to arrive, she walks towards the bar. She places herself beside him.

'Another vodka and Coke,' she demands, louder than necessary.

He turns to her with a raise of the eyebrows.

'Bastard hasn't shown,' she says, glaring at him as if to say, 'Whaddya want?'

'He's a fool.' He eyes her with frank admiration. The accent is English, south not north. A confirmation.

'I'm the eejit,' she says. Her drink arrives and she makes to return to her seat.

'You might as well stay and chat till he comes. I'll pull that stool over.'

She hesitates. It seems too easy. What's this man really like? From nowhere she imagines him hitting her. Where did that come from? Nerves, just nerves. Her heartbeat is racing. She gathers herself. 'I left my coat at the table.'

'It's OK, I'll keep an eye on it.' He chuckles. 'I'm good at that.' His remark startles her. She hopes she's not shown it. 'So who's the missing boyfriend?' he continues.

'Ex-boyfriend. Bastard,' she repeats. Is she overdoing it? She senses how miscast she is for this performance. She's a quiet student who should be buried in her books. Some even say she's gawky. Suddenly she sees that's maybe why Joseph's picked her. The copper will never suspect.

He shrugs and sips from his glass. Scotch and ice, must have been at least a double. 'Men,' he says. 'Can't trust them. Just like criminals and politicians. No wonder *they're* usually men, too.'

'Thatcher?' she says.

'Thought you girls said she was a man, too. Anyway, they got rid of her. Assassins all men.'

She makes herself laugh. He raises his glass; she raises hers and clinks.

'Cheers,' they chime together, grinning at each other.

'Bet they were glad round here when she was dumped,' he says.

'Aye, they banged the dustbin lids.'

He pauses for another sip. 'Sorry, should have introduced myself. Name's Peter.' The final confirmation.

'Annie.' Unless he's lying, like her.

'So whose side are you on, Annie?'

'My side. Fuck 'em all.' He frowns. 'Sorry, I should mind my tongue.' She sticks it out at him like a rude child. What came over her to do that? The job's become an act, two more hours on stage before the curtain falls.

His grin widens. 'I like your tongue. Agree with it, too.'

He's flirting hard now. Another pause. She doesn't want to seem like she's making the running. Eventually, he resumes. 'OK, I'll try another tack. What do you do, Annie?'

'Studying. Queen's. Just finished first year. I'd like to travel but I don't have money.'

'Can't you get a job?'

'A job here! In Belfast! You find me one.' A further silence. This time she feels safe to have her turn. 'And youse?'

The hesitation is just perceptible. 'My company's sent me over for four months. We're investigating setting up an office. The grants are good.'

'Whaddya do?'

He's thinking. 'Financial advice. Investment. All that stuff.'

'So you're rich!'

'That'll be the day.' He peers down at his glass.

She feels sweat on her neck and between her breasts. She moves her right hand to her left wrist to check her pulse.

He notices. 'Are you OK?'

'Yeah, just the heat.' She smiles. She can't take the tension much longer, not knowing if he'll bite. Maybe he's sussed something – but he hasn't come with his own prepared story, she's sure of that. She needs her moment of truth right now. She looks at her watch, finishes her drink and finds the line to close Act One. 'Bastard still hasn't shown,' she says angrily. 'Suppose I'd better be heading.'

His head jerks up and round. 'Don't do that, I'll buy you another.'

He's bitten. She inspects him, to make him feel he's undergoing an examination, to ratchet up his gratitude if she accepts. 'I probably shouldn't,' she says. 'I dunno you, do I?'

'I'm harmless as a butterfly.' His eyes plead with her. He's on the hook.

'OK, then, might as well get pissed. Nothing else to do, is there?'

'You're the local,' he says. 'I was hoping you might have something in mind.' It's his first openly suggestive remark and it's taken time. He's a cautious man, but now he orders a double vodka and Coke for her, and a double Scotch for himself.

They drink and chitchat, nothing personal or controversial, but a mutual hunger in the eyes. Occasionally she flashes a look around the room. 'Just in case the bastard's skulking,' she tells him. In a corner of the bar she spies a man she's seen with Joseph once or twice. He's always peeled off as soon as she arrives, back into his undergrowth. But not tonight. The exit door is jammed shut.

Just before 10.30, an alarm sounds, abrupt and deafening. A voice booms over the Tannoy. 'Ladies and gentlemen, we have a bomb scare. Please evacuate the building now.' The warning words are repeated every five seconds. They're on cue.

'I'll grab my coat,' she says.

'I'll wait for you,' he replies.

They walk out into Great Victoria Street to join the hundreds retreating behind the barricades. Bomb warnings are no longer scary – the age of nightly explosions and shootings has long gone. Now it's a meaner war. Individual murder, assassinations, suspected informers tortured and ending up with a bullet through the knees or head. A few weeks ago three IRA men were ambushed on a country lane and shot dead by the SAS. That had to come from a grass. She remembers it – no wonder Joseph, her brother and friends want an intelligence propaganda victory. Maybe what she's doing is OK.

She sets off south and he sticks to her limpet-like. Once they reach the other side of the yellow tapes, they stop to catch their breath. Sirens and shouts echo, nothing more.

'Bastards,' he says, 'why did they have to break that up? I was enjoying myself.'

'Me too,' she agrees. 'Fucking eejits.' She pauses. 'Well, I suppose this is it, my flat's not far. Better be away.' She's nearing the end of the second Act – moment of truth number two. She looks at him. 'And you should be, too,' she says cheekily.

'We shouldn't let them get away with it,' he says. 'Busting up the evening like that.' He takes a breath and exhales into the night air. 'Can I get you another drink?'

'Reckon I've had plenty,' she says.

'Coffee, then?' he pleads.

'Honest, I should be heading.'

'OK, coffee in your flat. And then I go home.'

She laughs at him. 'You don't give up, do you?'

'You make it hard to,' he says.

'OK, coffee in the flat.' Hook, line and sinker. She pounces, giving him a quick kiss on the lips. She feels him relax with pleasure and anticipation as they head towards Botanic and he puts his arm round her. Act Three is about to begin.

They've taken a short lease on a first-floor student flat in a street of Victorian terraces. She's been driven past it once – she wanted a second look but they said it was too risky. There's a Yale lock above and a mortice below – they've told her the mortice will be left unlocked to make it easier for her. They should be in position by now. While she and the man walk, she tries not to search for their car and them waiting inside. The street lamp is opposite the front door, illuminating the house number. She unlocks the Yale and pushes the door open.

'Don't you double-lock?' he says. He's drunk plenty but he's still a policeman.

'No petty crime in this town,' she replies without a beat. She thanks heaven her brain's quick enough to disarm him.

She switches on the stair light and leads him up. With the university on holiday, both the ground- and upper-floor flats are empty. At the top of the landing, she slots a second key into a bare wooden door and ushers him in. She's learnt the floor plan, memorizing rooms, doors, furniture, cupboard contents, electrical appliances. They'd better have got it right. She'd better have remembered it right.

'Sorry, it's a bit dire,' she says. 'My flatmates are away for the vac but I didn't wanna be trapped at home with my ma and da.' She pauses, feigning embarrassment. 'It means I'm sort of camping in the bedroom.' She nods towards the room at the back. 'TV's there if you want. I'll make coffee. Oh, bathroom's there.'

'Thanks,' he says. 'I could do with it.'

She puts on the kettle. When it begins whistling, she creeps to the front door and peers out. They're there. She puts the palms of both hands to the window, fingers and thumbs splayed out. Ten minutes. Ten minutes till the play ends and the job's done. She wants it over.

She's back in the kitchen just as he pulls the plug. She hears sounds of hand washing and face scrubbing. He's preparing, cleaning himself for her. More washing sounds. She imagines him taking out his penis and soaping it in the basin. The nerves have been there all night. Now there's a charge of fear.

He leaves the bathroom, turns into the narrow passage and stops by her in the kitchen. She's pouring coffee into cups. He comes behind her and puts his arms round her, moving down to the roll of her waist and round to her buttocks. She leans back against him.

'Look what I found,' she says. She picks up the dusty, half-drunk bottle of Teacher's that's been placed beside the coffee and tea jars.

'Scotch, not Irish,' he leers, 'must be my lucky night. She puts her left hand behind her, pats his buttock, then moves it around past his crotch. He's erect. She can feel the evening's drinks rising in her throat.

'You carry the Scotch and glasses,' she orders.

They retreat to the bedroom and she waits to see where he puts himself. He takes off his shoes; she follows suit. There's a double bed and double duvet, but cushions on one side only.

'Here looks comfortable,' he says, stretching out on the bed. 'And I can see the telly.'

'Is that what you've come for?' she asks, flashing her most alluring smile.

'And the coffee.' She pours two cups and brings him one. Then she pours Scotch into a tumbler and places it beside him. He puts his arms around her to draw her towards him.

'Not yet.' This is the moment she knows might come but can never fully prepare for. Joseph has suggested what to do if it gets this far – he says he knows what a man really likes. And it will incapacitate him, protecting her and making it easier for the boys after she's left. She doesn't even want to think about that.

Again she tells herself it's just a play – and she's just this evening's performer. She forces herself. 'Close your eyes,' she whispers in his ear. She walks round to the front of the bed and strokes him from the toes up. Through ankles, calves, knees, hamstrings, fingers moving up to the front of the waist. There they stop, unbuckle the belt, and slowly slide down the zip fastener. His eyes remain closed, though he's breathing faster and emitting soft murmurs. She pulls his trousers from beneath him and slips his pants down. The pants' elastic waist reaches down to his tip – as it passes over, he bursts out and upright, swollen to a size she hasn't seen on Joseph.

'My word,' she gasps. He opens his eyes, looks beyond his chest and stomach at her mouth level with the engorged tip. She gives it a short touch. He murmurs again. She feels burning in her throat. She mustn't retch.

'I just need to go the bathroom,' she says, 'make myself ready.'

'I can't wait,' he whispers.

'Course you can wait. Willpower. I wanna make it fun.'

'Oh, sweet Jesus,' he sighs.

She closes the bedroom door behind her, goes to the bathroom and runs a tap. She re-emerges and creeps towards the front window. With her left hand she forms a zero with her thumb and forefinger and holds it against the glass. With her right hand she waves inwards. She re-enters the bathroom, stops the tap and pulls the flush. Both the flush itself and the refill are inefficiently noisy, an unexpected bonus.

Against their background sounds, she edges on her toes to the flat's entrance, praying no floorboard creaks, and descends the stairs to the front door. As she opens it, they allow her to leave before they enter. Four of them, masked. She has a pang of sadness for the man she's left behind and the ordeal he faces, then walks, increasing her pace with each step. The pavement is dry and smooth. It's just as well as she's been unable to retrieve her shoes. Joseph and his friends will tidy up. At least she's wearing stockings.

She hurries past Botanic station, and over the roundabout into Great Victoria Street. Ahead the barricades are still up and no one is being allowed near the Europa. She stops; the fire in her throat rises. She runs to some railings, leans over, and retches. A tiny stream of bile, nothing more. It's not nerves – or guilt – that's brought it up, just the memory of touching him.

She straightens, skirts the crowd, turning right, then left towards the city centre. It's still only 11.30 p.m., a single, eternal hour since they left the bar. Now she can lose herself in the late-night revellers and make her way to the black taxis heading for Andersonstown. A girl who's had too good a night out and somehow managed to lose her shoes in the process.

Her heartbeat quietens. They may have made her complicit but, should they ever try again, she knows she won't do it, whatever the consequences. It may be their life, it's not going to be hers.

The curtain falls.

It's over.

CHAPTER 2

The next day, Sunday, she stays at home in her room.

'Coming to Mass, Maire?' her mother yells up.

She peers down from the landing and addresses the bottom of the stairs. 'Sorry, Ma, still a bit off colour. You and Da go on.' She wonders why they persist.

She spends the day in her room with the local radio on. All is quiet and she feels an overwhelming relief. By evening she decides she's calm enough to appear for tea. She comes downstairs, where her father's watching the six o'clock television news in the living room.

'Jeez, Maire, have a look at this.'

The screen shows the taped-off street, and the flashing lamps of police cars and an ambulance beyond. Nausea rises, this time from her midriff. She's missed the newsreader's introduction and a local reporter is taking up the story. 'It seems the male victim was lured to this flat off Botanic Avenue and then set upon by attackers waiting inside. It appears that some sort of fight may have broken out, during which the man was shot dead. It's not known at this point who the victim was or whether the attack was a purely criminal one or had a political or paramilitary connection.'

'What the hell was going on there?' Stephen exclaims. The news gives way to the Sunday sporting action and he buries himself in the newspaper. Another day, another shooting.

She wants to retreat to her room but forces herself to stay with her da until the end of the weather forecast. She looks into the kitchen. The smells of cooking repel her.

'Sorry, Ma, still off the food. Must be a bug or something I ate.'

Rosa watches as she goes back up the stairs. Something unusual is going on with her daughter but she knows better than to press. It will all come out in due course, or just go away.

Maire wants to go out, to run for miles, to lose herself in exhaustion. Anything to stop thoughts. But the summer nights are short and she's afraid of the daylight. By 10 p.m. she can stand it no longer and leaves the house without a goodbye or see you later. 'Must be something to do with Joseph,' Rosa mutters to Stephen.

She paces the streets for an hour, taking deep breaths, willing herself to restore the calm she's now lost. Did they, or rather Joseph, deceive her and always intend to kill? Perhaps the policeman was carrying a gun – though, if he was, he kept it well hidden – and managed to grab it as they entered. But she heard no shots as she walked away. It surely means they must have taken control of him.

Joseph gave her his word. He used the word 'promise'. Was it a lie? Or was *he* lied to? She has a horrible vision of her brother as the mastermind. Surely that can't be. More than betrayal, what she now feels is a sickening combination of terror and her own foolishness – the knowledge that she allowed herself to be deceived. She clings on to the hope that something went wrong in the flat – that he brought his death upon himself. That, in some sense, he deserved it. She wonders who will miss him and tries to banish the thought.

Without planning it, she finds herself near Joseph's street – he still lives with his family and they've used a friend's place to sleep together. Unable to stop herself, she approaches the house. At the last minute she delays, watching for movement through any gaps in the curtains. She sees none, but some ground-floor lights are still on and she rings the bell.

Joseph's mother answers. 'Maire, you're looking in late.'

'Sorry, Mrs Kennedy.'

'It's OK, love, come in.'

'I was just looking for Joseph.'

'Haven't seen him today, love. You know how it is with him. Always in and out.'

'OK, Mrs Kennedy, never mind. Thanks anyway. I'd better be away.'

The next day is worse. Silence. Alone. She's been hung out to dry. She tells herself again that this is what it must be like. Despite the falseness she feels ever surer of, she craves to see Joseph. Perhaps he really does have an explanation and it can still be all right between them. She listens out for Martin's footsteps and one of his cheery entrances into the house. It doesn't matter what's said, she simply needs someone who knows to talk to.

At lunchtime, the noose tightens. 'The victim was Inspector Peter Halliburton, who was on secondment to local police from London's Metropolitan Police Special Branch. Mr Halliburton, aged thirty-six, was married and had two children of six and eight. There has still been no claim of responsibility for his killing,' announces the radio news.

She thinks of him lying on the bed, his zip undone, his penis bared, a young man, husband, father, in the dying moments of his short life. She tries to justify it. He shouldn't have come with her. He betrayed his marriage and those children. He was a representative of the occupying forces. The words and excuses taste of sulphur.

Her one good fortune is that on Monday both her parents are out and she can stay in her room without need for explanations. In the late afternoon, shortly before her mother is due home, she goes out, propelled once again by some automatic, subconscious navigation in the direction of Joseph's home. She steels herself to ring the bell. No answer. She knocks on the door. No answer. She backs away to look up at the first floor. The curtains in Joseph's room are drawn. Either he's still away or deliberately avoiding her. The question jumps at her. Could they have arrested him? Are they holding him, forcing him to implicate her? Surely his mother would have known. Surely Joseph is too smart.

Early the next morning, 5.45, it happens. A violent beating on the front door, the sound of her father descending the stairs to answer it. She peeps behind a curtain of her bedroom window to see two armed police jeeps to the right and left and a police saloon, its roof light silently revolving. She hardly has time to take it in before two uniformed police enter her room with neither words nor knocking.

'Get dressed,' says one.

The second speaks more formally.

'Maire McCartney?'

'Yes.' She tells herself to resist the tears.

'I have a warrant to arrest you on a charge of conspiracy to murder Peter Halliburton on the night of Saturday the twenty-third of July. You have the right to stay silent. Anything you say can and will be used against you in a court of law . . .'

Even as she dresses herself, and they pull her hands in front of her to apply handcuffs, it's as if it were happening to another person. It belongs to a parallel universe. The person she really is could never have degraded herself to this.

The walk down the stairs and out of the front door freezes her into self-loathing. Her mother and father watch, their eyes aflame with humiliation. She's unable to speak, only to shake her head. Once inside the police car, she lacerates herself for being too weak to leave them words of hope.

They take her to Castlereagh, a journey that is a badge of honour for anger-fuelled young men, a spiral into blackness for her. How do they know it was she? They must have soon worked out that the victim had been lured. Were her shoes still in the room, showing that a woman took him there? Could Joseph and friends have been so careless? Did they suspect Joseph and make the connection to her? Perhaps they're just operating on that hunch and have no hard evidence.

She slumps in a cell for hours, allowed only to brush her teeth and visit the toilet. She's escorted to a bleak room where a woman in a white coat takes her fingerprints and a swab from her throat. She's brought food but her sense of time begins to fade. All she knows is that, when she's taken to an interview room, occasional shafts of light show that it is not yet night.

Two men in suits arrive, a recording machine is switched on. They introduce themselves but she doesn't catch their names. Again, she feels distant and disconnected. Her real self is floating on the ceiling above, looking disdainfully at the grotesque spectacle beneath.

'We know you were with him,' they say.

'I've nothing to say,' she says. It's all she says that evening, again and again. At least Joseph told her to do that if anything went wrong.

'Your brother's a Provo, your boyfriend's a Provo. You were with him in that bedroom. You leave, a few minutes later he's shot dead by a gang of your friends. You're going down, Maire. You've ruined your life, your career, dishonoured your ma and da. Think about it as the long night passes.'

As they foresaw, darkness brings change. The unreality, the distancing recedes. She's in a black tunnel with no light at the end. She knows she must not allow desperation to block her thoughts, but it's hard to not keep seeing the puzzled, frightened expressions of her ma and da as she was led away. The hopes they had for her, the trust in their golden girl – all blown apart. Whatever happens now, there will always be a before and an after in her life.

She needs a life raft, a narrative that gives her a chance of survival. She tries to peer into that night from the other end of a telescope. To live it from his point of view. To imagine that he's not a foolish man, but a bad man. Or a man made bad by alcohol and opportunity. She doesn't like forcing her mind to work it through – but this is no time to be nice.

The next morning, she asks for a solicitor. They tell her all in good time. She tries to insist on her rights, they ignore her. Perhaps her request accelerates their reappearance for she's back in the interview room within twenty minutes of making it. Their tone has hardened.

'You've no way out, Maire,' says the first man.

'Your fingerprints are all over the room,' says the second.

'Christ, there's even your saliva in his pubic hair.'

'You filthy little slut, Maire. You really want that to come up in court? You want your ma and da to hear you were sucking the dick of some poor bastard you were setting up to be shot?'

She's ready for them. 'You've nothing. Sure I was with him.

Sure he "picked me up". Not me, him. Sure he insisted on coming home with me. But he was drunk, became violent. He was trying to rape me, so I ran. What the hell would you have done?'

'Just at the very moment your good friend Joseph and his mates happen to arrive to murder him. What a coincidence, Maire. What a fluke of timing.'

'I dunno anything 'bout that. You've no evidence to say that. I was in a bar, he picked me up. I was fool enough to go with him.' Even if she's not kidding herself, maybe she can somehow dent their certainty. She forces on, trying to convey confidence not desperation. 'That's my only crime. Maybe there was some eejits following him. So what? Nothing to do with me. He's a bad man who tried to attack me. Look at the size of me – what chance would I have had? Now I wanna solicitor.'

'You can have a solicitor, Maire. Won't do you any good. There's only one way out. You tell us everything you know about Joseph Kennedy and his friends – it's OK, it'll just be between youse and us, no one else'll ever know – and maybe we'll cut you some slack.'

'It's your life, Maire. Your future. Think about it,' says the second man. They leave the room and she is escorted back to her cell, the barred door clanging shut behind her, the bare walls closing in on her life.

Later that day, she sees a solicitor and offers the same account she's given her interrogators. They were right; the solicitor tells her the evidence, the coincidence of timing are stacked against her. The rape allegation gives her a chance, but only a small one. She's come up with it late and there's not even any bruising.

Maire knows only one thing for certain. It looks like they don't have anything on Joseph. If she grasses – tells them Joseph did it – and his friends find out, she's dead. There's no greater sin than to turn informer. Not even Martin could save her – probably wouldn't even want to. The story always has the same ending. A lonely grave in some anonymous damp patch of field.

The next day, another spell in the interview room, this time with her solicitor present. Her interrogators arrive together and say nothing. Instead they produce a pair of shoes from a bag, the shoes she wore on the night, and hand them to her.

'We've cleaned them for you, Maire,' says one. 'You can have them back after the trial if your prison governor allows it.'

'Careless of your friends to leave them behind,' says the other. They walk out with a mocking grin.

'Might be best to own up, Maire,' says the solicitor later. 'Say you knew nothing about the plan to kill him. We'd go for aiding and abetting an abduction. You might get away with five years. You'd only serve half.'

Her third night in the cell is the worst. All exits are closed and it seems a one-way street to conviction and branding as a criminal. If she confesses, the full dirtiness of what she's done need not be revealed. Her ma and da can be spared that shame. After more than two decades of the 'war', her community will understand her getting caught up in it. Though what a pity, they'll say, that clever little Maire McCartney, with the whole world at her fingertips, chose to spoil everything.

What if there's not even that deal without their piece of flesh? Everything she knows about Joseph. The names of his friends. She feels a shiver of terror.

By the night's end, she's come to one conclusion. She's not a committed warrior willing to spend a lifetime in prison for the 'cause'. She doesn't know where it will lead – but it's time to negotiate and see what cards she's got left to play.

A woman police officer arrives with breakfast.

'I've been thinking,' says Maire. 'I wanna speak to my solicitor.'

'That won't be necessary,' says the woman.

'Whaddya mean? I've made a decision. I need to see her.'

'No, you don't. You're leaving.'

'What?'

'I said you're leaving. Seems like you're a lucky girl.'

'You joking? That's bad taste . . .'

'It's not a joke, Maire. Pack your things, your da's coming to fetch you.'

An hour later she finds herself walking past the front desk and out to the car park. It's a journey of utter unreality. Maybe it's some kind of trap. But there, in the flesh, is her da. Stephen has been allowed through the gates and security barriers and is waiting. As she nears the car, he gets out and hugs her. They drive in silence, no questions asked, no answers given. When they arrive home, it's the same, her mother waiting quietly for her.

'Welcome home, love.' It's all she says.

That evening, Martin comes for tea, the entrance as nonchalant as ever, the chitchat light and jokey. In front of her parents, no reference is made to the last three days. As they're clearing the plates, she catches Martin nodding at them. They retreat to the kitchen to wash up. He closes the door behind them.

'You'll get your scholarship at Trinity, you're that smart,' he begins. 'Working-class Catholic girl from the North – just what they need to move with the times. But you'll leave this city and head down to Dublin now. I got friends who'll put you up till we find you something permanent. Only a couple of months now. Maybe you can take some time abroad. I'll see if I can raise some money.'

'Did you know, Martin?' she asks.

'Know what?' He sounds sharp, hard even. It's unlike him.

'Joseph said you approved it. I mean using me.'

He shakes his head slowly, closing his eyes and rubbing them with his hands. 'Jesus, Maire, you should know me better. I'm not even going to discuss that.'

'Well, he said you would.'

'He said that?'

'Yes.' Her brother says nothing. 'And the plan itself? Seducing him? Shooting him?'

'Don't go there. It's past now.'

'Joseph told me it was just to interrogate him.'

'Fuck's sake, Maire, you're not that naïve.'

She wants to cry but mustn't let herself. 'I believed him, Martin. He promised. He said it was propaganda. To show they could run a Special Branch man out of town.'

'He said that?'

'Yes. Several times over.'

'OK.' He shakes his head and looks away from her. 'Look here, Maire, I'm not going to piss on Joseph. He's important in the movement. You can't expect me to do that.'

'I wanna see him. Ask him myself.'

'That won't be possible.' His eyes pierce her in that way she knows he won't be contradicted. She looks down, silent. 'You're not to see him again, Maire. There's to be no contact ever again. From you or from him.'

She feels tears welling and tries to suppress them. There's no point in arguing. Instead she asks the obvious question. 'Why did they let me go?'

'You're small fry, they've bigger fish. Maybe they didn't have enough on you. Maybe they wanna see where you'll lead them. Use you as bait against your own side. That's why you gotta leave.'

That's a reason you can never see Joseph again.' He pauses. 'Not the only one, mind.' She feels herself crushed. 'And there's another thing, Maire. Some will say they only let you go 'cos you grassed. Another reason you gotta go.'

'Jesus, Martin, you should know me better than that.' She grimaces. 'Christ, that's what you just said, isn't it?' He doesn't answer – there's nothing more to say. Her destiny, for now, is out of her hands. 'OK, when?'

'Tomorrow.'

'Tomorrow!'

'That's right. You better start packing.' Her brother grasps her shoulders and speaks with a searing passion. 'You were never meant for this, Maire. You're the lawyer. Maybe politics one day. You're the ballot, not the bullet. Never forget that.'

The next morning, her father drives her to Victoria Bus Station to catch the express coach to Dublin. She's been given an address and fifty pounds. She's never felt so alone.

A few days later, Martin visits her in Dublin. It's been arranged that she'll live with a Mrs Bridget Ryan, whose daughter, Bernadette, is serving time for possessing explosives. As a contribution to her board and lodging, Maire will help look after Bernadette's three children. The husband's no good – he was once in the movement but forced out because of his drinking. The arrangement will last the full three years of Maire's degree.

'You can call it your prison if you want,' says Martin, 'but it'll give you a better chance than the real thing. Now, you, work hard. Don't socialize. Don't look for friends. No boyfriends. Trust no one. Get your degree. And then get the fuck out of this island and make something of your life.'

As she watches him disappear, Maire begins to understand the worst of what she's done. It's not about being used, or luring a Brit peeler to his death, or shaming her parents, or losing Joseph.

It's that she made an error. A huge, life-changing, potentially life-destroying error. If she's managed to get away with it, if she's been given a second chance, she promises herself one thing.

She will never again make such an error. Not ever.

CHAPTER 3

Twenty-six years later, UK General Election night, Friday, 5 May. 2.41 a.m.

'I, the Acting Returning Officer for the constituency of Lambeth West, hereby give notice that the total number of votes given for each candidate was as follows . . .'

Anne-Marie Gallagher squinted down at an army of flashlights, TV cameras and microphones. The next five minutes would shape the next five years of her life. Yet, until one day and one conversation three months before, what now lay before her would have seemed unreachable.

'They're imploding,' cried out her head of chambers, Kieron Carnegie, flicking through the newspapers. 'Those smug idiots are imploding. Split from top to bottom.'

'There there, Kieron, we don't want you imploding too.' She spoke with a hint of Celtic tinge too polished to place.

He rounded on her. 'But it's our chance. This time, even after the last mess, we might actually get back into office.'

She observed him fondly – still, in his early sixties, a craggily attractive man with a rich voice and greying blond hair hanging down to his collar. He had a reputation as a Lothario of the law but had never tried it on with her. From the day she joined Audax, her body language had said no to affairs.

For his part, Carnegie still saw the smart, pretty, petite twenty-three-year-old with the quick brain and spiky wit who had brightened his office the moment she'd stepped into it twenty-two years earlier. The same straight, dark-brown hair that settled in a bob above the join of her neck and shoulders. The same fringe falling over her forehead like wisps of fresh grass. The elegant little nose. The small mouth and curve of her lips. The tiny gap between the whiteness of her front two teeth. The same aura of untouchability.

'I have an idea.'

'Oh?' She went on instant alert; Carnegie's ideas could be dangerous.

'I never personally wanted to enter politics.'

'You've always cultivated the party's leaders.'

'Me cultivate the leaders?' His eyebrows jumped in horror.

'Sorry, Kieron.' She grinned. 'They cultivated you.'

'I'd never have hacked it as a Member of Parliament. Don't have the discipline.' He paused. 'You do.'

She narrowed her eyes. 'I only joined the party a couple of years ago.'

'I know. But you're getting noticed. Appearances on *Newsnight* and *Today*, pieces in the *Guardian*. The go-to lawyer for comment on human rights.'

'It's nothing more than a sideshow to my work here,' she protested.

'Listen,' he said, pointing at the headlines yelling disarray at Westminster, 'there's no solution to this but an early election.'

'So?' she interrupted.

'There's going to be a vacancy in Lambeth West.'

'What do you mean? Harry Davies is the candidate there.'

'Not for much longer. Few know it but he's had a stroke. The medics have told him he's got to take it easy.'

'So?' she repeated.

'You live there. You're attractive and articulate. You have a rising profile. Put your bonnet in the ring, my dear.' He launched his most extravagant smile. 'And I will do a little moving and shaking in the background.'

For once, she did not return the smile. She felt a stirring, an echo of youthful ambition that had seemed irretrievable. 'If I were to do this, I'd enter the goldfish bowl. The media would scrutinize me, try to rake over my past, exercise their bloodlust.'

'Are you afraid of that?'

For a woman so quick on her feet, it took a split second longer than usual to find a response. 'The only thing we have to fear is fear itself,' she quoted.

'Franklin Delano Roosevelt, inauguration speech, March 1933.'

'Yes.'

'Then that's your answer, isn't it?'

Carnegie's forecast was accurate. The government moved from bickering to in-fighting to self-destruction. No alternative could be formed to command a majority. The only way out was an immediate General Election. There was a vacancy at Lambeth West.

Anne-Marie cross-examined herself, both present and past. Since her reinvention after Dublin and entry into a different world, she had not come face to face with anyone who remembered her. Standing as an MP would expose her but, in a national election, an unknown first-timer would attract only local attention. In any case, there had been no shame in adopting her new life. The circumstances could even win her sympathy. Which left the two jeopardies. The knowledge of the dead and disappeared had vanished with them. The chance of any credible, living witness emerging this many years later was too remote to stand in her way. She could not always hide from risk.

'OK,' she told Carnegie. 'I'll give it a go. But don't you forget it's your fault.'

The first hurdle was the panel to select a shortlist of candidates. The males were easy meat but then came the formidable Margaret Wykeham, the well-bred chair of a progressive school to which she would never have sent her own children. 'Ms Gallagher, your grasp of the issues is formidable,' she began. 'But perhaps we could know a little more about you.'

'Yes, of course.' Anne-Marie was prepared for it. 'After university, where I graduated with first-class honours, I joined Audax Chambers. There, over the years, I have been lucky enough to form firm friendships and eventually to oversee the expansion of its human rights practice.'

'You were at university in Dublin?'

'Yes, that is correct.'

'And, before that, one has rather little sense of your background. Your family, for example.'

'Mrs Wykeham,' stated Anne-Marie with cool deliberation, staring at the emerald brooch pinned on the bosom of her interrogator's cashmere sweater, 'this election is not about whether I was born with a silver spoon or a poor mother's saliva-wetted finger in my mouth. I am a self-made woman. I am happy to discuss my professional life, even happier to discuss the problems that confront our country. But the condition of my candidature is that I will not speak in public beyond those.'

The die cast, she fired a defiant stare at the panel. After a silence interrupted only by the rumble of a passing train, grins began to spread across the faces opposite, including Margaret Wykeham's.

At an open meeting three weeks later, constituency party members selected her as their candidate with an overall majority on the first ballot.

During these weeks Anne-Marie came to wonder at her gift for artifice. She felt a sheen of hardness beginning to cloak her like a sleek, well-tailored suit. What surprised her, once she had entered the fight, was her will to win.

'Jonathan Alfred Ashby, Conservative, 24,317,' continued the acting returning officer. The sitting MP maintained a rictus smile below bulging eyes.

'Brian Hugh Butler, Liberal Democrat, 2,318.' The forlorn loser failed to disguise a murderous intent towards his one-time partner in government.

'Joy Freedom, Hen Party "Backing Genuinely Free Range", 141.' A figure buried inside a giant yellow chicken costume did a hop.

'Anne-Marie Gallagher, 25,779.' An eruption of shrieks, youthful OmiGods, cheers and whistles exploded through the hall. 'And I declare that Anne-Marie Gallagher has been duly elected Member of Parliament for Lambeth West.'

Amid the racket, the outlandishness of the moment seized her. The cheers went silent; she was confronted by a mass of mute, mouthing faces. There was something unreal about it. She had a *déjà vu* of another moment of unreality in her previous life; it chilled her like a blast of arctic wind.

Catching herself, she moved along the row of beaten rivals, shook hands – a pat on the beak for the hen – exchanged false congratulations on a campaign well fought, and approached the microphone.

'There are so many people to thank, particularly the acting Returning Officer and his most efficient staff.' She spoke with crystal purity, realizing that any delay in this traditional act of courtesy would show an unwise contempt for election-night protocol. 'But before I give other thanks,' she continued, 'and while this hall commands its brief moment of attention, there is something I want to say.'

She paused, her smile yielding to a cool intent. Right up until the last minute, she had not been sure of what she might say. Now, in this crucible of democratic fervour, hundreds of eyes bearing up at her, TV cameras trained on her, an unexpected sense of destiny tugged.

Perhaps Kieron Carnegie had been right. Perhaps this was her time, her chance at last to cash in years of slog in the mire of law chambers and courts, and the frustrations of committee rooms and thwarted campaigns.

Heeding the instant, her audience ceased its cheering. An expectation created by her magnetic fragility reduced the hall to a hush.

'Are human rights a joke?' She fired the question like a crossbow bolt, puzzled faces beneath straining to understand its target.

'Sometimes you might think so. We read stories of voting rights for child rapists. Refugees granted asylum to look after their cat. Such stories are always distorted, if not invented. But what they betray is an attitude. Human rights are a nuisance. Or silly. Or something foreigners deploy to take advantage of us.

'Such a state of mind makes us an ungenerous nation. We give the impression of wanting to send asylum seekers into danger, not welcome them to safety. To keep families separated, not united. To make ourselves less civilized, not more.

'But what ultimately prevents us from so demeaning ourselves is law. The laws that enshrine human rights. I want to tell you on this extraordinary night that I have stood in this election for the lawful human rights of every individual in this nation. And of those who with just cause seek refuge in it.'

There were stirrings not just on the floor below her. A few minutes earlier, the party leader and his entourage had swept into Festival Hall, commandeered for a mass gathering of the ranks. Pummelled by jostlers and backslappers, they paused to watch the Lambeth West declaration, knowing that victory there would surely see them into Downing Street. After the announcement of the result, they made to move on but were halted by the remark- able speech of their winning candidate.

For a moment Anne-Marie thought of stopping there. But, almost despite herself, the words flowed on, an undercurrent of payback throbbing within her.

'No human right has been more trampled,' she resumed, 'than the right to live our lawful lives unobserved in the privacy of our homes, our meeting places, with our friends, with our families.

'Under the cloak of fear, of exaggerated threats from terrorists and other convenient enemies, technology – and a lust for control – has created the surveillance state.

'I condemn that state.'

She could hear the collective gasp around her. A single cough reverberated like a gunshot. In Festival Hall, the volume dropped again and the now Prime Minister in waiting watched on. In a few still-lit rooms in Whitehall, in two fortress buildings by the Thames, and on comfortable sofas in commuter belts, a network of men, and a few women, were taking note of this upstart lawyer just turned MP.

'There must be no more snooping on the lives of tens of millions of innocent people by NSA, GCHQ, CIA, MI5, MI6 or any other sets of initials and numbers the faceless, unaccountable watchers choose to hide behind.

'There must be no more dirty tricks, extraordinary renditions, unexplained disappearances.

'Every citizen of this country is entitled to a life that is private, unviolated, and free.

'I make you a promise. I will work to dismantle the surveillance state. Nothing will deter me from keeping that pledge.'

For a few seconds, the Lambeth West election revellers remained stunned in a frozen silence. Then came the first ripples of applause, followed by waves of cheering and chanting. At Festival Hall, normal service was resumed, though raised eyebrows were exchanged amid mutterings of, 'Did you see that?'

Social media buzzed. The speech began to trend on Twitter; party workers posted it on Facebook and 'likes' mounted in their thousands. Anne-Marie had hit a nerve.

But, as well as in the secretive recesses of Whitehall, other nerves were less favourably struck. Long-in-the-tooth politicians noted the rashness of her words. Patriotic support of the 'vital work' of the security services was a mantra – particularly if you wanted your own secrets to stay buried. One senior member of her party amused himself by wondering what skeletons might lurk in pretty little Anne-Marie Gallagher's cupboard.

Having stepped down from the platform, Anne-Marie found Margaret Wykeham alongside her, leaning in for a hug. 'Your speech was wonderful. But take care.' They locked eyes, two women in a stadium where the gladiators were still largely male. 'Get some rest. It's allowed, you know.'

It was past 3 a.m. Small groups were setting off to join the Festival Hall throng, beckoning her to come with them. She realized that all she wanted was to be rid of them, to find silence to take in what had happened to her. She waved happily, leaning the side of her face against joined hands to indicate sleep. While other newly elected MPs and defeated candidates retired to their homes with loving wives, husbands, boyfriends and girlfriends, she left the arena alone.

Melting into the night air and walking briskly to expel the fustiness of the crowd and the clamour, she cut through the side streets of low Victorian terraces towards the river, stopping occasionally to listen for pursuing steps. The further she walked, the more the sense of unreality took hold.

Within half an hour she was entering her apartment block, one of five modernist buildings its architect called 'pavilions' overhanging the Thames – just one element in the massive new city within a city housing fifty thousand people. A new embassy row. A new haven for rich oligarchs when the going back home got rough. Thousands of pods of secluded anonymity. Her shield.

She took the lift to the eleventh floor and entered the flat she had reserved two years before. Then, she had analysed the model in the sales suite and lined up the view she wanted. Now that imagined outlook lay before her in spectacular reality. It never ceased to take her breath away.

She flicked on the television. Nearly 4 a.m. Counting had stopped for the night but her party was certain of an overall majority.

She undressed, scrubbed her face and teeth, and changed into the comfort of her pyjamas. She walked to the swathe of glass revealing London and the river. To the right the Millennium Wheel was still alight and revolving on this long election night, catching its celebrating stragglers. Sweeping left came the tower of the House of Lords, the ugliness of Millbank, then, peeping through a tiny gap in the forest of concrete and brick, the face of Big Ben.

She stared at these icons of the British state, the alien fortress she would soon inhabit. Below, apart from one lonely tug crawling slowly upstream, water gleamed emptily. A few cars flowed along the Embankment opposite, then an ambulance flashing its light. Their motion was silent and ghostly, deadened by the thickly insulated glass. She looked down on the river below and then right as the towpath resumed its curl towards Vauxhall.

There she saw the figure.

Stooping, long coat, dark brimmer hat concealing his forehead and upper face. He – it was a man for sure – lifted a cigarette pinched between thumb and forefinger to his lips, puffed, and exhaled smoke that streaked into the night. He turned his head up and towards the window she was watching from. She caught a glimmer of chin and lip. There seemed something familiar about their contours. She felt she saw him start, as if he had seen an apparition. He threw the cigarette onto the path, turned on his heel, and shuffled away. It was his back view as he left, the brimmer raked at a hint of an angle over his neck, strands of hair falling beneath that made her shudder. A wraith dissolving into the blackness.

The moment passed and she told herself to snap out of it. The transformative events of the past hours must have dislocated her. She repeated her calculation: any man with any interest in tracking her down these many years on was dead or disappeared.

Cold logic dictated imaginings of coincidences.

CHAPTER 4

Post-election, Saturday, 6 May

The rutted lane snaked up the hillside and emerged into a broad flank of heather-dotted fields forming a shallow ascent to a flat summit. Grey drizzle cast a familiar gloom over Irish border country, a sullen response to the excitement at Westminster.

Peering through the monotonous beat of his windscreen wipers, Detective Chief Inspector Jon Carne felt he was disappearing into a primordial soup. Finally he could make out the working party a couple of fields away. He turned right through a gate and pulled up beside a four-by-four in the gaudy gold of the province's Police Service, its roof light flashing like an irrelevant lighthouse in a deserted sea of washed-out green.

Stakes were being driven into the ground and a wire fence assembled. He watched the mallet head swish down like an executioner's blade. The point of wood below broke smoothly into the soft squelch of earth. Inside the fence a temporary tarpaulin was being erected over the excavation site.

A sergeant stood guard. 'SOCO's inside, sir,' he said.

Carne crossed the fence boundary and approached the area where the tarpaulin was rising.

'Morning, sir,' said the scene-of-crime officer.

'Morning,' replied Carne. 'So how and why?'

'We got a call on the confidential line last night. Couldn't do anything till first light.'

'Credentials?'

'He gave a password. It was a genuine one, operating in the early '90s.'

'When did they stop using it?'

'1995, sir.'

'Go on.'

'His coordinates are spot on. The description of the field and where to dig, too. We found a few remains on the surface. Animal disturbance. We've done a preliminary dig. Skull's well preserved. Fair bit of clothing.'

'He didn't say who or exactly when.'

'Just you'll find an unlucky young man. That was it, sir.'

Carne looked down at the muddled remnants so far revealed. Fragments of what may have been dark-blue jeans, the rubber soles of shoes, the jacket oddly intact, the macabre shape of head. He imagined the different endgames. A simple execution of a known enemy – or an assassination – just a bullet in the head. More likely, the last hours of a tout. Kicks and punches, cigarette burns, electrodes, hammers on kneecaps, scalpels on skin, two bullets in the head.

What must it be like to be the parent of whoever who had become this set of bones and rotted clothes? An offspring who disappeared, never to return. Would they have had any idea – or suspicions? Were they ever told? 'We're sorry to have to inform you, Mr and Mrs . . .' Carne tried to imagine the platitudes of a ghastly conversation. If he and Alice had been able to have children, they would have come into this world at the time this young man was leaving it. They would now be the age his short life was extinguished. What might they have become? But no child had arrived. And as the years passed, her memory receded into a different, long-gone life whose future had died along with her.

'Pathologist's on the way, sir.' The scene-of-crime officer shook him from his distraction.

'Who's on call?

'Riordan, sir.'

'Good.' He looked again at the skull. 'I don't care how long he's been there. Any tiny trace, we want it.' Carne's bleakness conveyed little optimism. 'And no talking. No media, no publicity. You tell this lot, make sure they get it. I'll instruct the press office. I don't want anyone out there scurrying for cover.' He retreated from the covering canvas into the drizzle still driving across the rolling fields. A few mournful sheep, huddled against stone walls, munched disconsolately, occasionally raising their heads at the unfamiliar activity. This was a place where nothing ever happened.

A battered-looking Ford Fiesta splashed through the gate, halting with a skid of the front wheels. Out of it jumped a chubby woman with bouncing blonde hair, a pert snub nose and hint of double chin, accompanied by a male colleague. For the first time that morning a galvanizing beam illuminated Carne's face. He removed his cap, transforming the policeman's dourness to reveal a handsome, dark-haired man belying his forty-seven years. Working with Amy Riordan, in his eyes the single argument for the state pathology service, was guaranteed to cheer him up. He briskly greeted her.

'OK, make my life easy. Tell me who did it, why, when, and how.'

'Sure. I thought you wanted something difficult.'

She gave him an amiable punch in the ribs, headed up to the grave, laid out her evidence bags and carefully pulled on inner nitrile gloves and latex covers. She knelt beside the remains, spreading her weight to avoid disturbing the mud walls, and gingerly stretched down one hand. One by one, she removed shreds of clothing, passing them to her assistant to place in individual bags and mark. The work tensed her, beads of sweat forming around her mouth. After ten minutes of concentrated foraging, she came up for air and stood gazing at the skull.

'So, early 1990s,' said Riordan.

'Yes, the password he used dates him.'

'That fits. Twenty, twenty-five years.' She shrugged. 'Give or take a few. Looks like he had a bashing around the face. Signs of bullet damage in the skull. Doesn't seem much on the other bones that are bared.'

'Will we get anything?' asked Carne.

'Possibly,' she replied. 'The jacket's synthetic, so it's pretty intact. Might be something on it, or inside it. Jeans were denim, natural fibre, so not much left. But you never know. I don't want to poke around the shirt fibres yet. He had a plastic belt. It's slipped down his thighs. That's probably the result of the corpse swelling, forcing his lower clothing down below the waist.'

'Is that common?'

'Reasonably, though it's not widely studied. It can sometimes be interpreted as an indicator of sexual interaction with the victim. But actually, during decomposition this kind of abdominal bloating is frequent. Then, as the flesh and organs continue to decompose, it leaves this curious-looking position of the belt.'

As so often when watching and listening to Amy, Carne felt goose pimples of pride both at her manual dexterity and expert knowledge.

'Mind you,' she continued, 'I might get something on sex. Saliva, semen, DNA. Maybe what type too if you're dead lucky. Gay or straight, mouth or tongue.'

'Let's turn it into a musical,' Carne chimed in.

'Sure, you write the tunes, I'll do the words.' She gave him her full-on, inquisitorial stare. 'Now you tell me something, Jonny Carne. What in the name of God, the Devil and all creatures in between is this young man doing lying in this grave in this field in this desolate part of this island of poets, artists and balladeers with bullet holes in his head?'

'You tell me, Amy Riordan. Tout? Caught on the wrong side?'

'Unlucky in love?' she chipped in.

'We need a name.' Carne tensed. 'We will investigate and we will find out what happened to him. Doesn't matter who he is, or what company he kept. Or where it leads. Or who gets embarrassed. Or who ends up in a dock.'

'That's why I love you.'

She approached him, gave him a kiss on the cheek and put her arm round him. They enjoyed the trust of a relationship where physical contact could not impinge. Amy made no secret of her sexuality and Carne felt revulsion at older men salivating after women half their age. Instead he almost saw her as his consolation – the daughter he had never had.

He could feel a prickle in his eye; perhaps it was the life lost in the grave, the loneliness of the unpeopled hills, or the memory of loss. He needed to leave this place.

'Over to you,' he said. 'Just find me a smoking gun.'

Instead of driving north to join the motorway, Carne turned east. He could not yet face the desultoriness of the weekend office and its few occupants counting up their overtime. He wanted air, space, and time. He headed towards his favourite sight: the sculpted shapes of the Mourne Mountains rising stealthily from the sea to form their elevated pattern, even on as grey a day as this. He drew up to the vantage point he had made his own, switched off the engine and sat as still as the mountains in front of him – a hiding place where memory could not be disturbed.

There was something about the interdependence of each summit that made every peak play its part in a communal enterprise of nature, a harmony that never failed to restore his inner peace. They seemed to be saying temporary matters, lives, people will come and go – but we will always be here watching the absurdities of your brief lives. Perhaps they would be saying that about the loss of just one life more than twenty years ago.

But then it struck him, unprompted by the word itself, that they would instead be mourning; and that, like each peak, all life was mutually dependent. To dismiss one was to dismiss all. Whatever the aloneness of his own life, he would not write off another human being for the sake of convenience.

Enough poetic melancholy. A young man had not walked into a muddy grave in an isolated field to lie down for a rest: someone, more than one person, had buried him. This many years on, he knew there'd be pressure to let it lie – politics, amnesties, leave the Troubles behind. But, to him, a killing was a killing, wherever and why ever it happened. The rest was mealy-mouthed excuse-making. He would never allow himself to compromise with murder.

Carne switched on the engine, accelerated hard and turned north. There was one man he needed to talk to. He pushed the number for Castlereagh switchboard and engaged the hands-free set.

'Detective Sergeant Poots, please,' he demanded. Carne tapped his thumb impatiently on the steering wheel as he cruised through the rolling hills of South Down. Thirty seconds later, the familiar gruff voice was on the line.

'Yes, boss.'

'Billy, your great age is finally going to come in useful. Early-'90s disappearances – I want the almanac.'

'Christ, I thought we'd left all that behind.'

'To the contrary. We have a new body in a field without a name.'

'Ah, a ghost is coming alive.'

'Ghosts indeed,' said Carne. 'That's your department, Billy. Let's get resurrecting him.'

CHAPTER 5

October 1993

It's the same boy who was in the library two days ago, the one she gawped at, the one she'd never seen before. Only this time he's got there first and taken her seat. Maire wonders if it's coincidental or deliberate, then chides herself for being so soft. He's probably not given her a thought. Nor should she give him one. That's not what she's here for, and not what she's spent the last two years for.

This is the final year – the year she will propel herself on the future that will transport her from home, family, place, class. From the past. It's the year she'll get away. For twenty-six months – she counts them – she's stuck by the rules she agreed with her brother and devoted herself like a nun. No distractions, no entanglements, head down. No staring.

But two days ago it was impossible to avoid the curl of brown hair falling so silkily on his collar, seeming to surface from nowhere. She's buried in the close print of an American court's judgement not to return an IRA killer of a British soldier because it's a political act. It excites her. Law is not just dry argument or sterile litigation: it can bring political change, too.

She relaxes to let the moment of revelation sink in. Her eyes settle idly, unintended, twelve feet away on the other side of the study table and somehow lock onto him. He sits ramrod straight, head forced downwards with an awkward angularity, glued to the thickly bound volume on the rectangular oak slab, a statue of concentration. She reckons he's in his mid-twenties, glinting brown hair falling in soft waves over his ears and neck – and that one curl in particular. His pencil is held tight between his teeth – good, white teeth. She can see part of one leg encased in weathered blue jeans crossed over the other. He still has a black leather jacket on – it outlines broad shoulders and a flat stomach. He reads on. She stares longer than she means before rebuking herself and forcing her eyes back to her book. He never looks up – not that she notices, anyway. Thank God!

Now he's back.

She's suddenly conscious of the beads of sweat on her flushed cheeks, invisible to others, a torrent to her. Outside it's a balmy autumn's day, the early mist clearing, the sun breaking through. As she skirted the river on her twenty-five-minute walk to the library, warmth seemed to rise even from the water itself, the trees alongside glowing islets of deep ochre. Right now, the perspiration is an embarrassment, which only seems to feed the sweat.

She's hung her overcoat on the hooks outside. Within the overheated library, she raises her arm to remove her jumper. It sticks to her T-shirt, raising it above the waist of her jeans. She quickly pats down the shirt to cover herself. The jumper removed, she shakes her hair – and uses the movement as a cover to cast him the quickest of looks.

Where to sit? She can't go too near him and places her books at the opposite end of the table. But, if she raises her eyes, she will be forced to look inwards, unable to escape him as there is nothing beyond except the unbreachable wood panelling of the library walls.

She sits down.

His eyes seem held by an invisible glue to the thickly bound legal volume. After a few minutes, she glimpses him running his hand through his hair and furrowing his brow. She feels him straining to understand the complexities he's buried in. She trains her own eyes to her book.

A vibration in the table hints at his repeating the action. Twice. Each time, she holds her face down. Then, a furtive glance. Like two days before, he doesn't respond. As if he hasn't even seen her.

The minutes pass, she sticks in a frozen immobility. She takes a deep breath and lets out a sigh. No reaction. She feels her concentration wavering – unusual for her. She restrains herself for what must be a full hour, but then can't help a peep at him. She senses him lifting his chin and turning towards her. It's a tracer bullet, stunning her into dropping her head. Flopping from the executioner's blow. Her cheeks burn – she must be colouring like a strawberry.

Shortly after midday, she closes her volume, restores it to a shelf and makes to go. She turns her back and has an instinct he's watching her. She doesn't look round to check. She half hopes he is. Avoiding, as always, the library canteen, she heads outside, up Dawson Street to her regular sandwich bar in a lane just off to the right. Arriving there, she tells herself to catch on.

Routine is restored. She orders her usual toasted cheese-and-tomato sandwich with a pack of crisps, which she sits on a stool beside a long Formica shelf to eat. She will then get a coffee and head out for a quick breath of air and her one piece of shopping before returning to the library. She is unusually hungry as she licks stray strands of melted cheese from her chubby fingers and off her light-red, varnished nails.

He's coming through the door.

'Hey!' he exclaims.

She tells herself not to jump or shriek, but the sound of her heart beating drowns the words they exchange. 'Oh, hi.'

'I didn't know you used this place,' he says.

She must stay cool. 'I was gonna say the same to you.'

'Ah well.' He turns back, orders his own sandwich, then looks round at her again. 'Fancy a coffee?'

'I gotta go to the chemist. Then head back.'

'Can it wait?' She frowns. 'Tell you what,' he continues, 'I'll cancel my sandwich. Let me get the coffees and I'll walk with you.'

'OK.' The word seems to have auto-popped out – he's already ordering the coffees and she's suddenly walking down the street beside him.

'You're a Brit!' It's almost a shriek – she can't help herself.

'Does it matter?' he asks innocently.

'Does it matter? Christ!' She pauses. He shrugs his shoulders, as if to convey that it's nothing to do with him.

'Course it doesn't fucking matter,' she says. 'Why would anyone think that?'

He feels an idiot. 'Sorry, I—'

'But you're a bit of a posh Brit,' she interrupts. 'Whaddya gonna do 'bout that, then?' She's putting on the full accent and idiom of the working-class girl from the North. She doesn't know why. But transcending both is the restored timbre of her voice. Pure and unfiltered, the clarity of mountain water.

'I'll take lessons,' he replies.

'Hope you're a fast learner.' His apparent discomfiture makes her laugh.

She finds herself behaving skittishly, pricking him with tiny taunts and conveying nothing of the blast of pleasure she's feeling. Why can't she be herself? He doesn't seem to mind and, almost quaintly, stretches out his right hand with a theatrical show of formality and introduces himself.

'David.' And then, hesitantly, his surname. 'David Vallely.'

Shaking the hand with a mocking delicacy, she responds with her own introduction.

'Maire McCartney.'

'Moira. Nice name,' he says, mispronouncing it. 'I thought it was Scottish.'

She corrects him. 'You say it like this. More-a. OK? Spelt M-A-I-R-E.'

'Sorry, I never heard it.'

'That's OK. It's common enough here.'

'So Dublin, then,' he says, happy now to place her.

'Wrong city. I got away.' There's a sharpness that brings silence.

She thinks about his name. An English boy called David Vallely. A nice ring to it – Irish origin somewhere down the line. It occurs to her, now she thinks about it, that it's great he's a Brit. There may be plenty of those at Trinity but in her world he's a stranger, an outsider. Someone with no connection to home.

They walk down the lane and turn left into Grafton Street, past the statue of Molly Malone and her cart, erected five years before and still too unblemished.

'I wouldn't say she's pretty enough for Dublin's fair city,' he says.

'Not just posh, but sexist too, eh?' The accusation comes with exaggerated alarm.

'Just an aesthetic judgement,' he tries to assure her.

'Course she's not pretty. She was a street hawker and tart in an eighteenth-century, shite, British colonial town. Whaddya expect?' She flares her nostrils at him.

They have reached the chemist and she turns in while he waits on the pavement. She feels embarrassed – although it's only cream she's been prescribed for a couple of spots bugging her. What's he thinking she's in there for?

When she walks out of the chemist the thumping has quietened and she wills herself to scrap the artifice. No need either to give him the big smile she's suppressing, no need to encourage.

'It's such a great day,' he says.

'Yes,' she replies absently.

'How about a stroll?'

She hesitates, then raises an eyebrow as if to say 'give over'. He waits silently, a plea in his eye.

'I shouldn't,' she says. 'Time to get back to the library.'

'It's not a prison.'

'OK, just this once.' Her face at last breaks into a hint of a smile.

'Great.' He's the cat with the cream.

They end up in St Stephen's Green on a bench. He raises his polystyrene cup. 'Cheers.' She smiles and raises hers too.

'So,' he continues, 'you must be doing law.'

'Yeah. Third year, finals coming up. I work all day and night. No distractions.' She wants to make it harder for him. 'And I gotta finish my dissertation.'

'What's it on?'

'It's kinda on postwar evolution in international law. I'm mainly focusing on extradition treaties.'

'That's amazing,' he exclaims. 'The thesis for my master's—'

'You're doing a master's?' she interrupts. 'That's why I never saw you in the first two years.'

'That's right,' he continues. 'But here's the thing – my specialism is the International Court of Justice in The Hague. Maybe I can help you.'

'Or maybe I can help you,' she retorts smartly. They beam with shared pleasure at their common interest.

'Wouldn't it be great if every day was like this?' she suddenly says. 'Look at it, leaves turning but still golden, sun shining, heat in the air. Fuck's sake, this is Dublin in autumn.'

'I know,' he says.

'There's something unreal about it, isn't there?'

He looks at his watch and cries out, 'Hell, the time! I'll be late for my supervisor.'

'I should get back to work, too.'

They walk back to the library together. As they part, he says, 'It was great to talk. Maybe we can do it again next week?' She's suddenly deflated but tries not to show it. 'I'd say a drink tonight but there's a friend I promised to see.' He pauses. 'And then I'm away for the weekend.'

'Course you are, posh boy.' She states it flatly. 'Anyway, I forgot, Film Soc's showing *Battle of Algiers*. Been meaning to see it since I was born.' She hopes her recovery is swift enough to let him know they're parting on equal terms.

'Long live the revolution, then.' He smiles and turns in the direction of the Law Faculty.

Did he spot her tug of disappointment when he said he was away for the weekend?

Not that she'd have been able to spare him more than an hour or two. Mrs Ryan's staying overnight in Limerick, so away for both the Saturday and Sunday, and she's got the kids full-on – not a weekend to look forward to. Why did she blurt out Film Soc showing *Battle of Algiers*? No chance of escaping to see that. Maybe Blockbuster will have a VHS. If not, she should be able to find a review of it somewhere to clue herself up.

What will he be doing? As they part at the library, she watches him until he disappears through an arch. His broad shoulders taper down to slim hips and long, floating legs. She feels she's never seen such a perfect man's body. The unreality of it all strikes her again with renewed force.

As the slow weekend drags on she keeps seeing his disappearing backside. It's both a distraction and an irritant in the life she's made herself endure. She knows the kids well enough by now but keeping them fed and entertained on the single note Mrs Ryan left is wearying. Kevin's got a match for the under-elevens, which Roisin's still young enough to be cajoled to watch. Brian is contemptuous of his younger brother's sporting prowess and refuses to come, staying at home to play on his Atari. She tries to josh him into getting some fresh air but finally gives up. On their return, they pass him on a street corner slouching with his 'gang'. She suspects he's been smoking and hopes it's nothing worse. It's only a few minutes to the badlands of Sheriff Street and the kids start too early these days. She suspects there's too much in him of what of she's heard about his absentee father.

She manages to find a couple of hours on Saturday evening to work. Her eyes soon tire. She tries to resist slumping in front of the TV. She couldn't get a VHS of *Battle of Algiers* but the student mag has a preview of it, which should give her enough to get by.

She thinks of students thronging in bars, laughter, kisses, falling over drunk, falling into bed. The thought makes her sit up straight, wipe her eyes, stand up and open the front door to breathe the street air, and return to her book.

Sunday morning has Mass to fill the time and Brian isn't yet bold enough to duck out. She dutifully accompanies the children to the altar rail to receive Communion – just a blessing for Roisin, who's doing confirmation class this year – and senses a stroking of her hand from Father Gerry as he lays the wafer in her palm. She jerks her head up at him with a flinch of fury, but he's gone. He's youngish, mid-thirties, she guesses, the trendy priest of the Dublin badlands. Couldn't be a better match for it.

The church is well stocked with young couples trailing toddlers and babies who add their music of chirping and screeching. They leave her as cold as the church itself and the dirty priests that preside over it. Not so Roisin. On the walk home, holding Maire's hand, she's sufficiently emboldened to ask a question that has obviously been nagging her.

'Why don't you have a boyfriend, Maire?'

'How d'you know I don't?' she replies with a teasing smile.

'Well, he never comes to see you.'

'Well there you are, then, you can't believe what you don't see.' The nonsensical double negative flummoxes Roisin into silence.

Mrs Ryan returns around six. She looks exhausted, her face etched with thin brushstrokes of worry. Or maybe it's the cigarettes – as soon as she flops at the kitchen table, she lights one, inhales deeply, closes her eyes, and slowly allows smoke to drift out. Maire can smell it infusing her dyed jet black hair.

'Kids all right, love?' she asks.

'Yes, all fine, Mrs Ryan,' replies Maire, injecting an unfelt breeziness. She sometimes wonders why, in the more than two years she's now been here, Mrs Ryan has never suggested she call her Bridget. 'How was Bernadette?'

'She's OK.' Mrs Ryan takes another gasp. 'I asked her again about putting in for a transfer to Dublin, but she wouldn't. Says she's used to it down there.' Another puff, followed by a single rich cough. 'She says there's talk of some kind of negotiations going on. Maybe some'll get released.'

'That'd be good,' says Maire. It's a discussion she doesn't want to get drawn into. 'Better go up and catch up with my work.'

'Aye, you do that.' Mrs Ryan looks up at her. 'Thanks, Maire.'

She goes upstairs, sits at her desk, opens a notebook and the marked page of a book, *Anatomy of the Nuremberg Trials*. It's by Telford Taylor, an American lawyer who was one of the Nazis' prosecutors, and was published a year ago. Despite the good reviews, the library hasn't got a copy, so she's splashed out and ordered one for herself. She's been devouring it hungrily but, at this moment, her appetite has gone missing.

She peers around her box of a room: narrow single bed, bedside table with just enough room for lamp and alarm clock, school desk and chair, scratched brown chest of drawers, hangers on a rail, a wash basin in the corner. Two photographs sit on the chest, her ma and da getting married, and the McCartneys and Kennedys together by the sea in Portrush. She wonders who could have taken it, as they're all in the picture. On the back row, Joseph stares at her with an idiot grin on his face. She wonders how he's faring. At least there's been nothing of him or his friends in the newspapers.

Looking at him only brings that image of the boy's receding behind. She stands to inspect herself in a small square mirror nailed onto the wall. She peers closely to examine the two spots, one lodged just above her upper right lip, the other low on her chin. She touches them – not ready to pop and nothing she can do before the morning. Her hands move down her body to the growing tyre of flesh around her belly. She knows she's let herself run to seed. Bad eating, mainly – it's chips every night at the Ryans'. What's there been to look good for since she came here? Now she thinks of taking better care of herself. Just in case . . .

In case of what? She tells herself to wise up. David Vallely is a nice-looking English boy from another world she's met and talked to once and knows nothing about. He's probably a flirt who sees nothing more in her than a coffee mate with a mutual academic interest. She needs to see him that way too and remind herself that she's here to get a top degree and keep herself to herself. She probably won't even see him again anyway. Be better not.

On the Monday morning, he's there in the library. Same table, same chair.

CHAPTER 6

He walks towards her, flicks a smile and leaves the library. A few minutes later, he's back and drops a note in front of her as he passes.

'Fancy pizza this evening?' it reads.

She looks up at him with apparent disapproval, turns over the note and writes on the back. She holds it up so he can see the reply from the far end of the table.

'OK.'

Her end of weekend resolution has lasted the split second of hesitation it takes to scribble two letters. She can't believe what she's done. He sticks up a thumb, reads for a few more minutes and leaves again, this time not to return.

Her heart seems to thump all day. She's racked by a jumble of feelings. Guilt, anticipation, dread, excitement – reverting always to guilt. She knows full well Martin would say she's breaking their deal if she goes out with him. She tries to think back to that conversation two years ago. Martin gave the orders – she stayed silent. Why should her silence mean acquiescence? She's too smart not to know that's sophistry. But she's maintained the isolation for more than two years – there has to come a time when she can relax. What could be more harmless than a posh English boy with whom she's nothing in common and who knows nothing of her island or where she's come from? Anyway, she's already said yes.

When they meet up at the pizza place and exchange opening pecks on cheeks, she calms. He's easygoing, soothing, even nicer to look at close up across the table. She's struck again by his teeth and feels self-conscious. The gap between her two upper front ones has never much bothered her – doesn't Madonna have one? – but now she wonders if he minds. And there are the 'incisors' the dentist once remarked on – not to mention the uneven bottom row. They were never bad enough to get done on the National Health, and who'd want to waste their own money on teeth? Not that it was ever an option. He truly doesn't seem to care. Lightly creased in smiles, he contentedly gazes at her eating her pizza slice by slice, her tongue slithering through the melting cheese on her hands. They share a bottle of Soave – she finds herself drinking faster than he is.

'How was your weekend?' she asks.

'I packed the rucksack and got a bus to Wicklow.'

'Really?'

'Yeah. Walked up Lugnaquilla. It was great. Fantastic views.'

'I love mountains!' she exclaims.

'Maybe sometime we should climb one,' he suggests shyly.

'Yeah, be great,' she replies almost under her breath, then buries her eyes in her plate.

'And you,' he says after a second or two. 'How was *Battle of Algiers*?'

'Brilliant.' He expects her to go on but her eyes stay silently down.

'Yes, it is,' he agrees.

'It sorta manipulates you,' she says, looking back up with a smile. 'You know what they're doing is wrong, but you kinda feel it's right.' She feels a tiny thrill at coming up with the judgement out of the blue.

'Like here?' he asks. She doesn't answer and itches to change the subject.

'So tell me 'bout youse,' she finally says.

'Not as much to tell as there should be,' he replies. 'Irish father, as it happens—'

'Would be with a name like yours,' she whips in.

'Though they left a long time ago. The family did OK.'

'I can see that.'

He blushes modestly, then casts his most beguiling grin, his eyes twinkling. 'My mother was English, though. Bit of French blood. She was a good-looking woman.'

She notices the tension. His smile disappears. 'Yeah, both gone.'

'I'm sorry.'

'There we are, nothing to be done.'

She thinks of asking how and why, but decides from the sadness in his expression that he doesn't really want to discuss it.

'So it's me alone against the world,' he continues, proclaiming it like a manifesto.

'No brothers or sisters?' she asks.

'Just me. A lonely orphan in Dublin.' He reverts to his default mode of self-mocking. She sees him as the standard male who deals with past regrets by avoiding them. Silence follows for a second or two of memory and consolation.

He's chatty enough and reticent only about himself – she understands that's in a boy's nature. Above all, he's a good listener and she finds herself chattering away in all sorts of unintended directions.

'So what about you?' he pipes up.

'Not much to tell either. Not yet rags to riches. My da's a mechanic, never had a proper academic education.' He watches her break into a smile of fondness. 'Mind you, the wee man's now a self-taught philosopher king.' Unlike him, she's not holding back. 'Ma's a classroom assistant since my brother and I grew up. Working-class Catholic. They reckon they never had a proper chance so they were damned – well, my da used another word – if it was going to be the same for my brother and me. They pushed me. Scholarships mattered. That's what got me here.'

'And your brother?'

'Oh. He's a clever boy. Committed to the cause. You know.' She sounds embarrassed. 'He's the philosopher windbag. Hot air and purple prose.' She feels she's gone too far and tries to row back. He concentrates fiercely on his pizza and eats hungrily.

'I'd have been the same,' he says between mouthfuls.

'Not that he's ever up to anything, just a whole load of blather. Gets boring after all these years.' She forces a grin. 'Thank God I got away.'

'I'm glad you did.'

His hand creeps slowly across the table and ends up resting on hers. She lets it linger. She means to pull hers away, but, if she's failing at that, there's no way she'll let him know where she lives. She imagines Mrs Ryan, cigarette hanging from lip, looking down on her through the curtains of the front bedroom.

He offers to drop her home, but she declines, giving him a peck on the cheek before setting off down the dimly lit lane. There's a spring in her step. He's nice. Really nice. Pity she can't let it go anywhere. But there's no reason not to be friends.

Imperceptibly, they fall into a routine, controlled by when he happens to appear at the library – lunch breaks together when he's there, sometimes supper out when she's ahead of her work and doesn't have the kids to do. Though she only ever uses work as an excuse for being busy – she's not going to mention her life as a childminder.

Occasionally they see a movie – he loves discussing them as much as she does. *Schindler's List* keeps them going for hours – he's fascinated by the different ways a 'good' man can behave in the face of evil. At his suggestion, they go to *Indecent Proposal* – she feels her cheeks going redder and redder as the story unfolds and Demi Moore undresses. He turns to her, appears to notice despite the darkness, chuckles, pats her on the thigh, then withdraws his hand.

She's impressed by how hard he's working, and his sympathetic understanding that she needs space and time for her own studies. Sometimes they walk round the city; on cold days he might hold her hands to warm them. They give each other chaste kisses as they part. He offers no hint of sex or love.

As these days and early weeks pass, a puzzle begins to trouble her. She's thrown by how much she's liking this man – as she now sees him – and how much she wants to spend time with him. He's amiable, relaxing, interesting. There's no side to him. He's also gorgeous – she feasts on him every time she sees him. There's no avoiding it – she wants him and has tried at times to convey it in her eyes. The puzzle is how slowly they seem to be moving – or, rather, he is.

She's sure he's attracted to her. She thinks she sees the desire in his eyes – yet he seems content to go on playing it for friendship. Perhaps that's one reason why she's grown to like him so much. Over a supper out – he's not short of money and will never allow her to contribute, which is a relief – she tries a gambit to move it on.

'It's great eating out, but sometime I'd like to cook for you myself,' she begins.

'That'd be good,' he says, 'another of your talents to explore.'

'Trouble is,' she goes on downcast, 'where I live is girls only and the landlady's a witch. No men allowed.'

'That's Stone Age.' He grins.

'I blame the priests,' she says.

'Well never mind, we'll just have to live on pizza.'

Why doesn't he take the bait and invite her to his place instead? A nasty thought surfaces. Has he got a girlfriend hidden away somewhere? But on that her instinct is certain: he hasn't. So what's stopping him? Is there something she's missed? God, maybe he's not even into girls. No, he is. She's sure of that too.

If, in those early days, they'd ended up in a pub, had a few drinks, gone back to where he lives – even checked into a cheap hotel or behind the bushes on a rug for God's sake, warmed by alcohol – desire would have taken over. That would have suited her after such long abstinence – an escapist fling with a dreamy boy hailing from a different planet, no strings attached. Now it's gone too far and they've spent too much time together for it to be just that. The implications of eventual sex begin to weigh more heavily. Yet, though he always tries to answer everything she asks, she feels she still doesn't really know this man she's getting in so deep with.

'So,' she asks once, 'you've never told me about your student days.'

'They were pretty average,' he says.

'Hey, doesn't matter what they were. I don't mind.'

He's silent, even gloomy, then speaks. 'OK, I confess. I did history at Exeter. Now you're going to really despise me.'

She laughs out loud, shaking her head at him. 'You oul fool, I already know you're a posh boy.'

Titbits like this are frustratingly meagre. Perhaps she has too idealized a view of what a relationship, even just a proper friendship, should be. Isn't it about not just answering questions but immersing yourself into each other's life, family, prejudices, experiences, all the pieces that make you the person you are – knowing there's nothing you can't share? It nags her that she's only scraped his surface.

'You know something,' she says another time, idly twirling spaghetti on her fork, 'we spend all this time together and it's great. But I still feel I dunno anything 'bout you.'

He laughs. 'What do you want to know? What *is* there to know? I'm all yours to see.' He thinks, seeking to justify himself. 'I've always told you anything you've asked.'

'I know you have. I know you try. But it's like . . . it's like you've no family. No friends. None I know of, anyway. No past – sometimes what you tell me just feels like lines in a CV. We talk 'bout stuff but we never really talk 'bout you.'

'I told you, I'm not very interesting. And I don't have friends here.' He pauses. 'And, hey, I don't quiz you about you. You said you'd got away. Maybe I'm the same.'

'Fair enough,' she says, 'can't argue with that.'

That's it, and they change the subject, chatting as easily as always. But his face momentarily droops and she realizes she's struck a nerve.

'Remember you said you wanted to climb a hill?' he says a few days later during the lunch break.

'Yeah?' She wonders what's coming.

'Weekend after next my mate Rob's coming over. We're driving to Connemara. We'd like you to come.'

'We?'

'Yes, we. He's my oldest friend. I was thinking of what you said.' She looks puzzled. 'About knowing about me.'

'Oh, right.' She frowns. 'Didn't mean you to take it that literally.'

'I didn't. He was coming anyway. He's good fun, clever too. A reporter for *The Times*. I'll show you his byline. Rob McNeil.'

'OK. Sounds great.' The frown gives way to a beam and then to bleakness. 'Look, I'd love to but I can't.'

'You can't!'

'I got a commitment: my flatmates are having a gathering.'

'Can't you get out of it?' he pleads. 'Just this once. Just for me.'

The beseeching in his eyes alarms her – he's never exposed himself like that before. Has the moment come? Is this his foot pushing the accelerator? If so, she wants more than ever to be on the ride, though her strength of feeling has made it scarier.

Her arrangement with Mrs Ryan is one weekend a month off – and the dates clash. She needs a plan.

'I was just wondering about something, Mrs Ryan,' she says as tea that evening is ending.

'Yes, love,' she says, looking up from her plate. It's cheese on toast with beans and chips – the kids are gone, having bolted theirs down and rinsed their plates.

'I was gonna ask if it might be possible to swap my weekend off this month.'

Mrs Ryan's eyebrows rise disagreeably. 'That wouldn't be very convenient, Maire. You never asked it before.'

'I know, it's just that something's come up for my studies. Bit short notice but there's a symposium the weekend after next in Cork – it's about international law and war crimes.'

'Sorry, love, you've got me there, what's that?

'It's like . . . a symposium's like some of the world's experts on it'll be gathered there. Lectures and discussion groups. Could help with my degree.'

'It's to do with your degree?'

'Yes, Mrs Ryan. They're laying on a bus for the third-years.'

'OK, Maire, I'll think about it. Maybe Margaret can help out.'

'That'd be great, Mrs Ryan, thanks.'

She knows that Margaret, Mrs Ryan's pregnant younger daughter, won't be doing anything better – but also won't want the bother. It's down to how hard Mrs Ryan wants to push it.

Later that evening, she hears Mrs Ryan on the phone. She edges her room door ajar to make out what she's saying, but whoever's on the other end of the line seems to be doing most of the talking, only odd phrases wafting up. 'Yes, that's right . . . there's a bus taking them . . . she says it's good for her degree.' She guesses Mrs Ryan's trying to persuade her daughter – not that Margaret would be impressed by helping anyone get a degree.

As she's leaving for the library next morning, Mrs Ryan pops her head out of her bedroom door. Her hairnet's still in place, along with the cigarette.

'Before you go, Maire – I had a chat with Margaret. You can go on your weekend for whatever that occasion is you mentioned.'

She's startled, never believing it would work. 'Thank you, Mrs Ryan, thanks very much.'

'But no partying, OK?'

'That's great, it's only for work.'

It seems too easy to be true – but what's to worry about that? She's off to Connemara with her posh English boy and, no doubt, his posh English friend. She closes her eyes and takes a deep breath – eight days to wait.

It's going to happen.

CHAPTER 7

On the Friday afternoon Anne-Marie Gallagher had called into Audax Chambers. A 'Congratulations' banner hung and they gathered in reception to applaud as she entered. Her timing was fortuitous; the TV was showing the new prime minister, Lionel Buller, leaving Buckingham Palace after 'kissing hands' with the monarch.

'You did it,' said Kieron Carnegie.

'You did it, Kieron,' she replied.

'Wrong. It's entirely your achievement. And it doesn't surprise me one jot.' They exchanged happy smiles. 'That was some speech.'

'I'm not sure what took hold of me.'

'The risk taker that lurks within.'

He leant close to whisper. 'You may find you get a phone call soon.'

'What?' For once she seemed genuinely puzzled.

'I'm afraid this may be the one and only time you have to allow me to know something you don't.'

'You're incorrigible,' she murmured, turning to mingle.

The call came at 8.30 on the Sunday morning, the number showing private.

'He wants to see me? Yes, of course, name your time.'

She was lying in her bath, soapsuds playing around her toes, incredulity around her eyes.

'Four-thirty. I'll look forward to it. Oh, and where do I arrive?'

The instruction was brief. 'Sure, I'll remember to smile.'

She dialled Kieron Carnegie's number. 'You set me up again!'

'Not at all,' he protested. 'They called me out of the blue.'

'Checking me out?'

'Just one of Lionel's boys. He was only asking if there was anything they needed to know.'

'And?'

'I said you were the most remarkable young woman I had ever met. It seemed to satisfy him.' He paused. 'Good luck. Don't worry if he doesn't smile, he left his sense of humour behind in the womb.'

At 4.28 p.m., conveying herself elegantly on black, lightly heeled boots, she was ushered through the gates of Downing Street by the duty policemen. 'Good afternoon, Ms Gallagher.' Their recognition shot a dart of pleasure through her. For the cameras parked outside Number 10 she affected a shy smile. 'What's he giving you, Anne-Marie?' came a shout. She raised an eyebrow at the offender.

At 4.30 p.m. the black front door opened. A young man with floppy hair, a boy, it seemed to her, at the heart of government, shook her hand and addressed her with a silky maturity.

'Welcome, Ms Gallagher. Philip Wells, private secretary to the Prime Minister. You're the last by some way and he's retreated to the flat. If you could bear to follow me up . . .'

Lionel Buller was dressed in charcoal grey suit trousers and a white shirt, top button open. In the corner, she saw a jacket and tie folded carefully over a chair.

'Anne-Marie, good to see you.'

'And you, too, Prime Minister,' she replied.

Without a handshake or embrace, he gestured her to sit down. Somehow she had expected him to forgo formality and ask her to call him by his first name.

A second man looked on, similarly dressed but with tie in place, topped by retreating sandy hair whitening at the edges. 'You know Rob McNeil,' stated Buller. It was an assumption that neither of them challenged.

'Good to meet,' said McNeil stretching out his hand.

'Yes, indeed,' she replied, shaking it. She felt not just shock but a punch of dread. Over the years, she had occasionally noticed his rising profile and ultimate appointment as political editor. As she herself grew in her smaller world, there was little danger of their careers crossing paths – until her selection as a parliamentary candidate. Even then a little known, would-be MP was too small fry for a national political editor.

Now, without any rehearsal, she was pitched together with him. She told herself to stay calm and show nothing – there was no reason, in such a different context, why he should suddenly start thinking about a weekend twenty-four years ago.

'I'll be announcing Rob's appointment tomorrow morning as the new Number 10 press secretary,' said Buller. 'Unexpected no doubt, but, given he's done six years as *The Times'* political editor, we might at least keep that paper onside.' He grimaced. Hooded brown eyes, snuggling beneath heavy brown brows, bore in on her. 'Well, congratulations.'

'Thank you.'

'It was a seat we had to win.' He looked down at an untidy cluster of papers on the glass table in front of him. 'I happened to arrive at Festival Hall just in time for your declaration. A turning point.'

'Yes.'

'I watched your speech.'

'Oh.'

'I watched it again yesterday. We recorded the night.' He paused. 'It was remarkable.'

'Oh, good.' She realized she was scuffing her hands together and told herself to stop.

'Is there anything I ought to know . . .?' His voice tailed off.

She suspected he had been told to ask the question. 'No. I live to work. That's it.'

'Curiously enough,' he resumed, as if he had not heard her, 'I tend to believe the Security Service when it tells me it does not vet ministers.' God, she thought, what's this leading to? 'Unless, of course, they think someone's going to blow up Parliament.' He manufactured a twisting of the face, intended to be a smile.

'I'll try to resist that temptation,' she said. The face untwisted itself.

'I want this to be a moral government.' He blurted it out, his eyes coming alive, shining through the hoods. 'We said that once before and it didn't work out. This time it will.'

'That's why I joined the party,' she said. 'Why I stood for parliament.'

'There are obstacles.' Again he did not speak directly to her. 'Not just from outside, but within the party too.' He sprang up from his seat, walked to the window and peered down at the Downing Street garden below.

'Steve Whalley.' He stopped. She resisted any temptation to

nudge him. 'Stalwart of the party. I have asked him to be Home Secretary.'

She nodded, maintaining a strategy of silence. 'One of my strongest backers for the leadership. He's a traditionalist. Needs support from a strong, modern voice. Someone with an unblemished record in human rights.'

He walked back, sat down and fiddled again with the papers. Was it an act that allowed him to judge her reactions – or was he hamstrung by a social gaucheness? Especially, perhaps, with women. 'The Home Office, as presently structured – a structure I see no need to change – has three Ministers of State. One oversees crime prevention, the second policing and criminal justice, the third security and immigration.' He paused. 'You know all this.'

'Yes,' replied Anne-Marie, breaking her silence, 'I've had dealings on the other side of the table with the outgoing Minister for Security and Immigration.'

'Of course.' A hint of a smile appeared and instantly dissolved. 'It's a difficult portfolio. Asylum, extradition, national security.' He paused. 'The surveillance which makes that possible.'

'All areas of great professional interest to me,' said Anne-Marie. 'And now political interest too.'

'We should not always be a predictable government. I'm determined that now, right at the beginning, we show that we can be bold.' He looked up and, for the first time, fully locked eyes with her. 'I would like to offer you a post in my government as Home Office Minister of State for Security and Immigration.'

'Jesus.' Her language relapsed, the astonishment was so real. A welling of emotion caught her unawares. She swatted it like a fly. 'I don't know what to say.'

McNeil caught her eye. 'I think what the Prime Minister

would like you to say is whether or not you accept his offer,'
he said gently.

She had that odd sensation – not for the first time in her life – of
her words emerging ahead of her thoughts. 'Yes, of course.' She
did not hesitate. 'Of course I do.'

'Good,' stated Buller without emotion.

'I have no experience in government.'

'Few of us do. But you have expertise.'

'What about Steve Whalley?' she found herself asking.

'Don't worry about Steve,' replied Buller, 'you'll find a way.'

She sensed the conversation was over and stood up. This time,
unlike at her arrival, he stretched out a hand and she shook it.
'Any problems you ever have, just ring Rob. He'll be my eyes
and ears.'

'I'll see you out,' McNeil said with a nod.

He waved her ahead of him and followed her down a modest
corridor lined with nondescript watercolours before emerging
at the grand staircase. Anne-Marie considered the scions of the
British establishment looking down on her. The blessed Theresa,
fleshy Cameron, glowering Brown, Blair, the grinner in anguish
by his end, Major, the nothing man, Thatcher, the *femme fatale*
who had haunted Anne-Marie's teenage years.

'History's proving kind to her, isn't it?' remarked McNeil,
scrutinizing Anne-Marie's eyes trained on the famous face and
bouffant hair.

She stopped to look more closely at the portrait. The journey
she had made suddenly seemed so improbable. To think that the
idea of Thatcher as the mortal enemy was one of the certainties
of her political upbringing. And yet here she was stepping down
the very staircase this iconic foe had once graced. Of course, it
was not only she: the one-time leaders of the IRA now too were

politicians, collaborating with a British state they had wanted
to destroy.

'In that case, history is being somewhat premature,' Anne-Marie
replied tartly.

'Perhaps that depends on when history begins,' Rob continued.

She turned sharply, again feeling the dread. 'What do you
mean?'

'Only musing.' He smiled. 'Just thinking of how quickly they
can come and go.' She thought she detected admiration in his
eyes. Perhaps it was nothing more.

She turned away and accelerated down the stairs. McNeil
skipped down them behind her. As they crossed the chequerboard
floor and approached the front door, she stopped again. He
caught up and she inspected him more thoroughly. The furrowed
seriousness was even more apparent, enhanced by the widow's
peak of his pale hair.

'I should have congratulated you in there,' she said. 'It's a great
achievement. A huge job too – the voice of government.'

He smiled again. 'That's rather an intimidating way of putting
it. I meant to congratulate you too. Yours was an important victory.' He paused, looking around. 'And now all this.'

'I know. Doesn't quite feel real, does it?'

She spun on her heel, nodded to the policeman at the door,
and left to the clicking of photographers and yells of reporters.
Despite her trembling knees, she paused, smiled, waved, took a
deep breath and strode off up Downing Street.

She had anticipated the return walk would be a celebration,
wordless though with a smile for the camera. Now, the smile
fought the thumping in her head. Coming face to face with McNeil
had brought the past abruptly to unwelcome life. She sensed
walking invisibly beside her the three men – one brother, two

lovers – who had truly mattered in her life. All long gone, swept away from her, disappeared. Who knew where? Or how? Were they now to be the ghosts at her banquet?

She crossed the Embankment, red flashes of passing buses appearing abstract, almost unreal. What if I stepped out now? She caught herself, reflecting on the idiocy of the thought, worse still the failure of nerve, and headed for the pedestrian lights.

Over Westminster Bridge she increased her pace, wanting to run, but knew she must not. There could be more photographers, followers, pursuers even. She found herself watching out for men in hats. Her pulse raced. Calm it down, slow deep breaths, smile, admire the reflections of the river, enjoy the rainbow colours of tourist groups.

Big Ben struck five – she could only have been in there twenty minutes; it felt not just an eternity but a distant one.

She reached the other side of the river, crossed and flitted down the steps onto the Thames pathway. To the right the Houses of Parliament, a mile or so ahead the boorish shape of MI6's grandiose contribution to the London skyline and James Bond films. The monstrous palace of games.

The South Bank unshackled her. She took off her heels and, despite the constrictions of her skirt, broke into a jog. As the last neo-Gothic vestiges of the Houses of Parliament slipped from her eyeline, the building rhythm of her movement slowed her heartbeat. A sense of mission seeped down and reinforced her.

CHAPTER 8

November 1993

She's told Mrs Ryan the bus to Cork leaves from BusAras at 8 a.m. To avoid seeing her or the kids, Maire creeps out of the house with her rucksack an hour earlier. Night is clearing to a biting crispness as the sun breaks through the late November fog.

The bus station's less than a mile away but she takes a detour via Talbot Street, instinctively glancing back for prowling eyes. She tells herself not to be an idiot and heads for the junction with O'Connell Street. They're picking her up outside the General Post Office – whatever the historical connections, at least they can't miss it. Because of the early departure she's half an hour to kill and finds a side street café to warm her hands over a cup of tea.

At 8 a.m. a sporty-looking car draws up and toots its horn. David leaps out and helps her into the cramped back. 'Sorry,' he says, 'you're the only one who'll fit there.'

As they pull away, he does the introductions. 'Maire, this is my friend, Rob.' The driver takes one hand off the steering wheel, turns and offers it.

'Hi, Maire.' He doesn't sound quite as posh as David but the nicely cut and brushed straw-coloured hair and green jacket suggest wealth.

She shakes the hand. 'Hello, Rob.'

They head west, Rob driving too fast and David urging him to go faster. David swivels. 'His choice of car, not mine.' Rob grimaces.

The space in the back is so tight that even she, with her short legs, is forced to put them across the seat. She can't help her face being close to the hair falling on his collar and has an urge to blow on the soft skin of his nape. In the rear-view mirror, she sees Rob now smiling. He turns to David, 'Well, you said she was a looker.'

She glows. She realizes she's never felt so well – her skin feels fresh, even the spots have gone. She feels the tyre of flesh around her waist – still there but tauter. Is that what love can do? She bats away the question. This can never be about that.

They drive past Maynooth, through Kinnegad and into Athlone, where David suggests stopping to inspect the dull, grey stone fortress by the river.

'His culture only extends to wars and battles,' Rob says as they stare up at it.

'He doesn't talk 'bout that with me,' says Maire.

'That's because you're broadening my horizons,' says David.

'About bloody time someone did,' says Rob, winking at Maire. 'Has he bored you with his rugby stories yet?'

'Didn't even know he played.'

'Ah, the many talents . . .' He stops himself, breaks into a chuckle and stretches out his left hand to slap David on the shoulder. 'The many talents of the amazing Mr David Vallely.'

Then it's on to Galway city for a bacon sandwich and, in

deference to their notions of Irishness, pints of Guinness around a rickety wooden pub table.

'So,' Maire says, turning to Rob, 'tell us more about the secret life of David Vallely.'

'Now you're asking.'

'I wanna know. He never talks 'bout himself.'

'What can I say?' Rob reflects, looking fondly at his friend. 'I've known this comedian for, let me see, twelve years off and on. It's not been easy for him . . .' He leaves the thought unspoken.

'Did you know his ma and da?' she interrupts, getting it.

'Not his father, he died a while ago. His mother was lovely.' He allows a silence to hang.

'I'm sorry,' says Maire, turning to David, who's looking away, out of the pub window.

'Anyway,' resumes Rob, 'in all that time, we've hardly had a cross word. There've been periods when he's been travelling – he's a bit of a hobo – but we just take up where we left off. Nothing changes.'

'That's great,' says Maire. 'Great to have a friend like that.' Her voice tails off and she too stares out of the window, feeling her own aloneness.

'Anyway' – Rob's eyes are trained on David – 'after all that wandering, he looks settled now, doesn't he?'

'I am, mate,' agrees David, 'I really think I am.'

'And about bloody time too!' exclaims Rob, puncturing the moment of gravity.

They pass another castle, the gaunt ruins of Menlo, which David doesn't inflict on them, and finally, in the early afternoon, the mountains of Connemara loom beneath a lowering late autumn sky.

'I need to climb a hill,' exclaims David. 'You on, Maire? You said you'd like to.'

'Yeah, I'm on.' She glances at him, throwing a challenge, the car pulls up and he helps her climb out over the front seat.

'Race you to the top,' she says. 'Loser pays all.'

'OK, you're on.' He pinches her and grins.

Before the two men can move, she's running through a springy field, splattering mud over her jeans. She finds a path along a stone wall and begins to climb, sheep watching her haste with incredulity. She hears them chasing her. 'We're coming to get you,' yells David.

She forges on, flicking looks behind as they close. She reaches a gate, hops neatly over it and feels drops of rain on her hair. She looks up and the skies are blackening. She stops, closes her eyes, opens her arms, and feels a gush of water burst over her face. At the same moment, he's behind her, throwing his arms around the fold of her waist, his body tight and hard against hers, breathing heavily.

'OK,' he says, 'you win. Now let's get the hell back to the car before we drown.' He's never held her like that before.

They reach the modest, pebble-dashed guesthouse in Clifden as dusk falls. A swirling wind beats rain against windows and the sea against rocks. The landlady recoils at the drenched, shivering arrivals.

'Hot showers for you, then.' She peers down at her reservations book. 'A single and a double?' There's a question mark in her voice.

'The single's for me,' says Maire.

A couple of hours later the rain subsides and they find a pub serving up easygoing food, a crackling wood fire, and a live band. It's an out-of-season Saturday evening but the place is crowded with locals of all shapes and ages: wizened old peat cutters wearing black jackets matching the darkness of their stout mingling with ruddy-faced country girls displaying brightly coloured skirts and muscled calves.

With speakers turned up to deafen, the band strike up a jig. Maire motions David to the dance floor. She tries to set steps for him to follow but it's a lost cause as he narrowly avoids her toes and grasps her instead in close embrace. The music ends and he leads her back to their table.

'He sings better than he dances,' Rob tells Maire with a curiously dull edge. He sees her notice and perks himself up. 'Go on, get him on stage.'

'It's gotta be an improvement,' she says. 'His dancing's shite.'

David glares at Rob but is too late to stop her skipping over to the band leader. She points to David and heads back towards the two friends. She sees them break off their conversation, still glaring at each other. The edge between them is odd – she assumes David's embarrassed by his friend.

'Ladies and gentlemen,' announces the lead singer, 'we're joined on vocals by David from Dublin.' David walks over and whispers in his ear. 'And he'll be singing for us that beautiful folk song which originated the other side of the Irish sea but we've adopted as our own. You all know it – "The Nightingale".'

The fiddle and guitar play their opening bars. David, gazing into Maire's eyes, lifts the microphone to his lips and softly and shyly sings.

As I went a walking one morning in May
I met a young couple so far did we stray
And one was a young maid so sweet and so fair
And the other was a soldier and a brave Grenadier

With his free hand, David beckons the audience to join in the chorus.

> *And they kissed so sweet and comforting as they clung to*
> *each other*
> *They went arm-in-arm along the road like sister and brother*
> *They were arming along the road till they came to a stream*
> *And they both sat down together, love, to hear the*
> *nightingale sing.*

The song ends, the audience clap and cheer. David, now confident and enjoying the moment, bows. Maire has a new sensation – she feels proud of him.

'You could almost pass for an Irishman,' she says.

'I love the music,' David replies. 'Listen to it endlessly.'

'And now you're in the country itself.' She turns to his friend. 'Do you know Ireland, Rob?'

'A bit,' he says. 'I did a six-month stint in the North for the paper.'

'Oh,' she says, her voice rising an octave. 'When was that?'

'Not so long ago, summer of '91.'

'So, pretty quiet.'

'Yeah, not much,' he says casually. 'Only real nasty was the murder of the Special Branch guy, poor bastard.'

She's motionless. 'I read about it. I'd left by then, thank God.' The memory kills conversation and their eyes turn back to the band.

Later, Rob withdraws to the guesthouse and Maire and David find themselves walking along the harbour front. The clouds have cleared and he puts his arm round her. She doesn't sink into him.

'You're shivering,' he says.

'It's not exactly warm,' she says with a touch of frost.

'What's wrong?'

'Nothing's wrong.'

'I can tell,' he says. 'Was it the pub? Or Rob?'

She pipes up. 'Well, I did wonder why you looked as if you wanted to punch each other.'

He laughs. 'It was nothing. Though I might have preferred him not to act the impresario.'

'I though it might be that.'

'There's something else, isn't there?' he insists.

'No, not really.' She puts her arm round his waist. 'Just the fears and hopes of life.'

He doesn't pursue it, instead rubbing her warm against the piercing cold. Out to the west, away from the lights of land, the moon casts onto the blackness of the sea a shimmering pathway of brilliance, which seems to stretch to infinity. In the distance, the silhouette of the Twelve Bens mountains draws a curtain against the island and continent that lie behind them. She arches her neck to look up at him. He leans over her and they kiss fully and deeply for the first time.

'Here and now, in this magical place, it's as if we're . . .' He pauses, breaking away, trying to find the word. 'As if we're invulnerable. Untouchable. There's no need for fears.'

She pulls herself to, breaks away and gives him a gentle slap. 'That's unlike you,' she says, cheeriness restored. 'I guess I'll have to get used to the singing poet.' She flings her arms round his neck and plants a kiss on his mouth. 'Christ, it's bloody freezing,' she exclaims. 'What the hell are you doing keeping me out so late, Mr Vallely?'

Arms back round each other's waist, they walk briskly to the guesthouse. Despite the length of his stride, her thickset legs spring along beside him. They open the door. She puts her hand over his mouth and quietly hushes him. They creep up the stairs, trying not to giggle as floorboards creak. On the landing at the top, he makes to leave her and go to his room. She looks into his eyes, takes him by the hand and leads him to hers, all the time keeping him silent.

Inside her room, he begins to speak, 'Maire, are you sure—' She puts her forefinger over his lips, then inside his mouth and strokes his milky teeth with it. He licks the finger and kisses it. She breaks away, takes off her coat and folds it over a chair. Then her shoes and jeans. She pulls her sweater over her head, causing her long tresses of hair to lift and then fall back in floating descent. She unbuttons her shirt and lays it over the sweater, and unclips her bra and lets it slip to the ground. She puts her hands through her hair and brings strands to her front. She stands facing him and beckons.

'Too much blubber,' she says shyly.

'No,' he answers, 'the more of you, the better.'

'Now you.'

He undresses and she steps back to lie on the bed and pull him over her.

They make love three times until it lasts long enough for her to share in the full pleasure of it. 'I'm sorry,' he keeps saying, 'I've been wanting it too much. Storing it up.' She shushes him, saying it doesn't matter. At the end, after they've been lying sleepily in peace for a few minutes, she props herself with a jolt on an elbow and looks over him.

'If you wanted it that much, what took you so long?'

He opens his resting eyes. 'I wasn't sure. You know, you might have disapproved. Not liked me for it. Attitudes are different here. Like the rules in your flat.'

She chuckles. 'Christ, I was glad to get rid of that hang-up.' His eyes widen. She continues more softly. 'But it's been a while since.' She pauses. 'You can't have hearts breaking and get a first at the same time.'

'You're clever enough to have anything you want,' he says.

The sleep that seemed ready to overwhelm them has turned elusive.

'I wanna tell you something,' she says.

'There's nothing you have to tell me – you are as you come.'

'No, it's about the flat. I somehow couldn't tell you straight.'

'What couldn't you tell me?'

'I lodge with a woman who's got three grandchildren living with her. Her daughter's in prison, the father's no good. Part of my rent is to look after the kids. That's why I could never invite you.'

He doesn't seem offended or even taken aback – instead he puts his arms around her and pulls her close.

'I'm glad you told me,' he whispers. 'It's great not to have secrets from each other.' He sits up and beams. 'Hey, perhaps I'm allowed to ask you back to my place now!'

She sits up too, smartly pushes him back down, lies on top and begins to touch him again. 'I thought you'd never ask.'

The only sourness in this unmatchable moment is the mental effort to dismiss the exchange in the pub. Part of her wants to tell him everything, even why she first went to Mrs Ryan. But she knows that can never be.

CHAPTER 9

On the Monday morning, he's not in the library. She'd never asked, just assumed he would be. Her concentration keeps wavering as she imagines him walking through the door. He doesn't. Tuesday morning he's not there either. She has a premonition of something wrong.

Just before the lunch break, he arrives with a grin.

'I thought you'd be here yesterday,' she says on the way out. She didn't mean to – it just comes out.

'Hey,' he says, putting his arm round her. She doesn't pursue it and they head to the sandwich bar. It's turned cold, grey winter and they eat inside.

'I'm really glad you told me about the kids,' he says. 'I know not to ask too much of you.' She wonders if this is some kind of explanation for the day before.

'I'd like to spend more time—' she begins.

'Me too,' he interrupts. They munch silently for a few seconds.

He looks up, a glint in the eye. 'We could sometimes work from my flat in the afternoon.'

'Work?'

'Sure,' he says, 'why not?' She knows he's deceiving himself as much as she is.

'OK, maybe day after tomorrow?' she suggests. He's skipped a day, so she can too.

'Done.' He stretches out his hand – she shakes both it and her head.

He doesn't arrive at the library till mid-morning, takes down a bound volume, buries himself in it for an hour and a half, closes it, and walks behind her, brushing her neck with the back of a hand, to replace it. She follows him out.

'I bought a car,' he announces.

'A car!'

He grins inanely. 'Let's pick up a sandwich and go.'

'OK.'

He says he's parked the other side of St Stephen's Green so, lunch in bags, they cut through the bared winter trees, his arm around her shoulder reinforcing the warmth of her coat.

Suddenly she feels him flinch. He jerks to a stop, whisks her under some branches, pulls his hood over his head and buries himself in a hug with her. She's too surprised to resist, then tries to pull away.

'What the—' she begins, but he puts his forefinger over her mouth to silence her. He has a quick glance behind, repeats the signal with a finger over his own lips and hides himself within her again. A minute passes, he breaks away and they resume the walk.

'What the fuck was that all about?'

'I thought I saw a ghost,' he says. 'Well sort of.' She can see he's thinking it out. 'Actually, it looked like a girl I once knew. Had no idea she could be here. It would have been awkward.'

'Awkward?'

'Yeah, it sort of ended messily.' His eyes drop to the ground. 'Probably my fault.' He says it to mean anything but. 'It was a while ago. Hey, I'm sorry.'

'What's her name?' she asks.

A beat. 'Her name?'

'Yeah, her name.'

'If you really want to know, she's called Susan. It just could have been really difficult,' he repeats. 'She was upset.' Another beat. 'So was I.'

'Exactly how long ago?' she asks.

'Couple of years,' he replies briskly. He's more confident now.

'Oh, well, guess it happens,' she says. 'Weird, though, she turns up here.'

'Yeah, I know. I mean I didn't know. It's nothing, just coincidence.'

She doesn't push but it's a knife to her heart. She berates herself for letting it get to her – of course he's had other girls. How could a boy like him not have?

They reach a bright-red hatchback car.

'What do you think?' he asks.

'It's flashy,' she says without enthusiasm. She tries not to go on thinking about what happened.

'It's an RS turbo, not just some crap Fiesta,' he explains. 'After last weekend, I thought we could hit the road some more.'

'That'd be good,' she says, 'if I can ever get away again.'

She detects his deflation. He wants the car to be for the two of them but the incident in the park has soured the surprise.

They draw up in a broad avenue of well-kept Victorian villas. He opens the door of his first-floor flat and ushers her in ahead of him and through to the sitting room.

'Wow, it's big,' she says.

'I'm lucky,' he replied. 'I inherited a bit of money. Though I guess that wasn't lucky really.' A cloud passes over his face. She suddenly feels for him, gives him a hug and a kiss, and pulls back to look around.

One wall is a tableau of portrait posters. Martin Luther King, Lawrence of Arabia, Muhammad Ali, Karl Marx, Bobby Sands set alongside Jesus Christ, Ayrton Senna holding the 1991 World Championship trophy.

'Friends of yours?' she asks him.

'Ha-ha, funny girl,' he replies, restoring the big grin and giving her a deep kiss.

'All right,' she says when they ease apart, 'why them?'

'All men who changed the world.' His eyes range over them before settling on Senna. 'And he's just brilliant. He'll be number one again next year for sure.'

'Can't say it's my scene.'

'You'll love it when I get you close up to the noise.'

She ranges towards a small round table with a handful of framed photographs. He hovers over her as she picks them up one by one. Colour snapshots of a good-looking young couple by the sea and among hippy-dressed crowds at a festival.

'Mum and Dad,' he says, 'Isle of Wight 1969. When Dylan came over.'

'They look too straight for that.'

'Some people went for the music. The Who, Moody Blues, quite a line-up.'

She replaces it and picks up David himself on graduation day wearing black gown and cap.

'You haven't changed much,' she says.

'Christ, it wasn't *that* long ago,' he protests.

'What about your year?' she asks.

'By the time they got round to the group photos I was going stir crazy,' he answers. 'Mainly a bunch of twats, anyway.'

She works something out. 'Is that why you're living out here, then? Among the posh?'

'If you mean did I have enough of squawking undergraduates, the answer's yes. I don't like the crowd. Never did, really. I suppose I'm a bit of a loner.' He checks her expression. 'Sorry, is that sad?'

'Not at all,' she replies. 'I'm the same.' She puts the photo down. 'So, better get to work.'

'I've got a better idea,' he says, wrapping his arms around her front. She leans her head back into his neck and sighs. Their lovemaking is sublime in a way she'd never imagined possible.

An hour later, as they're spread peacefully in his bed, he stretches out a hand to the drawer of a bedside table and pulls out a photograph lying flat inside it. He places it face down on his chest and turns to her.

'Since we first met, I always wanted to tell you something,' he says, 'but I was scared to.'

She has her back to him and rolls alertly round. 'Whaddya mean?' She can't hide her alarm.

'It's OK,' he says, 'it's just that when you told me about you having to look after the kids, I knew we couldn't have secrets between us. We want to know everything about each other, don't we?'

'Of course.'

He raises the photograph and holds it out in front of them. A smiling young man in uniform stands beside a bride in a white dress holding a bouquet of roses. Behind them stretch two rows of four men, also in uniform, holding up their swords angled at forty-five degrees to a summer sky. A church porch is just visible, traces of unlit faces in the shadows waiting to emerge. The newly

married couple are the same couple, though less windswept, as at
the Isle of Wight festival.

She peers at it without speaking, trying to understand.

'1967,' he says.

'Your mum and dad,' she says. 'I don't get it.'

'It's their wedding guard of honour. My dad was a soldier.'
A hushed pause, then the low growl of a passing motorbike
reverberates through the front bay window to the bedroom at
the back. 'A British soldier.'

'Jesus.'

'I'm sorry. It's not what you'd have wanted.' Silence. 'It's not
what I'd have ever wanted, either.'

'Whaddya mean?'

'I feel pride in him but not in the institution. The one thing I
never inherited from him is a love of the British Army.'

'Did you tell him that?'

'No, I realized it too late. It's probably for the best.'

'What happened to him?'

'He died in the Falklands. Tumbledown. 1982. When I was
thirteen.' A tear forms in a glistening brown eye and rolls slowly
down. She moves close and licks it off his cheek.

'I'm sorry.'

He breaks away and sits up. 'It was a shit war over a piece of
fucking rock. Dying for the greater glory of Margaret Thatcher.'

'You could say the same for Bobby Sands,' she says. Her remark
electrifies him – she has never before even hinted at the troubled
history of her island and instantly wishes she hadn't.

'You mean they've something in common,' he suggests eagerly.

'I dunno what I mean,' she says. 'It's kinda confusing.'

'That's why I was scared to tell you. But we're here together
now. So I had to.' He waits while she processes the information.

'It's good you told me,' she finally says. 'But never tell it to anyone where I come from.' She throws off the sheet. 'Gotta do some work now.' She needs more time.

An hour later, sitting at his desk in the front room while he reads in an armchair, she turns and casts him a frown. 'What 'bout your mum?'

'My mum?'

'Yeah, you never told me 'bout her.'

'I think she never got over it.'

'That doesn't kill you.'

'No. But ovarian cancer does.' He states it brutally.

'Shit, I'm sorry,' she says. She gets up, gently places herself on top of him in the armchair and embraces him. They stay locked together till finally his lips pluck her ear lobe.

Intertwined by shared shocks and confidences, they find a rhythm in the weeks leading up to Christmas. Two or three afternoons each week in his flat, maybe a weekend day when she is free. She never stays overnight and, when he drops her off, she never lets his car enter the immediate neighbourhood, let alone her street.

'Whaddya doing for Christmas?' she asks one afternoon as he's driving her back.

'I spend it with Rob and his family,' he replies. 'It's like they've adopted me.'

'Bet it's a big country house.'

'How did you ever guess?' She inspects his profile, the crease of a grin stretching his left cheek.

'And you?' he asks, keeping his eyes on the road.

'I'll go up and see Ma and Da. Couple of nights, three maybe, no more. The city gives me the creeps these days but I can't leave them on their own.'

'What about your brother?' he asks.

'He'll look in as it suits him.' She sounds as frosty as the December day. He draws up short of Sheriff Street. 'I'll be away to Mrs Ryan's mansion, then,' she says, hopping on to the pavement and striding off as fast as her legs will carry her.

She gets the return bus to Dublin the day after Boxing Day. He's not said when he'll be back but she knows by now he doesn't like to be tied down by dates. She assumes it will be at least another day or two, maybe not till after New Year.

Two p.m. she arrives at Central Bus Station. He's there, waiting.

'What the fuck are you doing here?' She doesn't know whether to smile or frown – it's too unexpected.

'I came back early. Wanted to see you.'

She examines him, touching his unshaven face. 'Look at you. Did you join the down-and-outs?'

'I'll explain.'

'I dunno what you're expecting. I gotta get back to Mrs Ryan.'

'Spend the afternoon with me,' he pleads. 'It's Christmas. She'll have loads of people to help. You could phone her.'

'Where from?'

'There'll be phone boxes here. I've got change. Tell her the bus has broken down.'

'Christ, you have all the answers, don't you?' He grins sheepishly and she rolls her eyes. 'You look like a tramp and smell like one, too, but you're still a handsome bastard.' He broadens the smile. 'OK, let's find a phone box,' she says with a sigh.

Snug in bed in the lazy late afternoon, he suddenly sits up and looks down on her. 'I understood something this Christmas,' he begins.

'Oh?' She is sleepily relaxed.

'When you've had no family for too long, you forget what you're missing.' He strokes her upper lip with his forefinger. 'So what I understood is that I want to be part of you, Maire. Part of where you belong. Part of who you are.'

'Whadda you mean?' she asks, shifting uneasily beneath him and propping on an elbow.

'You've become my touchstone. I lie here with you and define myself against you. This, here, now, is my world.'

'What about your friends? And Rob's family. You said they'd adopted you.'

'Yes. But that's just an illusion. Escapist wishful thinking.' He lies silently, as if wrestling with some great dilemma that is crushing him. 'I want you to take me to meet your family.'

She jerks up to sit ramrod straight beside him.

'David, they're a world apart.'

'I know that. But if they are, so must we be. And we're not, are we?'

She wants to turn away from the imploring in his eyes and the timbre of his voice but she's frozen in the enormity of the moment. He allows her time. 'No, we're not,' she at last agrees.

'In that case, there can't be borders between us.'

'It's not that easy.'

'Nothing in life that's good ever is.' She has no response. 'I love you, Maire,' he whispers.

She stays silent, burning with an overwhelming tenderness for him. She wants to say the word back but can't bring herself to let it out.

CHAPTER 10

Post-election, Monday, 8 May

'So, William MacGillivray Poots.' Carne threw the challenge like a punch to the gut, 'The early '90s. Imagine I've dropped in from Mars. What's going on here?'

'It's raining,' replied the grizzled face sitting opposite him, the close-cropped whitening hair and square face with its jutting chin showing his near-sixty years. 'Linfield win the cup. Two years running. Then it rains more. My wife refuses to leave me, however hard I try. The kids are a pain up the arse.'

'All right, you gloomy bastard, tell me something new.'

Carne enjoyed the dourness – and the mordant wit beneath, a welcome riposte to the modern day of 'Human Resources' assessments conducted according to 'behavioural pathways' by humourless managers. After nearly four decades in the force, Billy Poots was nearing retirement, still a detective sergeant. In a changing world where terrorist violence was replaced by political compromise and paramilitaries became professional racketeers, he was a man of rugged integrity who took no prisoners and sought

no favours. Carne viewed Poots as his greatest blessing since he
and Alice had decided to escape their troubles in south London
and come to live in her homeland. For some reason the Ulster
salt of the earth had adopted the young English greenhorn and,
whenever the chance offered, they had been a team ever since.

Wanting Billy to relax and allow the memories to flow, Carne
had forgone the prying eyes and ears of the office and summoned
him to a mid-morning get-together within the Victorian enchant-
ments of Belfast's Crown. Its restored columns and capitals, tiles
and brocades made it something of a tourist trap these days; but
the snugs were still places where you could hide and shut off
the world. Carne ordered a Scotch for Billy and a diet Coke for
himself. The drink of the reformed alcoholic, he had heard it said.

'You want a reason why a young man disappears in the nineties
and is found buried in a field over twenty years later,' began Poots.
He paused, sipped his Scotch, and cast a wary eye outside the
snug. He spied a young American couple in jeans and rucksacks
on shoulders, eyes locked in lovers' embrace, on honeymoon
perhaps in the 'old country'. Two scrawny-looking men sat sadly
on stools at the bar. The Crown's day had just begun.

'1994 was the year the pigs finally came to the trough.' Poots's
harsh accent and crusty voice projected a world-weary contempt.
'I'd been in the force five years. Sure, there were still murders and
killings, sectarian stupidity, but it was slowing down. Most people
had had enough. At the head of the queue, though they'd never
own up to it, were our friends at the top of the IRA. Because, you
know what, when you've been campaigning and struggling and
lying and fighting and watching informers and gangsters behind
your back for over twenty years, you fancy just a little warmth
and comfort. And there's nowhere more comfortable than the big,
fat, cushioned seat under the big, fat politician's arse.'

Behind Poots's flat forehead and watchful eyes, Carne could feel the burning intensity of a historic rage.

'It was called the peace process, Billy,' Carne said quietly.

'Peace process! Jesus Christ, self-enrichment process at the point of a gun and a bomb. Don't worry, boss, I'm not biased, my aisle of the church was just as bent.'

'So what's this got to with a corpse in a field?'

'You call me a gloomy bastard. You're an impatient bastard all right.' Carne smiled. Poots looked down at his glass.

'Another?'

'No, let's get out of here and walk.' Without waiting for an answer, Poots rose and strode towards the door. Carne leapt to keep up.

Across the road the Grand Opera House stood proud in all its restored, misplaced, oriental glory. Beside it the Europa Hotel, bombed twenty-eight times, giving its name to the newsman's appetiser 'Avocado Europa', which exploded in your face. It all seemed a long time ago – another age – yet Poots still cast a look around before turning left towards Botanic.

'Just shadows,' said Carne.

'My rational mind knows that,' replied the older man. 'But you weren't here then.'

Though that was true, Carne also felt the ghosts. Looking around, there was no visible sense of them. This was a contemporary city of hotels, restaurants, clubs, cinemas, theatres, into which a treasure of peace money had been poured. But sectarian passions still flourished, national flags still provoked political fistfights, the marching season still brought mob violence to the streets. Every year or two a prison warder or policeman or soldier or reservist was murdered. Letter bombs were sent in the post. There was still a residual organization, with changing names but the same core personnel, willing to bomb, kill and maim in the name of 'unity'. Atavistic needs for revenge still lurked. The pigs who had come to the trough could never feed in total comfort.

'They don't kill coppers now, Billy,' said Carne.

'Last one just a few years ago,' replied Poots. 'A prison officer two years ago. That's milliseconds in Irish history. Remember the early sixties. You weren't even born then, I was only a kid. This was the most peaceful place in the world. The only murders we ever had were cows in abattoirs. And then, three and half thousand people dead.'

'Plus one,' said Carne.

'Yes, plus one. Just part of history, eh?'

'Stop it, Billy. Now . . . talk.'

Striding down Great Victoria Street, the two men made an odd couple. Carne tall, slim, with that full head of dark hair and long face, calm, concise; Poots six inches shorter, cropped hair, florid, more than a hint of stoutness, pugnacious, talkative. Their differences, Carne often thought, must be what glued them together.

'OK,' continued Poots, 'we go back to the early '90s. The Provos are tired of fighting, the Brits are tired of fighting, even the sad benighted side I'm born into, we bigoted Prods, we're tired of fighting. They all want a deal. But there's one problem. Some of the boys want to fight on at any price. The idealists, the revolutionaries, the true believers.'

'The fanatics,' broke in Carne. 'Yes. OK, here's what's interesting. By early 1994 we – Special Branch, Army, MI5 – know who the main deal breakers are. It's not a secret, they've even got a name – the "Gang of Four". Martin McCartney, Brendan O'Donnell, Sean Black, Joseph Kennedy. If there's a leader, it's McCartney – intelligent, highly political, committed, an ideologue. Until recently he's been quartermaster-general of the Belfast

Brigade. He knows where all the weapons are. We're pretty sure that when he sees the split inside the IRA coming, he stores away a whole arsenal for himself and his friends.

'Black and O'Donnell are different. Hard, brutal, unreconstructed. Remember Enniskillen?'

They fell silent. Even a generation later the wreckage-strewn square of a quiet market town on Remembrance Day remained an unforgettable vision of horror. Eleven innocent people killed, sixty-three injured, the lives of the families who mourned them unalterably blighted.

'No one was ever arrested,' continued Poots, 'but we knew damn well Black and O'Donnell were at the heart of it. The IRA claimed the bomb went off prematurely but those two bastards meant every bloody bit of it.' Poots bristled with quiet, visceral contempt.

'And Kennedy?' prompted Carne.

'Kennedy's the most interesting. He's a fusion of everything. Politically radical, extreme nationalist and a killer – though we never nailed him. We're sure he broke his virginity with that visiting Met Special Branch officer – Halliburton. Nasty business. And Kennedy's ambitious, charismatic in his way, a leader in waiting if ever McCartney falls by the wayside.'

Carne could feel the agitation in Poots's voice. The older man was varying his pace, slow, fast, slow, fast, flicking a look behind each time he did so. He was back in troubled times, unable to escape. Sweat formed around his brow, his breathing becoming heavier. They reached the bottom of Great Victoria Street. To the left barbed wire and barricades still cloaked Donegall Pass police station. Across a wasteland of parked cars, the resplendent façade of the new Radisson hotel tried to contradict it, the present denying the past.

Poots could feel Carne watching him, checking him over. 'Too early for that whiskey, boss. Let's grab a coffee.'

They headed over the roundabout to Botanic Avenue and bought two double espressos from a coffee bar. As Poots drank his, Carne knew better than to interrupt him; he would finish the story at his own pace in his own time. Poots turned right into Crescent Gardens and settled on a bench overlooking a neat oval of grass. In a corner, two tramps slumped with crooked backs over empty bottles of cider beside their feet. A young mother pushed a pram, an overweight indeterminate dog circling around her. Pigeon shit decorated the pavements.

Poots drained his coffee, got up to throw the cardboard cup into a wastepaper basket and sat down again. They had not talked for nearly ten minutes.

'The Gang of Four, Billy. The obstacles to peace,' prompted Carne finally.

'Yes, the Gang of Four,' Poots resumed. 'Something strange happens. In the spring of '94: one by one, the Gang of Four disappears. First Black, we're down to a Gang of Three. Then O'Donnell, and it's a Gang of Two. And then, pretty much at the same time, Kennedy and McCartney. The Gang of None. There's no noise, no claims, no bodies, they just fade out of the picture. And no one knows how or why. Or wants to know.'

Poots's attention was caught by two men entering the far corner of the park and heading diagonally across towards their bench. As they neared, they could be seen to be in their mid-forties, one bearded, the other vigorously making a point with his unlit pipe. Poots stopped talking and watched them. They were just yards away. He felt inside his pocket and touched the reassurance of his pistol. The men looked at him with sudden suspicion, increased their pace and walked past. One of them cast back a glance of fright.

'Hey, Billy,' said Carne quietly.

'Now I'm the one seeing ghosts,' murmured Poots. 'Perhaps my time's come, boss, I'm finally losing it.'

Carne paused to allow him time to recover. 'Does the story have an ending?'

'The Gang of None? No, just a black hole. But you know the history. August 1994, ceasefire declared. OK, the first ceasefire's not the final one but it's the breakthrough. A few ups and downs and three years later, it's official, the Troubles are over. Everyone lives happily ever after. More or less.'

Carne looked up. A few more mothers had arrived with prams and toddlers trotting happily around, not a care in the world. The shouts and screams of tiny joys broke through Poots's funereal silence.

'That's the story of your body in the field, boss. Perm one from four.'

'OK, Billy. So who fired the bullet?'

CHAPTER 11

January 1994

She says they'll just go up for the day. Her parents' house is too modest to stay in, it'll be too awkward, there are only three bedrooms, unspoken questions about the sleeping arrangements will hang in the air. She sees his disappointment.

'I want to get to know them,' David says, 'just as I've come to know you.'

'I just don't really wanna go there,' Maire replies. 'I told you before the place gives me the creeps.'

'It's your home town!'

'Yeah, I got away.'

In the days leading up to the visit, her nerves show, making her irritable. Martin will be sure to have been told. Will he stay away, or come to inspect? Why even ask herself when she knows the answer. Maybe he'll have told Joseph to come too. She avoided him over Christmas and dreads the thought of it.

She expects David to drive but he insists they take the bus. Nearly four hours there, more door-to-door, and four hours back – at least the journey will shorten the visit. They arrange to meet at BusAras at 7.30 a.m. on the Saturday.

'Christ, look at you.' She says it to scold, not tease. Gone are the jeans and bomber jacket; in their place dark trousers, a corduroy jacket, simple striped shirt and tie, his hair trimmed. She gets the look, even admires him for it – smart but not posh, clean, ordinary, classless, respectable. Her mother will love it.

'I've got to look my best,' he says. 'First impressions are every-thing.' He flashes a sparkling eye. 'Aren't they?'

Conversation during the bus journey is fragile and intermittent. As they cross the border north of Dundalk, just two small signs showing the change of state, she turns to him warily. 'I never asked, did you ever go to the North?'

'No,' he replies, 'I told you that before. When we were in Connemara.' He dons the grin. 'Virgin territory.'

'Not sure I'd say that after the past twenty-five years.' There's an unfamiliar sourness in her voice. 'I wish we weren't doing this.'

'They're your family, Maire.'

'Who I made the choice to leave.'

'Do you mean the family or the place?'

He's niggling her and she scorns him. 'Where I was born, there's not much of a distinction, is there?' She doesn't require an answer and he has the sense not to offer one.

Mid-morning, the Bus Eireann coach draws into the neat concrete rows of the Europa bus station, built two years before beneath a multi-story car park – just one monument to the money splurged to dampen the violence.

'So where now?' he asks as they dismount.

'Bus down the trouble tourist trail – Divis, Falls, then the delights of Andersonstown.' He's still inhaling her chill. 'Unless you want to go by black cab.'

'Sounds great,' he says.

'Do you know what the black taxis are, David?' she sneers.

'Yes, Maire, I read and watch the news. Communal taxis ultimately controlled by Sinn Féin. Or the IRA, some would say. It would be interesting.'

'God, you mean it, don't you? OK, just don't open your mouth.'

'I can do Irish. You heard me singing.' The grin is back.

'Don't you fucking dare.' But, though damn him she might wish, she can't help smiling. He gives her a discreet peck on the cheek.

'Friends?' he asks.

'If you behave.'

He's as good as his word, keeping silent in the black cab while she chats away to keep their fellow passengers at bay. His overcoat conceals the dissonant jacket and tie beneath.

They get out at Glen Road and she leads him through neat roads of semi-detached and terraced houses, some with well-kept front gardens, others with concrete paving, but none despoiled. A place of gnomes and dangling chimes where neighbours watch out for each other – where comings and goings are recorded by twitching noses and eyes behind half-drawn net curtains.

She stops at a house, clean plastic weatherproof windows recently installed, brick walls partially coated with pebbledash, in the front a narrow stone path curling around a central rose bush. She presses the bell and it sounds a musical ding-dong. After a few seconds a bespectacled bald man of middling height in his sixties opens the white front door with its central oval pane of multicoloured glass, beams on Maire and embraces her.

'Good to see you, girl,' he says.

'Hello, Da,' she replies.

He looks over at the young man beside her and offers his hand. 'And you'll be David.'

'Hello, sir,' says David.

'Ach, for heaven's sake, lad, name's Stephen.'

A woman of the same age bustles down the narrow corridor from the kitchen, patting down her dress with her hands.

'Hello, love,' she says, kissing Maire on both cheeks.

'This is David, Ma.' She gives him a quick up and down.

'Hello, Mrs McCartney.'

'You can call me Rosa, David,' she replies. Her shyness makes her seem almost tart. 'Right, I'm away, you'll be needing food on the table.'

'Lovely smells,' says David, but she's already halfway back to the kitchen.

Stephen leads them into a compact sitting room with a central maroon settee and accompanying chairs, arms shielded with white linen cloths. Above a wood-effect gas fire is a mantelpiece with miniature china dogs and cats and a photograph each end, Maire in her sixth-form uniform and her brother Martin in Gaelic football kit. On one side are book shelves from ceiling to floor, the great Russian novels, Dickens, Joyce, a shelf primarily of World Wars One and Two history, and on the bottom political philosophers. Rousseau, Marx, Proudhon, Bakunin.

'Will you have a wee drink, David? Whiskey? Beer?' asks Stephen.

'Whatever you're having, Stephen, be great, thanks,' he replies and turns to look more closely at the shelves of books. 'You must be a history man?'

'Aye, well, I try to take an interest,' he says modestly.

'You'd be a PhD, wouldn't you, Da, if life was different,' says Maire.

'Not got your brains, kid.' His pride in her illuminates the room.

'Course you have, you oul fool,' she says. 'You just never had the chance.'

'Never know now, will we?' He rises stiffly and disappears to the kitchen. David shoots Maire a grin; she repels it with a grimace and raised eyebrow. Her father returns with a bottle of Jameson's.

'Unless you're a Scotch man,' he suddenly wonders.

'No, that'll be great,' says David.

'That's handy, not sure I got any.'

Stephen turns to Maire. 'Sorry, love, I was forgetting.'

'It's OK, Da.' She rises and gives him a peck on his bald head. 'I'll go and help Ma.'

'I see you've got the philosophy shelf, too,' says David, after she has closed the door behind her.

'Aye, well, that's all down to Martin.' His tone contains a hint of wistfulness. Momentarily subdued, he looks away from David at the lower shelf, then perks up. 'I stick to the history myself.' He smiles.

In the kitchen, Rosa bastes a topside of beef.

'Ma, you shouldn't be spending money on that,' Maire chides her.

'Course I should, love. Any friend of yours needs a proper welcome.' They're both silent as she concentrates on the juices and returns the joint to the oven. 'He's a fair-looking wee man.'

'I'm glad you think so, Ma.'

'You like him?'

'Yes, Ma, I do. He's fun.'

'Is he kind?'

'Yes, he's kind.'

She takes a tray of roast potatoes – they seem a vast amount – and carefully revolves them, inspecting every side for brownness. While she's returning them to the heat, with her back to her daughter, Rosa mumbles, 'Not like us, is he, though?' She turns to Maire, wearing a worried smile.

'Does that matter, Ma?' asks Maire gently.

'Not if you really like him, love.' She pauses. 'And his intentions are good.'

Lunch, which takes place around the kitchen table, is not the ordeal Maire's imagined. Her mother's food is always delicious and David relishes it. He is, she knows all too well, a practised charmer and he and Stephen range over twentieth-century history, which David explains was his special course during his degree – something he's not previously told her. They even compare Ireland's Gaelic football teams, another area of expertise he's not previously laid claim to. He's shameless, she tells herself, but can't help admiring him for it. By the time pudding, a massive apple pie with ice cream, has largely disappeared, he has his mother and father dangling on a hook. A half-bottle of cognac is even produced to accompany coffee.

A key rattles the front door lock; she tenses. Martin walks in, hangs up his coat and joins them in the kitchen. 'Don't get up,' he commands. 'Jeez, Ma, smells cracking.'

'I've kept you a plate,' she says. 'Wasn't sure youse were coming.'

'Aye, I meant to be earlier but something come up.' He looks over at David.

'This is my friend David,' says Maire.

Martin offers his hand, 'Pleased to meet you, David.' David jumps to his feet to shake it. Martin's face is a blank, neither warm nor cool. 'Just a slice of that there apple pie would be great, Ma. Then I'll need to away.'

'No beef?' She sounds disappointed.

He pats his stomach. 'Gotta watch myself.'

Maire catches David's eye. 'Almost time to go if we're gonna catch that bus.'

'I'm just beginning to enjoy myself. You're no sooner come than gone,' Stephen says. 'Go on, stay. Stay the night. David can go in Martin's room. He's living out the house now.'

'No, Da,' Maire interrupts, 'honestly we've got to—'

David cuts across her. 'I don't need to get back, Maire.'

She casts him an icy stare. 'There we are,' says her father.

'I didn't pack,' says Maire.

'I'll have whatever you need,' says Rosa. 'Be nice if you stay, love.'

With a flourish, David produces two objects from his jacket pocket. 'Toothbrushes,' he announces triumphantly. 'Never travel without them.'

'Looks like you're beaten, love,' says Stephen.

Martin has been listening quietly. 'Sure, that's OK, I'm never sleeping here now.'

Early winter darkness is setting in. 'Fancy a walk, David?' asks Maire. 'Show you the neighbourhood.'

'That'd be nice.'

Her parents nod in approval. 'You two go on,' says Rosa, the mother orchestrating the young lovers to have their time.

They walk in a cold silence that matches the air. The Black Mountain is a silhouetted line in the dark, lowering over them; the streets deserted, neighbours huddled behind closed doors watching television in warmly lit rooms.

'You shouldn't have done that.'

'Done what?' he replies with the innocence of angels.

'You fucking well know what, David,' she snaps.

'Good God, you're really angry, aren't you? Is this going to be our first row?'

He's refusing to take her seriously; this time the charm and the grin won't work.

'You planned it,' she accuses him.

'No, not planned.'

'What about the stunt with the toothbrushes? How stupid do you think that made me feel?'

'I was prepared, that's all.'

'Not good enough, David. I told you, I didn't wanna stay here long. I don't like this place.'

'Why? It's your home town.'

'You dunno anything, do you, David?'

'Not if you don't tell me, no, I don't.'

'And I thought you fucking understood history.'

He addresses her with a deadly earnest. 'Maire, I meant what I said. For us to be one, I have to be one with them. This is my chance to overcome that history. I know it's costing you. But I've got to grab it.'

'You tricked me.'

'Maire, look at me.' He's imploring her. 'I love you for God's sake.'

She allows the word to linger. A sliver of moon is showing, occasional stars dotting the sky between the street lights. 'You always have an answer, don't you?' she says.

'Love's not a contest.'

Tea, as her parents call it, or supper, as David does when with her, is mushroom omelettes with home-cut chips. The front door latch sounds. She hears the voice of Martin reappearing and a second set of footsteps behind. She immediately knows.

Martin pokes his head around the kitchen door, followed by Joseph. He's still the lanky, beguiling figure with long dark hair, but now a cigarette stuck in his hand and a gauntness in his cheeks. She's cold with fear of him.

'Hello, Maire,' he says. 'Been a while.'

'I've too much work ever to get away.' She wants to be anywhere but here. 'It's good to see you, Joseph.' She doesn't want to touch him and introduces him to David.

'Pleased to meet you,' says Joseph. 'You're a lucky man. There's plenty like to be in your shoes.' David grins while Joseph makes a show of inspecting him up and down. 'Good luck to you. Any true friend of Maire's a friend of mine.' The chill in the word 'true' is unmistakable.

After tea she and David go up to her room. David admires her trophies: the silver cup for 'outstanding academic achievement', the photograph of her in the school cycling team, family photos of windswept holidays on the Atlantic coast.

'Mum and Dad insist on keeping them there,' she says. 'I'd get shot of them all.'

'You can see how proud they are of you,' he protests. He peers at a portrait photograph of the teenage Maire in her school uniform.

'So who's our friend Joseph?' he asks idly.

'Why do you wanna know about him?' Her reply is not warm.

'He can't take his eyes off you.'

'Unrequited adoration, I expect.' The sarcasm tells him not to pursue it.

At 11 p.m. she packs him off to bed in Martin's bedroom with a promise that he'll stay there. Even if she's in the mood, she can't spend the night with him in her childhood home.

And then they come.

CHAPTER 12

One a.m. The turbulence of the day sabotages her sleep. She hears the front door click open, the flick of a light switch and tiptoeing footsteps. A minute later, a tap on her bedroom door.

'Maire.' It's Martin whispering.

She rubs her eyes, switches on the bedside light and pulls the door ajar. She's wearing her pants and shirt.

'Whaddya you want, Martin?' He puts a finger over his lips and shushes her.

'Just come down for a minute, kid.'

'Why?'

'Just do it, Maire, OK.'

It's an order not a request; she puts on her sweater and jeans and follows him down.

Three figures are grouped in front of the gas fire. Joseph Kennedy is one. She recognizes the other two from occasional visits to the house in past years: Sean Black, denim jacketed with sleeked back, jet black hair; Brendan O'Donnell, narrow brown eyes darting about, pallid cheeks below. She nods to them all. She is in the presence of men with blood on their hands – men who won't turn a hair at disposing of anyone they deem an enemy or traitor.

'Sorry to disturb you, Maire,' says Joseph. 'Nothing to be alarmed about, I'm sure.'

'Something's come up,' says Black. 'We need to check it out.'

O'Donnell takes over; it strikes her that they've rehearsed. 'Your friend David. There's a question of identity,' he says more roughly.

Martin takes charge – as he has always done. 'The name rings a bell,' he says.

Maire instantly remembers what David's told her about his father. 'Whaddya mean?' She sounds as puzzled as she can.

'Vallely,' continues Martin. 'As I say, it rings a bell.'

'It's just a name,' she says. 'What sort of bell?'

'It's not that common, though, is it?'

'It's another Irish name,' she says.

'But he's a Brit, isn't he?' interrupts Joseph.

'Yes, Joseph, he's English,' says Maire. 'Is that a sin?' She gets no answer.

'The thing is,' says Black, 'your brother recalls the name Vallely as having a military connection. A Brit soldier.'

'I dunno what you're talking about,' says Maire. 'When was this?'

'That's the trouble,' says O'Donnell. 'Your brother can't place the timing.'

'Can't my *brother*' – she stamps the word with heavy emphasis – 'speak for himself?'

'Don't get angry, Maire,' says Joseph. 'It's for your own good.'

'That's why you were inspecting him, then,' says Maire, scornfully rounding on him.

'I'm still looking out for you, Maire.'

'I can look out for myself,' she snarls.

'Actually, you should be grateful to Joseph, Maire,' says Martin, watching her closely. She's reminded how much she has come to dislike his assumption of authority over her. 'He doesn't remember the name like I do. Do you, Joseph?'

'That's right, Martin, I don't. Doesn't ring a bell to me.'

Maire shivers. She's grateful for the excuse of the cold house in the middle of the night. She looks at the four of them, in their different ways all living reasons not to return to this place.

'I'll tell him what you say,' she says. 'but he won't know what you're talking about. What's the big deal, anyway?'

'We're not saying there is one, Maire,' says Black, 'but unexplained Brits lurking in our home territory . . .'

'He's not a lurker,' says Maire, 'he's my friend. I'm not such a fool.'

'You need to know something, Maire,' says Martin. She senses her brother about to embark on one of his lectures. 'These are delicate times. Treacherous times. There are men in the leadership wanting to give up the struggle. Talking about some kind of peace process with the Brits. We've got to hold the line. We four have committed ourselves to do that. We'll do whatever's necessary. So we've got to be careful, keep our eyes and ears open. This is a situation which breeds traitors and spies.'

'He's a student,' she says. 'He lives a hundred miles away. He's a nice boy. I like him. Maybe he's happy-go-lucky, maybe his big stupid grin's sometimes too wide. But those are sins I can put up with.' She's trying to stay calm. Desperation is her most dangerous opponent.

'OK,' says Martin, 'we'll decide overnight if any further action is necessary. That's it. Till the morning, anyway.' He looks hard into her eyes. 'And youse keep an eye on him.'

Joseph follows her out to the hallway, planting a restraining hand on her shoulder.

'You got away OK, didn't you, Maire?'

'Whaddya talking 'bout?'

'Just that.'

'You'd best make yourself clear, Joseph.'

'Never even said goodbye.'

'Jesus Christ, what the fuck did you expect?'

Kennedy neither answers nor lets her go. 'Handsome, your Brit, isn't he?'

'Yes, he's handsome.'

'Need to be careful.'

'Whaddya saying, Joseph?'

'A lotta touts around.' He cast her a curious smile. 'Know what I mean?' He puts a finger to his nose as if to imply a shared secret.

'I dunno what the fuck you're talking 'bout, Joseph.' He raises his eyebrows and removes his hand from her shoulder. She swivels on her heel and climbs the stairs as swiftly as quiet allows.

Reaching the landing, she thinks she sees the door of Martin's room, where David is sleeping, silently closing. Perhaps it's her agitation. The burble of voices below is audible for a few minutes, then the sound of the front door opening, footsteps departing, and the latch snapping slickly shut.

She realizes she's at a crossroads in her life. She makes her decision – after it, there can be no turning back.

Instead of retreating to her room, she eases open the door she thinks she saw shutting. He's lying in bed, apparently asleep.

'David?' she whispers.

He's instantly alert. 'Yes, Maire.'

'Listen to me. Just for once don't speak, don't ask questions, don't argue, don't try tricks. In thirty minutes, you and I'll leave this house silently. That'll give them time—'

'Give who time?' he interrupts.

'Just shut up, would you?' she hisses. 'We'll give them time to split up and get to their own homes. We'll then walk to the Europa bus station. We'll look like late-night lovers. It's only a few miles. We'll not take a local bus there, or a taxi. The early bus for Dublin leaves at four a.m. We're catching it. Understand?'

'Yes, Maire.' It's the first time he has complied with her so instantly. 'What about your parents?'

'I said don't ask questions.' She tiptoes from the room, turns into her own, and puts the rest of her clothes on. Her and David's overcoats are on hooks in the hall downstairs and will have to wait until they're ready to leave the house. She puts on her bedside lamp, angling it onto the floor to throw as little ambient light as possible. Her old school desk is still in the corner – in it she finds a scrap of paper and a biro. She picks it up, recoils at its childishly chewed end, and writes:

Dear Ma and Da

Sorry David and I had to away early. Forgot we're meeting friends down south for Mass tomorrow. Been great to see you and thanks, Ma, for the great food. See you soon and will ring, love Maire xx.

She doesn't know whether to feel pleased with herself or ashamed.

She leaves her room, closing its door tight. David hears her, creeps out onto the landing, and closes his. Her father's snoring drifts through the house. It is helpful cover. Downstairs, they collect their coats and slide into the night. Maire pulls out a woolly hat and stretches it down over her ears and forehead. She unfurls David's coat collar and pulls it as far as she can up his neck. She whispers in his ear.

'So we're lovers. Been drinking the night through, staggering home, a bit far gone. No one talks except me.'

At one point, she sees a man in the distance, pushes David against a hedge and kisses him passionately. After the man has passed, she brusquely withdraws and marches on. They pause in dark corners to allow time to pass and arrive at the bus station at 3.40. She places them on a bench and they conceal each other in long hugs. The time comes to board the coach. It is a quarter full. They sit together and continue the burial of each other in embraces. As the bus pulls away, she speaks.

'Don't look out of the window.'

'OK,' he says.

'Shush.'

The coach follows its slow meandering route, past pickup points heading out of Belfast via Lisburn. The motorway offers protection, but there is still the Newry stop to come. Much of the time Maire tells herself she's being paranoid. It seems preposterous that some kind of revenge against a long dead British soldier could be visited on the son. But she knows these men. And she remembers Martin's severity – her brother, now disunited in blood. She tries to forget Joseph speaking in riddles. She disobeys her own instructions and glances at overtaking cars.

It is still dark when they cross the border and turn into Dundalk, the last stop before Dublin. The driver announces there will be a fifteen-minute wait.

'I need to stretch my legs, Maire.'

'No.'

'I need to piss.'

'No.'

He sits in silent pain.

'Jesus Christ,' she whispers. 'Stay.' It's a command to a dog. She steps out, woolly hat back over her head, and heads towards a kiosk in the bus station. He watches her negotiate with a toothless old man encamped in the stall and return with a plastic shopping bag. The other passengers are sleeping or taking a break outside. She hands him the bag.

'Use this.'

'Is this really necessary, Maire?'

'Shut up. Use it.'

He undoes his fly zip and she leans over him while he fills the bag.

'Give it me.'

She takes the bag, trying to catch any leaking drips in her hand as she dismounts the bus. She walks over to a garbage can and throws the bag in. She wipes her hands with distaste.

An hour and a half later they're in Dublin. It is nearly 8 a.m., the early-morning cold and damp.

'I wanna walk along the river,' she says.

'I'm famished, Maire,' he answers. 'Any chance of some breakfast?'

'Walk first.'

'Did you remember my lead?' he asks.

'Not funny,' she snaps. Her agitation silences him.

They walk towards the river, turn left along Customs House Quay and find an empty bench. Its stone is hard and flat, no back and no arms. They sit down together, backs straight, untouching, looking through railings to the river. She wants to speak, to unlock the shock of the night. Instead she slumps, unable to talk.

He stretches a hand across her leg. 'So,' he says gently, 'what was all that about?'

Her eyes glisten. 'I dunno,' she whispers.

'Tell me.'

She removes his hand and sits up again. 'Was your father in the North?' She forces herself to be calm, but firm.

'What?' he exclaims. His surprise rattles her.

'Your father. Your British soldier father.'

'What's that got to do with anything?'

'My brother remembered his name.'

His astonishment rises. 'Look,' he says, 'that couldn't be. It's not possible.'

'Why's it not possible?'

She sees him gathering his thoughts. 'Christ, Maire, it's not as if they released their names. It wasn't an invitation to a ball.'

'But he was here,' she states.

'Yeah, he probably did a tour. But that was nothing. They all did.'

'Did he do anything bad?'

'No.' He reflects. 'Not that I know of. Not that ever came out. They were troubled times. Lots of bad stuff happened. But getting hold of his name. That just couldn't be.'

'Then I don't understand it,' she says meekly.

'Look,' he says, 'I don't want to go against your brother but maybe he thinks saying something like this will put you off me. I know he'll hardly see me as ideal company for his sister.'

She slumps again and turns to the river. 'You don't understand those men,' she says.

'And you need have nothing more to do with them,' he replies. 'I'm sorry to have caused you such a fright.'

He buries his head in her crotch and lies there, still as a statue. She remains motionless, but allows him to stay. He moves his arms around her waist and gently strokes her, digging his fingers beneath the belt of her jeans to touch the top of her buttocks. She puts her fingers through his thick dark hair and pulls his head up.

'All right, you beautiful, mixed-up fool,' she says, 'let's get some breakfast.' She looks at her hands. 'God knows what I've just left on your hair.'

CHAPTER 13

Post-election, Monday, 8 May

Cloud stretched motionless throughout the day across the Thames and the city beyond. The fog of office, thought Anne-Marie. Office – the word kept on rearing up at her. She had been propelled by the moment to accept the new Prime Minister's offer. With time to think, she was amazed at her impulsiveness.

It was not just the scare of her encounter with Rob McNeil. Her whole career had been about taking sides, fighting causes, standing up for the underdog. Now she was entering a world of compromises, where right and wrong were shadows. The state would not just try to shackle her judgements. The day's very first official act – stepping into the ministerial car – was the first small step in shackling her life.

'This is spoiling, Mr Hinds,' she had said. Her driver angled his rear-view mirror.

'Please call me Keith, Minister, it's traditional.'

'Yes, Keith. And you may call me, Anne-Marie.'

'I'm afraid that's not traditional, Minister.' He smiled.

'And I'm afraid I'd rather be on my bike. I truly can't see myself getting used to this.'

'Don't worry, Minister, I'm told that's what they all say.'

'Oh, does that mean you're new to the job?'

'That's right, Minister,' he replied breezily. 'You and I can make up our rules as we go along.'

He returned the mirror back to its correct position. Despite her driver's chirpiness, she felt the closing of the cell door.

She had expected to be dropped at the main Home Office entrance in Marsham Street. Instead Hinds turned left at the traffic lights with Horseferry Road and then right to descend into the strip-lit concrete of the basement car park. Two men in grey suits and white shirts waited outside bare automatic swing doors resembling the entrance to a cancer ward.

'Welcome, Minister,' said the older man. She took in a stocky figure, mid-fifties, a large, no doubt brain-packed, shiny bald head with a fringe of close-cropped black hair. No glasses, but an irregular squinting suggested unfamiliar contact lenses. 'George Jupp, Permanent Secretary.'

'Hello, Sir George,' she said.

'George will do splendidly, Minister.' He gestured to the younger man, around thirty, swept-back sandy hair. 'May I introduce you to your private secretary, Alan Dalrymple.'

She gave him her most dazzling smile and detected a shy blush in return. 'Hello, Alan.'

'Welcome, Minister.' A classless voice, impossible to tell whether it was once laced with Essex or Eton.

They escorted her through the doors into the lift to the ministerial floor.

'So, Minister, poacher turned gamekeeper,' said Sir George. Small talk not his strength, she thought.

'No, George,' she replied, 'the poacher within.' The private secretary's eyes popped. She gave him an arch of the eyebrow. They exited the lift and walked down a corridor past Steve Whalley's suite.

'The Secretary of State has asked for morning prayers every Monday with his ministerial team,' said Sir George. 'Not literally, of course, just one of our expressions.'

'Yes, I can't imagine Steve Whalley invoking the Lord,' replied Anne-Marie. 'He wouldn't want to lose face.'

'In that case, we have half an hour to prepare to meet our maker – and breaker – here on earth,' chipped in Dalrymple. Sir George cast him a silent reprimand. By contrast, she grinned and Sir George's disapproval was magically transformed.

They arrived at a door with a newly mounted sign. 'Anne-Marie Gallagher, Minister of State, Security and Immigration.' Three people rose as one from their desks.

'Minister, this is Jemima Sheffield, your diary secretary. She's joined us today as her predecessor has been switched to different pastures,' said Dalrymple. Anne-Marie shook the hand of an efficient-looking, fair-haired woman in her early forties, dressed in a knee-length, straight, grey skirt. 'Jemima,' continued Dalrymple, 'has the reputation of being Whitehall's briskest enforcer of train and plane timetables. We must share her with others, so that allows her only to pop in and out as needs demand.' Anne-Marie raised an eyebrow. 'Our first contribution to the new government's war on bureaucratic waste, Minister,' he continued with an archness she found herself liking. 'And Nikki and Dan, assistant private secretaries.' Two more handshakes.

Beneath the courtesies, the entrance of the new Minister was pregnant with uncertainty. Usually, a private office had some warning of the goods it was going to receive – or have dumped on it. It could picture a face. It could research what the likely Minister stood for and prepare briefs and policies in advance. Sometimes legislation if the party manifesto was specific enough.

But Anne-Marie Gallagher was nowhere on their radar. Dalrymple and the two assistant private secretaries had spent that Sunday night Googling, Wiki'ing, and trawling news sites. Her chambers' own website offered résumés of a career and recent cases that were the standard fare of extradition and asylum appeals. She had represented whistleblowers and written opinion pieces for the *Guardian*. *Newsnight* interviewed her on weekly payments for asylum seekers. But it was a curiously blank personal canvas: no background or context, no sense of origin, family or place.

The one sign suggesting something out of the ordinary was that speech after her election. As the young civil servants laboured through the night and studied her words again and again, they could not help whispering whether they had a cuckoo in the nest.

'Your speech was amazing, Minister,' enthused Nikki, mid-twenties, short blonde hair, white silk shirt.

'Absolutely, Minister, totally,' chimed Dan from the white collar and mild striped tie of his grey suit. 'It was such a different tone from your predecessor.'

'Thank you, Dan,' she replied. 'Yes, he did sound as if what he'd really like to do is wreathe the nation in barbed wire. So' – she cast a challenging stare at them – 'what's the way to get things done around here?'

Alan Dalrymple moved quickly to speak first. 'The key for a minister, Minister, is to have the ear of the Secretary of State. Without his backing, it's hard to wade through the morass. Unless' – he paused, engaging her eye to eye – 'you feel you have a direct line to the Prime Minister himself.'

'Let's first see how the land lies with the Secretary of State, shall we?' said Anne-Marie, smiling sweetly at them all.

She had seen Steve Whalley on podiums and screens but never in the flesh. Flesh, it struck her on shaking his hand, was the word. Drooping jowls, two, maybe three, chins; stomach shamelessly pushing into trousers held by braces; gold cufflinks shining from formal white shirt and mauve tie; above, a full head of strong steely-grey hair and thick spectacles obscuring the gimlet eyes. He was a man with a reputation for combining avuncular charm and political brutality.

'Anne-Marie,' he said pressing bulbous fingers into her hand, 'no doubt a surprise to you as much as to me.' He had asked to see her alone before morning prayers – not, it seemed, to pay compliments.

'Sit down, lass, sit down,' Whalley continued. 'You're a mystery woman to me. I don't mind that, I can see you've got something. So' – he took a deep breath – 'what were Lionel's instructions?'

'Instructions?'

'That's right, instructions. What did he tell you?'

She felt his eyes bearing in.

'It went in such a blur, I can hardly remember a word he said.'

'I'm not stupid, but I won't push you – this time.' He stood up, stretched his braces and shamelessly stuck out his belly. 'Mind you, he's given you the poisoned chalice, hasn't he?'

'I'm sorry . . .'

'Immigration, country being overrun, you thinking you want to let 'em all in.'

'I've never said that.'

'It's not what you don't say, kid, it's how you don't say it. And all your refugees and asylum seekers, what's that going to cost?'

'It's about a different mindset—' she tried to interrupt.

'He's a crafty bastard, Lionel,' he forced on. 'Probably setting you up to fail.' He walked round the desk and looked down on her, grinning amiably. She stood up in response, feeling the heat of his breath.

'Why on earth would he want to do that?'

''Cos he's a fucking politician who's now Prime Minister. And you're a pretty little loose cannon, who shoots her mouth off.'

'Has it ever occurred to you he might mean what he says?'

'No, lass, I can't say it ever has.' He paused and she bit her tongue.

Whalley shuffled back round to his chair. 'You play it right with me, Anne-Marie, and I'll see you right. You can have as many human rights as you want as long as it doesn't affect the efficient working of this department,' he ground on. 'I know you've whistleblower friends but no blowing whistles here. No leaking, no shitting on the boss. To anyone. Including Lionel Buller.'

'I'm not a fool.' She felt the fury rising inside and sprang from her chair.

'One thing before you go, Anne-Marie. No skeletons in your cupboard, are there? Funny boyfriends, girlfriends maybe – not that I care – dirty money, buried bodies? Don't mind if there are and you tell me 'cos I'll sort it. If you don't and anything comes out, you're dead.'

This time, she could not repress it. Brought up on rough streets where young men learnt to fight and young women learnt to lance old men's leers, she leant across the desk and, enunciating each word, whispered in his ear, 'If you ever speak to me again like that, I will squeeze your balls so tight you will scream.'

She stood upright, stretched out her hand to shake his and spoke in her loudest voice: 'Thank you, Secretary of State, it will be a privilege to serve in your team.'

As, with measured steps, she made for the door, he murmured, 'You can call me Steve, you know.'

Outside, Sir George Jupp approached. She realized he would have been listening in and flashed him an extravagant smile. An unwelcome thought intruded. Could a man like Steve Whalley know anything about her? If so, how? And why?

Back at the private office, Dalrymple handed her a printed sheet. 'I've taken the liberty, Minister, of organizing a round of briefings to begin half an hour after the Secretary of State's morning prayers.'

Anne-Marie looked down. Meetings with the Director-General of the Border Force; the Chief Executive of the Passport Office; updates on asylum tribunals; on contentious exclusion orders in the offing; finally, an evening welcome drink with senior officials.

'When do I get time to think?' she asked Dalrymple.

'Don't worry, Minister,' he replied, 'that's for night-time when you're with your red box.'

Eleven hours later, she returned to the office to collect her coat and go home. Dalrymple was still at work.

'You should be home, Alan.'

'A private secretary cannot leave before the minister, Minister.'

'Is that a rule or a tradition?' He could see she was teasing him.

'Neither, Minister, it's a sackable offence.'

She felt a tiny thrill of pleasure at his smiling as he said it. 'Thank you, Alan, for organizing such an interesting and productive day.'

Thank you for thanking, Minister.' He hesitated. 'It never happened under your predecessor.' Dalrymple shuffled some final papers, closed her red box and handed it to her. 'Your overnight reading. Rather a lot, I'm afraid. A logjam tends to build up over elections. Appointments for you to sign off, extradition decisions which need your approval.'

'How can I approve decisions to extradite?' she asked, understanding instantly that it could only be a question addressed to herself.

'Oh, one last thing, Minister,' continued Dalrymple, 'a man called Joseph has rung the office several times. Initially we palmed him off but he really did seem to know you and want to speak, so we took his number. He said to mention the Botanic flat. It sounded as if it might be some rather urgent property issue.'

He handed her a note with a phone number; she looked down at it, repressing the sinking in her gut. 'Thank you, yes, that's probably the reason.' She picked up the box and headed for the door.

'Your driver's waiting, Minister, solo travel on city streets with your red box is not recommended.'

'You'll train me yet.' She stuffed the note into her handbag and, avoiding the lift, headed for the back stairs. Checking that she was alone, she stopped at the top, stood tall, and composed herself.

Joseph. The one person above all she had assumed would never – could never – reappear. Who'd had to hide, to vanish for ever. She'd imagined him long dead, probably with a bullet in his head. How he must have waited. And waited. And now he had delivered his shock. She hoped she had managed to betray nothing when Dalrymple mentioned the name. She suspected the blood must have all too visibly drained from her face.

Hinds was leaning on the bonnet of the car, puzzling over a crossword. Hearing the click of heels, he sprang to his feet and opened the back door. She slid in, collapsed into her seat and dropped the red box beside her.

'Straight home, Minister?' asked Hinds.

For once, she wanted the safety of company. 'Keith, would you do something for me?'

'That's what I'm here for, Minister.'

'I've just had some sad news. An aunt I'm fond of. They're saying she may not have long. Could you drive me around for half an hour? Doesn't matter where. I just need to let it sink in, phone one or two people.'

Hinds looked round at her. It was the first hint of vulnerability; she had seemed so organized, brisk, confident, at ease with herself. 'I'd be happy to, Minister.'

He drove across Parliament Square, east along the Embankment, past the Inns of Court on her left and, across the river, the bizarrely and massively elongated pyramid that was the Shard; discordant notes in a city moulded in power and commerce rather than beauty or elegance. She allowed the images to float past; their effect was hypnotic.

She stirred herself to consider the options. She could report Joseph's approach to the police and ask them to stop him harassing her. She assumed any police file would show him as a missing person, probably presumed dead. But his reappearance would raise awkward questions. And answers that could spill over onto her.

She could seek advice from Kieron Carnegie. It would mean taking him into her confidence – but that was a decision she would have had to make a long time ago.

She could ignore him. But, if she did, she was sure he would never leave her alone. He would remain outside, a loose cannon.

In the end, she knew, in her heart, that there were no options. She must flush him out herself. She had to know his motivation, and what he intended to do. Or, more likely, wanted her to do. Before taking action, she would allow herself the night to think it over. Over the past four days, among the triumphalism, she had felt nausea and occasional dread. Now, for the first time, she smelt fear.

She turned to Hinds. 'So what were you doing before, Keith?'

Hinds adjusted the rear-view mirror to see her. 'Me, Minister?'

'Yes, you, Keith.' She smiled.

'Just a humble police driver for the Met, Minister,' he replied. 'This is where one or two of us lucky ones get pensioned off.'

'I see,' said Anne-Marie, 'the policeman's rest home. And the politician's graveyard.'

'Don't worry, Minister, we'll get you out alive.'

CHAPTER 14

March–April 1994

'I was thinking, Maire,' David begins cheerily, walking over to put his arms round her neck. It's a couple of weeks since the night flight from the North and their afternoon routine is regaining normality.

She peers over her shoulder. 'Yeah?'

'It wasn't necessary to do that runner from your home.'

Alerted, she rises and breaks away to stand by the window, studying the traffic below. She whips round. 'Whaddya talking about?'

'I'm just thinking it was a pity, that's all. I've nothing to hide, I can't be blamed for being my father's son. You've nothing to hide. We could have stayed on and said so.'

'Christ, I get that. But these guys don't. I tell you again, David Vallely, you have no idea. No fucking idea.'

'What do you mean, I have "no fucking idea"?' He repeats her words with sour emphasis.

'Do you know the sort of people we're dealing with?'

'No, why should I? Except for your brother – and you told me he's a windbag.' She's riled. 'Your words, Maire, not mine.'

'You shouldn't have such a good fucking memory.'

'As for Joseph Kennedy, the only problem there is that he's obviously sweet on you.'

'Let me tell you something.' She's shown him before her spikiness. Now she adds fire. 'Forget about Martin and Joseph, I don't wanna discuss them. But those other two – they're called Sean Black and Brendan O'Donnell by the way if you wanna commit that to your brilliant fucking memory – they wouldn't even need the evidence if they took against you. You'd be bundled up, shotgun to your kneecaps, cigarette burns in your eyes, and then two bullets in your head before they leave you to the wild animals in some distant bog.'

'They seemed polite enough to me.'

'How the fuck do you know how polite they are?' She seeps suspicion.

'Maire,' he replies calmly, 'the walls of your house are thin. I may not have heard the words but I could make out the tone. It seemed friendly enough.'

'If you think that,' she says, 'you're an eejit. You should be too smart to be that.'

He walks to the window. 'OK. I touched a nerve I didn't understand.'

'No, you don't understand.' Her cheeks are flushed. 'You don't understand how corrosive it is, how people get sucked in. Christ, when I was a twelve-year-old kid, I was out there cheering my fucking head off when they nearly blew up Thatcher. Sure I was. I was a fucking teenager in West Belfast. Bomb the bastards. But then I began to use my brain. And I discovered something called the law. That's what we came here to study, isn't it?'

She glares at him, her passion and anger electric, laying down some kind of challenge.

'I won't mention it again,' he says.

'Good. Don't. None of it. And you remember, it could have gone the other way for any of us. I escaped, so never remind me of it.'

She returns to her seat and her books. He approaches and she looks up warily, but all he does is put a set of keys on the desk. 'I got these cut for you. Come and go as you like. I want the flat to be a refuge for you. To show our trust in each other.' She looks into his eyes and feels foolish.

One evening in March she lets herself in, climbs up the stairs to the first floor, enters the narrow hallway and sees him silhouetted in his bedroom at the far end, holding the phone.

Not wanting to interrupt, she quietly pushes the door to and slips into the kitchen. Phrases waft down the passage. She tries to stop herself listening but the curiosity is too much. His voice floats over. 'That's great, at least he's feeling better.' 'And how about you, my love?' 'And the job?' 'How's that shit of a boss?' 'You should tell him where to get off.' 'I'm hoping to get back for a weekend in a few weeks, maybe.' 'There's a couple of things to finish here, then it will be over.' 'OK, just remember, won't be long. Tons of love.'

There's a clunk as the phone is put down. She can sense him sitting for a minute or two, almost hear his brain whirring as he reflects on something. Then the slow beat of his footsteps speeding up as he notices the kitchen door ajar and a strip of light shafting through.

His voice precedes him. 'Maire?'

She raises her eyes as his face peers around the door. He offers his most angelic look. 'I didn't hear you come in.'

'I know. You were on the phone.'

'Yes.' She turns her back, puts the food she's bought for supper into the fridge, and flicks the kettle on. She doesn't look round. 'Who is she, David?'

'She? Why she?'

Now she does turn round to confront him. 'Oh, come on.'

'OK, if you're really that interested, it was my sister.'

Her eyes stay locked on him, her bewilderment turning to a sad deflation amid an oppressive silence.

'You don't have a sister, David,' she finally says.

For the first time she can remember, she sees fear in his eyes.

'Shit,' he says simply.

'Yes, shit,' she says.

His calculating is all too transparent – and he's floundering. She waits to see what he'll come up with.

'It was a girl.'

'A girl?'

'She was nothing. Is nothing.'

'The girl you left behind?'

'Sort of.'

She scoffs. 'That ghost of a girl you saw that time in the park.'

She detects something akin to relief – maybe because the secret he's been harbouring is now coming out. 'OK, yes.'

'Called Susan, yeah? The girl you're going back to. When you leave here. What was it you said? When it's over.'

'No. No.' He's beginning to shake, a tear forming in his eye. 'It's you I want to be with, Maire. You have to believe me. But I can't tell her over the phone. Can't hurt her like that. I have to do it face to face. Then it will be over. And I'll be with you.' He smiles. 'And we'll live happily ever after.'

'And who's the he who's feeling better, David?' There's a millisecond of hesitation.

'Her dad,' he answers. 'He's been ill.'

She turns from him again, busying herself with slicing an onion, finding a pan, dripping oil into it. The sulphurous fumes from the onion bring her own tear.

'You've lied to me, David.'

'I'm sorry. Truly sorry. I'm telling you the truth now. I just always want to make it easy for you. Not to hurt you.'

She puts down the knife, rinses her hands, and takes a tissue to wipe her eyes. She swivels to face him.

'Don't ever lie to me, David.' There's a chill in her voice.

He winces. 'I won't, Maire, I promise.'

It may be a small lie. It may be she should take his explanation at face value. But she can't help it – distrust lurks. Invisible, unspoken, silently polluting.

It's been their pattern before to let tensions settle before resolving them. He consumes her far too much to allow one lie to break them so, a few days later, she refers back to it with a lilt in her voice.

'OK, then, what's she like?'

He's puzzled, genuinely it seems. 'What's who like?'

'Susan, you big fool.'

'Oh, her.' She feels him droop.

'Yeah, her. Thought we might exorcise her.'

He perks up. 'OK. She's tall, willowy, fair hair, you'd say she's posh.'

'In other words, everything that's not me.'

'You got it in one.' He's beaming now. 'That's why you're so adorable.'

'Christ, it wasn't that bad, was it?'

'Course not. It was great for a long time. We met as students, kept together even while I was travelling, bit of licence on each side. But then, I don't know why, she got possessive. Clammy.'

'Perhaps she loved you,' says Maire. 'Wanted to marry you.'

'If she did, it wasn't the way to show it,' he replies. 'You'd never be like that.'

'How do you know?' she asks archly.

He ruffles her hair. 'I know.'

'So what was she doing over here?'

He removes his hands. 'The interrogation continues.'

'Not at all, I'm just interested.'

'I have absolutely no idea.' He reflects on the sighting. 'I didn't ask. I'm not even sure it was her. Maybe I didn't need to take fright.'

'What were you frightened of?' He doesn't answer. 'That she was stalking you?'

'Hey,' he says, lightening up, 'perhaps it really was a ghost I saw.'

She understands he wants closure and lays off. 'Right, my turn if we're exorcising,' he continues cheerfully. 'Your two nasties, Sean and Brendan, perhaps it's just that you were pissed off with me for staying the night and they were your excuse to leave early. I still reckon they're not as bad as you say.'

She glowers. 'I dunno why you'd think that, David. The world would be a lot better place without those two evil bastards.'

'I'm sorry.' His switch to remorse is immediate. As before, he seems to want her forgiveness.

'Don't mess with what you don't know.' This time, she's not granting it.

The reconciliation is only partial. Her mind tells her to freeze the relationship but whenever she looks at him with that thought – a thought he seems able to read – he looks so destroyed and the feeling he stirs in her is so powerful that she cannot bring herself to. But she's beginning to see how it could end. The university year will wind down to its natural conclusion. Then won't the differences between their worlds loom so large that he'll go back to his and she'll be alone again?

Work consumes both their days. He's even told her he needs to get away occasionally to find the peace to focus on his thesis. He says it's the most difficult thing he's ever done – perhaps he'll decamp for the odd day or two to Connemara and find solutions in mountains and oceans. She stops herself telling him that he should try being like her; just close the door, sit down and work.

She's revising in the flat alone and the front doorbell rings. She leans out of the window to see a familiar figure. Her heart jumps but he's spotted her and there's no hiding. She pulls herself together, walks calmly down the stairs, and opens the door.

'Martin!' she exclaims, feigning pleasure at seeing her brother. 'How did you know I was—'

'I'll come in, Maire, if I may,' he interrupts. It's not a request for permission. He's already crossing the threshold and pushing the door behind him. He gives her a peck on the cheek. Peremptorily, she returns it.

Once inside the flat, she tries again to tackle him. 'How did you know I was alone?'

'I waited for him to go,' he replies.

'Have you been spying on me?'

'No, Maire, watching over you.'

'It doesn't feel like that.' He's silent, biding his time. 'Well,' she says, 'what is it? Not Ma and Da, I hope.' She looks in any direction but his.

'No, they're fine, Maire. Missing you, though.'

'My last time home wasn't great.'

'It's because we wanted to act in your best interests.' He pauses. 'That's why I'm here.'

Now she engages him, steel in her eyes. 'Whatever you're gonna say, I don't wanna hear it.'

'I understand that.' He sounds soft and conciliatory. 'I know what you see in him. Good-looking, fun, clever, charming. But, for your own sake, I want you to end it now. I promise you no good can come of it. I'm your brother. I want you to have a good life. You know that from everything I've done for you. So, just on this, trust me.'

'Why should I trust you? What was all that rubbish about his name ringing a bell?' He doesn't answer. 'Was it to make me get shot of him?' She's never stood up to him like this before and fears his reaction. He does no more than sigh.

'You'll have to make your own judgement on that,' he says.

'OK. Is there something you actually know, Martin, that I ought to know?'

'That's not the point. I'm just asking you to disentangle yourself now, before it's too late.' He may be evasive but at least he's pleading, not threatening.

'*What's* too late?' She softens her voice too.

'I can't tell you. I'm not in control of it all, anyway.'

A terror grips her. 'Christ, are they gonna do something to him?' She pauses. 'Are you?'

He shakes his head. 'Jeez, Maire, whaddya think I am? Whaddya think *they* are?'

'I sometimes wonder, Martin.' Again he stays silent. 'I won't do it, Martin.' She walks over to the window and leans against the radiator, peering down at her hands. She prepares her words and turns to face him. 'Whatever his faults, I can't just dismiss him without a proper reason. And an accident of birth is certainly not that.'

'Whaddya mean,' he asks, '"accident of birth"?'

Of course, she realizes, he doesn't know about David's father, unless he's found out more. For sure, she's not going to tell him.

'I mean him being a Brit,' she replies.

'It's nothing to do with him being an Englishman. You should know me better than that.' This time, she stays quiet. 'Do you love him?' he asks.

'That's not the point. It's about being fair.'

'Does he love you, then?'

'That's not the point either.'

'Jesus, Maire, you're so fucking obtuse sometimes.' It's the first time he's raised his voice.

'You should go now, Martin.' She's imbued with a calm that surprises her.

'If that's the way you want it.' He pauses. 'Will you be home for Easter?'

'After what happened that weekend, whaddya think?'

'OK. Look, Maire.' Now he's pleading, voice softened. 'You'll never forget where you come from. It'll always be with you. And I pray that one day, with all your talent, you'll have the chance to make a difference.' She says nothing. 'I'll give your love to Ma and Da, then.'

She turns back to stare blankly out of the window, his words jarring in her head. His brisk footsteps echo up the stairs, followed by the closing click of the front door. She sees him hurrying across the road and disappearing into the city. He has not even taken his coat off.

She decides never again to be alone in the flat without David.

It's no longer a refuge and she'd rather be in the security of the library or Mrs Ryan.

Saturday, 23rd April 1994

He's been no less caring but has become more distant, sometimes fretful. Whenever she tackles him, just gentle questions as to whether anything's wrong, it's always the same answer. 'It's the thesis, Maire. Still so bloody much to write.' He blames the deadline – less than a month to deliver – his lack of fluency, how it's unlike any other writing he's done before. Watching him suffer, she determines to banish Martin's warning. To interrogate him will, in itself, be a breach of the trust she still hopes to restore. It's unthinkable even to tell him about her brother's visit.

He heads off on one of his escapes, then, three days later, reappears in the library. He sidles round her back and puts a note down over her shoulder on the table. She almost shrieks with the surprise, only the library walls enforcing her silence: 'Meet 7 p.m., this Sat, BusAras. Fix away night with Mrs Ryan!! xxx'. She's no sooner read it than he's gone.

He's already there, the grin as broad as she ever remembers it, and throws his arms round her.

'You got round Mrs Ryan!'

'Yeah, told her it was the Law Faculty spring sleepover.' She breaks away to examine him. 'I reckon she didn't believe a word of it, not sure what's come over her.'

'Who cares? You're here.' He links arms and heads away from the bus station.

'Hey, where are you taking me?' she asks with mock alarm.

'Nowhere on a bus,' he says. 'We had enough of them.'

They head down Talbot Street towards O'Connell Street. 'This is the way I walked when we went to Galway,' she says.

'We're staying nearer home this time.' He's enjoying the mystery. They turn right into O'Connell Street and walk a couple of hundred yards, and he stops by a top-hatted commissionaire guarding a grand entrance. There's a question mark in her wide-open eyes.

'Come inside,' he says.

He sweeps her past the commissionaire beneath the chandeliers of the Gresham hotel lobby and motions her to the lifts. They rise several floors and exit. He marches her down a corridor, finds a room number, produces a key from his pocket, unlocks the door and waves her in.

'What the fuck is this all about, David?' She walks over to a spread of window and takes in the cityscape. She's never seen it like this. She turns to see him walk over to a low table, lift a bottle from a silver bucket, fire its cork into the ceiling and pour pale, bubbling liquid into angled flutes.

'I'll tell you what it's all about.' He grins. 'I'm celebrating. I've cracked it.'

'You finished the thesis!' Her surprise is genuine: she never quite thought he would.

'Almost,' he says, 'just dotting and crossing final *i*'s and *t*'s.'

'That's fantastic,' she says.

'Yeah, I think I finally found a solution.'

'A solution?'

'There were two propositions fighting each other, a kind of conflict. I found a way through. Just the conclusion to do.'

'You'll have to tell me about it.'

He rolls his eyes. 'Maybe not tonight?'

She smiles. 'OK, I'll let you off.'

He orders dinner from room service – prawns the size she's

never seen before, foie gras she's never tasted before, a chocolate tart to die for.

'Christ, David, what's this costing you?' she asks, munching in a dream.

'You only live once,' he says. 'I'll never care what I'll spend on you.'

She notices his use of the future tense and feels a combination of thrill and fantasy. The memory of how unreal she found their first meeting hits her – irritated, she tells herself to dismiss it.

They scroll the movies on the hotel TV menu. 'Hey, that's impressive,' he exclaims, 'they've got *Four Weddings and a Funeral*. It's only just come out.'

'Never heard of it,' she says.

'Then it'll be an education for you.'

They snuggle up – she winces at the foppish young Englishman and friends from another universe but can't help finding them funny. 'Are there really people like that?' she asks when it's over.

'I thought you were with one of them.' For an instant, she can almost believe him, then he says 'ha-ha' and starts kissing her with an exciting deepness. There's something febrile about his lovemaking but second time around he relaxes and they find an ease with each other she feared had gone missing.

He kisses her goodnight on the forehead and rolls away on his side. Within seconds, she can hear his even breathing as he appears to sleep, but every now and then he twitches and she's not sure. At one point, she stretches out a hand to graze his shoulder. He stirs and turns. He cups her face and moves closer.

'I want you to know, Maire, that I love you. Never believe anything else. I love you more than you could ever understand.'

She sees a tear in his eye. 'And I want you to know, David, that I feel more for you than I ever thought it would be possible to feel for anyone.' She still cannot say the word. He doesn't ask for it or seem to mind. Instead he smiles and rolls over. Soon, all she can detect are the tiny risings and fallings of the rhythmic breathing of sleep.

She cannot imitate him. She's unusually restless as her stomach fights the unfamiliar richness of food and her mind churns too many inchoate thoughts. She remembers how she sprayed the word *love* into her pillow talk with Joseph. How wrong a word it was to describe her teenage idolizing of a selfish boy who ended up exploiting her. How right it would be, if their worlds could ever be aligned, to describe the wondrous feelings she's had for this man. She starts. What did he mean by 'Never believe anything else'? Why ever would she?

She inspects his silhouette, outlined by a shaft of street light. Inch by inch she follows the curves from his head, around his shoulder, the decline to his slim waist, the rise over his buttocks and waist, and the descent to his heels. The rising and falling has almost ceased – his breathing barely audible. The twitching has stopped. There's something about his stillness that seems unnatural. She watches until, finally, exhaustion overcomes her.

She awakes just after nine o'clock, daylight streaming through a gap in the curtains. She stretches out a hand. Nothing. She turns over. He's gone. In his place he's left a slender silver bracelet and matching earrings which dangle in the shape of a capital D. When she leaves the key at reception and asks about the bill, she's told it's all been paid.

That evening, she sits alone in her room at Mrs Ryan's, trying to work it out. It's ended – she's sure of that. He's gone, maybe he's already back in England. He's handed in the thesis and rejoined his people, leaving her behind. It doesn't fully add up. *He* doesn't add up. He loves her, she's sure of it. Something's driven him away. She thinks back to what Martin said. No sense there either. She thinks back to David's behaviour in recent weeks – his stress, his absences, his apartness at times. She thinks back to the whole period since the visit to her family. Perhaps they could never fully recover from it. Perhaps the distance between them was always going to be too much.

She asks herself again and again why she could never bring herself to use the word – to tell him she loves him. Because, now that he's gone, she knows she did. And does. She has an overwhelming sense of something unmatchable being lost. That, wherever he's gone, there's a part of him that remains unreached.

However unreachable it may now seem, it's a part she must not allow to escape.

CHAPTER 15

Post-election, Tuesday, 9 May

Checking her private phone was in her jacket pocket, Anne-Marie took the lift down to reception, exited left into Marsham Street and over the lights, and headed north past Church House towards St James's Park. Just past the entrance to Churchill's war rooms she crossed Horse Guards Parade, intending to lose herself among the plane trees sparkling with early summer leaf and mallards flapping around the lake. She had the half-hour she had told Jemima to clear from her lunchtime diary.

She dialled the number Joseph had left. It was answered instantly with a single word.

'Yes.' The voice was hoarse but there was no doubt.

'Joseph?'

'Yes, Maire.'

'Is it really you, Joseph? How can I know?'

'You know all right, Maire. You got my message, didn't you?'

She resigned herself. 'Yes, I did.'

'Then that's that.'

'Where are you? Where have you been? For God's sake, it's over twenty years. What are you doing suddenly contacting me?'

'There's nothing sudden. I just took my time.'

'What is this, Joseph?' She told herself to stay calm, not to betray her fear. 'You know you can't show your face again. You'd be shot. Even now.'

'Is that right, Maire?'

'Christ, Joseph, you know that's fucking right!'

'Maybe I don't care. Maybe I want the truth.'

'What are you talking about?'

'Who pulled the trigger? Eh, Maire? That'd be one truth.'

'You're mad.'

'No, I'm very sane.'

She paused, sensing a whole elaborate web unravelling. 'Have you been following me?'

'No.' Another pause. She did not believe him. 'I've been watching your progress, though.'

'Where from? Where are you?'

'Doesn't matter. You can be anywhere these days. Not like then.'

'Why now, Joseph?'

'I decided it was time.' He said it perfunctorily. They both held the silence. 'I phoned them about a body.'

'A body? Whose body?'

'Christ, Maire, whaddya mean "Whose body"?'

'I'll ask you again. Whose body?'

'You playing some kind of game?'

'OK. Just tell me what you did.'

'I phoned them. The police. Confidential line.'

'What made you do that?'

'Whaddya think? You getting elected. That's what made me

do it. And look at you now.' He paused to splutter. 'You've risen high and fast, haven't you, kid?'

'You sound out of your mind, Joseph.'

'You can't explain me away like that, Maire.'

'What did you tell them?'

'I gave the coordinates.'

'For Christ's sake!'

'When we've done, I'll be phoning again with some clues to who it might be.'

'Might be, Joseph?'

'Christ, you've come some way.'

'Where is it?' she interrupted.

'You don't need the coordinates, Maire.'

She tried to think – nothing came but the obvious and desperate. 'Whaddya want, Joseph?'

'Christ, Maire, the accent slipped there.' He paused, allowing time for the barb to sting. 'As I said, it's time.'

'Time for what?'

'You made it, didn't you? Infiltrated the bastards.'

'What do you mean, "infiltrated"?'

'You know what I mean.'

'No, I don't.'

'Doesn't it mean anything to you, Maire?'

'I don't know what you're talking about, Joseph.'

'Christ above, it killed your brother, didn't it?'

She said nothing, feeling the sinking in her heart and the return of crushed hope.

'Anyway, doesn't matter now,' he rasped on. 'I'm dying. I want it to come out before I go.'

'What do you want to come out?'

'I need to see you. So I can explain.'

'I can't see you, I can't even know you.'

'It'll only be the once.' His voice was now reduced to a diseased moan, a note of surrender she had never heard before. 'There's something you need to know.'

'All that's gone, Joseph. It's over. The past. I'm not Maire any more.'

'Sure, you'd like it that way. But it's never over.'

'Are you trying to threaten me?'

'Now I wouldn't do that, would I? Jesus, Maire, don't you remember what we once were?'

'I've never forgotten that, Joseph.'

'Then that's something, isn't it?'

She heard the old bitterness. 'So tell me why.'

'I heard your speech.' He paused, breaking into more splutters of coughing. 'It was a trick. We were all tricked. David too. It wasn't like it seemed.'

'You're speaking in riddles.'

'It's the state. You said it yourself. That's why we have to meet.'

'I'm sorry, Joseph, I'm going to ring off.'

'Don't. Just see me one time. Then it'll be done. Then you'll know. And you can decide. I won't threaten you.'

She said nothing, hearing only his rasping wheeziness.

'I promise,' he said.

'What's your plan?'

'Is this your private phone?'

'Yes. They've given me a new one for government business.'

'I'll text you a time and place.'

'I'm not saying I will, Joseph. I need to think.'

'I've given you my word. This'll be it, Maire. Closure. I promise. But you don't have a choice. It's not about me, or you. It's about the fucking British state. That's what you gotta understand. That's what I figured out. That's what's gonna blow them apart.'

The phone went dead. She heard a voice calling. 'Minister?' She started, as if woken from a bad dream, her heart banging, and looked around. It was Jemima. She forced a smile.

'Hello, Jemima. Here to talk to the ducks? Probably get more sense from them than our colleagues.'

'They don't answer back, do they?' Jemima looked at her, wafting a rush of sympathy. 'It's a strange place.' She paused. 'And very male.'

'Oh, I can handle them,' said Anne-Marie. 'They just want to be dominated really.'

Jemima laughed. 'Well, you're better placed than me as a mere servant to do that.' She tried again. 'I just want you to know that if there's ever anything . . .'

'That's kind of you, Jemima. But I must look after myself.' She wondered if she had snubbed her and softened. 'It's the only way I know, I've been on my own too long.'

Her weakness, she was all too quickly realizing, was that she was not.

The skeleton, recovered piece by piece from its lonely field, was laid out on a steel trolley as coherently as the bones allowed. Carne could imagine the short back and long legs but anything else eluded him. He watched Amy inspecting her handiwork with pride, occasionally rearranging pieces of bone by what seemed no more than a millimetre or two. He failed to see the difference but it was giving her quiet satisfaction. She walked up to the head and gazed at the holes where eyes would have been.

'What do you see?' asked Carne.

'I'm a scientist, not a seer,' she retorted. 'But, now you ask, I'll look at my crystal ball. I see a man scared of something. Not of death, he isn't a coward, but something unresolved.'

'Stick to the science?' suggested Carne, seeing he was being teased.

She walked over and patted him on the chest. 'Then watch how you phrase your questions.'

'OK. Cause of death?'

'Shot in the back of the head. Two separate bullet traces in the skull. There's a marking on the back of the right femur.'

'Anything else?'

'He was given a beating, probably crude. Maybe with a large spanner or similar.'

'Burns?' He paused. 'Electrics? Fingernail extraction?'

'Can't tell,' she replied. 'Make your own assumptions.'

'But he didn't walk into a field, shoot himself and disappear.'

'No.'

'You see,' reflected Carne, 'it's the idea of disappearance. Disappearances don't just happen.'

'Of course they do,' Amy retorted with surprising sharpness. 'Disappearances happen all the time. Sometimes folk reappear, kids come home, fathers leave the lovers they run off to. Sometimes they don't.'

'Disappearances like that never happened here.'

'Sorry, Jonny, you're beginning to lose me. Come in, ground control.' She smiled at him, as if to commiserate with his mental waywardness.

'What else?'

She walked over to a grey, aluminium cabinet and pulled open a drawer. Inside, neatly pinned in regimented lines, were fibres from tattered cloth. In another drawer, the almost intact Gore-Tex jacket. It was a forlorn display – Carne felt an involuntary welling of sadness.

'Did you confirm his age?' he asked.

'Mid-twenties to early thirties.'

'Pointless.'

'You don't know that.' She sounded like a schoolmistress ticking off an unthinking pupil.

'Know what?'

'Whether it was pointless. You don't know.'

Amy was leaning back against the filing cabinet, her eyes shining with triumph. 'I have something.' She opened another drawer to reveal three small Perspex bags. From one she removed a plastic box, two inches square, dull worn red in colour, and held it up in triumph. 'It's a jewellery box. Faux leather, made from plastic so it's lasted. It was in the inside pocket of the jacket. Guess what I found inside.'

'The killers' name cards?' suggested Carne. This time, he got more than a pat in the ribs.

'A gold signet ring. And a lock of hair.'

'And it belongs to . . .?'

'That's your department. The ring's in the lab. It's just possible there might be a print on the inside of the signet because it's flat. From the lock of hair we'll get mitochondrial DNA. Won't give you a single individual, but it's shared by the female line.

'A parting gift?' mused Carne. 'Wife? Mother? Lover? Sister?'

'Back to facts. If you can find me the family, there won't be too many of its women in the wrong place at the wrong time.'

'Clever girl.'

Carne wanted to hug her, but the skeleton on the table was too disconcerting a witness.

Carne's phone rang. 'Yes, Billy.'

'There's been a second call on the confidential phone. Same source. Said, "I got some clues for you." Then gave another name to check out.'

Half an hour later Carne swung through the gates of Castlereagh and strode down its soulless corridors past the interrogation cells. Echoes and ghosts of the past darted by, confessions being extracted from bombers and assassins, hard-drinking interrogators who made this building their fortress, the daily threat of mortars. The nearest they got these days to serious crime was an improbable spate of local serial killers and sex fiends on television. Of course they could only be caught by star investigators specially imported from London and New York to alleviate the dull ineptitude of the foggy-brained local coppers.

Now he had a real-world, unsolved murder on his hands with a body and a name. He flung open the door into the detectives' open-plan office and marched towards Billy Poots. 'So?' he demanded.

'I've a surprise for you, boss,' replied Poots with unusual zest. 'And for me, too.'

'What?'

'Disappearance number five. No form, no record. Zero, sod all. The silence of the damned and the dead, not even a whisper or a breath in the wind.'

'What's the fucking name, Billy?'

CHAPTER 16

April 1994

The next Friday – nearly a week's passed, she goes early to his flat. An estate agent's board displaying '1ST FLOOR 2 BED FOR RENT' is mounted on the front railing. She opens the front door with the key he gave her and climbs the flight of stairs. The second key no longer fits the lock to his flat. She knocks – no answer. She kneels and lays her head on the floor to peer through the slit under the door. She can see floorboards and legs of furniture still and silent. The emptiness of his rooms compounds her sense of loss. The abandonment of place matches his abandonment of her. She's alone with an unshareable grief.

She retraces her steps into the street and waits until a tenant from one of the other flats leaves for work. She intercepts him.

'I'm looking for David Vallely,' she says. 'I thought he lived on the first floor.'

'You mean the young Englishman?' the man replies.

'Yes.'

'He must have left. They came yesterday to move his stuff and put up the sign. Not much, just a few boxes.' The man is about to move on, then examines her more closely. 'Didn't I see you come round once?' he asks.

'No, couldn't have been me,' she answers. 'He was a friend of a friend. I never met him.'

'I beg your pardon, then.' He's confused. 'Must have been someone like you.'

'Well, it wasn't me.' She sounds sharper than she intends. He retreats and hurries off. She feels low and mean. She must not allow his absence to demean her.

On Sunday, a week after he's left, there's a phone call to the house.

'It's for you, Maire,' yells Mrs Ryan up the stairs. 'Your da.'

Panic seizes her. She takes a deep breath, tells herself to calm down and descends the stairs.

'Hi, Da.'

'Hello, Maire. How are you?'

'I'm fine.'

'We missed you at Easter.'

'Yeah, I'm sorry, too much work on.'

'We understand.' Silence. He's trying to find a way of saying something. She knows it's bad. 'We were wondering if you'd seen Martin lately.'

'He was down just before Easter. Not since then. Why?'

'He always looks in once or twice a week and we haven't seen him.'

She doesn't know how to reply. Ice enters her heart when she thinks of her changed brother, then begins to melt at the memory of his parting words. He is her blood, her family – she wishes she could do more for her father than offer hope. 'I'm sure he's fine, Da. You know Martin.'

'Aye, I know. But your ma was asking round and it seems Joseph has disappeared too.'

'Joseph?'

'Aye, Joseph Kennedy. Don't suppose you'd have seen him either, love?'

'No, Da, I wouldn't have reason any more to see Joseph.'

'It just seems odd. Your ma's worried.' There's a pause – she waits for him. 'Jeez, Maire, I'm worried too.'

Again, she doesn't know what to say. 'Look, I'm sure it's nothing. You know how things come up.'

'All right, love, just thought I'd phone to check.'

'Is Ma OK?'

'I'll do my best with her. Anyways, how's things with you?'

Here, at least, she can try to inject some brightness. 'Exams start next week, got my head down.'

'You just stick to that, girl. No need to worry for us.'

Two weeks later, her father calls again to say there's still no sign of Martin. Or Joseph.

May 1994

She's in the library, one exam to go, one last burst of revision. She steps out into a cloudless late May day, promising the warmth of summer, and heads for her customary sandwich bar. As she bites her melted-cheese sandwich with a hunger born of fierce concentration, she hears a male voice with an English accent over her shoulder.

'Excuse me.'

Startled, she jumps to her feet, remembering the last time an unknown Englishman approached her in this place. This one is older and wearing a suit – late forties, slim, fit, thin moustache, smoothed dark hair, a golden pin holding a striped tie in place. A figure from an alien world.

'Who are you?' Her tone is not friendly.

'I'm sorry to trouble you but I'm looking for Maire McCartney.' He pronounces it correctly. 'I think you may be her.' He projects a languid smile and easy charm.

'You got the wrong person,' she says sharply and heads out to the street.

He follows. 'Please allow me to introduce myself. We have a friend in common.'

He's now beside her and she won't make a spectacle by running to shake him off. 'What friend?'

'David Vallely.'

She stops. 'I see.' She scans him from top to bottom. Who is this man? What does he know?

'My name is Jimmy,' he continues as if she'd asked the question out loud. 'I'm David's uncle.'

'I don't get it,' she says quietly.

'Shall we walk to the park and chat there?' he asks.

They walk, her legs buckling under the double weight of fear and anticipation. He offers to buy her a coffee from the stall by the pond – which she accepts. He returns with two polystyrene cups, whistling nonchalantly, and sits on the bench beside her.

'Dublin can be delightful at this time of year, can't it?' he remarks. She stays silent, staring rigidly ahead. Once or twice she flicks a look at him. How can he seem so detached? Though, she realizes, she does not know what things he knows or does not know.

'David never told me he had an uncle,' she says.

'No, he probably didn't,' he replies. 'He's rather a private person. Doesn't like to talk about himself.'

'You can say that again.'

He smiles – a tiny piece of common ground. He sips his coffee and takes out a silver cigarette case. 'Would you like one?'

'I don't smoke.'

'Would you mind if I do?'

'I've changed my mind, I'll have one.'

He takes out one cigarette and offers it to her, takes one himself, produces a gold Dunhill lighter, and lights hers and his. She splutters and feels a wave of giddiness as she inhales – it's nearly three years since she smoked her last cigarette that night in the Europa hotel bar. He draws easily and fully – she notices how little smoke emerges when he exhales.

'So,' he says, 'David—'

'Do you have any ID?' she interrupts. 'I don't wanna sound paranoid but how do I know you're who you say you are?'

He smiles. 'Of course. David told me you had a real law-yer's mind – so I've come prepared.' He removes a wallet from his inside jacket packet and then a passport. She examines it. 'James Bernard Vallely'. The issue date is August 1993 and the photograph a true likeness. He fishes around another pocket and produces two snapshots. One is recent – of him and David against some sort of sand or desert. The second shows a head and shoulders of him younger and David in his early teens, sea behind them.

'Thanks,' she says. 'You said you're his uncle.'

'Yes, I think that's right,' he replies with a mannered uncertainty. 'I'm the son of David's grandfather's brother, hence the shared name. Whether that makes me an uncle or a cousin once removed I've never bothered to work out – genealogy not the strong point I'm afraid. Suffice it to say I was always Uncle Jimmy.'

She examines him. 'Were you a soldier like his father?'

He laughs uproariously. 'Good heavens, no. Who'd want to live life on an army officer's pittance?'

She shrugs. 'So whaddya do then?'

'Put it this way, my dear, I'm a dabbler. Middle East oil fields, African diamonds are my sorts of milieu.'

'Is that where the photo is?'

'Yes, David visited me in Africa not so long ago.' He takes another drag and looks straight ahead, avoiding her. 'After his father died, we became close. I suppose I became a substitute. A rather poor one, I fear. But we communicated with clockwork regularity. David has always written to me or phoned at least once a fortnight, wherever he might be in the world.' Now he turns to her. 'I have not heard from him in over a month.'

'Neither have I,' she says.

'So I thought I should come over,' he continues, appearing to ignore her. 'I visited his flat.'

'So did I.' She considers something. 'How do you know about me?'

'Oh, he's written and spoken a great deal about you. He's extremely fond of you.'

'Yes.' She's aware of a missed answer. 'How did you know where to find me?'

'As I say, David delighted in telling me about your comings and goings. Even down to where you have your lunch break.'

'Dunno why he'd want to do that.'

'Perhaps it's another indication of his care for you,' he replies smoothly. 'And I'm sure you care equally for him – which is why I'm hoping you may know where he could be.'

'I don't. One morning he upped and went. He's done it before but always been back in two or three days.' She tries another puff – this time it's easier.

'I don't mean to interrogate you, my dear, but did you notice anything amiss with him?'

She considers for a second how to answer him. 'No. He was fine. Said he'd cracked his thesis. Solved its contradictions.' She smiles briefly. 'I never found out what they were.'

'So it seems he has disappeared.'

'Yes. Mind you, I always suspected he'd go off and leave me when he'd done his master's. Look, I'm trying to get over it so all this isn't too great.'

He becomes serious. 'I do not believe that was his wish, Miss McCartney.'

'You can call me Maire.'

'Indeed, I believe that he was struggling to envisage a future life with you. One thing he did say to me was that if anything ever happened to him – he's done some hair-raising things on his travels – he wanted you to be looked after.'

'I don't need looking after,' she says fiercely.

'It may feel like that now but circumstances change. Because he was away so often, David gave me power of attorney over his finances. He inherited a little money after his mother died and the house was sold.'

'Yes, he never seemed to want.'

'I know that he would want you to make use of that money.'

'I don't want it.'

'Well, the offer's there.'

She's mystified by this man with his suggestion of some sort of weird legacy. Her first instinct is to have nothing to do with him. He rises to his feet and produces a card. 'This is my phone number in the UK. If you get the answer machine just say it's Maire with a message for Jimmy. I shall take that as meaning you'd like to meet again and I will come straight over. The next day at noon, you will find me on this exact bench in this park, rain or shine.' He takes a final drag and stubs his cigarette on the pavement. 'I hope we'll stay in touch.'

She watches his back disappear behind the trees.

Maire determines not to think about 'Uncle Jimmy' and his offer until finals are over and maintains that self-discipline. But, the afternoon after the last exam, her thoughts turn to him. There are things she knows and things she doesn't know. Time spent in that territory of unknowns and unknowables is time wasted. She won't go there. There is the night she is already obliterating from knowledge and memory. She will never speak of it.

She remembers Martin's words of three years ago: '. . . get the fuck out of this island and make something of your life.' Though she's still not sure exactly how, she feels she's been used – there's something about Jimmy that's oblique and impenetrable. Yet what are her options? Martin, David – Joseph too, though she would never have turned to him – all gone. She can never return home. Even if she could, there's nothing her ma and da can offer except affection. She's become oddly fonder of Mrs Ryan, but there's certainly no future there. She needs to become hard. Above all, after everything that's happened over the past three years, she needs a new life. She can't make it alone – and her tutors can't help with what she really wants. Next morning, she phones the number he's given her.

'I'm glad you got in touch,' Jimmy says, standing by the park bench the next day, umbrella over his head. 'Our last meeting must have been the false dawn of summer. Perhaps we should find somewhere dry and quiet.'

He leads her to a hotel bar opposite the park. 'Coffee or something stronger?' he asks.

'Coffee,' she answers. What is it about this man that stops her saying 'please'? 'Before we talk about what you said, I wanna ask you something.' She needs a way to test him. Is he more than he seems? Why is he being so helpful?

'Fire away.' He places the cigarette case on the side table between their armchairs and offers her one. She declines and he takes one for himself. 'My brother's disappeared too.'

'Your brother?'

'Yeah, my brother Martin. Didn't David tell you 'bout him? And what happened when we went to my home?' He's momentarily thrown. 'You said he told you everything.'

'Yes, but about you and him. He may well have mentioned something but no importance was attached to it.'

'So you dunno anything 'bout what's happened to my brother?'

'My dear girl, how on earth do you think I'd know anything about that?'

'Dunno. Just thought I'd ask.'

'Well, you've certainly surprised me with that one.'

'Never mind that.' She wants now to be businesslike. Uncle Jimmy may be useful but she will never like him.

'You said you could help me,' she begins.

'David's money and the wishes he's expressed can help you,' he corrects her.

'OK, I'm gonna believe you.'

'Of course you should believe me.'

'It doesn't matter if I do or don't,' she says harshly. 'I could do with cash for something right now.'

'How much?' She names a figure and he produces a wad of notes from his wallet. He doesn't ask her what it's for.

'And then I want out of here. Out of this island. I don't have friends here – there are reasons.'

'Yes, David told me you led a rather isolated life.'

'That's why he suited me. An outsider. And I wanna get rid of any leftover connections.'

'Are you saying you wish in some way to reinvent yourself?' he asks gently.

'Yeah.' She pauses. 'I hadn't thought of it like that but that's exactly what I want.' She wonders whether to articulate something, then says it quietly. 'It's best not to be my brother's sister.'

'I see.' He makes no comment and considers her. 'Do you want to change your name?'

'Maybe. Nothing illegal 'bout that, is there?'

'Nothing whatsoever,' he assures her. 'I can help arrange it.' He pauses. 'And your appearance?'

'Maybe that too. A bit, anyway.'

'For you, it would be easy. May I suggest an idea?"

'Carry on.'

'David's money will allow you to take a year out. You could perhaps travel. During that period, nothing more complicated than weight change – loss or gain, it hardly matters—'

'I'll lose it,' she interrupts.

'—expert dentistry to straighten your teeth and close the front gap, and finally change your long wavy hair to something shorter, straighter and either fairer or darker.'

'I wanna straighten my nose too.'

He smiles. 'Of course, why not? When you return, only people who have been very, very close to you would recognize you. And how many of those are there?' She notes his apparent expertise but says nothing. 'What is your preference after that?' he continues.

'I wanna go to London. Start over. Pursue a legal career.'

'I can help with that too.'

'What can't you help with, Uncle Jimmy?'

He ignores her. 'You can begin your training immediately after the year out – and as a new woman.' He pauses. 'There's enough money for all of that.'

She looks hard at him, searching for clues, wanting to unravel the continuing mystery of this man. She's sure that, in some way or other, he's not who or what he says he is. Yet his name, his identity, his knowledge of David all stack up. She makes one last try – it comes out cruder than she intends.

'So, why the fuck are you doing all this for me, *Uncle* Jimmy?' She enunciates the word *Uncle* with leaden irony.

'Because, Maire,' he replies with a pale smile, 'you and I have one thing in common. It so happens that, like you, I loved him.'

They agree a name change from Maire Anne McCartney to Anne-Marie Gallagher – which is more generally 'Celtic' – and for that to be recorded as the name under which her law degree is registered. Her good brain and hard work achieve a first-class honours degree. She spends August in London, during which her change of look is begun before she heads off on a year of travel.

When she returns to London, she receives an invitation for an interview with Audax Chambers, which has been recently set up by a dynamic young QC called Kieron Carnegie. They offer to finance the completion of her solicitor's qualifications with the promise of a career at Audax to follow. Jimmy leaves a new phone number, which he says will remain a permanent point of contact in the years ahead if she ever needs any help.

The past fades, becoming a distant bad dream. But sometimes – and as her memory of him reverts to sweeter times of childhood – the voice of her brother still rings in her ears.

And the more she reflects on David Vallely – the more she rationalizes the relationship – the more, like Joseph, she makes a deliberate choice to see it as an error. The second huge error of her life. She will not make a third.

CHAPTER 17

Post-election, Thursday, 11 May

She wore jeans, trainers and beret, as anonymous as she could make herself. She had told Hinds that she would visit her sick aunt on the way to the office and change into ministerial clothes once there. Jemima Sheffield had adjusted her diary for a later-than-usual arrival.

Anne-Marie instructed Hinds to drive down Nine Elms, around the Vauxhall Cross roundabout and back along South Lambeth Road. He could wait in one of the cafés of 'Little Portugal' while she made her visit.

She got out at the junction with Meadow Place. Despite the early-morning chill, smokers were sitting outside on the small tri-angle of pavement puffing cigarettes and sipping coffees. The road was a line of commuter traffic, buses emitting wisps of sulphurous smoke, helmeted cyclists on their drop-handled frames jostling for position on the narrow blue cycleway. A few suited men and black-skirted women marched along the pavement towards Stockwell to catch the Northern line to the City.

Anne-Marie felt reassured by the bustle around her and increased her pace. After three hundred yards or so she turned left into a side road, stopped and pulled out the sheet of map she had printed. Joseph had simply texted her a date, a time, 8 a.m., and an address, 11a Ironmongers Mews.

The narrow roads and buildings were now a silent, deserted muddle in stark contrast to the cacophony of the main road. A four-storey block of council flats stood ahead. She searched for a name and eventually found it. It was not Ironmongers Mews. She walked alongside the block trying to orient the map to the concrete and tarmac shapes around her. At the end of the block, past a row of overflowing dustbins and their nauseous smell of rotting food, she saw an alleyway to the right. It was unmarked. After forty yards or so it arrived at a row of garages. She could see no road sign but each lockup had a number. One of them was 11A. The roll-up door was ajar and a faint light from inside cast a shadow onto the pavement. Could this possibly be the place he meant? She reminded herself that she had not seen Joseph for over twenty years and could not know the sort of life he was leading.

Even back then it seemed to her that he had come to inhabit a paranoid world of conspiracies and smoke and mirrors. Perhaps he had been unable to lose the habit. She knocked faintly on the garage door. There was no response. She knocked again, harder. Still no reaction. She looked around – she was alone. She bent down and slowly began to roll up the door. As she did, more and more of the garage's concrete floor was revealed.

Suddenly Anne-Marie felt that this was not right. Perhaps she had rushed to an assumption and it was the wrong address. Or it was simply a location he had given her and Joseph was, at this moment, walking up the alleyway to meet her. She backed away from the door and retraced her steps. There was no sign of Joseph or anyone else. Her watch said 8.11. Eleven minutes after he'd said they'd meet. He was always a stickler for punctuality. He was not here.

She returned to the garage and told herself to stop being so timid. She raised the door in one deft, swift movement.

'Oh, my God!' she whispered, covering her mouth with her hand. 'Oh, my God!'

She flinched and turned away, bile rising from the pit of her stomach. This could not be. She forced herself to look back, to check that she was not seeing some horrific apparition, some trick of the brain. She walked slowly forward, hand outstretched, steeling herself to touch.

A bearded man hung from a rope suspended on a meat hook. A single, unshaded light bulb cast a flat light on the limp body, shrouded in a scuffed donkey jacket and dark-brown corduroy trousers. Strands of greying brown hair had fallen haphazardly over the forehead. Standing on tiptoe, Anne-Marie stretched out both hands to separate them and reveal the uncovered face. The skin was cold. The eyes, bearing the dull glaze of death, bulged horribly, their whites dotted with livid red spots. A blackened tongue protruded from lips turned blue, beads of saliva dripping from the mouth. The air smelt of leeching body fluids. She tried to close the lids over the enlarged eyes but they were stuck, set in their misshapen rigor mortis. He hasn't changed, she thought. Even the clothes. The hair was still luxuriant, the beard strong.

She stepped back from the hanging corpse, driving back the nausea, trying to take deep, even breaths. She heard a car starting up and moving. She rolled down the door, trapping the odours of death. The car must be reversing as it abruptly stopped, then, after a few seconds, accelerated fiercely past. Despite the smell, she could not face the light and mundanity of daily life outside. She cast around for somewhere to drop and saw a pile of tyres in the corner. She forced her legs towards it, sat and slumped, burying her head in her hands. After a few seconds she allowed her eyes to peer through gaps in her fingers, wishing that somehow the body would have disappeared and it was all a sick invention of her imagination.

The body still dangled. A rush of wind blew through the small gap between the concrete ground and door bottom and she thought she saw his feet and ankles judder. She closed the gap between her fingers but kept her eyes open. Joseph. An image of his boyish figure in swimming trunks by the sea came to her: skinny, covered with sand, an innocent smile covering his face, playfully baring the gap in his mouth as adult teeth waited to grow, then pulling his face with his hands, turning it into a hideous, comic monstrosity to frighten her. She closed her eyes and a smile of memory gave way to the bitterness of loss. She sniffed, found a tissue in her pocket and wiped her face. As her rational senses began to return, the stink from the corpse grew stronger. She could not go on sitting here in this dark cell of unnatural death.

She raised herself to her feet – it felt like a gigantic effort of will – and stared at the body. She looked up and down it several times, beginning to feel more familiar with it, less sickened. The visceral recoil of her guts gave way to the first prompting of questions about why, and how, he could have ended up like this. Certainly, whatever the secret was that he had wanted to tell her had now gone with him to the dust.

She tried to remember his words in those scattered fragments of phone talk. 'Who pulled the trigger? Eh, Maire? . . . You made it, didn't you? Infiltrated the bastards . . . It was a trick. We were all tricked. David too. It wasn't like it seemed . . . It's about the fucking British state. That's what you gotta understand. That's what I figured out. That's what's gonna blow them apart.' She had instantly, and sickeningly, understood one of his allusions. But what did he mean about a trick? What was the truth about David that, even now, could be so explosive?

Her thoughts were disrupted by catching sight of a corner of brown paper sticking out of his coat pocket. She removed it – a rolled-up envelope, A4 size, too thin to contain more than a sheet or two of paper. Sensing too much time had passed, she hurriedly folded it into a small square and stuffed it into a pocket.

She walked to the roll-up door, took one last look back at him, and pushed it back up. There were no signs of activity. She stepped out, turned to lower the door, patted herself down and retraced her steps to the alleyway. She walked back past the block of flats, flicking glances in all directions as she went. She did not notice at the far end of the side road, beyond the turning into the alleyway, a parked car with a man in it reading a newspaper. Nor did she see him putting his newspaper down.

Back on the main road, protected by the sounds and shapes of rush hour, Anne-Marie slowed down. After the shock and revulsion, she understood that she had choices to make, choices that could be correct only if based on cool calculation.

I am a public figure entrapped by a secret that is of the here and now, she told herself. It may have emerged from a past which, unfairly and arbitrarily, has returned to haunt me, even play with me. But, whatever risk the past might bring, I must play my cards for the present.

The cardinal rule of political scandal was that it was never the deed, but the cover-up, that destroyed. By staying silent about what she had seen, she would take a first, irreversible step in the wrong direction. To avoid that step, she had to share her knowledge, or, at the very least, a part of it.

The Portuguese café came into sight; Hinds, seeing her, jumped from his table and walked over to the car. She called to him to get in and opened the front passenger door to sit beside him.

'Minister?' Her agitation was obvious.

'Just drive please, Keith.' The note of command was strident and unusual. Hinds looked at her – she was fighting to control something.

'Are you all right, Minister?' he asked.

'I've had something of a surprise. More than that. A nasty shock.'

'Yes, Minister.' She looked at him. There seemed an inner decency about him, a protective sympathy. She made her decision.

'Keith, I was rung by an old family friend yesterday, not a sick aunt. I hadn't seen him for more than twenty years. He sounded worried about something and asked me to meet him at an address he gave me, 11a Ironmongers Mews, Stockwell. It's a garage. Inside it his dead body is hanging on a cord suspended from a meat hook. I'd be grateful if, on my behalf, you could inform the police. No one else knew that I was meeting him. I'll leave it you to decide precisely what you tell the police. Oh, his name is Joseph Kennedy.'

'I was a policeman, Minister,' he said gently.

'Yes, you told me,' she replied. For the second time he sensed vulnerability – a possible softness inside the shell.

'So, in one sense, you have informed the police, haven't you, Minister?'

She turned her head to him, the colour returning to her face. But those words of Joseph – 'That's what's gonna blow them apart' – rang ever louder in her ears.

Only the collar of a grey suit creeping over the back of a white lab coat marked out the man standing over the covered slab.

Carne, despite his astonishment when told both of the caller and his request, had given immediate permission for a visit to the mortuary. He allowed him a minute and then approached, offering an indeterminate police-to-army salute.

'Good afternoon, General.' He was not going to 'sir' him.

'Good morning, Chief Inspector, er . . .'

'Carne. We met once at Lisburn, one of those pointless love-each-other days.'

'My apologies.'

'Forget it, it was enough to cry yourself to sleep.'

'As you see, I am not here in uniform. This is a private visit.' Carne noted a defensiveness unusual in such a senior figure – Kenneth Bowman had been General Officer Commanding, Northern Ireland, for nearly a year. 'I'd imagined,' he said, reasserting himself, 'they'd have put a local officer in charge.'

'I am a local,' replied Carne. 'They welcome English coppers here.' He felt irritated by Bowman's assumption of superiority. 'Romanians and Bulgarians, too.'

Bowman forced a smile. 'I understand you have some new intelligence.'

'Initially the location of a body was reported on the confidential line,' replied Carne. 'Yesterday a second call gave clues to a further, unreported disappearance in the early '90s.' He looked sharply at Bowman. 'General, this is not a military matter, it is a police investigation. I have not yet officially released news of the body's discovery. And certainly not of who it might be. May I ask how you came to know what you call "new intelligence"?'

Bowman shrugged. 'Isn't that rather by the by?'

'Not if there's been a breach of security.'

The two men stared each other down. Both tall, over six foot, both slim, both inscrutable.

Finally, Bowman spoke. 'For heaven's sake, Chief Inspector, what in this hi-tech day and age is the one phone line above others in this part of the world our security service friends are going to be monitoring?'

Carne slowly shook his head. 'So much for confidentiality.'

'How the information was obtained hardly matters to the man under there, does it?' said Bowman.

'So why is this of interest to you, General?'

'The disappearance and death of any young man is relevant to me.'

'That wasn't my point.'

'I'm sure it wasn't. But I'd remember something if I was you, Carne. You've done your job, finding him. Young men come and go and some live, some die – drugs, fast cars, fighting battles, falling off mountains. And that's it. I'd remember another thing. We've had peace here, more or less, for twenty years. Don't allow relics of the past to disturb it.'

'Is that something your intelligence friends asked you to convey, General?'

'I'll forget you asked that, Chief Inspector.' Carne was surprised to get even that much of an answer.

Amy Riordan's arrival interrupted them. Bowman introduced himself and stretched out a hand. Amy got a faint nod from Carne and shook it. 'Good morning, General. Amy Riordan, state pathologist.'

'Can we remove the cover, Miss Riordan?' asked Bowman.

'Yes,' she replied, peeling back the white sheet, 'but no touching, please.'

Stock still, Bowman stared, then began to ease ever closer. Carne, quietly taking up a position opposite him, saw the emotion in his face.

'Am I to take it that, if the identity is finally confirmed, you knew this young man,' said Carne softly.

'There may be a complexity.' He hesitated. 'I knew the family.'

'I'm sorry.'

'Thank you. I'm grateful to you.'

After a few more seconds, Bowman suddenly and briskly straightened. He addressed himself to Amy, ignoring Carne. 'Thank you, Miss Riordan. Now please forgive me, I must make some telephone calls.' He turned, marched to the exit, flung his white coat onto a trolley and disappeared without a further word.

Watching him go, Carne and Amy exchanged raised eyebrows.

'What the hell was that about, Jonny boy?'

'I think it's what they call a warning. Keep off my turf.'

At the day's end, back in her flat, there was one final task. Anne-Marie took the jeans she had worn to the garage out of a shoulder bag. She retrieved the envelope she had removed from Joseph's hanging body, unfolded it, broke the flap and pulled out a single sheet, a copy of a newspaper front page. From it, the smiling face of a fair-haired man in his mid-thirties, with his wife and two small children happily grouped around him, stared back at her.

'Oh, God,' she whispered.

CHAPTER 18

Post-election, Friday, 12 May

She was being hurled along a twisting lane, her eyes blinded by taut cloth, flashes of light breaking in rapid signals through the veil of black.

'Why me?' she whispered. 'Why me?' The response was as dark and silent as the night.

'Why me?'

The rubber of wheels hissed over tarmac, swerving and skidding. Lurch, acceleration, the road to oblivion.

'You'll kill us!' she tried to cry but words refused to escape. Her throat was sore, blocked, strangulated by an alien pressure.

'Why me?'

The car sheered to the right; rubber spat out stones and the wheels slithered to a juddery halt.

She heard the click of the door handle and felt pressure at her back, propelling her across damp grass. She wanted to lift her feet, to stride out, to run. But each step was an excruciating effort, her toes bare, sinking into glutinous mud.

'Why me?'

Her feet stuck, she stumbled and fell to her knees. The veil was lifted and stars circled above in a brilliant show of force. Though the night was dry, steaming beads of sweat dripped onto her nose and lips, slipping into the parched, rasping drought of her throat.

A black-gloved hand raised a torch, a second hand yanked back her head and a beam speared into her. Her eyes froze against its blinding harshness. Light seemed transformed into the slim sharpness of a dagger, coruscating with a thousand flickers against the moonlit backdrop, a symphony of macabre and lethal beauty.

More hands gripped her shoulders, compressing her like an onrushing avalanche. She gasped for breath and her palms closed in supplication. Into them was thrust not the bread of communion but the polished weight of heavy metal, her forefinger wrapped around a cocked trigger.

A figure strapped to a chair rose in front of her, its head slumped and hands flailing, a seat of crucifixion. With agonizing slowness, the revolving head revealed an earlobe, the line of an emerging jaw, a partially blackened cheek, a chipped edge of nose, a flickering eyelash.

'Shoot, fuck you, shoot!' the figure screeched.

She tried to close her eyes and was blinded by an ear-shattering starburst of piercing light.

Anne-Marie Gallagher jerked awake and sat bolt upright. Only the low glow of the city night crept through the gap she had left at the bottom of the blinds. She pressed the remote control to raise them fully, checked her iPhone – 4.45 a.m., Friday the 12th – rose from her bed and walked over to the wall of glass. She looked down at the river pathway. Empty. No one watching, no men in hats.

After so many years the nightmare had returned – the second

time in four nights. She felt her pulse – racing. She tried to blame exhaustion, excitement, trepidation at her bewildering elevation. She knew she was kidding herself. The image of Joseph's hanging body dangled.

She recalled his words about another body. Was he telling the truth – or trying to scare her? She forced herself to be rational. Joseph had probably made it up; an invention like that would stem from the creature he had become. He had meant to frighten her. Why? What had he wanted from her?

Why was he now a corpse?

She went into the bathroom and switched on the mirror light. The traces of crow's feet around her eyes seemed to glare back, the green irises bleached, veiled in a misty yellowing. She picked up a flannel and immersed her face in it. Forcing her woken mind to redirect itself, she began to see and hear the blues of sea and sky, a child's laugh in the distance, speckled tips of waves glinting in the sun. She lifted her face from the basin and leant her head back, eyes shut, bob of brown hair falling from her neck. Droplets of water fell languidly onto the floor one by one.

She returned to bed. Five-fifteen. Sleep would not come. She craved distraction and retrieved from the floor the red box she had put down four hours earlier.

Aziz Al-Dimashqi. United States citizen. Until a few days ago, her client. He had travelled from Syria to Britain, finally entering on a flight from Schiphol to Heathrow, claiming asylum on arrival. His grounds were that he would be subjected to inhumane treatment on arrest in the United States and an unfair trial. Audax Chambers, in the form of Anne-Marie and her junior, Zara, took up his case.

They had grown both to like and believe him. He had come to understand the futility of Islamist wars and now only wanted to work for peace. The extradition request from Washington was backed mainly by hearsay evidence. As the case passed through its appeal stages, Anne-Marie believed there was an outside chance that she could use the lack of concrete proof to win him asylum. But, two weeks before, the final appeal was lost. It was a decision for the Home Secretary – which he would take on the advice of the Minister for Security and Immigration. When she initially opened the file, her first thought was how Zara would judge her if she ruled against Aziz. She put the case to one side and worked her way through the rest of the box.

Her car arrived at 7.45 a.m. Keith Hinds looked at her in the mirror. 'Working late, Minister?'

'Does it look that bad?' she replied.

On arrival at the office, she raised the Al-Dimashqi case with Dalrymple.

'Can I get out of it, Alan?' she asked.

'Have you been thinking about it all night, Minister?' he replied gently.

'God!' she exclaimed. 'First Keith, now you.'

'Minister?'

'Forget it. Just advise me. It's what you're here for, isn't it?' He backed off and she silently damned herself.

'You have three sources of advice. The Department's legal department. The Permanent Secretary. Or the Secretary of State.'

'What would you recommend?'

'I'm afraid, Minister, that really is one for you.'

'Yes. Can you see if the Secretary of State can spare me a couple of minutes?'

Later that morning, she sat opposite a grinning Steve Whalley massaging his hands with glee. 'Well, lass,' he said, 'you're finding out what it's like to be a politician. No easy choices, eh?'

'Let's say some are easier than others,' she replied, forcing herself not to rise to him. 'And I have a personal connection to this.'

'Not any more, you don't.'

'I should pass it to another minister. Indeed to you yourself.'

'No, no. It's just the sort of case I need your advice on. You're the expert. You've read the file. You know the law. Is there sufficient evidence for our American partners to be justified in asking for this man's extradition?'

She tried not to appear a supplicant. 'You won't help me out with this, Steve?'

'No, Anne-Marie. Nor should I. Nor should you ask for it.'

If she were to be politically credible, she knew what the decision had to be – and what Zara would think of her. She cursed the state that made it so. She trudged back to her office. A fretful Dalrymple greeted her. 'The Prime Minister's press secretary phoned. Said it was urgent. And, er, private.'

'Does my private office listen in to my private calls?' she asked lightly.

'Not perhaps in this instance, Minister.' It was the first time she had seen Dalrymple ruffled and put it down to the spell of Number 10.

'So where do I make a personal call?'

'I tend to use the ladies',' piped up Nikki.

'Of course,' Anne-Marie replied, 'wherever else?'

She checked the row of cubicles – all unoccupied – leant against a window ledge and dialled Rob McNeil's direct line.

'McNeil here.' He sounded brusque – she wondered if he was liking power too much.

'It's Anne-Marie. You called.'

'Yes, Anne-Marie, of course. Sorry.' He was flustered and she took back the thought. There was a moment of silence. 'Look, this is going to sound odd. And it may be totally unnecessary but I thought I should—'

'Say what you want to,' Anne-Marie interrupted. It was as if electricity were fizzing through her body – she knew something bad was coming and was already working out her options.

'It's just that,' continued Rob, 'to put it briefly, a body has been found in Ireland. It was named as a certain David Vallely. He was a postgraduate student in Dublin in the early 1990s. He disappeared shortly before the end of his studies.'

Anne-Marie took a slow, deep breath. The silence hung oppressively.

'As I say,' McNeil stumbled on, 'this may mean absolutely nothing to you and my apologies if it doesn't. But, since I heard this news, I began reflecting on those times and—'

'It's OK, Rob, you can stop explaining.' She said it harshly.

'So . . .' he resumed after few more seconds.

'It means something.'

'I see.'

She heard his slow breathing on the other end of the line – the world around her seemed shut off, barricaded. 'I'd like you to go on.'

'The body's location was pinpointed a week ago by an anonymous caller. The day after the election in fact. A second call rather mysteriously referred to a fifth disappearance and said check out David Vallely. Something like that, anyway. The name caused some initial confusion.'

'Why's that confusing?'

He hesitated. 'Anne-Marie, it is you, isn't it? Maire? That weekend? Dublin, Connemara?' She did not reply. 'After I heard this news, I thought back to seeing you at Number 10. I checked the Dublin dates in your biog. You look so different but your

voice, your eyes. They're . . . they're unforgettable. Tell me if
I'm wrong.'

'You're not wrong. But David left me. Disappeared without a
word. I'd no idea what happened to him. I had to restart my life.
And now you're telling me he's been dead for more than twenty
years.'

'Yes. I'm sorry. It's horrible.'

'You'd better tell me everything. You said there was some initial
confusion.'

'If you want to know it all – I mean as much as I know – you'll
need to prepare yourself.'

'Give me a few seconds.' She laid her phone on the window
ledge, walked over to a basin and splashed her face with cold
water. She rubbed furiously, scraping herself, then dabbed her eyes,
cheeks and hands. She returned to the window, stared listlessly
at the frosted glass, sat on the ledge and retrieved the phone. 'I'm
ready.'

'Right.' He sounded more businesslike – she was glad of it.
'This may come as rather a shock. Vallely was not his real name.'

'I see.' She determined to match his tone, despite the nausea
rising in her stomach.

'It was an alias David was using in Dublin.'

'An alias?'

'Yes, his actual surname was Wallis. David Wallis. I've no idea
why he was using a false name.'

She couldn't stop herself. 'Did you know?'

'Anne-Marie, this isn't the time.'

She took a deep breath. 'OK, how did he die?'

'It appears he was shot in the head. Twice.'

'I see.' She thought again of Joseph. 'Are you sure this isn't some
kind of weird trick? Maybe it's not the same David.'

'I'm told there's no doubt.'

'How did you find out about all this?'

'The Belfast police phoned Fiona to tell her.'

'Fiona?'

'Yes, Fiona.' There was a tinge of impatience. 'David's sister.'

'He had a sister?'

'Yes. His sister. And for the last eighteen years my wife.'

'Your wife?'

'Yes. Two years after my best friend disappeared, I married his sister.' He paused, expecting some reaction. There was nothing. 'Read into that whatever you like,' he continued, immediately wondering what had made him say it.

She dabbed the cold sweat on her face with a tissue and stood up to repress the faintness. 'David told me he had no family. His parents were dead. He had no sisters, no brothers. He called himself an orphan.'

'He said that to you?'

'Yes.'

'In that case, he was not telling you the truth.'

'I don't understand.'

'I'm sorry. Truly sorry.'

'I mean why?'

'I've no idea.'

Again, she had to ask him. 'Did you know, Rob?' Silence. 'That weekend, Rob. Did you know he was using a false name?'

'Anne-Marie, I can only assure you that, if you were deceived, I was deceived too.'

'What else is there?'

She sensed him wavering. 'I'm not sure what more is to come. I thought I was close to him. I wanted to trust him.'

'Just tell me this. Was he at Trinity to do a master's?'

A further slight hesitation. 'Yes. Yes, he was.'

'OK. If you can't tell me more, let's cut it.'

'Anne-Marie, I'm more sorry than I can say. When it sinks in, perhaps we can talk.'

'I don't think I'll want to talk.'

'Perhaps not. I hope you will.' He took a sharp breath. 'In the meantime we must try to avoid any blowback. Political, I mean. Not that there should be. But we must be careful. Maybe it wasn't before, but it could become an issue for you now.'

'God in heaven above, Robert McNeil!' she cried. 'Isn't the important thing that the body of your friend and my friend has been found?' She clicked her phone. The line went dead.

She went inside one of the cubicles and locked the door. She was unsteady, now burning hot, the sickness rising uncontrollably. Leaning over the bowl, she vomited until there was nothing left. She stood up, flushed the lavatory and shook herself. This was not the place to show frailty or hide away in self-doubt. She heard a tapping, and a voice outside.

'Minister?' It was Jemima. She wiped her face, shook herself again, tidied her shirt and skirt and opened the door.

'Sorry, Minister,' said Jemima, 'I was a little worried.'

Anne-Marie ran cold water and bathed her face. 'It's all right, Jemima, must be something I ate. Don't worry, it's not morning sickness. I don't suppose a diary secretary's duties include supplying a toothbrush and toothpaste, do they?' she asked, managing a smile.

'Of course, Minister, 'I'll fetch one from the office. Was your phone call with the press secretary satisfactory?'

'As he said, it was just a private matter,' replied Anne-Marie. 'Nothing much really. Nothing important.'

She inspected herself in the mirror while the toothbrush was found, but all she could see was that curl of his hair that first beguiled her. The unreality of it all, both then and now, was over-whelming – some improbable film noir that she was caught up in.

Unreal. The word resonated like a thunderclap. The reality of David Vallely was the corpse of a man called David Wallis that had lain in a field for over twenty years.

Now, with his body disinterred from an Irish mountainside and the discovery of his false name, she understood that, from the very first, he could not have been what he seemed. It was the order of things that mattered. When the final crisis came, he had begged her to believe one order. Right up until now, she had.

Now she must face up to the alternative. Had he known at the outset that she would be there? In the library. At that table. Studying extradition law.

General Bowman had asked for one final look at the skeleton of David Wallis, a.k.a. Vallely. Carne quickly agreed – it was a chance to pump him, however tortuous he suspected the conversation might be.

'First, General, may I thank you for facilitating the contact with David Wallis's sister.'

'I will always help where I can, Mr Carne.'

'It takes this investigation into unusually high places.'

'Mrs McNeil told me she hopes the discovery of her brother's body will be treated with the utmost delicacy and discretion. You can imagine what a shock this is to her.'

Carne stopped himself bridling, his standard reflex to anyone trying to tell him how to do his job. He allowed a second or two's silence.

'Of course, this is your, er, bailiwick, Chief Inspector, but I felt you should be aware of these additional sensitivities.'

'I will try not to be heavy-footed. To that end, it would greatly help me if you could fill in some background. When you phoned with David Wallis's name and the connection to Mrs McNeil, you mentioned there was a military connection that would need careful handling. I didn't want to push you at that moment.'

Bowman turned to the skeleton. 'This is not a place to speak ill of men.'

'Let us hope we won't need to,' said Carne.

Bowman gathered himself – Carne felt the rules of engagement being rewritten. 'David Wallis's father was a soldier. Major Hugh Wallis. I was his commanding officer.'

He stumbled – Carne could sense a long shadow veiling him. 'Go on, General.'

'He was killed in the Falklands. He was posthumously awarded the Military Cross for his actions on Mount Tumbledown.' Bowman turned to Carne and thrust out his chin. 'The significant – and problematic – matter is that David Wallis joined the same regiment as his father. He was a British Army officer under my command for much of his short military career.'

'I see. Did he serve in Northern Ireland?'

'Yes,' replied the general flatly.

'When?'

'Now let me see . . .'

'The year and role please, General.'

Bowman sounded resigned. 'It will be in the public record that in 1988 he did a four-month tour in West Belfast. In uniform.' He hesitated, Carne waited. 'And 1990. Intelligence liaison.'

'Intelligence.'

'Yes.'

'What sort of "intelligence" precisely?'

'He was on secondment. I don't possess the details.'

'In that case, just tell me where.'

'He was mobile. Mainly South Armagh. Though I saw him at Lisburn a few times.'

'And then?'

'Wallis left the army in early 1993,' continued Bowman bleakly. 'What happened to him after that I don't know.'

'You don't know?' Carne struggled to hide his incredulity.

'Correct. It is only since the discovery of his body that I have learnt he ended up in Dublin.'

'With respect, General, You were his commanding officer, you must have taken an interest in his future.'

Bowman's eyes, half closing, were drawn again to the skeleton. 'I wish I had. Perhaps if only I had. The truth is he disappeared from my sights.' He looked up and smiled wanly. 'To be honest, the common view amongst those who knew him was that he'd gone off on some madcap do-gooding expedition, probably in the most godforsaken part of the world he could think of. Now, it seems, we know differently. What a stupid waste.'

Both men peered down again, trying to reconstruct the vigour the young body had once contained.

Bowman made to leave, then stopped dead in his tracks. 'David Wallis was a good, intelligent young man, certainly the David Wallis I knew as a schoolboy, a teenager and then all too briefly as a soldier. I wish it had been possible for him to stay in the army. We needed, and still need, brave young men who bear some nobility in their heart.'

'Why was it not possible?' For the first time there was an edge in Carne's voice.

'Sorry?'

'You said it was not possible for him to stay in the army. Why?'

'Did I?'

'Yes, General, you did.'

Bowman was trying all too obviously to recover. 'You mis-understand. I meant that he didn't want to stay in.' The general resumed his departure – as before without a goodbye.

You're a bad liar, thought Carne, not displeased. It was an asset for a detective. Bad liars were honest men. They understood the difference between truth and falsehood.

'Right, Billy' said Carne, back at Castlereagh.

'It's the dating, isn't it?' replied Poots. 'Second half '93, first half '94. When the Gang of Four vanish into thin air.'

'And a young ex-soldier called Wallis, a.k.a. Vallely, does too.'

'Yes.'

'Except, unlike them, he's come back.'

'Dug up. And dead.'

'The fifth disappearance, the fifth man,' mused Carne.

'Who's seeing ghosts now?' exclaimed Poots.

Carne grinned. 'Anything else?'

'Not sure it's relevant, boss.'

'Billy!' Carne knew Poots hated speculation.

'OK,' he replied reluctantly. 'Back in 1990 there are some other disappearances. In border country. A bunch of Provos known as the South Armagh snipers. They're doing well – then it all goes quiet. Three go missing. Never heard of since.'

'At a time when General Bowman says Wallis is in those parts seconded to intelligence liaison.'

'Yes.' Poots looked down at his hands, embarrassed by how far he had gone. 'Probably just coincidence, boss.'

'Sure, Billy.' Carne patted him on the shoulder.

Anne-Marie engaged her auto-pilot to negotiate the rest of the morning's business – with one exception. Audax Chambers had asked formally for a meeting on the Al-Dimashqi case and the new government's interpretation of asylum and extradition law. She knew she could not refuse the request; she also knew that Audax's two representatives would be Kieron Carnegie himself and Zara Shah.

When Dalrymple showed them into her office, she saw Zara as herself fifteen years before – the only difference was the olive skin, translucent against the bright blue scarf, and the clarity about right and wrong granted to the young.

They began with chitchat: how strange her life must be; the surrounds of a private office and staff all to herself; the requirement to meet those she despised as well as those she respected. Perhaps the idea of respect was the prompt.

'So, Al-Dimashqi?' asked Zara.

'I tried this morning to get out of it,' she replied feebly, 'but the Secretary of State won't allow me to escape.'

'In which case he was correct,' said Carnegie. 'It's the bargain you've struck.'

'What will you decide?' asked Zara.

'I already have,' she murmured.

'It's bad for him, isn't it?' said Zara.

'Yes. I'm afraid it is. I know you'll hold me in contempt.' She looked from one to the other, seeking the verdict in their eyes.

'Not at all,' said Kieron.

'No,' added Zara. 'You had no choice. That's what we came to tell you.'

She looked at them and, after the terrible shocks of the past days, fought back the tears. Watching them leave, she hated her submission.

CHAPTER 19

Post-election, Monday, 15 May

The mourners filed out – a desolate procession, in pitiable conformity with the surroundings.

The gaunt, early Victorian building, with its squat central tower, sat squarely on the site of the ruins Thomas Cromwell's destroyers had left behind. Around it lay an undistinguished jumble of late-nineteenth-century school boarding houses and ugly modern add-ons. It was the May half-term week. The greying brick walls were silent and deserted, bar an occasional monk in black cassock blending timelessly with the silence.

From the vantage point he had staked out the previous evening, Carne could take in the setting of the Abbey in a dip surrounded by shallow, rolling hills still veiled by soft streaks of morning mist. He felt himself in an ancient England, imagining its people once cowering before their god.

Yet primitive urges had continued to rule here. As in other institutions like it, stories had emerged of child abuse and degradation at Bowlby Abbey school. The bleakness without had been matched by a darkness within. Monastic frustration and divine authority had produced a noxious cocktail.

Carne knew his investigation of David Wallis's death would develop its own toxicity. Secrecy – and an instinct to cover up – were bound to be the reaction to a trail connecting David Wallis via his sister to 10 Downing Street. Immediately the dental records had confirmed the identity, Carne had asked for the body to be repatriated and the funeral held without delay. Fiona McNeil, Wallis's only surviving relative, was quick to agree and, without any publicity, arranged a private ceremony. Carne's best chance was that, somewhere out there, a shadowy figure or two might break cover to see David Wallis laid to rest.

A 500-millimetre lens and doubler would give him facial detail. On the way into the abbey, the mourners had steadfastly looked forward, offering him only their rears. He prepared himself for their return. He was shooting with a camera but felt like an assassin.

The coffin, borne by two young and two much older men – a retirement job for Billy Poots, he had the perfect face – emerged. Immediately behind was the officiating monk, tall though stooped, thin, narrow-faced, and bespectacled. Well over seventy, guessed Carne. Then came Robert McNeil, whom he recognized from photographs at the time of his appointment. Beside him, presumably, his wife, Fiona, the dead man's sister. There was a handful of others, more distant relatives perhaps, then the erect figure of General Bowman in a civilian suit.

Alongside was another man of military bearing, ten or so years older. He had crisply parted, silvery hair and a gold tiepin. Even to a camera lens two hundred yards away, it gleamed against the dark backdrop of his tie. One or two lone souls, less pristine, lagged behind – probably villagers for whom a funeral was a welcome distraction.

The coffin headed for what must be a small burial ground beyond the abbey. Carne allowed the procession out of sight. Having snapped his prey, he would copy the photographs onto his phone later, then email them to Poots and tell him to get an ID on the man next to Bowman. For now, he waited. After some twenty minutes, the party hove back into sight and disappeared into a boarding house.

Carne strolled carelessly towards the abbey. He pushed open the west door. A woman was tidying flowers by the pulpit; he smiled at her and she smiled back. Otherwise he was alone. A book of condolence was open. Bowman had signed it but immediately above and below his line were two women's names. The man with the gold tiepin had not signed.

He heard a door creak and slam shut behind him. Instinctively he checked his rear and reached for his back pocket. A pointless reflex as he had brought no gun to this doleful place. He saw a hooded shadow retreating beyond a pillar. He rounded it and came face to face with the old monk who had presided over the funeral. Carne felt an involuntary guilt. The picture of David Wallis's bullet-scarred skull and the collection of mourners watching the wooden box containing it unnerved him.

'Can I help?' asked the monk.

'I was paying my respects,' replied Carne.

'I did not see you at the service.'

'No . . .' Carne hesitated. Why did this kindly man in his white collar and black vestments make him feel so awkward? 'I did not wish to intrude.' Faced by the monk's gentle gaze of enquiry, he found deceit impossible. 'I'm a policeman,' he explained. 'It's my

unfortunate task to investigate how this young man met his death.'
Carne showed his ID to the monk. He brushed it away.

'This is God's house. All are welcome. Even detectives.' The
monk smiled. 'My name is Father Simon.'

'Chief Inspector Carne.' He stretched out his hand. The monk
took it.

'Hello, Mr Carne.'

'May we chat? Informally.'

'Let us walk to his grave.' It was an instruction.

The monk led him to a small plot beyond the main group of
buildings and invisible from them. The mist had lifted to clear the
folds of moorland beyond, divided by straight lines of grey-stone
walls, the sun bestowing an iridescent early summer green. It was a
hidden cemetery, the only spectators a few chewing sheep. Modest
headstones formed a pattern of remembrance. In one corner, the
earth was freshly dug.

'This is where we monks end up,' said Father Simon.

'So why him?' asked Carne. 'Don't tell me he was a monk too.'

The monk laughed uproariously, out of all proportion to
the frail body. 'David Wallis a monk? Good heavens, perish the
thought!'

'So why, then?'

'His sister rang me to ask. She knew David loved this place.
After so many years in an anonymous field, I think she wanted to
restore his identity. His humanity. And she wanted it done quietly
and quickly. I could hardly say no, could I?'

'How well did you know him?'

'I loved him.' Carne's eyebrows rose. The monk noticed. 'Oh
for heaven's sake, not like that. We weren't all sinners here.' He
looked down at the churned earth and small temporary wooden
cross. 'I saw David as of another age. A romantic idealist in a

cynical world. "I was sent to these Arabs as a stranger, unable to think their thoughts or subscribe their beliefs, but charged by duty to lead them forward."'

'T. E. Lawrence,' interjected Carne.

'Yes, Lawrence of Arabia. That was David. Change the world. A young man on a mission. "The dreams of waking men". Schools like this tended to encourage that.' The monk looked down again at the grave. 'Not always with happy endings.' Silent memories clouded his face. 'I'm talking too much.'

Carne felt a rush of sympathy for the old man, consumed by a raw sadness. He turned to the business at hand. 'Did you have any contact in the period leading up to his disappearance?'

The monk seemed grateful for the question. 'As a matter of fact, I did. In the year before he . . . he left us, he came to see me twice. I was surprised. Delighted too. If you'd ever met him, you'd have seen how he could light up even this dank fortress.'

'How did you find him?'

'His first visit must have been in the autumn of 1993. We watched the boys' boxing. He was a good boxer, David. Crude technique, but brave as a lion, too brave. I sometimes sensed a bloodthirsty streak in him. The sort of young man to glory in war. Like Churchill, another great British hero.' The monk paused, allowing the reflection to float into the distant curve of hills. 'Anyway,' he resumed, 'he seemed happy. He said he'd left the army – he sounded disillusioned with it but I didn't want to probe – and was doing something truly worthwhile at last. He mentioned a girl he'd met in Dublin.'

'And then?'

'That was later, early 1994. The boys were on half term. It had snowed and he wanted one of his epic walks. Even then, I was becoming too old for it.'

The monk's voice tailed off; Carne needed him to keep talking. The old man had something to say but a sense of protection, or perhaps fear, was obstructing him. A tear formed in his right eye. He took a white handkerchief from his black pocket, wiped it away, and blew his beaky nose.

'I apologize,' said the monk. 'It does no good to think about mortality, does it? I once believed there was a heaven.'

His remark shocked Carne. The monk noticed. 'I have surprised you. Perhaps I have offended you. I'm sorry.' The monk straightened; he had made his decision. 'I will tell you what I know,' he said. 'That happiness of the previous autumn had gone. David said something strange and striking. "I am caught between duty and love." Those were his exact words. He asked me which he should opt for. I told him there could never be an absolute. I could only answer if he told me the circumstances. He replied that, even if we were in the confessional box, those were secrets he could not inflict on me. In that case, I told him, only his conscience could decide.'

The monk glanced down at the freshly dug grave and turned smartly on his heel. Carne followed him.

'When I heard he had disappeared—'

'How did you hear?' Carne broke in.

'I didn't in that sense,' he replied. 'His friend, Rob McNeil – he was at the funeral – phoned me to ask if David had been in touch at all. I said not. Rob explained that no one had seen him for nearly a year and he hadn't contacted anyone – mother, sister, friends.'

'I see,' said Carne. 'Sorry, I interrupted.'

'Don't ask me why,' he said with a curt finality, 'but I knew instantly that David was dead.' The monk gave Carne a distant look. 'Now, if you'll forgive me, I must go and join the mourners.'

Carne waited until the black cassock had disappeared through the schoolhouse gate. He returned to his car, drove slowly down the lane, parked, and prepared the camera. The funeral had given him a list of witnesses worth staying over for. The departing number plates might give him something more.

He tried to imagine the optimistic face of the idealistic young man that had been described to him. All he could see was a recurring image of corrupted youth. As an image of David Wallis's final moments floated in front of him, he sensed the menacing shadow of a murderous history.

CHAPTER 20

Post-election, Tuesday, 16 May

Rob McNeil's answers were perfunctory. Yes, he had met David Wallis at Bowlby and they remained friends. Yes, he had met him once for a drink in Belfast in 1990 when he was a young reporter doing a stint there for *The Times*. No, there had seemed nothing unusual about his conduct. No, he was not aware of any 'intelligence' role. The last time he saw Wallis was in October 1993 at his godfather's annual shoot in Devon. Yes, he had appeared as 'chipper' as ever. No, he had not seen him in Dublin. No, he only knew that Wallis was changing career and doing an MA.

In other words, concluded Carne from the twenty minutes he had been allowed, nothing. Except everything he was holding back. The poacher-journalist turned Number 10's gamekeeper. He passed the gates of Downing Street and headed towards the dull, grey, rectangular façade of the Ministry of Defence for his desultory day's second appointment.

His phone rang – McNeil's private number.

'Carne here.'

'It's Rob McNeil again, Mr Carne.'

'Hello, Mr McNeil.'

'There was one matter I'd been thinking of raising with you. I've now decided to do so.'

'I'm listening.'

'But in confidence.'

'All right.'

'When he was in Dublin, David Wallis had a girlfriend. I did in fact visit him once there and met her. I apologize for not mentioning. It didn't seem relevant to his disappearance.'

'That's for me to decide, Mr McNeil. If you're telling the truth now, I'll overlook it.'

'Thank you.' McNeil paused. Carne held the silence, his brain buzzing as he thought of the lock of hair. 'That girl is now a senior figure in British public life.'

'I see,' said Carne.

'There's no suggestion that she was in any way involved in the disappearance of David Wallis. Or would know anything about it.'

'Her name?'

'Instead of giving you her name, I'm going to give her yours. She should not be dragged into this by anyone except herself. As for me, I'd like to know the truth about my friend's death. I don't see any point in your investigation extending beyond that to his life. I shall have nothing further to add.'

'Goodbye, Mr McNeil.' A man who has shed a burden, thought Carne, and also drawn his line in the sand. Even so, it felt like the first crack in the veneer of denial. Perhaps the soulless corridors of the Ministry of Defence would provide a second.

General Bowman greeted him with a geniality in marked contrast to his demeanour at the cemetery. 'I thought I'd stay over and network in this ghastly place for a day or two,' he began, waving him to a sofa. 'What more can I do for you?'

'You mentioned David Wallis's intelligence secondment in 1990. In border country.'

'Yes, as I understand it, he spent time there.'

'Do the South Armagh snipers mean anything to you?'

'You'll have to remind me,' replied Bowman warily.

'Expert IRA assassins armed with Barrett M82s and M90s.' Carne waited for Bowman's acknowledgement of facts he must have known. 'Come on, General, you know what happened. Some kind of operation was mounted and they disappeared. Never to return. No bodies found.'

'If that was so, we were thankful.'

'If David Wallis was involved, that could have made him a long-term IRA target.'

'For heaven's sake, Mr Carne, this is a blind alley.'

Carne could see Bowman's impatience – and a value in testing it. 'Why?' he asked simply.

'If you really want to know,' Bowman replied testily, 'Wallis was seconded to a unit run by a man known as Jimmy. Jimmy Snu, actually. Stands for surname unknown. A little joke. And I can assure you of two things. Firstly, I have zero knowledge of this unit's activities. Secondly, they were faceless men, invisible to the IRA enemy.'

'Thank you, General,' said Carne. He paused to open his briefcase and locate a folder. 'Just one further matter.'

'Oh?'

Carne pulled from the folder the photograph of the man with the tiepin at the funeral. 'Is this Jimmy?'

Bowman affected to examine it carefully. 'I'm afraid I wouldn't know.'

Carne pulled out a second photograph of the man with the tiepin talking to Bowman.

'Is this the real reason you came to see me, Chief Inspector?' asked Bowman coldly.

Carne stayed silent, his eyes fixed on Bowman looking down at the picture. He could see the general was unnerved, wrong-footed both by the question itself and the trick played on him.

'The funeral was the first time I met him,' he began.

'Really?'

'How would you know, Mr Carne? Were you ever of that world?'

Carne resisted the challenge. 'Perhaps you could tell me how he introduced himself.'

'I don't see why not. I only half caught the name. Something like Brock. He rather mumbled it.' He stopped to remember; Carne allowed him whatever time he needed. 'As a matter of fact, I began to think he was there more to see who else had turned up than anything else.' Bowman looked up at Carne. 'Like you, Chief Inspector.'

Carne rolled with the punch. 'What did he say about Wallis?'

'I'm afraid I can't remember.'

'Funerals are to exchange memories of the deceased, General Bowman. I'll ask you again. What did he say about Wallis?'

'He wasn't forthcoming.'

'Why did Wallis leave the army?'

'Mr Carne, I really can't see—'

'There must be something in the records.'

'The records will show,' stated Bowman icily, 'that Wallis satisfactorily completed the short-term commission which he signed up to in return for funding through university.'

'General, you told me when we met before that Wallis had to leave the army.'

'If that is your recollection, Mr Carne, I must have unwittingly misled you. Now, your questions are becoming irrelevant and I have work to do.'

Carne retrieved the photographs, slowly inserted them in their folders, rearranged with great deliberation the papers in his briefcase and quietly closed it. The whole exercise took well over thirty seconds during which no word was spoken. At its end, Carne looked up at Bowman with a just perceptible raise of his eyebrows and rose from his chair.

'Goodbye, General.'

'Goodbye, Chief Inspector.'

'The Sundays are after you for profiles,' said McNeil.

'Can't I settle in first?' asked Anne-Marie.

'They've said they only want the personal angle. They understand it's too early for the political. Makes it hard to refuse.' He smiled ruefully.

'Whatever once happened, I've nothing to hide.' It came out more stridently than she meant. 'And nothing of any interest, either.'

McNeil was presiding over a photoshoot of the new Prime Minister and the women he had fast-tracked into his government. 'Lionel's Ladies' or 'Lionel's Lovelies', according to media taste. Anne-Marie had been asked to sit next to Buller – *lovely* was not the word for Lionel's other ladies.

She saw Steve Whalley step through the French windows onto the terrace. She thought about the opportunistic rise that had brought him to this garden of power. Young trade union militant in the late 1970s; ruthless organizer of flying pickets; leading light in the Trotskyite 'entryist' tendency that made the party unelectable in the late 1980s. Then the lurch to the right, which had been so destructive of his former 'comrades', rewarded with a rising ministerial career in his party's last term of office. He had served his masters with brutal efficiency and now, in his sixties, was a player whom the leader had to accommodate.

Buller headed towards him and the two men buried their heads together. She spotted them turn towards her. Who's watching whom now? she asked herself.

Buller, Whalley, Jupp, McNeil – even her private secretary, Alan – all men, all in the real rungs of power with women packaged neatly around them, from ministers in less significant departments to the junior girls in her office. Despite two women prime ministers, it seemed that in her party male bonding still held sway and she was just part of the window dressing.

'You make a good story,' continued McNeil. 'A woman who's risen from humble beginnings to the epicentre of power.'

'You know fuck all about my womanly beginnings, Rob,' retorted Anne-Marie. 'Nothing. My life starts on the day I graduate.'

'Whoa, sorry!'

'I shouldn't have reacted. It's just that all this,' she waved her hand around the garden, 'it's rubbish. You know that.'

'It's politics, Anne-Marie. We both decided to join the game.'

'OK,' she relented. 'You can give them Kieron. Kieron Carnegie.'

'Yes, I know of him.'

'He can tell them I'm a selfish, ambitious workaholic. He'd have every right to. He won't, of course.' She paused. 'And they can have a couple of men I've had relationships with who'll know how to play your game. Will that do?'

She looked around at Lionel Buller, who had left Whalley and was awkwardly working his women. McNeil noticed. 'Don't underestimate him. And don't cross him. He's got you marked for the top.' They watched him together, both feeling the tension between them. Seeing the evasion in his eyes, she decided to challenge it.

'What you said on the phone . . . blowback . . .'

'It must have sounded crass. But thinking of what might have happened to him is too awful. I'm just trying to deal with the here and now. Eventually, stuff will come out.'

'Maybe. First, I have to talk to you about that weekend.'

'I can't discuss that here. I thought he was just playing his usual silly buggers.'

'All right, not now. OK?'

'OK.'

She moved closer to him, putting her hands on his shoulders, not caring who was watching. 'So let's discuss "now". Others may remember me, recognize me. But you may be the only living person who knows about David and me. We spent our time together alone. Usually in his flat. Except that one weekend with you. He never wanted anyone else to know. I didn't understand why – it was just the way he was, or liked to be.' She hesitated. 'And it suited me.'

She caught sight of Whalley pawing one of the new women ministers. With a shudder, she turned back to Rob. 'Towards the end it became difficult, I thought he was being secretive. Then he disappeared. I tried to find out more but couldn't. Now I know part of the reason – I didn't even have the right name. As far as I'm concerned, it never happened. You remember something, Rob. Maire was the one he left behind. She was entitled to rebuild her life. To redefine herself. To have her career. To rise above it, as far as fate took her. There was nothing wrong in it. There's no need for blowback, as you call it.'

'It's not that simple,' said McNeil. 'Things will come out.'

'Then deal with "things", Rob. That's what you're here for, isn't it?'

McNeil's eyes stayed trained on her as she spun on her heel. Her red dress hugged her small frame, which was as striking as ever, just leaner. The hair, smart clothes and make-up, and the adult slimness had changed her appearance. But the spirit within was the same. As she walked evenly and purposefully on her black heels, it seemed to him that ambition had given her courage – or perhaps it was the other way round.

His thoughts drifted back to that weekend and spat at him like a hornet's buzz. Had he really been nothing more than his best friend's patsy?

The photographs had caught him on the hop – he should have been prepared for a ruse like that. Altogether, reflected Bowman, he had played the unearthing of David Wallis badly. Trying to interfere when it would have been best left alone. The important thing now was damage limitation. His only personal jeopardy was the incident in Saudi. It may have happened long ago, but murder remained murder for life.

In the second week of January 1991, with Wallis restored to his command, Bowman, by now a full colonel, hand-picked him, the experienced Sergeant Nickold and four others to cross enemy lines into occupied Kuwait. Their orders were to kidnap an Iraqi outpost guard, and bring him back to Saudi for interrogation. The snatch was textbook and the Iraqi deposited in a cell, stripped, hooded, yelled at, kicked about, deprived of sleep, food, toilet and washing facilities and left to fester in the stink of his own body and its emissions as an encouragement to spill everything he knew. All standard stuff.

Only one thing had gone wrong. They appeared to have alighted on the one man in Saddam's forces with such fanatical loyalty to his leader that these inducements produced nothing more than grunts and silence. Bowman told Wallis and Nickold that the potential intelligence was so vital that they should up the ante. More beatings followed, head holding in tubs of water, pincers on fingers, a slavering Doberman breathing and snarling in the Iraqi's face and taking a chunk out of his leg. Again, all fair game, but still nothing.

Bowman only discovered later from Wallis that Nickold then introduced his cut-throat razor. With Wallis in attendance, he sliced into the back of both the prisoner's heels, rupturing the Achilles' tendons, opening a jagged gash in the pink sinewy flesh. The Iraqi, perhaps familiar with such matters, may have known that, even if he got out alive, he would never walk properly again. He still remained silent. Nickold did not stop there, moving up the body to slash the prisoner's wrists. His draining blood coloured the festering cell floor a bright pink; unchecked, the blood loss would kill him. Wallis, having condoned the older sergeant's brutality, now called for cloths to staunch the flow. He also later claimed to Bowman that he thought of summoning medical help. But, he said, Nickold told him not to be so 'fucking stupid' asking, in these precise words, 'Do you want this to get out, you fucking cunt, and see us both done for murder?'

Over the next two days the Iraqi prisoner lost consciousness, becoming too weak even to try to save his life in return for information. His body was spirited from the cell and deposited in the desert. Knowledge of the incident was kept to a tiny circle, stopping at Bowman himself. He decided that it should be viewed as an accident of war and go no further.

However, there was a consequence. Bowman did not directly blame Wallis for what took place in that cell. Rather, he blamed himself for allowing Nickold, a savage man, too much licence. But Wallis, as the presiding officer, was in charge. He argued to Bowman that it was right, good and in line with his orders to pursue all avenues to extract vital information that could save many of their own soldiers' lives. The ends justified the means. Bowman came to an unwelcome conclusion. Wallis's near-Jesuitical justification of the use of violence, even outside the law – which he had also displayed against the South Armagh snipers – combined with his maverick strain, made him too risky a character for a modern, rule-bound army.

Over the next year he gently conveyed this to Wallis. Two years later, Wallis, knowing his army career was going nowhere, resigned his commission, accompanying it with an embittered letter to his commanding officer. To soften the blow, Bowman offered to contact Jimmy on Wallis's behalf to see if he might like to renew their association.

Thank heavens his own responsibility, and knowledge, ended there – but it did not stop him now ruing the day he put the two of them together.

CHAPTER 21

She had often thought of throwing away the piece of card and losing all trace and memory of it; some instinct had always prevented her. Now Anne-Marie retrieved from her purse a phone number she had kept for more than two decades. The park seemed to offer an anonymous blanket of comfort, ducks and geese honking their pleasure in the shimmer of midday sun illuminating the lake.

Using her private mobile, she dialled the seven-digit number left by 'Uncle Jimmy'. His passport photo flashed before her – James Bernard Vallely – just another play in the deceit. Perhaps the number was fraudulent too. An answer came after a single ring.

'Hello?' A female voice. 'Can I ask who's calling?'

'I was told to say Maire from Dublin and ask for James.'

'Thank you, Maire, please stay on the line. I'll route you through as quickly as I can. It should not take more than a minute or so but, to repeat, please stay on the line.'

Anne-Marie was seized with wonder. In some ways, it might be better if the number – and she – had been forgotten in the mists of past turbulence. The instant answer meant Jimmy represented some sort of continuing reality. She looked back through the trees

to Horse Guards Parade and the old Admiralty buildings, once
the hub of British imperial power and which long predated the
grandiose pomposity of the upstart Foreign Office next door. She
had escaped from a small island and ended up in this unlikely
destination in a rather larger one. Now, two dead men, David
Wallis and Joseph Kennedy, meant she had never got away after
all.

The voice came back on the line. 'Thank you for holding. Can
I confirm this is Maire?'

'Yes. I asked to speak to James.'

'James has moved on. Our obligation to you has not.'

'Excuse me, who are you?'

'The person who has inherited his responsibilities will be at
the Marine bar on the river, just west of Battersea Park, at 8 p.m.
this evening.'

'I need to check my diary.'

'It has been checked' – there was an almost imperceptible
pause – 'Minister. Unless you have a private engagement not
recorded in it.'

'Jesus!' murmured Anne-Marie, feeling all sense of control
slipping away. 'I have no other engagement.'

'Like you, your new contact is a cyclist. She will be wearing cycling gear and reading *Hello!* magazine. It is your choice
whether or not to meet her – but she will be there. Goodbye.' The
phone went dead.

In the afternoon Anne-Marie was driven by Hinds to a symposium in Oxford with the subject 'After ISIS – Dictatorship or
Democracy?' Dalrymple had tried to exclude it from her diary as
it was not of departmental relevance. She protested that it was
the one commitment inherited from Audax Chambers that she
would not renege on – she must be there to defend the rule of law.

Steve Whalley caught her on the way out. 'Remember our government is here to represent British interests. That means arms sales – though I didn't say that.' His tone was almost friendly. 'And just you remember, kid, I'm watching you.' He laughed mirthlessly. 'In a good way of course.'

On the drive back to London, she had a text from Rob McNeil:

Hi A-M, a Chief Inspector Carne is investigating David's death. He's an OK guy. Told him David had a girlfriend in Dublin, up to you whether you decide to contact him. Rob x

Her first reaction was to feel like a bird captured in a pet's cage under endless scrutiny. Her second was a sense of McNeil protecting his rear and passing the buck.

As they passed the wired perimeter of Northolt air base, Hinds leant to his right to engage her in his rear-view mirror.

'Mind if I speak, Minister?' he asked.

'Of course not, Keith.'

'I've talked to my contacts in the police. There's nothing to worry about that body you discovered this morning.'

'Oh, how's that?'

'Turns out it's a case of mistaken identity.'

'What!'

'It wasn't that man, Joseph Kennedy, you thought you were going to see.'

'That's impossible.' She felt a nasty tug of suspicion. 'Who are you getting this from?'

'I've a friend in the investigation, Minister.'

'You're certainly a fount of knowledge, Keith.'

'Thank you, Minister.'

She hesitated to pursue the conversation but curiosity overtook her. 'So what else did they say?'

'Apparently he had a credit card and driving licence on him. He's been identified as Brian Fitzgerald, a resident of Southend-on-Sea. There's no mystery about his death. He had advanced lung cancer and only a few weeks, if that, to live. He left a note, too. Just saying he wanted to save any further trouble.'

'There was no note,' she stated calmly.

'Remember, Minister, you had a bad surprise. Easy to miss things.' She realized he was trying to help without condescending. 'I know from my time in the force. Very understandable in circumstances like that.'

'I wouldn't have missed it.'

'Anyway, Minister, with or without a letter, it's a relief, isn't it? One less thing to worry about.'

Anne-Marie tried to make sense of this bizarre turn of events. She had seen the man close up and dead. She had parted his lifeless hair and looked into his cold eyes. He was Joseph Kennedy, a man she had known well, albeit long ago. But too well ever to forget. The truth was that there was no sense.

Past deaths and disappearances were one thing – a suspicious death today was another.

A few minutes after 8 p.m. she arrived at the Marine on the river, locked her light-framed racing bike to some railings, took off her helmet to reveal a tied bob of brown hair, removed her yellow jacket and made straight for the far corner of the bar. A familiar-looking woman with fair hair bunched in a headband lifted her eyes from her magazine, ran over and embraced her in enthusiastic greeting.

'Jemima!' hissed Anne-Marie.

'Wonderful, isn't it?' exclaimed Jemima Sheffield. She leant into her ear and whispered, 'Let's catch up with everything outside.' Moving back, she smiled broadly. 'Darling, you're looking marvellous. Circuits, then a drink?'

Jemima marched outside towards a bicycle, mounted and pedalled off towards Battersea Park, Anne-Marie in tow. After two circuits they pulled up by the Chinese pagoda, dismounted and walked over to the Thames to admire the silhouetted Lots Road power station.

Anne-Marie's cheeks flushed angrily in the evening light. 'What's going on, Jemima?' During the few minutes of bike ride she had recalled how Jemima always seemed to be there at crucial moments – in the park just after she had phoned Joseph, in the ladies' after Rob had told her about the discovery of David's body. 'You've been spying on me.'

Jemima was trying to lock eyes. 'It might appear that way, Minister. But it's not spying; it's exercising a duty of care.'

Anne-Marie felt a surge of anger. 'Who exactly do you work for? You're not a diary secretary, are you?'

'I am in government service.'

'For God's sake, Jemima, if you're not going to give me straight-forward answers to—'

'I am employed by the Security Service.'

'MI5.'

'Yes, some call it that. Incorrectly, of course.'

'As was "Uncle Jimmy", I presume.'

'Yes, Minister.'

Anne-Marie realized that the implications of the admission would require her to redefine her adult life. For a start the cash that had helped her reinvent herself. Not David's money, but dirty money. There would be time for all that and she could only dismantle the edifice of deceit brick by brick.

'What is your assignment? And how did it come about?'

'Minister, I inherited your file, that's all. It shows that you were accidentally caught up in a British operation in Ireland in '93 and '94.'

'What British operation?'

'I will need guidance on explaining that, Minister.'

'Guidance!'

Jemima ploughed on. 'Most importantly, the file shows that you were to be given lifetime care and protection by the Service, should any need ever arise. When you were appointed minister, there was no need for the Service to intervene as there is no suggestion in the file of any wrongdoing by yourself. However, as soon as your appointment was announced, the Service decided that, for the first few months at least, it should carry out its obligation by placing me at your side.'

'You *are* spying on me.'

'No, Minister.'

'You always seem to be hovering when anything potentially awkward is happening.'

'If you have gained that impression, it is purely coincidental.'

'I wish I could believe you, Jemima.'

'So do I, Minister. I truly do.'

They fell quiet, a lull descending after the first shots. Anne-Marie, voice now composed, broke the uneasy calm. 'I had an unpleasant experience this morning.' She engaged fully with Jemima. 'For God's sake, you probably know about it already.'

'I'm not aware of anything, Minister,' Jemima replied evenly. If you're lying, you're good, thought Anne-Marie. She scanned their surroundings, searching for other eyes and ears.

'There's no one unfriendly,' said Jemima. 'I obviously did not want this conversation in or near the Ministry. We're out in the open, so we've followed a protocol.'

'All right,' continued Anne-Marie. 'After my appointment was announced, an old friend of my family, Joseph Kennedy, got in touch. I had not seen him for many years. He wanted to see me urgently. That I'm sure you do know.' Jemima's face was a mask. 'He arranged a meeting for this morning at an address he gave me. It turned out to be a garage. I arrived to find him dead, hanging on a rope.'

'I'm sorry. It must have been a horrible shock,' said Jemima, combining surprise with sympathy. Either it was indeed news to her or, as Anne-Marie again reflected, she was an accomplished actor. The latter now seemed more likely.

'Jemima, it's not comforting I need,' she stated coldly. 'He told me in the phone call that he was dying. There was clearly something he needed to unburden. I have, of course, ensured that the discovery of his body has been reported to the police.'

'Good,' said Jemima. 'As you had no possible connection to his death, I can see no reason for you to be dragged into this. Who else knows?'

'My driver, Keith Hinds. You probably know that too. I asked him to contact the police for me.'

'We will speak to Hinds.' Jemima conveyed the weight of authority.

'That is not now my main reason for re-establishing this contact with you.' Anne-Marie cast a sceptical smile. 'Although it seems you have pre-empted me in re-establishing contact.'

'Please go on,' said Jemima. This time, it was she who looked around. A couple of hundred yards up river were two other cyclists, both male, sitting on a bench drinking from water bottles.

She looked at them and turned to Anne-Marie. 'Shall we walk with our bikes while you tell me more?'

Anne-Marie followed Jemima's eyes to the two cyclists.

'Who are they?' she demanded.

'They're friends,' replied Jemima. 'You must trust me when I say that you can speak to me in confidence.'

'Trust is not the point,' she said. 'A bonus perhaps, but not what matters.' Anne-Marie halted, turned her bike towards the river and looked west. The sun was almost set and the sky darkening. A red glow seeped through the power station's chimneys and above the rows of Victorian terraces beside it. A chill whipped up from the water. 'You will know from the file that I had a relationship with a man calling himself David Vallely in Dublin. You will also know that his body has been found. I cannot be sure whether that is what Joseph Kennedy wanted to talk to me about, but the coincidence is obvious. I want one thing from you.'

'Yes, Minister.'

'I would like to know the truth about David Wallis, as I must now learn to call him: what exactly he was doing and – it's hard to find the right way to express this – how he perceived his relationship with me.'

'Minister, that is an operational matter.'

'Don't try that with me, Jemima. For better or worse, I'm a Minister of the Crown. Whether or not it's in my interest, I'm willing to go wherever this leads. There are now two dead bodies, one of them in the here and now. Don't force me to make a public issue of this.'

'I will see what I can do, Minister.'

'No, Jemima, do better than that.' Anne-Marie turned her bike round and gripped the handlebars. 'And never forget that duty of care to me.'

'Yes, Minister,' replied Jemima.

Anne-Marie mounted her bike. 'Will I continue to have the pleasure of your occasional visits to my office?'

'Perhaps that would now be inappropriate, Minister.'

'Yes, perhaps it would.'

'But I want you to know that I am on your side.'

'What other side is there, Jemima?'

Fuelled by adrenalin and suppressed fury, Anne-Marie headed for the park's exit, forgetting that the path she was taking was barred to cyclists. When she realized, it could hardly have seemed more irrelevant.

There was only one person in the world she could trust: herself. Now she had compromised that by confiding in others. Her destiny was slipping from her grasp. She stopped short of her apartment block and checked the text from Rob McNeil with the name and number of the investigating policeman. She would sleep on it but she knew already that in the morning she would ring the number. It would be the first step in wresting back her life.

The uncovering of David Wallis's body, the reappearance of Joseph Kennedy and her own elevation were no coincidence. They amounted to a perfect storm. Nothing had been erased. It was not going away after all.

CHAPTER 22

Post-election, Wednesday, 17 May

She's done well, thought Carne, looking up at the structure of shining dark veneers and tinted glass – elegance for high achievers, reflecting the gold sky and reddening sun. He rang the bell.

'Hello?' Just a whisper of Celtic tinge.

'It's DCI Carne.'

She buzzed him in. 'Come on up, eleventh floor.' The security camera watched him enter.

The curt phone call that morning had astonished him. She gave her name, address and a time, and then rang off without a further word. In a Google search, the most detailed piece was in *Daily Mail* online, headed by the group photograph of the new government's women ministers. 'LIONEL'S LOVELY FIRECRACKER' was the headline. 'Among Lionel's new ladies she stands out for her petite charm and remarkable election night speech.' Carne could see her attraction – vivacious with a glint in her eye. The article gave the bare bones of a career propelled by an outstanding law degree from Trinity College, Dublin; articles with Audax, an emerging left-leaning London law chambers; a speedy rise to partner and a spell making serious money. Then she set up Audax's Human Rights Department, recruiting the eminent QC wife of a former prime minister to join them, a key political entrée.

For a tabloid there was little about her personal life. Audax's head of chambers, Kieron Carnegie, called her 'a brilliant and attractive woman, but a solo operator who keeps herself to herself'. The paper claimed it had spoken to a former lover of Ms Gallagher who said that her commitment to her work 'overrode any thoughts of marriage or even long-term relationships'.

The question is, the article concluded, 'can Anne-Marie Gallagher, Britain's prettiest, and most mysterious, minister, make it a national hat-trick of women leaders?'

There was a mirror in the lift. Carne checked himself, patting down his suit and pushing any stray hairs back into place. He was unaccountably nervous. You're a policeman going to a routine interview with a potential witness, he told himself. Except that there was nothing routine about any of this. He was breaking every procedural rule in the book. He rang the bell of her flat, heard 'Just a minute' through the door and waited.

'Sorry to keep you,' she said. 'I was out on my bike. Bit of a rushed change.' Her eyes were sparkling from the exercise and what must have been a breakneck shower and throwing-on of old jeans and a light-blue blouse. Her feet were still bare. 'As you can see,' she continued.

'I shouldn't have been so punctual,' replied Carne, frowning to hide his embarrassment.

'It's fine. Come on in.' She crisply ushered him through the door into a sitting room with an unbroken spread of glass overlooking the Thames. The setting sun was now more clearly visible over the two giant fingers of the old Lots Road power station across the river, casting a glow that seemed to flood the whole horizon.

He could not stop himself admiring it again. 'It's dazzling.'

'Yes, I'm lucky,' she said, liking his approval.

'Lived here long?' he asked, feeling stupid as he did.

'I bought it when the block went up a couple of years ago.' She flashed him a grin. 'Mind you, a politician's salary's not great for the mortgage.'

'So your election was unexpected?'

'It seemed incredible.'

'Congratulations.'

'Thanks.' She was sizing him up like a tailor fitting a new suit. 'Drink?'

In return he wanted to examine every inch of her but knew he must not. 'Better not. I'm on duty. Aren't I?'

'Perhaps we should agree the rules of engagement.'

He took a risk. 'OK. In the meantime, I'll have a glass of something.' She smiled. He had done the right thing. 'Whatever's easy.'

She walked through a door and returned with a bottle of white wine and two glasses. 'I'll join you,' she said. 'Just a glass, anyway. I don't really drink.'

She motioned him to a pale beige sofa, placed the wine glasses on a small square glass table in front of it and poured. He could not recall, imagine even, another politician like her. She was small, neat but not skinny, hints of auburn in the brown hair, highlights perhaps, which rested just below her nape. The top two buttons of her shirt were undone and, as she leant over, he allowed himself a glimpse of small breasts, starting a flutter in his heart. It was impossible not to compare any woman with Alice, the strong broad shoulders and long blonde hair hanging down over them.

Yet, for the first time he could remember, the comparison seemed irrelevant. This was a woman who seemed so slight and fragile that you could carry her like a child. It was a ridiculous thought – she must be tough as teak to have risen so far.

She finished pouring the wine and looked up, noticing him trying not to watch her. 'So.' She flopped into a matching seat placed at precise right angles to the sofa.

'So,' he repeated.

'I asked for this meeting,' she said. 'What does that make it? On the record, off the record – official, unofficial?'

'Off the record's fine.'

She liked his voice, mellow without being too deep, an aftertaste of accent she could not quite recognize. 'OK.'

'You made the contact. Why?' he asked.

She looked out at the river. 'Not quite. Rob McNeil gave me your name and number. Let's start with what led you to him.'

'All right. Late on the Sunday night after the election,' Carne began, 'we received an anonymous call giving the precise location of a burial site. Two days later the same caller said check out a name: "David Vallely". It turned out that he was a postgraduate student in Dublin who'd disappeared in 1994. Shortly afterwards I was visited in the mortuary by General Kenneth Bowman, the present GOC, Northern Ireland.'

'How did he know?' she asked.

'He'd been told of the calls on the police confidential line.'

'These people have no rules,' she sighed.

'No,' agreed Carne. 'Shortly after his visit the general rang to tell me it was his certain view that David Vallely was an alias and the real identity was David Wallis.'

'How could he be so sure?'

'I've never been fully clear about that, though I have my

suspicions. But he was right. Within hours dental records proved it. He went on to say that Wallis's sister was married to the new Prime Minister's press secretary.'

'That must have set wires buzzing.'

'Yes.' Carne grimaced. 'The next part may, I fear, distress you. General Bowman asked to return to the mortuary for one final look at Wallis. I took the opportunity to have a further conversation with him. He told me that Wallis's father had been a British soldier under his command, killed in the Falklands.'

'I knew that. David told me,' exclaimed Anne-Marie. She felt a wisp of victory. Something had been true.

'I'm afraid that's not all. Bowman then said that David Wallis himself had followed his father into the same regiment. He had also been a British Army officer under his command.'

'Jesus.' The tiny moment of vindication was crushed. 'Could you stop there for a minute?' Anne-Marie rose from her chair, picked up her glass, looked away and drank. She walked over to the window. After a minute or so, she turned and offered Carne a refill. He refused with a wave of his hand, and she topped up her own glass. He could see that she had suffered a shock and stayed silent.

'You're saying that David Wallis was a British soldier.'

'At one time, yes. Bowman said he left the army in early 1993.'

'You're one hundred per cent sure.'

'Yes.'

'There is no possible doubt that Vallely was an assumed name.'

'No.'

She allowed herself a deep sigh. The last vestige of hope, however irrational, had just died.

'What sort of soldier was he?'

'That's sketchy. He spent some time in what has been described to me as "intelligence liaison".'

'Intelligence.'

'Yes.'

'I see.' He marvelled at her equilibrium, a reed standing firm against such a cruel buffeting. 'OK, go on.'

'I formed the impression,' Carne continued, choosing his words carefully, 'that General Bowman considered it would be unhelpful to investigate David Wallis's life and death too deeply.' He searched for any hint in her eyes. They remained locked on him, expressionless. 'I disagree with that view. I believe that David Wallis's killers should be brought to justice. And the key to explaining his disappearance is to understand what exactly he was doing in the years and, more specifically, the months leading up to it.' His last sentence had a note of finality. It was her turn now.

She flicked a straying lock of hair over an ear, and exhaled, disturbing the strands of her fringe. She stretched out one leg, clenching and relaxing the calf and hamstrings, and then the other. He was not sure whether she was buying time or merely reflecting. He tried not to follow the legs.

'Do you believe I know something that will help you?' she asked.

'You'll know that better than me.'

She rose again to her feet. He cursorily wondered if he had made a mistake and alarmed her.

'We may come to that,' she said, 'but for now there is a more immediate matter.' He felt a hit of relief – she was simply asserting her control of her agenda. 'My reason for seeing you is another death. Shortly after the announcement of my appointment, I received a call from a man I had not seen for more than twenty years. He was a close friend of my family. My brother in particular. In his teens, he was a likeable and amusing boy. His name was Joseph Kennedy.'

Carne, recalling Poots's summary of the disappeared Gang of Four, almost choked on his drink.

'He asked to see me, said it was urgent. He was dying and had something he needed to tell me. I was afraid. As he grew into manhood, he became harder. Perhaps foolishly, I agreed to meet him a few days later at a time and place he gave me.'

She caught one last glance of the disappearing sun, and glared at him. 'I arrived at the meeting place. It turned out to be a scruffy garage not far from here. He was hanging from the ceiling, a rope around his neck. Dead. I know that. I parted the hair that had fallen over his face and inspected his eyes. Very dead.'

This time, it was she giving finality to her words. Carne tried to remind himself that on this night he must not be a police interrogator. Yet there was one obvious question. 'Are you sure this man was Joseph Kennedy?'

'Do you seriously think I would make a mistake like that?'

He had irritated her. 'I'm sorry,' he said, meaning it. 'It was a stupid question. Old habits. Bad habits.'

She relaxed. 'You're forgiven. The real point – the reason I have decided to see you – comes next. Yes, I was shocked. I found it hard to decide a course of action. I couldn't say silent, so I asked my driver to report my discovery to the police.'

'That was the right thing to do,' he said. She felt the warmth of a support she had not anticipated. It emboldened her.

'Later that day,' she continued, 'my driver – he seems remarkably well connected – told me there must have been a case of mistaken identity as the dead man's name was not Joseph Kennedy, but Brian Fitzgerald. And, further, he'd left a suicide note.'

She walked over and waved the wine bottle in front of him. 'Thanks,' he said. She again refilled her own glass.

'I am telling you,' she said with clinical deliberation, 'this man was not Brian Fitzgerald. And there was no suicide note.' He felt her calculating whether, or how, to add something. 'In his coat pocket there was an envelope containing a document. It would have meant something only to him and me. It told me there could be no possible doubt that this was Joseph.' She finished abruptly, sat down and awaited him.

'Can I ask you some questions?' Carne asked softly.

'Can I trust you?' she asked.

'I believe I am a trustworthy person.'

'That's not what I mean.' She searched for the words, moving an inch closer, her eyes piercing him. In what she now knew was a treacherous path ahead – one that could destroy her – she needed an irrevocable ally. A partner to help her reclaim her fate. The customary mutual suspicion between politicians and policemen made him an unlikely one. But they had one critical thing in common: they were both outsiders.

She inspected him again. The dark-brown hair with hints of greying curls at the edges; the slightly long nose and face conveying a sorrowful yearning; the firm chin above broad shoulders. There was a gravity and straightforwardness in him. He was a decent man and an instinct – one she disliked in herself – told her she could lead him.

'I mean, truly trust you,' she continued. 'I have to be sure that you're on my side. That you will protect me.' He looked away, seeking refuge in the gloaming of the darkening sky. 'Wherever that takes you.'

Carne eased himself up from the sofa and went to peer through the glass. He wanted the lights of the city to give him an answer, some sign at least. A police car rushed along the embankment, its lights flashing, its siren just audible through the thick pane. An ambulance followed in its wake. He turned round. She was sitting, her eyes devouring him in a silent plea. He felt he was making one of the most important choices of his life – perhaps *the* most. It would not be rational but a leap of faith. Faith did not lead to predictable outcomes.

Who really was this woman he had known for no more than minutes? He recalled the newspaper profile. She had 'come from nowhere'. A woman apparently without a past. The mere fact that she had been involved with Wallis might of itself seem suspicious. Not to mention her knowledge of Joseph Kennedy. Whose side, if any, had she really been on? Both then and, perhaps, now? He stopped himself. To begin thinking like that would mean he must now – instantly – turn his back on her and walk through the door of her flat. That he must lose any chance of a friendship – of coming to understand who she really was.

'Yes.' The word seemed to come out of his mouth before he had completed the internal debate. He stared at her, propelled by some reflex that was visceral and now irreversible. She breathed deeply again and closed her eyes.

'Thank you,' she said. 'Now ask me your questions.'

He resumed his seat on the sofa, now at the end nearer her chair.

'You mentioned Joseph Kennedy was a friend of your brother. Who is your brother?'

'His name is – was, I mean – Martin McCartney.' For the second time, Carne stifled his shock. 'I was born Maire McCartney. Maire Anne McCartney to be precise. I reversed the names and changed my surname after David disappeared.'

'Why did you do that?' He instantly regretted asking it. If, having come so far so quickly, he lost her by reaching too far, the error would be unforgivable.

She fell silent. 'Why do you ask?' she finally replied.

This was a test he must not fail. 'Because, knowing it, how could I not ask?' She did not answer – he had to give her more. 'You must have thought about this when you started becoming a public figure. Former friends, acquaintances, family. Even more than twenty years later, someone would know you.'

'I have no family.' She was whispering.

'But others?'

'I had no friends left. I was living an isolated life in Dublin.'

'Why isolated? A woman – a girl – like you . . .'

'That's not for now. But then David came. Like the sun bursting through clouds.' She paused, seeming to look into his eyes with a plea he could not interpret. 'And then he went. And I wanted to leave it all behind.'

'But others might know you. Joseph Kennedy did.'

'Yes.' She paused. 'Rob McNeil, too, though we only once met face to face. I suppose there may be one or two more. But so few.' She sprang up and rounded on him. 'And so what? I had every right to seek a new life. I was the victim. There was nothing illegal in changing a name, in wanting to get away, to be a new person. I have nothing to reproach myself for. Or for others to reproach me. I had reason.'

'People will still ask,' he said gently.

'Let them. It doesn't matter. I had reason,' she repeated.

There was a bitterness he had not suspected in her. He was struck by the absence of family photographs in the room. He should have noticed it before. 'You spoke of your brother in the past.'

'Yes.' The single word hung in the air.

'This is not easy for you.'

'No.'

'I have to know.'

'Yes.'

She walked over to a desk on the corner, also glass-topped with a laptop on it. Down both sides were rows of black metallic drawers. She opened one, pulled out a photograph frame and brought it over. A young man with wavy fair hair and clear blue eyes smiled out of it. 'He disappeared shortly before the 1994 ceasefire.' She stood the photograph on the table, angled so that they could both see it. 'I haven't seen him since.'

'What happened to him?'

Was there a hesitation before she spoke? 'I don't know.' She lifted the photograph and examined it, stroking his hair with a finger. 'As we grew up together I loved Martin very much.'

'And then?'

'We went our separate ways. I'd rather not speak further of him.' She walked back to the sofa and slumped opposite him. 'For God's sake, it would not have been a smart career move to be known as the sister of Martin McCartney. As I said, I had reason.' She took a long, slow breath, the force subsiding.

'I understand,' said Carne softly. He allowed the moment to pass. 'Let's return to Joseph. You said he and Martin were friends.'

'They were like brothers.'

'And continued to be?'

'Yes. As far as I know.'

'Did Joseph Kennedy give any further detail in his phone call of why he wanted to see you?'

Was she hesitating again, or trying to recall? He felt every image and noise beyond the few feet between them screened out.

The only sounds were her precise, deliberately even breathing and the background hum of ventilation. The only smell was her.

'He said something about it all being a trick. I can't remember exactly.'

'And this was just a day or two after you were appointed a minister and David Wallis's body was found.'

'Yes.'

'Wallis also disappeared at around that time in 1994.'

'Yes.'

'You must have thought about that.'

'Of course.' She abruptly grabbed the photograph, jumped from her chair, and walked over to her desk. She returned and sat down, pushing her chair back from him. 'I'm sorry, I can't talk about this any more now.'

'Please . . . forgive me. just one more thing. You mentioned a document in Joseph's pocket.' For the first time, he thought she showed a glimmer of fear. 'What was it?'

'I can't tell you that yet.'

'All right. But I ask you to tell me this. Would anyone else, anyone at all from your past, also know what that document implied?'

He realized his window of opportunity was closing. 'What I'm getting at is whether any other person could have put it there to convey some sort of message to you.'

'It's possible. Now, no more.'

She wiped an eye, pushed her fingers through her hair and cast a politician's smile. The spell was broken, the buzz of traffic audible again, the night city panorama now vast and in focus behind her small face. 'So you, Chief Inspector . . .'

'It's Jon. Jonny to some.'

She smiled, this time meaning it. 'I'll start again. So you,

Jon – I'll stick to that for the moment – you have an unfair advantage over me. You get to read about me, I get to know nothing about you.'

'I'm not interesting.' He grinned ruefully. It was the first time he had broken into a full smile. The act of transformation was surprising. It confirmed not just that he was an attractive man – handsome, even – it also seemed to take years off him.

'You're interesting to me. I'm sure there are lots of things. Famous cases. Starring in court. Wife. Nice family.'

'Not even that.' The grin subsided.

'Alone in the world, then?' She had a sudden apparition of David. The same colouring, the same grin, even. She remembered those words: 'a lonely orphan'. But David's grin had tended never to disappear.

'My wife died,' he said bleakly.

'I'm sorry, I was prying.'

'It's fine. She was Irish too – though the other side of the fence from you. Not that she gave a damn.' He could not understand what possessed him – perhaps because her example gave him the confidence – but he took out his wallet and produced a tiny photograph of a rosy-cheeked, fair-haired woman.

'Pretty,' she said.

'I met her over here. She was a trainee psychiatric nurse at the Maudsley. I was a young copper in south London. She was homesick so I followed her back.' He paused. 'That was one reason, anyway.' He noticed the question in her eyes and chided himself for the slip. 'She died seven years later. Ovarian cancer. It was aggressive.'

'I'm sorry.' Ovarian cancer. The memory of David's description of his mother's death flashed before her. Now just another lie.

'You get over it. I wondered looking back if that was why we could never have children.'

'I never had children either.' Her remark cast them both into silence. She broke it sharply. 'I'm surprised you stayed there.'

'I like the hills.' He hesitated, wanting to explain to this woman why to return was impossible but knowing it was too soon.

'I like the city,' she said. 'Oh, hell, it's nearly eleven and I have work to do.'

Carne realized his time was up. He had not talked even this much about himself for years; an incandescence flowing from this woman was unlocking him. He wanted to linger, to delay the solitary night. He gathered his coat and case.

'Thank you, Jon. You have more to ask. I know that. But there's time. First, I want to find out what happened to Joseph Kennedy. That's in the here and now.'

'And, er . . .'

'Anne-Marie.'

'Anne-Marie, I don't want to frighten you but you were the last person to speak to Joseph Kennedy. You were the person who discovered his body. If I am to investigate his death properly, I'll have to share that investigation with the local police. And it's a habit of detectives to look upon people who discover bodies with suspicion.'

'I've nothing to hide over the death of Joseph Kennedy,' she replied sharply.

'One last thing,' he said. 'You told me that you reported the discovery to your driver. Have you discussed this with anyone else? Anyone at all?'

She looked into his eyes and placed a hand on each of his shoulders. She gripped hard in a way that disturbed him. 'I won't tell you lies. But there are some things which I will tell you only when I choose to. In the same way that I trust you, you too must trust that I'm on your side.'

'In that case,' he said, 'until we know precisely how Joseph Kennedy died, I urge you to take great care.'

'I can look after myself,' she replied. 'And now I have my guardian angel, don't I?'

Carne stepped out into the night, and set off down the river pathway. It was clear but not cold, yet he shivered, heavy with the responsibility she had placed on him. He felt afraid for her and an overpowering desire to give her the protection she wanted. Yet he had only scratched her surface and had no real understanding of what beat inside. He was the artist trying to paint an elusive, entrancing, energizing model, but seeing nothing.

He counted eleven floors up and saw a dim beam from a lamp casting a pale glow onto the expanse of glass. He imagined her sitting in the half-light alone. An elusive woman of contradictions. She was self-assured, confident, controlling at times. She seemed to need to live in the present; the past, like her birthplace, to be swept aside. She did not want to travel there. He must somehow prise the full story of that past out of her to help solve not just the disappearance and bullet in the head of David Wallis, but the death of Joseph Kennedy too. He shuddered at leading her on that journey.

Unless . . . unless she was leading him – the imagining he must kill.

It was midnight. He headed on through Battersea Park – a couple of sprint cyclists doing late circuits passing him on the roadway to his right – finally arriving at Chelsea Bridge. He steeled himself for the walk to Sloane Square Underground station and the retreat to his budget hotel jail. He checked his phone – there was a message from Poots. 'Any more clues re tiepin man? Billy.' Carne texted back: 'Need Amy here tomorrow. Another body.'

Bodies. A tramp was slumped across a park bench, telltale cans of cider scattered beneath. Briefly the moon illuminated him; Carne could smell the stains on his scuffed jacket and grease on his straggling hair. Wasted lives, reducing to universal black holes. Then he thought of her, alive and glowing, the small breasts showing in the blue blouse, the allure of the green eyes.

Stop fantasizing. She was a tough, successful career woman who, once upon a time, and in circumstances for which she was not responsible, had become unwittingly embroiled in some lethal game. Unless – the imagining was refusing to die – her eyes had been open all along.

From her window, Anne-Marie could see him by the river, disappearing into the shadows. The uncanniness of the resemblance pulsed within her. She wondered if memory was deceiving her – and David in middle age could only be imagined. Yet the clean-lined smoothness of youth would surely have turned into the attractive cragginess; the dark hair now cut short would, if allowed to grow, retain the curl tipping over the ear; the brown eyes would still have been twinkling at her. The voice – there lay the difference. David's accent was posh – there was no other word for it – the policeman was not. She was no expert in the dialects of England but the burr was unmissable – most likely West Country. A provincial man with nothing grand in his background.

She had to believe she had captured him, that he would never renege on the trust he had promised. It was what the conversation had been about; everything else was trivial. If her judgement was wrong, she was making the third great error of her life.

She looked at the red box perched on the desk, forced herself towards it and sat down in the hard-backed chair, sufficiently uncomfortable to keep her alert. She hoiked the case onto her desk, engaged the lock and snapped open the lid. At the top were briefing notes for another conference on extradition and individual rights – once the subject of her undergraduate dissertation. She should be ticking with anticipation. Instead, she felt detached from it all; it was just talk. She put down the notes and stared out of the window. Her favourite, consoling sight – the city that had become her refuge, and her opportunity. Now it was beginning to feel like a city of lies.

Damn you, David whatever your name was! Damn you not just for what you did to me, but what you did to yourself! Did you mean to be a good man? Were you a good man? Doing what you thought was right, whatever the betrayals and the costs?

Again, Anne-Marie had a sense of going round in circles, of some disembodied narrative loop revolving around her, which she could not break out of, past and present circling in opposite directions on a fateful collision course. Perhaps that collision had to happen to allow her to free herself.

She felt an overpowering weariness. It shocked her – she never tired. She collected the papers scattered in front of her, patted them together and replaced them in the box. She closed the catches, reset the lock and let the case drop onto the floor with a dull thud. She rubbed her eyes, walked over to the window to lower the blinds, headed for the bedroom, stripped off her clothes, and collapsed onto her bed without even removing her make-up or brushing her teeth.

CHAPTER 23

Post-election, Thursday, 18 May

Amy Riordan ran her fingers over the dead man's face and neck, raised his head, parted the long dark hair and gathered it towards the back of the neck. His full features were revealed: deeply cleaved forehead; sunken brown eyes; neglected, yellowed teeth, the colour of decades of nicotine; bristle on chin and cheek, the skin now drained bloodless and white. She hovered over him, apparently trying to summon some sort of judgement.

'He must have been a good-looking man,' she said. 'Once upon a time.' She pulled at the skin around his eyes, opening them wide, and then closed them again. 'What age do we have for him?'

The local CID inspector flicked through a notebook. 'Born 1969. Late forties.'

'Ravaged body, ravaged life,' said Amy.

'Do we know anything about him after '94?' asked Carne.

'We've made brief enquiries,' replied the inspector, 'but, till you came along, there didn't seem any need for more. Man with a terminal illness, maybe came up to London to meet someone who stood him up, rope around the neck, jump from chair, QED. Neighbours didn't see much of him, said he was a loner, a few sightings around the building sites, that's it. Unless there are police records, there'd hardly be photos of him. No Facebook then.'

'And the letter?' asked Carne.

'Short and simple. I'm dying, time to end it, don't want to be a burden any more.'

'Handwriting?'

'Yes, we can look at that. Don't know what there'll be to go on. Maybe a signature at the surgery or something.'

Carne leant down towards the face. 'So, my friend,' he said, stroking any remaining wisps of hair off his forehead, 'are you Joseph Kennedy? And why did you vanish without trace?' He straightened his shoulders and back, and put an arm around Amy. 'OK, did he hang himself? Or was he hanged?'

Using the thumbs and index fingers of both hands, she cupped the corpse's neck. 'The marks of the ligature on the neck should be the telltale. I understand he was found hanging on a thicker-than-average rope. This can confuse the picture. But there's a reasonably clear single ring of bruising. See it?' Carne leant over to inspect the neck: the ring seemed less clear-cut to him but he took Amy's word for it. 'That indicates he was probably alive when the rope strangled him. If he was dead beforehand, the mark would be less precise.'

'So he died by hanging? Rather than being dead first, then strung up?'

'I would say so, yes.'

'Self-inflicted hanging?'

'That's a different matter. You have to create a scenario where the killer – or killers it would have to be in this case, I think

– either persuade him to hang himself or, while he's still alive, hang him themselves.'

'Tranquillizing, anaesthetizing him?'

'We're into hypothesis here,' replied Amy tartly.

'OK, Amy,' said Carne respectfully, 'I'm hearing you. But, assuming our friend didn't simply agree to a polite invitation to hang himself, it would require more than one killer.'

'Yes.'

'And drugging him?'

'If they'd used chloroform, I'd expect to find signs of irritation on the skin around his mouth. Or there might be a needle mark. The problem is that he's been lying here too long. If the original pathologist made the assumption of suicide, which would have been wholly rational given the other circumstance, he'd have had no reason to look further.'

'I'm trying to imagine a doable scenario. They hold a gun to his head, handcuff him, or somehow restrain his arms and legs, hoist him, let him drop, then remove the restraints.'

'Yes, all of that's possible,' agreed Amy, 'though they would have to take care to avoid bruising. The point is that expert killers could find a way of making a killing look like a self-inflicted hanging. I can't prove it from the body.'

'If this was murder, it was expert. A professional job.'

'Yes. So you'd need evidence that goes beyond the corpse. And a motive.'

'Unless this poor bastard,' reflected Carne, 'really is a sad loner called Brian Fitzgerald who decided he didn't want to die a ghastly, painful death and tried to end it.' He paused and turned to Amy. 'Billy's checked at Castlereagh. There's sod all in the file, no prints, no nothing.'

'They never pinned anything on him, did they?' affirmed Amy.

'No. Whatever was once there, the cupboard is now bare.'

'And he disappeared a year before the DNA database came in.'

'Correct,' agreed Carne. 'There's only one way to know for sure.'

She had said he could ring her private mobile, though texting would be better. To his surprise, her response was instant: she would clear the evening to visit the mortuary.

At 7.30 p.m. Anne-Marie was there. 'My driver brought me,' she said breathlessly. 'He's in the loop on this. I told you that, didn't I?' She had changed from the controlled figure of the previous evening. Now Carne saw a coiled spring, agitated, wound up by the pressures of being on political parade throughout the day.

'Would you like a moment to relax?' he asked.

'No, let's get on with it.' She engaged him for only the briefest moment. Carne wondered what precisely Joseph Kennedy meant to her. He led her into the white hum and chemical odours of the postmortem suite where Amy was waiting for them. She pressed a button to open a refrigerated compartment. The gleaming metal slab on which Joseph's body lay slid out. Carne noted that it had been tidied after the afternoon examination and had the more benign appearance of a man in repose.

Anne-Marie stood gazing at it, expressionless. Carne had feared that she would flinch, or be repelled by it. Instead she remained motionless and silent. The only sounds were the heavy ticking of a dated, crude wall clock, and the irregular hum of south London's evening traffic.

She bent down over the head and kissed it.

'Yes, that's Joseph.'

'Thank you,' said Carne softly. 'I appreciate you doing this.' The warmth of his tone attracted a look from Amy.

'Ms Gallagher,' said Amy, 'it would be of great assistance if you were able to point to any identifying marks.'

Anne-Marie froze for a few seconds, lost in memory, then addressed Amy with a wary roughness. 'Look on the inside of his upper left leg. High. Just below the testicle. There's a birthmark. Shape of a half-moon.'

Amy lifted the cover and eased the legs apart. She bent down beneath the cover, the light of her torch casting a faint glimmer. She closed the legs together again and straightened the cover from neck to toes.

'Thank you,' she said with simple finality.

'Is that it?' she asked Carne.

'Yes, I think so. Amy?'

'There's one small favour, Ms Gallagher.' Carne detected an unaccustomed nervousness in his colleague. 'As you came into contact with the deceased shortly after he died, there may be DNA traces from you on his clothing. It would assist the investigation if I could take a DNA swab and fingerprints as what we call an elimination test. So that we don't confuse your DNA with—'

'I'm a lawyer, I understand why you need it,' Anne-Marie interrupted scratchily.

'It won't take a minute.'

'I'll wait for you by the exit,' said Carne. She shot him a wary look. Was she warning him about assuming any familiarity?

Ten minutes later, she reappeared with Amy alongside.

'Done,' said Amy.

'Good,' he replied. The three of them stood awkwardly together. 'Can I, er . . .?' he began.

She intervened. 'My driver's waiting outside.' Was he being cold-shouldered or, with onlookers present, kept at arm's length?

'Will you be all right?' he asked.

'Of course I'll be all right.' It was said harshly. She turned to leave without looking back and the door gave an ugly slam as she disappeared behind it.

Amy saw his dejection. 'More to the point, are you all right?'

'Not entirely,' he replied.

'By the way, he *was* murdered, wasn't he?'

'Of course he was.'

Anne-Marie walked to the car, eyes fixed far into the distance, emotions locked in chains, brain disconnected from the screeches and squealings of the grinding urban machine. Hinds jumped to open the rear door. He had observed her closing down once before and tried to snap her out of it with cheery chitchat. This time, he knew better.

'How long to the flat, Keith?'

'Twenty minutes or so, Minister,' he replied.

'Make it an hour, would you?'

She stared out of the window at the falling dusk, day slowly giving way to the car lights and street lamps of night, shapes she converted into softened contours and sounds. She tried to remember the year – 1980 was it? – when the McCartneys and Kennedys, sharing a caravan, first went on holiday together. Portrush in the summer, long sweeping beaches, on sunlit days the peaks of Donegal to the west, to the east somewhere in the distance the coast of Scotland and that other world that lay beyond her island. She was eight, a pretty little girl, they used to say, despite the puppy fat, with shiny auburn hair bouncing on her neck, neatly side-parted and held by grips to the front. Martin was fourteen, six years older. Later, she sometimes wondered whether there were just the two of them because her parents had exercised a restraint unusual in Catholics or whether there had been difficulties conceiving. It was a question she never got round to asking her mother and would never have dreamt of asking her father. Too late now. Too many questions came too late now.

Ahead of her was Joseph sprinting into the sea, urging her to keep up with him. Even aged eleven, he was tall and strikingly lean. His legs reached out like a racehorse's. She put the image into slow motion and he was floating ahead of her, hitting the edge of water, spraying foam into a mist of sparkles, screaming with delighted horror at the cold collision of the ocean, kicking his legs higher and higher as he urged himself on through the ever-increasing waves. Then he stopped, turned, saw her at the water's edge and yelled. 'Maire!' And what had he said? Yes, that was it. 'Don't be afraid.' Not 'don't be scared' or 'don't be a coward' or 'don't be a girl'. He had run back towards her, grasped her by the hand and said, 'Come with me, the waves are our friends.' And she had looked at the waves, curling with their white tips of surf, rolling over onto the water, flattening out into the level sea, and she realized there was nothing to be afraid of as each one of these waves' lives was so short that they could harm only themselves and not her.

Later, they were back on dry land, his body rough with salt and sand, his hair bleached and stiff from the sea spray. She found a rock pool and returned with a bucket full of water, crept up behind him and poured it over the back of his head and down his back. He turned round, pulled the corners of his mouth to each side, contorted his face into an idiot's leer and said, 'One day, Maire McCartney, I'll give you a wet kiss for that.' She stuck her tongue out at him and said, 'You're rude, Joseph Kennedy. And, anyway, you wouldn't dare.'

It had taken him seven years to summon up the courage.

'What took you so long?' she asked him when he finally did.

'I didn't want you to think me rude,' he answered. He must have stored the line for all that time.

'We're here, Minister,' said Hinds. She shook her head and rubbed her eyes. Her hands were dampened by a moistening of which she had been unaware.

'An hour passes quickly when you're . . .' Her voice tailed off; anything she said would be trite, a feeble cover-up.

'Yes, Minister.'

She gathered her handbag and box and went to open the car door but he was there before her.

'Goodnight, Minister.'

'Goodnight, Keith.'

He hesitated. 'Are you all right, Minister?'

'There seem to be a lot of people asking me that today, Keith.' She patted him on the arm and walked away. Then she realized she had forgotten to tell him and turned back.

'We were both correct, Keith.'

'Minister?'

'Brian Fitzgerald was once called Joseph Kennedy. It appears he changed his identity. I hadn't seen him for a long time.'

'I'm sorry, Minister. It's been an ordeal for you. But over now.' She gave him an ironic smile, turned and headed towards the glass doors of the apartment block.

Her flat, pristine as always, seemed barren and lifeless. It was the cleaner's day and she could smell polish and bleach, but none of the comforts of home: coal burning in the fire, a cake rising in the oven, meat sizzling under the grill. Arriving home from school, she would always find her mother cooking something, insisting that she sit down, rest and eat. Now she felt the solitariness of her single-minded ambition and success. In such moments, work was both her distraction and her interest, but the red box seemed no more than an inanimate conveyor of trivia set against the reappearance of two dead men's bodies.

Carne's phone buzzed. The message read: 'Sorry. Can I offer you coffee and sweets? A-M.'

Amy's eyes were flashing with curiosity. 'Billy?'

'No, not Billy.'

'It's her, isn't it?

'Amy, with you I have no secrets.'

'Secrets?' Seeing his reddening face, she grinned.

'How can someone like that be so self-contained?'

'She won't be deep inside,' replied Amy. 'She was raised a Catholic. She'll still have the confessional urge somewhere.'

'What does she have to confess?' Carne asked. The blushing had vanished.

'It's more there's a question she has to answer, isn't there?' He nodded. 'An agent or a victim perhaps?' she continued.

'Yes. Doer or a done-to.'

'What do you think, Jonny?'

'I don't think, Amy. I just gather evidence.'

'And theories.'

He gave her a peck on the cheek. 'You're a funny girl, Amy Riordan.' He walked out into the street.

CHAPTER 24

Thirty minutes later he was in the lift going up to her flat, buzzed by an irritating sense of Groundhog Day. She opened the door and stretched out her hand to shake his. 'I won't make a habit of it.' The image disappeared in an instant.

'I felt we hadn't finished our conversation,' she continued. 'Drink?'

'I think I'll stick to that coffee you offered,' he replied.

'Me too. Let's chat while I'm making it.'

She led him into the galley kitchen. Small oven, tall fridge-freezer, microwave, toaster, impeccably clean white hob, unstained and unchipped white china sink, state-of-the-art coffeemaker. Not the kitchen of a woman who did much cooking. She noticed him casting his eyes around.

'Are you interested in kitchens?' she asked. 'Or are you trying to analyse me?'

'Sorry.' He looked rueful. 'I can't stop myself.'

'Well, it's all German.'

'I have limited interest in kitchens.'

'So do I.'

She handed him a cup of coffee and stretched up to a cupboard in search of something. He could not help his eye ranging over the flexed legs and narrow heels lifting from her shoes, the hem of her black skirt rising above her knees, her thighs sharply delineated against the taut material. 'Let me,' he said, catching himself.

'There are chocolates there somewhere,' she said. 'The cleaner's probably hidden them.' He easily found a box of dark Belgian truffles and handed them down to her. 'Looks like this is tonight's supper.'

He followed her back to the sitting room, where she placed herself on a circular pouffe, kicked off her shoes and tucked her legs beneath her, leaving him to sit alone on the sofa. It seemed that she wanted to affirm a gap between them.

'You wish to continue our conversation,' he said, deflated.

'Same rules, Jon?' She was still using his first name; a childish relief flooded through him.

'Yes, Anne-Marie, same rules.'

She stood up with her cup of coffee, walked over to the mantelpiece and inspected herself in the mirror hanging above it. 'God, what a fright!'

'You won't expect me to agree with that.'

She angled her head so that she could see him in the mirror's reflection. He remembered Amy's words; was she the penitent in the confessional box calculating whether to say it or not? Whatever it was.

'Joseph was my first.' With a finger she wiped the tiniest smudge of mascara by her right eye and walked past the pouffe to sit on the other side of the sofa. Like the priest facing the invisible sinner, he stayed silent, while she told him about the childhood holidays. As she finished, she sipped her coffee and offered him a chocolate. 'Have one, they're just sitting there.' He did as he was told and she took one too, dark with a strawberry filling. She bit elegantly into it, a tiny line of pink falling on her lower lip which she retrieved with her tongue. He felt that patter in his chest.

'A few months after I turned sixteen,' she continued, 'we fucked. I could tell he'd done it before, he was too familiar with the condom. I hadn't. I felt annoyed with him for that.' She stopped, remembering, and smiled. 'Not very annoyed though. He told me I was the one he'd always wanted.' She looked up at him. 'Am I embarrassing you?'

'No,' he replied. 'You're making me sad.'

'Let's have a drink, for God's sake.' There was a roughness in her voice. 'Not every day you get to see the corpse of the man who took your virginity laid out on a mortuary slab.' She took a deep breath, and covered a sniffle with her wrist. 'Would you mind getting it? Should be bottles in the fridge.'

He went to the kitchen, and found a bottle, two glasses and a tray. She ought to eat. He opened the fridge: berries, sheep's yoghurt, skimmed milk, yellowed broccoli and faded lettuce in the crisper, oranges, lemons. At the back lay a pack of smoked salmon a day beyond its use-by date. He heard the sounds of water running in the bathroom, giving him the time to search for something to accompany it. A pack of crackers was all he could find. And black pepper. He located a plate and a knife and fork, laid out strips of the fish, added the lemon and returned with the tray. He heard the toilet flushing, more running of taps and she was back.

'Heavens!' she exclaimed.

'A woman can't live on chocolates alone.'

'You're sounding like my mother.'

'I'll take that as a compliment.'

She ground black pepper and squirted lemon over the fish. 'Today was almost worse than finding his body because I knew what to expect. It gave it a reality, and a finality.' She took a mouthful and he could see her suppressed hunger; adrenalin must be the main ingredient in her diet. Her last thought had silenced her and he watched while she ate. Just the salmon, not the crackers. The calm was companionable and he did not want to seem too curious.

She took the last bite. 'Protein injected. Thank you. Where were we?'

'Talking about Joseph.'

'What more do you need to know?'

'Why he ended up like this, I guess.'

'You'd have to enter his heart and mind to know that.'

He hesitated, afraid of pushing too far. 'Can you try?'

'Joseph always looked up to Martin. Odd, really. You'd think Joseph would be the leader: better-looking, taller, even eloquent sometimes. But Martin was three years older. He was fifteen in 1981, when the hunger strikers died. It radicalized him. I was only nine, so I felt their anger but didn't properly understand it till later. Anyway, Martin joined the Provos, rose to be a top man. As a boy, Joseph hero-worshipped him, grew up hugging his coat tails. They were thick as thieves. I started hearing "Martin says this", "Martin says we should do that" all the time. Not operational stuff – I didn't know about any of that. But it was like he became the repository of the wisdom of Martin McCartney.'

She stopped, like a schoolteacher checking her pupil was taking it all in. 'You see, Martin wasn't just a simple Republican: he saw himself as a revolutionary, too. That's why he couldn't stop. I looked up to him, too, my big brother, bit of a hero when I was small, but it all became . . . I don't know . . . oppressive somehow.' She hesitated. 'With Joseph, too.'

She lapsed into a silence of memory. Carne followed the moment until enough time had passed to re-engage her.

'How did it end with Joseph?'

She looked sharply up, colour rushing into her cheeks. He sensed her choosing words carefully. 'How can I best put it?' she finally said. 'I began to feel he was keeping secrets from me. I guess that was inevitable, given his involvement. But the trust went. I upset him. I upset myself too.'

'Did you love him?'

She smiled. 'I think that begs so many questions about what lies in our hearts that you need a cleverer person than me to answer it.'

Carne smiled back. 'I doubt that.' He wondered what really had caused the break with Joseph – there must have been some sort of final catalyst. He itched, too, to explore what David Wallis had meant to her but could see he had gone far enough. He tried to imagine her growing into womanhood but found himself distracted by a reflection of the young man on the mortuary slab who must have adored her. 'So where are we now?'

'1991, I guess. I was trying to make my big escape to Dublin.'

'When did you last see him?' She seemed about to answer but then he felt a frisson of that earlier frost.

'That sounded like an interrogation.'

He winced. 'Sorry.'

She topped up his glass without asking him. 'I've done enough talking about me. What about you?'

'I'm better at asking questions than answering them.' She looked up at his still-unlined face and, perhaps prompted by the earlier memories of Joseph, saw the child in him – the residual, unfaked, shyness. He had begun to twiddle his fingers on the glass table.

'I'm not just changing the subject,' she said. 'I'd like to know.'

'OK.' The twiddling stopped. 'My father was a musician, electric piano and organ. He was good, did recording sessions with some of the big name groups. Gigs too. Trouble was, he saw himself as a free spirit of the sixties. Sex, drugs, rock and roll. My mother was a teacher – they'd married before his career took off. He drifted away leaving her and this one-year-old baby boy behind. But it turned out I'd inherited some of his genes. Just the musical ones, I hope. So it was the church choir for me, respectable south London church school, practise my piano every day.'

'Do you still play?' she asked.

'Sometimes. I lost the appetite after Alice died.' There was an immense pain in his eyes. Again he felt the urge to tell more and the sureness that this was not the time.

'I'm sorry,' she said.

'Death brings no recovery.' He was peering down at his hands, momentarily disengaged, stopping himself. He found a way of reverting to her. 'It's worse for you: Joseph, David, your brother.'

'Yes. But they were all victims of political conflict. I tell myself that makes it different. And that's why politics can't be sorted by violence. It took me a bit of time to get there but the rule of law really matters. And politicians make laws.' She stood up and walked towards a desk in the corner of the room. Halfway there she glanced back. 'Quite a lot of the time I believe myself.'

She opened a drawer of the desk and returned with a small box covered with red velvet. She gently lifted from it a silver bracelet, matching earrings, and a silver ring with a single red ruby. 'From David,' she said.

She gave him the pieces of jewellery and he examined them in his hands, running his fingers along their smooth, cool surface.

'Were they just a present?' he asked. 'Or was he meaning more?'

'Or was it just another little deceit?' Her question cut through the air that separated them.

He handed her the box. 'I don't believe he was deceiving you with these.' He paused. 'Whatever else he was up to.'

She restored the box to the desk drawer. 'So' – she reverted to the pragmatic tone she had initially greeted him with – 'you can have one more question tonight. I need my sleep.'

Her brusqueness stung him. Was she mercurial – and therefore unreliable? Or embarrassed by lapses into sentimentality? Perhaps she was just showing that characteristic he had first noticed: the need for self-control, the fear of slipping up, of giving too much away. But, if she was offering him this one more question, he must take one more chance. He pulled a photograph from his pocket and placed it on the table in front of her. She inspected it in silence.

'Do you know him?' he asked.

'Where did you get this?' she demanded. She sounded brittle.

'I took it.'

He felt her flinch. 'You took it!' It was an accusation.

'Yes.'

'Where?'

'At David Wallis's funeral.'

'How come you were invited?'

'I wasn't.' He could feel his heart beating and the blood draining from his face. Each time he asked a difficult question, he felt it might destroy the possibility of friendship with her. If that happened, he had now come to realize that something within him would die.

'You were snooping.'

'Yes.' Her back was turned away again. 'It's my job.'

He spoke with a profound regret that he hoped she would see. As the room shrieked with her silence, he searched for the reflection of her face in the glass. It was washed out by the room lights and the black of the night. He had never known time pass so slowly. Finally, she turned round, walked very slowly back and sat down on the sofa.

'Yes,' she said, 'it's a part of your job. I have one question for you. Have you ever snooped on me?'

'No. I would never snoop on you. Never.'

'Even before you knew me?' She paused. 'Someone did.'

'I promise you from the bottom of my heart that I have never snooped on you.'

She picked up the photograph that showed the man with the gold tiepin. 'He's aged. Sorry, that's obvious. Hair greyer, though it was starting to go even then. Still got the moustache.' She looked closer. 'My God, even the tiepin. He called himself Jimmy. He claimed he was David's uncle, even showed me a passport. Uncle Jimmy Vallely. I remember the date it was issued. August 1993. No doubt he had several.'

'Yes, I'm sure he did. Thank you. I realize you've crossed a line.'

'Time for you to go now.'

He stood up, and wondered whether to offer a handshake, give her a farewell kiss, or maybe put an arm round her. In the end he just nodded, collected his coat, and opened the door to let himself out.

'By the way,' her voice interrupted, 'she's a pretty girl, your forensic colleague.'

He looked back in astonishment that she had noticed and might even care. He heard himself saying, 'It's all right, I'm not to her taste.' Descending in the lift, he almost did a jig.

As soon as he was out of the apartment block, Carne texted Poots:

Two sources say known as Jimmy, assume James. Surname beginning with B, maybe Br. Second source confirms he made appearances in Dublin early 1994. Check Foreign Office based at British embassy there '93 to '95.

At the same time Anne-Marie also sent a text – to the woman she knew as Jemima. 'I wish to meet tomorrow. Expect to receive full progress report from you.'

At Thames House, Jemima Sheffield was less than surprised by the message. The conversation she had just listened in to showed an emerging collaboration between the policeman and the Minister that had not been factored in. She wondered if the Minister was playing some deeper game that had also not been factored in. The meeting would need careful handling.

CHAPTER 25

Post-election, Friday, 19 May

Early-morning joggers passed by, illuminated in bright streaks of sun. A slightly built, dark-haired woman elegantly stretching her legs reminded Carne of Anne-Marie reaching up to her kitchen cupboard. The image filled him with unease, even a sense of prurience. His phone buzzed. A one-word message from Billy: 'Bingo'. Carne chucked the empty polystyrene cup into a waste bin, strode to the railings overlooking the river and dialled his number.

'I've gone cross-eyed in the process,' said Poots, 'but I finally nailed him. Guess where.'

'You tell me, Billy.'

'Well, boss, in this wondrous age and all its friggin' Facebooks, Twitters and other bollocks, there's just one place the silly bugger was too vain not to reveal himself: *Who's Who*. The old faithful. Got pen and paper?'

'Yes, Billy, I've got pen and paper,' replied Carne, iPhone in front of him.

'Right. James Beresford Brooks. Foreign Office, 1976–2012.

Postings include Dublin, 1992–1994. Immediately before that, Saudi Arabia, 1991–1992. Looking at the gaps, majority of his time seems to have been in London. And never got a top position in an embassy. Therefore . . .'

'He's a spook.'

'He's not parading it. Interests listed are gardening, bridge, church and flower arranging. In that order.'

'Collecting tiepins?'

'What's that?

'Don't worry, Billy. Address?'

'Rectory Garden Cottage, Old Witham, Devizes, Wiltshire.'

'A day out in the country for me, then.'

'You get all the fun. What's the news on the body?'

'Definitely Joseph Kennedy. Clear ID.'

There was a pause on the end of the line. Carne could feel Poots calculating.

'Messes up the theory, doesn't it?'

'How's that, Billy?'

'Joseph Kennedy was alive a few days ago. David Wallis's been dead for well over twenty years. So there's at least one of the Gang of Four David Wallis didn't make disappear.'

'Precisely,' agreed Carne. 'Meaning the score was three–one.'

'Four–one, boss, now Joseph's dead. Wonder if it's the same scorer – or they had to buy a new striker.'

'Nice one, Billy,' said Carne. 'I keep meaning to ask. Why the hell did you never make Chief Constable?'

'Too busy doing police work, boss,' replied Poots.

Heading west out of London, Carne's eye was caught by aircraft floating over Windsor Castle as they carved through the easterly breeze into Heathrow dazzled in the midday sun. Giant birds of prey diving to consume the concreted earth. Once past Reading, the skies cleared of metal, and rolling fields of corn alternated with clumps of woods. He tapped his fingers on the steering wheel as the final movement of the Trout Quintet sprinted. The warm rush of sounds and light did not distract long.

He needed a witness to murders, both past and present, who was alive, not dead. As he entered the county of Wiltshire, he was sanguine about the prospects of finding one who might like to help.

Old Witham lay a couple of miles down a narrow, twisting lane that descended into the depths of a darkened beech wood before rising to a narrow plateau. The first sighting of its church's squat tower brought Carne to a halt. He left his car on a verge and walked into the village, alongside neatly cut strips of grass and a succession of immaculately kept, nondescript houses of uncertain architecture. Their rectangular flowerbeds, front doors adorned by decorative glass and carriage lamps hanging in modest porches spelt out a comfortable middle England for retirees who shared one colour only. Not quite the Lord's waiting room, he reflected, but certainly the front parlour.

Fifty yards from the church, he passed a Georgian rectory, composed of weathered red brick and precisely symmetrical wood-paned windows, and almost missed a thin wooden sign pointing down a path to Rectory Garden Cottage. He looked around the still lifeless lane and headed down it, reaching a narrow gate marked 'PRIVATE'. He released the latch and the path narrowed from the encroachment of sprawling hedge and bramble. After a few more yards, it gave way to lawn and what seemed the back of a broad, single-storey, modern house. By it a figure, wearing, despite the warming sun, a floppy grey rain hat and waterproof jacket, was bent down over a flowerbed. As he appeared from the bushes, the figure rose to reveal a severe-looking woman, steely hair matching the hat and leathery voice the coat.

'Who are you?' she barked. 'Do I know you?'

'I'm looking for Mr Beresford Brooks.'

'You won't find him here. Try the church.' She bent down again to attend to her flowers.

'Thank you, Mrs Brooks. I'll track him down there.'

She raised her head, lowered her nose and peered at him over her glasses. 'Don't make any assumptions about that, young man.'

Carne beat a retreat, unsure whether she was referring to her marital state or the whereabouts of her husband. He could see why James Beresford Brooks might not spend too much time at his home.

A lychgate, its small wooden roof giving off a faint smell of recent varnishing, opened onto a smoothly tarmacked path leading to the church porch. Gravestones, several covered with small jars of commemorative flowers, dotted the weedless, closely mown lawn along with discrete gatherings of daffodils allowed to grow wild. This was a place well cared for. As he rounded the transept, the land fell away into a sharp escarpment, revealing a sun-soaked valley of fields and trees stretching into the far distance. At its furthest end, a chimney trailed faint wisps of smoke, foretelling a town that must lie beyond. Carne stopped to soak in the view, admiring a beauty and eternity that befitted the dead.

'Lovely place, isn't it?' The rich baritone voice burst the bubble and he turned round to see the weather-beaten, grinning face of a large man, perhaps in his early seventies, wearing a dark blazer over a twill shirt, dark red corduroys and a diagonally striped tie of reds and browns kept in perfect line by a gold tiepin. There was something porcine about the bridge and upturn of his prominent nose. Below, the broad chest was followed by a spreading girth, imposing rather than potbellied. A strong man. The picture of a boar flashed before Carne, down on all fours, foraging greedily for truffles in the forest.

'Yes,' replied Carne. 'Good place to die.'

'That sounds rather gloomy. Come in and see the church.'

Carne followed, wondering whether the tour would be preceded by any introductions. It was not. 'We are pretty sure there was a Saxon church here though no one's been able to match any of the foundations. Certainly there was a Norman building, replaced and expanded over the years in early English. And finally the spire in Victorian times. Not, unfortunately, an architectural gift to God.' He stretched his mouth and cheeks to form a well-rehearsed smile. 'As I'm sure you noticed on your way.'

'I can't pretend I'm an expert,' said Carne.

'Yes, I didn't think it was an interest in English church vernacular that had brought you here.' The smile fell away. 'DCI Carne, I presume.'

'Yes.'

'James Beresford Brooks. I knew you were on your way of course.'

'Excuse me?'

'My dear chap, don't be naïve.' He stuck out his hand, restoring the smile. Carne shook it and was held by the warm grasp uncomfortably longer than courtesy demanded. 'Usually known as Jimmy.' The hand was removed, along with the smile. 'Welcome to Old Witham Church.' He paused and winked. 'Where the bodies are buried. Do you like my flowers?' He pointed to two overpowering arrangements each side of the aisle. 'Marvellous time of year for chrysanths. Or course, we're lucky down here – it's like having a nursery garden in the wild. Nothing like the English seasons, is there, Mr Carne?' The question was not put to elicit a reply. 'But I don't think flowers brought you here, either.'

'No,' said Carne.

'In that case, I am all ears.'

'I'm investigating the death of a former British soldier called David Wallis more than two decades ago and the much more recent death of a man called Joseph Kennedy, who was once suspected of being a senior member of an extremist IRA faction. I believe you may be able to assist me with my enquiries.'

'Do you, now?' The smile reappeared. 'Shall we sit? And inside or out? Out I think, don't you? Such a lovely day. And these walls might have ears, too. Eh?' He led him out of the church to a bench, overlooking the valley.

'You talk of places to die. Hitler once opined,' said Brooks mellifluously, 'that there was only one piece of music to die to: the "Liebestod" from Wagner's *Tristan und Isolde*. Of course, as far as we know, he was disappointed in that particular wish. As, indeed, in so many others. But, ever since I first saw it, I have thought that this is the outlook to die to. Who knows? When I am old one day, decrepit and diseased, I may walk out here one summer evening with a pistol and achieve precisely that.' He looked down the valley and took a long breath of deep contentment. 'Apologies, Mr Carne, your talk of death has set me on this wholly irrelevant train of thought.'

'You knew David Wallis,' stated Carne, telling himself not to be led down blind alleys.

'What makes you think that?'

'You attended his funeral.'

'Yes, indeed I did. But, my dear chap, you make a leap of logic. My attendance at David Wallis's funeral does not mean

that I actually knew him. I may instead have been represent-
ing others, a family perhaps, or an organization for which he
worked, a charity, even, which believed it owed him this mark
of respect.'

'You knew him, Mr Brooks.'

'Please, it's Jimmy. And you're Jonny, I believe.'

Brooks turned to him and patted him twice on the leg,
then gently stroked it. Carne tried not to squirm. 'Let us try
another approach, Jonny. I am unfortunately still bound by
the Official Secrets Act and therefore must be most careful
with anything I say. After all, I would not wish you to charge
me with breaking it. So why don't you tell me everything you
think you know and I will try to help you and put you on the
right track where I can?'

Carne assumed some sort of trap was being laid. But, if he did
not take the risk and accept the deal, the day was over and his
journey pointless.

'I agree your terms. For now.'

'For now? Whenever else did you have in mind?'

Carne ignored him. 'In the autumn of 1993 David Wallis, using
the alias Vallely, began a master's at Trinity College, Dublin. At
that time, you were based at the British embassy in Dublin. In
mid-'94 David Wallis disappeared. Shortly after his disappearance,
you visited his girlfriend, Maire McCartney. Wallis never told Ms
McCartney that he was a former British soldier who had served
under the present GOC, Northern Ireland, General Kenneth
Bowman. You attended the funeral of David Wallis, where it was
clear you knew General Bowman.'

'How would that have been clear?'

Carne produced the photograph of Bowman with Brooks at
the funeral. Brooks inspected it with a disdainful lack of curiosity.

'I won't embarrass you by asking how you come to possess this photograph, so do carry on.'

'During the first half of 1994, four senior IRA men, all leading opponents of the ceasefire with the British that the IRA leadership was negotiating, disappeared. They were known to some as the Gang of Four. Their most prominent member was Martin McCartney, the brother of Maire McCartney, whom David Wallis was using subterfuge to cultivate. One of those four, Joseph Kennedy, recently resurfaced in London and died in suspicious circumstances. His death is the subject of an ongoing investigation. The obvious conclusion is that you were running David Wallis as an agent as a means of penetrating the McCartney family, Martin McCartney in particular, and gaining intelligence on the activities of the Gang of Four.'

'Were this so, Jonny,' said Brooks, 'it sounds to me precisely the sort of legitimate operation you would expect a nation threatened by terrorism to mount.'

'However,' continued Carne, 'engineering the disappearance of these men would not be either legal or legitimate. Nor would the murder of Joseph Kennedy.'

'Oh, come, come!'

'There may also be question marks about the safety of the operation which led to the killing of David Wallis.'

'Oh, my dear, sweet man,' exclaimed Brooks, 'do you seriously think David Wallis was such a delicate flower!'

'So you did know him.' Carne felt it was the first blow he had landed.

'Come with me, Jonny,' said Brooks, putting his arm on his shoulder and squeezing. He rose and walked slowly among the gravestones, stopping every now and then to read the inscriptions. Boys and girls who had died in childhood in the reign of Victoria.

Young mothers in childbirth. More recently, longer-lived parents and grandparents in the age of Elizabeth II. The Ivy's and Rose's of old England, names of both people and plants. He picked up a pot of flowers, smelt their perfume, laid them down again, peered up at the sky and along the valley and released a sigh of contentment.

'Tell me,' he asked, 'what do you see here? What do you feel?'

'Sadness,' replied Carne.

'Do you? I don't. I feel a nation and a people at peace. The heart of England, of what we stand for. Of goodness, mutual respect, order. You may not approve, Jonny, but that is what I tried to work for. So did David Wallis. Perhaps, like these people, we should leave him in peace.'

Carne knew he had reached the end of a cul-de-sac. 'All right. But in one matter, I will take up your offer to put me on the correct track.'

'I am here only to help.'

'Joseph Kennedy resurfaced. David Wallis's body has been found. Where are the bodies of the other three that disappeared? Sean Black. Brendan O'Donnell. Martin McCartney.'

Brooks walked back to the bench, sat down and rested his eyes on the valley. Carne allowed a minute to pass before moving to join him. As he did so, Brooks rose and intercepted him. 'I have some advice for you, Chief Inspector Carne. Do not waste your time searching. And let me give you an assurance. Everything was approved. At the very top. On both sides of the political spectrum.'

'Who approved it, Mr Brooks?'

'If I told you that, Mr Carne, I would have to kill you, wouldn't I?

All humour in Brooks's face had vanished. Carne watched

him march down the path, through the lychgate and towards his house. He did not look back.

As Brooks emerged from the overgrown path into his back garden, the bent figure straightened to her feet, threw her gardening gloves to the ground and wiped her brow.

'I presume he found you, Jimmy,' she said.

'Yes, Dorothy.'

'A satisfactory conversation?'

'Oh, I don't think the ghosts of the past need disturb us too much.'

'Does that imply there are ghosts not of the past?' she asked with a remarkably arched eyebrow.

In stony silence he marched on, opened the French windows, entered the house and carefully closed them behind him. There were some documents he wanted to reread before deciding whether to continue to store them against a rainy day of nursing-home bills exceeding government service pension, or to consign them to the dustbin of betrayals.

As so often before, he reflected on the elegance of the plan – Operation Hawk, as he had called it. In the summer of 1993, he, now based at the Dublin embassy, had been the one and only person in possession of two pieces of intriguingly connected information. Maire McCartney, sister of the Gang of Four's leader, Martin McCartney, was living in the city as a student at Trinity College. David Wallis, drummed out of the army, needed a new outlet for his particular gifts.

Put the two of them together – and allow the game to unfold.

He discussed it with one extremely senior official only, the rising young star of the service. In turn, the official advised one senior minister only, as was Whitehall protocol in such matters. The official also informed an opposition party shadow minister with the relevant expertise in order to hedge against future changes in government.

Perhaps if he had felt able to tell Wallis the real point of the game, it might have saved him. But, if he had done that, Wallis could never have played the role of David Vallely so well.

Until the unforeseen happened.

CHAPTER 26

'I have some information for you, Minister.' Jemima Sheffield was perched, chin thrust forward, on the edge of an armchair. Anne-Marie sat straight-backed on the circular pouffe opposite. In the chill of the audibly ventilating air, Jemima produced a bound folder.

The day had begun with Anne-Marie's first visit to the chamber of the House of Commons. It was two weeks after the general election – MPs gathered to elect the Speaker of the Commons, many using the occasion to swear the oath of allegiance. Lining up by the Speaker's table among a throng of ministerial colleagues and MPs, Anne-Marie felt again like an exotic bird flown in from some obscure paradise, an object of extreme curiosity to be stared at, congratulated, shaken by hands and arms thrust from all directions. The bewigged Clerk of the House offered her a copy of the New Testament.

Observing the hypocrisy all around, she took it and swore her 'faithfulness and true allegiance to the monarch and heirs and successors, according to law. So help me God.' Royalty and God all in one day – I've travelled far, she told herself, smiling fraudulently at the clerk.

Steve Whalley ranged alongside, with surprising stealth for such a bulbous figure.

'I trust your friends the asylum seekers are feeling the benefit of our enlightened new administration,' he chirped. He leant to whisper in her ear, blowing a rank combination of cologne and halitosis. 'By the way, kid, I believe we have an acquaintance in common.'

'I beg your pardon,' she replied tartly.

'Yes,' he murmured, elongating the word. 'Chap called Jimmy. I bumped into him the other day.'

'I've no idea what you're talking about,' she said.

'Don't worry, love,' he soothed. 'He only wanted to tell me to be nice to you.' He turned and strode through the doors of the chamber towards the Central Lobby, leaving Anne-Marie in a cramp of confusion and dread that lingered through the day.

'I activated your request,' continued Jemima, handing over the folder. 'I hope you will feel this addresses the issue you raised with me.'

'Thank you.' Taking the folder, Anne-Marie walked slowly over to the glass frontage of her flat. She kicked off her shoes and stood, watching the still-light evening cloaking the humming city. She swivelled. 'Perhaps, Jemima, you could first put this in context.'

'It pertains to what was called Operation Hawk.'

'Hawk?'

'Yes, Minister.'

'A bird of prey, I believe.'

'I understand that David Wallis had pet kestrels in his childhood and it had no greater meaning than that.'

'How convenient.' Anne-Marie retraced her steps, sat down and began to read, determined to quash any emotion.

'You asked me, Minister,' said Jemima, searching for any signs of reaction, 'to know the truth about David Wallis's attitude towards you. While clearing his flat, we found a small dictaphone.'

'Dictaphone?'

'Yes. And microcassettes. Nothing sophisticated, what any office would have for standard dictation.' Jemima paused. 'It turned out he was recording an occasional diary. I understand no one knew about it. If they had, he would have been asked to desist.' Another secret, thought Anne-Marie. Was it another deception, too? 'There was no professional reason for it. His communications with his supervisor were face to face. Intentionally so.'

'Supervisor?' mused Anne-Maire. 'Would that be the man called Jimmy by any chance? Uncle Jimmy to some.'

'Yes, Minister.' Jemima was inscrutable. 'After Wallis's disappearance the diary was transcribed and added to his file. The folder contains extracts which are relevant to his contact with you.'

'So it is censored.'

'Only for operational reasons, Minister. But there's very little of that. It seems the recordings eventually became more of a respository for his . . . his emotions.'

It seemed to Anne-Marie that emotion was an alien word to Jemima.

Wednesday, 13 October 1993

I followed her this morning from her house to the library. Grey day, drizzle. The walk took her 25 minutes. She has short, stocky legs, I was surprised by how fast they move. I watched her go into the library. I allowed half an hour, then went in myself. Sat opposite her at the other end of a long study table. She took a quick peep at me – I didn't look back. Jimmy was not being very flattering. She's nice-looking with long tresses of auburn hair. Almost red. And not podgy, it's just puppy fat and only shows because she's short. I'll stay away tomorrow except to track what she does for lunch. Don't want her to think I'm chasing her.

Anne-Marie was smouldering. 'You shits!'

'Minister, I—'

'This is vile, Jemima.'

'Perhaps I could explain the thinking behind this operation, Minister,' replied Jemima evenly. 'Insofar as it has been explained to me.'

'In a minute.' Anne-Marie turned to the next entry.

Friday, 15 October 1993

I got to the library early. Took the seat she sat in two days ago. She arrived at her usual time and was bemused for a moment. She went to get her book and sat down at the other end of the table. So our positions were reversed. As planned, I could command the view beyond her. She was sweating from the walk. Maybe seeing me in her seat too. There were hints of looks by both of us.

Eventually we exchanged a smile. I decided to go for it and waylaid her in the sandwich bar. We walked down the street and chatted. I think her nerves made her sound sharp but she settled down. No problem with me being a 'Brit'. Seemed cool with it. She was fun. Easy to talk to. I did Jimmy's idea of mispronouncing her name – not knowing it was Irish etc. Felt a bit slimy. We discussed our work. If I wasn't coming home for the weekend, it could have gone on. But, as discussed with Jimmy, I guess slow is best. She needed to go to the chemist. Seemed flustered by it.

Anne-Marie lowered the folder. 'All right. I begin to see it all.' Her voice was ice. She sensed Jemima gathering herself for a rehearsed speech.

'Around that time, Minister, it was in fact the Metropolitan Police, Special Branch, which pioneered this intelligence-gathering tactic. Their initial focus was animal-rights activists. Some presented a lethal threat to animal-research laboratories and scientists who worked in them. Reports of this later surfaced in the investigative press.'

'Yes, I read them. Undercover policemen leading double lives who seduced vulnerable young women, impregnated them, made bigamous marriages with them.'

'Yes, Minister. In retrospect, it feels . . .' – she searched for a word – 'unwholesome. But the danger was clear and present. It was perhaps therefore not unreasonable for the intelligence services in Ireland to take advantage of any similar opportunity.'

'Jemima, how long have spies used seduction as a means of obtaining information?'

Beads of sweat formed on Jemima's brow. 'I'm afraid I, er . . . I'm not—'

'One hundred years? Two hundred? Two thousand, perhaps, back to Roman times? Egyptian?'

'Yes, Minister.'

'Shall we read on?'

Sunday, 17 October 1993

Got the last flight back. I want to be at the library early morning to catch her. The weekend was a mistake. I'd promised to go with Rob to his uncle's shoot in Devon. They like to show me off as their expert shot. For the first time really, I saw it for what it is. A game of rich men paying to drink, kill and be merry. I drank too much myself. Then after lunch I lowered my gun following snipe. A beater saw me. It was ghastly, embarrassing. Rob noticed. He tried to interrogate me on the way back. Brought up leaving the army again and all that. Like before, I told him to f— off. None of his business. Made up later. We overnighted with Mum and Fiona. I think she and Rob are finally getting together. I was in my room, looking at photos of Dad and then me in uniform. I realized I just wanted to get back here. New life, new start, new adventure. Wherever it leads. The cause is good.

Monday, 18 October 1993

I passed her a note suggesting a pizza and she gave the thumbs-up straightaway. Then a rueful smile. I returned it. We got along nicely at supper. I think she quite likes this sad, lonely British boy. It's an identity that suits me right now. I find it easy to slip into. The stars are in the right place.

I got her on to her family. She mentioned the brother – then stopped herself saying too much. It made me wonder if she fears him. Or what she might let slip about him. I should be careful not to probe too obviously. There's something about her that suggests secrets within. Sometimes she shows

her spikiness and flashes her eyes. Throws down some kind
of challenge. I like it. 'The green-eyed girl of the Emerald
Isle'. Intriguing days ahead.

Anne-Marie's face burnt with the dawning comprehension of the
full extent of her blindness – even if she still held to the hope that
something more complex might emerge. To Jemima she would
show only her contempt. 'So they targeted me to get to my brother.'

'In effect, yes, Minister.'

'Even though I'd managed to get away from that environment
to pursue my studies?'

'Yes.'

'Do you not see a difference between a potentially violent
animal-rights activist and a third-year law student?'

'They were both means to an end.'

'No, the difference is that I was going about my lawful business.
I was not suspected of illegal activity.'

'Not as far as I know, Minister.'

'What do you mean by that, Jemima?' She could feel the anger
returning.

'They may have seen you as a suspect, Minister. By association,
perhaps. The file doesn't shed light on this.'

'You people will invent anything to justify yourselves, won't
you?' Anne-Marie thought of that first weekend when David said
he'd been climbing Lugnaquilla. 'It was all a lie from the outset.'

'Yes. That's certainly how it began.'

'What do you mean?'

Jemima hesitated. 'If I may, Minister, I suggest you read to the
end and come to your own conclusions.'

'Are you going to just sit there while I do?'

'My instructions are not to let this material out of my sight.'

'For God's sake, woman, at least give me one night on my own with . . . with him.' Anne-Marie could see the hesitation, and then a frown cross Jemima's face.

'I'm not authorized to do this. I'll need to retrieve the folder before you leave in the morning.'

'So be it. Now you may leave, Jemima. You can see yourself out.'

The deputy director-general of the Security Service, MI5, listening in to the conversation in Anne-Marie Gallagher's apartment, was satisfied. In the rehearsal, they had anticipated that the Minister would demand to be allowed to read the file alone. Jemima Sheffield's concession might therefore be seen as an act of personal loyalty to her, which could begin to repair their relationship. From that, further confidences might follow.

It was also possible that Ms Gallagher might be prompted by reading the file to perform some action – make a phone call, for example. If so, it could throw a chink of light on the final moments of David Wallis's life. More than two decades later these remained a mystery to the Secret Intelligence Service, whose operation it then was, and the Security Service, which was charged with monitoring any blowback. Interrogation of Anne-Marie Gallagher, a.k.a. Maire McCartney, had been ruled out at the time as unlikely to be productive, and potentially counterproductive. Surveillance, however, had never been excluded and this moment could be a unique opportunity in the long aftermath.

The 'voice' of the diary shared a tone Anne-Marie recognized from the David who had first shown himself to her: boyish, fun, adventurous, signs of fragility. But he was leading a double life. She wanted to know if the diary would shed light on how he resolved it.

Friday, 12 November 1993

I may be taking it too slowly. Giving her too much time for thought. (She remembered that long hiatus before he made his move.) *Making her ask questions that might not have reared their heads if I – well, we – had just got on with it. We'd have certainly both been up for it. She said out of the blue she was worried because she didn't really know me.*

I was thrown. It was as if she'd become unsure about me. Needed someone to vouch for me. I could only think of one solution. Phoned Rob to come over for a weekend. Climb a mountain and meet my new girl. Bit of trouble persuading him. I apologized for being an arse at the shoot. Eventually he agreed. Obviously I couldn't tell him more at this stage or he'd have pulled out. Preparing myself for an awkward conversation when I meet him at the airport.

Monday, 29 November 1993

The weekend worked – just. There was nearly a fall at the first hurdle. I waited till Rob was safely inside the car. Then explained the name change. I said my chances with her would be ruined if she ever discovered I was a British soldier. Especially that I'd served in the North. Even trickier to explain the orphan thing. No family left and all that. He blew a gasket. Accused me of playing tricks like I always did. He shouted at me. Demanded I turn round and put him on the next plane back to London. I did my best pleading. All being done for love, she really could be the one. Finally he cooled down. He was a bit sour with me whenever she was out of sight. But he played the game.

He had suckered his best friend, too. There was no need now to interrogate Rob McNeil. He'd been nothing more than a gopher for David 'Vallely'. Just as he was for his new boss at Number 10 now.

I think Rob believed it when I told him it was all for love. The odd thing was that I began to as well. My hours alone with her were almost dreamlike. Something beautiful happening. But which me was it happening to? While we were lying together, she told me about her life with Mrs Ryan. Said that was the real reason she could never invite me to her flat. I remembered to act with surprise. Part of me is getting in deep. I'll leave her alone for a day.

Wednesday, 1 December 1993

Saw Jimmy to report on the weekend. He wants me to tell her my father was a soldier. I said it wasn't a good idea. He was insistent. Said her telling me about Mrs Ryan and the kids was a big deal for her. I needed to tell her something big in return. Something really awkward for me to face up. He said it will solidify us. I kept suspecting he had another reason. Asked him. He denied it. You never know with Jimmy. I said I didn't actually seem to be doing anything. He reminded me 'slowly slowly'. Said wait till after Christmas.

Thursday, 2 December 1993

I collected her from the library. As we walked across the park, I saw a bloke from Exeter who did the same course as me. Not a friend but he'd have recognized me. Like I did him. Nasty moment which I didn't cover too well. Pretended I was avoiding an old girlfriend. I think it ended up OK. The car didn't impress her – should have known. It went well in the flat. I had a sense of something needing to be made up after what happened in the park. It suddenly became the right moment to tell her about my father. She was shocked. But it was surprise not hostility. She's too open-minded for that. In fact it led to an interesting discussion about politics and violence here. First time that's come up. She'll want it to be the last too.

Tuesday, 21 December 1993

Saw Jimmy. Says I should make the next move after Christmas when the chance comes. It's a relief. The inactivity makes it harder to sustain things. She's going home just for a couple of nights. Says she doesn't want to but owes it to her ma and da. I'm the same. Don't want to but owe it to Mum and Fiona.

Monday, 27 December 1993

Midnight. Just got back after dropping her near Mrs Ryan. Everything's changed, opened up. I feel a mix of excitement and emotion. Apprehension too. I left home late morning Boxing Day. It was good to see Mum and Fiona. But I felt like that last time after the shoot. Just wanted to be back here. Got a late afternoon flight yesterday. She'd said she was coming back the day after Boxing Day. I couldn't face being in the flat alone. So I drove west, not east. Just headed off to where we'd spent that weekend. But this time it was dull cloud. I started climbing one of the Bens but looked back to see land and sea merge in a dark, grey nothing. Came back down and stopped at a pub. Inside there was a row of black-jacketed men, peat cutters with black caps. Sitting uniformly on stools all along the bar. One by one, the heads swivelled. Dark, sunken eyes inspected me. I turned round and left. Never felt further away from home.

Back in the car, I checked the petrol gauge. In my rush from the airport I somehow hadn't. The needle flickered around empty. Boxing Day at the end of nowhere. The Atlantic in one direction and peat bog in the other. I headed back to Galway city. The engine faltered near a garage. It was closed. I coasted to a stop by a petrol pump. It was 7.30 p.m., the place deserted. Had to sleep in the car. This morning someone finally arrived. Gave me a funny look and filled up the car. I drove back. Decided to wait at the bus station and hope to intercept her. Just before two, she was there. She said, 'What the fuck are you doing? You're not supposed to be back.' I said, 'I want to be with you.' Didn't mind her being spiky. I've never before been so pleased to see someone. She resisted at first but came back to flat. Afterwards, in bed, it all came out naturally. I said I had to meet her family. We'd never be properly together otherwise. She fought but gave in. I told her I love her.

Sunday, 23 January 1994

The trip home is done. Her 'Ma' and 'Da' were great. Really welcoming. I even was beginning to wonder if this could all sort itself out. Then the brother looked in. Came back with Joseph later. The brother is numero uno. You wouldn't think him a hard man, but it's there in his eyes. I suspect Joseph would like to step up to be leader. Also suspect he and the girl were once sweet on each other.

The plan to stay the night worked. She was seriously angry. Then trouble. The four of them came back together in the middle of the night. Interrogated her about me. The walls are thin, I could hear most of it. The way the brother drilled her was heavy. I could smell Joseph thinking windbag when he was giving her the sermon. O'Donnell and Black said little. Doers, not thinkers. Then the weird thing happened. It turned out the reason for the interrogation was the brother said my name rang some kind of bell. A connection to Brit military. In the North. I didn't get it. Maybe he came up with it as he's suspicious of me. It'd be a way of her getting rid of me. She took fright. We left in the small hours. Back in Dublin, she told me what he'd said. I was screaming to say the brother was wrong. There was never a Brit soldier name of Vallely! But, because I'd told her my father was a soldier, she could trust me. So we're intact.

The weirdness now hit Anne-Marie. What had Martin really known about David? Did he discover more than he was saying and was he trying to offer her a way out? Without damaging her? Perhaps without even damaging David – instead giving him a sign that he knew something and he should get out? With a recurring sadness, she knew it was a mystery she could never resolve.

As she thought back, it seemed remarkable to her for how long David maintained his duality more or less intact. Eventually, the crack in the double life widened – and she herself was the unwitting cause.

Thursday, 17 March 1994

I need to wrap this up soon. I slipped up today. Got away with it. But one more mistake and suspicion will begin to dominate her other feelings towards me. I was on the phone to Fiona – I'd wanted to speak to her about Uncle Bob. It seems he's got prostate cancer. She overheard my phone call. Asked who I was talking to. I forgot myself and gave a truthful answer. 'My sister.' She said, 'You don't have a sister.'

I'd laid a minefield for myself. Reckoned the only way to crawl through it was pretend I was using the 'sister' for cover. So confessed I was actually talking to an old girlfriend ahead of chucking her. I'm realizing that deceit in my relationship with Maire cannot go on for ever. It's just not practical. Never mind the damage that could be done to her – or me even. When I'm the person I'm being with her, I tell her I love her. And I do.

She read it again, and then for a third time, trying to interpret the full meaning. Ultimately, he had failed as a deceiver both of her and of himself. An overwhelming pity for him swept through her as she realized, for the first time, the crushing weight he was carrying.

With stark clarity, she saw that the victim of this tragic play was not her, but him. '*Or me, even.*' They should have noticed the crack and pulled him out.

CHAPTER 27

James Beresford Brooks did notice the crack. Now, as he lay in bed on the night of Carne's visit, his normally untroubled sleep was interrupted by recurring thoughts. He rose, retrieved the full file for a second time and descended to his study.

It never occurred to him to withdraw Wallis. On the contrary, he needed to keep him firmly in line because, by the early spring of 1994, the clock was ticking. Secret ceasefire negotiations between the IRA and the British state, brokered in part by the United States and supported by President Clinton himself, were progressing. The influence of the anti-ceasefire faction, specifically the Gang of Four, loomed as an ever larger spectre. IRA leaders themselves were raising the problem of the four, while also trying to use it to win concessions from the British.

In March 1994 the IRA attacked Heathrow Airport. Two mortars hit runways, five missed. Miraculously, no one was hurt and air traffic hardly disrupted. But Brooks and the senior official with whom he had instigated the Hawk operation decided that 'action' was now urgent.

The Heathrow attack had been approved by the IRA leadership as a concession to the Gang of Four to show the organization could still mount a spectacular at will. But, to Sean Black and Brendan O'Donnell in particular, the operation was an abject failure. No deaths. No planes shot down. One surveillance report stated that Black had been overheard saying he was going to do something that would make Enniskillen look like 'kid's stuff'.

Brooks's senior colleague confided in his minister and the friendly shadow minister that, unless 'action' was taken, the possibility of an outrage so barbaric as to scupper the peace talks for years, a generation even, was horribly real. He explained the problem of any such 'action'. The Gang of Four had become so watchful, ingenious and agile that 'exceptional' tactics were required.

The solution hung pregnantly, but silently, in the air; impossible to discuss, unthinkable as a state or government-approved operation. The politician said one sentence only to the official: 'We must not allow this once-in-a-lifetime chance of peace to be blown away.' It was the green light. And there was one big plus. This would be a limited operation with a clearly defined endgame; those to be taken out of the picture amounted to no more than the fingers of a single hand.

Operation Hawk meant that Wallis's penetration of the McCartney home in Belfast gave him an up-to-date observation of the targets. Wallis was also seeking a conclusion and had complained to Jimmy that he was sitting in Dublin doing nothing. Brooks, in possession of his fuller picture, ordered him to stay put and keep a low profile.

In late March 1994 Brooks decided he needed to test Wallis's resolve. He suggested an evening stroll by the river. Their paths met just beyond Wood Quay and they walked slowly east towards the darkening mouth of the Liffey.

'Last time,' Brooks began, 'you expressed some concern about our friend, the sister.'

'I wouldn't want her to come to any harm,' replied Wallis.

'What harm do you have in mind?'

'I'll have to leave her sooner than later, won't I?'

'Has she grown too fond of you, dear boy?'

Wallis stopped by a railing and leant over it, watching the river flowing calmly by on its way to its embrace by the sea.

'It's not easy, Jimmy.'

'You didn't have any trouble with that little honey pot in South Armagh.'

'That was different. Her brother had an M90 in his hand.'

Brooks cast him a narrow-eyed glance. 'Bloody hell, David, don't tell me it's the other way round and you've got too fond of her!'

'For God's sake, it's not that,' Wallis rounded on him. 'I'm a professional, damn it. But do whatever's going to be done.'

'In that case, your timing is perfect. It's been agreed that we will engineer their disappearances one by one, with suitable intervals between.'

'You didn't tell me it would lead to that,' said Wallis coldly.

'For fuck's sake, David,' began Brooks with an anger so out of character that Wallis recoiled.

'OK, OK,' replied Wallis.

'We're not a charity,' continued Brooks.

'All right. I get it.' He paused. 'Including Martin McCartney?'

'Yes.'

Wallis pushed off from the railing and marched away. Brooks caught up and fell in beside him, breathing deeply. Zeal displacing his habitual game-playing, he looked fiercely into Wallis's eyes.

'Remember Enniskillen?'

'Of course.'

'Black and O'Donnell have been overheard planning something that, in their words, will make that look like child's play.'

'I see.'

'It won't just kill and maim: it will blow up the chances of peace. And God knows who Kennedy's got on his kill list. They have to be stopped. Quickly. And efficiently. No trace.' Brooks left the thought hanging and fell silent for a few seconds. 'There's no one better than you.'

He could sense the calculations going on in Wallis's head – the agonizing over good and bad, right and wrong, loyalty and betrayal. Understanding his man more completely than ever before, Brooks played his best card. 'This is the right thing to do, David. Morally right. The means are a tiny number of deaths, the end is peace for a nation. How can that possibly be wrong?' Further seconds passed, Brooks holding his breath, nothing left in his hand.

'I won't do McCartney,' Wallis finally said. 'The others, OK. Better than some paramilitary cowboy you rope in messing it up.'

'When it comes to McCartney, we will only require you at the point of capture. We need your skills to help with that and to confirm identity. Your visit to Belfast has put you in a unique position. You will then be free to leave Ireland.'

'Immediately?'

'Yes.'

'With a job offer?'

Brooks replied without blinking. 'Yes.'

'I'll need a reason for taking these mini-breaks.'

Brooks could see Wallis beginning to narrow his focus to the business in hand. He appeared on-side. 'You'll think of something.' He patted him on the shoulder. The only risk was any return of sentimentality when he was back with the girl. 'One piece of friendly advice, David, from your uncle Jimmy. Cool it with her. She's served her purpose. See if you can wind it down a bit.'

'You're a hard-hearted bastard, aren't you?' He said it ferociously. The mention of the girl had made him flare up. Despite the satisfactory outcome to the meeting, it left Brooks with a niggle of discomfort.

'And you must be, too.' They glowered at each other and walked off in opposing directions.

The Gang of Four had decamped from Belfast to South Armagh. These were men embedded in the harsh rolling hills of the border country who saw any compromise by their smooth-talking city colleagues as surrender. There were plenty of supporters and safe houses to protect them – and rest and recreation was easy to find in the border town of Dundalk. It was there, outside United Kingdom jurisdiction, that Brooks earmarked for his operation. What no one else knew was that he was in possession of information that would give him potential times and locations to carry out a snatch. How smoothly the first one went would always remain a source of wonder.

It required a squad of three: Wallis, Brooks and a third man brought in by Brooks for the job. Brooks knew that Sean Black was having lunch with an associate in a café just off the high street, after which he was likely to attend a local Gaelic football match. They waited in a car within sight of the café and Wallis, using old-fashioned, lo-tech binoculars, was able to confirm a preliminary ID on Black. The associate was wearing a high-collared coat with his back to the window, making him less easy to pick out.

Around 2 p.m. – Brooks had decided daylight was safe given the stealth of the operation – the two men left the café, Black casting glances around him. His associate headed straight for the driver's seat, his back constantly to the watchers and still preventing any identification. They tailed the car as it headed out of the town. After a mile or so, it stopped by a tobacconist and the associate got out, presumably to buy cigarettes or other refreshments for the match. They drew up behind the car.

Brooks and Wallis were both dressed in duffle coats, Wallis wearing a beret and Brooks a brown cap. Wallis walked to the rear passenger door, climbed in and stuck a pistol to Black's temple. Black, confused and shocked, failed to put up the instant show of resistance that could possibly have made a difference. By the time he tried to struggle, he was already in Wallis's grasp. One crunching blow to his solar plexus, enhanced by the knuckleduster Wallis wore on his left-hand fingers, snuffed out any further fight.

Brooks jumped into the driver's seat, started the engine – the key was still in the ignition, though a reserve plan was in place to force Black into the tailing car if necessary – and drove off. The tailing car followed. A few seconds later, when they were a couple of hundred yards away, Brooks could see, through the nearside wing mirror, the associate emerge from the tobacconist, cast bewildered glances and walk away.

A few minutes later, they turned into a country lane and stopped. Brooks and Wallis applied handcuffs to Black's wrists and bound strong adhesive tape around his mouth and back of his head. They moved him and themselves to the tailing car, abandoning Black and his associate's original car. Its number plate might be rapidly communicated to those with an interest in retrieving Black.

They embarked on a silent drive southwest on minor roads that took them through small market towns with long names: Carrickmacross, Bailieborough, across the main N3 road to Ballyjamesduff. Their careful, lawful progress, mindful of speed limits, amber lights, and blind corners, brought them after an hour and a half or so to a stretch of water, Lough Sheelin. They pulled up in a wooded cove by a bay. Black was shaking, trying to mumble through his gag. They said nothing to him, and not a single word to each other. There was no interrogation. Nothing needed to be known or was not already known. The car smelt of his piss and the bowel contents that he had been unable to restrain.

A modest fishing boat with an outboard motor was moored to a jetty. They loaded Black onto it like a limp pack of cargo, the driver pulled the cord and, with a few wisps of exhaust, the motor chugged into action. It was late afternoon and as they made their way out into the lake, a few fishermen dotted the shoreline. They steered away from a couple of other boats and the driver began to circle, speeding up the engine and increasing its noise. One shot was fired to the head, a second to the heart. Lead weights were strapped inside Black's trousers and jacket and clipped securely with steel cord. Brooks never forgot the curious spectacle of the driver making the sign of the cross over the corpse before it was gently and carefully pushed overboard.

They headed back towards Dublin. The driver dropped Wallis and Brooks at a shopping centre car park on the outskirts, where they had left their car. Only when they were inside it did the two men talk. Brooks remembered well precisely what Wallis had said.

'I feel like I've just taken part in a Mafia execution. It could have been a scene from *The Godfather*.'

'There is one difference, David,' Brooks replied. 'We are not criminals.' That response afforded him as much satisfaction today as when he uttered it twenty years ago.

'What about the driver?' asked Wallis.

'What about him?'

'Criminal or angel?'

'No need to ask, David. We'll just call him "the man". He

comes highly recommended, though not, perhaps, from a source one might have expected.'

'Does he know who we are?'

'If you mean, did I give him CVs, of course not. The cash advance showed our credentials.'

'Well, he'd bloody well better keep his mouth shut.'

'Stop worrying, David. It's a walk in the park. Three to go. We succeed, we've served our country.'

The second disappearance, of Brendan O'Donnell, followed a similar pattern. Its course was less smooth.

This time the snatch was in Drogheda, where O'Donnell had family. At the point of capture, O'Donnell, unlike Black, tried to jump from the car. This required Wallis to smash his face with the butt of his pistol, resulting in blood seeping unstoppably from O'Donnell's mouth and teeth. The disposal of the body in a different lough went smoothly.

Brooks realized that O'Donnell's DNA would be all over both the car he was captured in and the car in which he travelled to his death. The latter presented no problem as 'the man' would dispose of it. The former was more awkward. This was not because of any trail of evidence: Brooks himself was sufficiently clothed and gloved to have left no trace. As for Wallis, it was the height of improbability that the Irish police, the Gardaí, would ever make any connection that would put him under suspicion. However, the abandoned car, with O'Donnell's blood all over it, provided a wealth of clues as to how he had disappeared.

The messiness of the snatch meant that Brooks would have to devise a new strategy for the two remaining targets: Joseph Kennedy and Martin McCartney.

There was a further awkwardness – the parting conversation with Wallis.

'That was a fucking mess, Jimmy,' Wallis began when they were alone in their own car after 'the man' drove off.

'It was a successful operation,' replied Brooks. 'But, I agree, not a work of art.'

'My blood's in that car too.'

'You'll be out of the country in no time.'

'We've got two. Isn't that enough?'

'We need to remove the head, David. Stop the beast rearing up again.'

'Why not do that first?'

'It's like a tree. You lop off the branches, then chop down the trunk. Same principle.' He could see that Wallis was unconvinced. So too would he have been, had he only seen the same partial picture.

'OK, let me think about it.'

'You can't pull out now, David. It's your duty to your country. And to your fellow citizens. Peace or terror. Your choice.'

'Christ, Jimmy, you make it hard, don't you?' They drove in silence through the detritus-strewn suburbs of north Dublin. After a full five minutes, Wallis uttered a single, familiar word. 'OK.'

Brooks understood that Operation Hawk was compromised; but not, in his view, fatally. A source told him that the news of a second disappearance, combined with the telltale evidence of blood in the abandoned car, had produced a justified paranoia in Martin McCartney and Joseph Kennedy. They were travelling everywhere together, linked by an umbilical cord, attended by escorts almost every waking hour. Their capture would now have to be both opportunistic and risky.

Brooks heard that the two men and their hangers-on were intending to celebrate a birthday at a pub called the Black Brimmer. It lay just on the Irish Republic's side of the border. He told Wallis that McCartney, as the leader of the faction, was now the priority target but repeated his promise that he would restrict his involvement in the McCartney disappearance to the capture only. It would require surprise and split-second timing.

As before, Brooks chose the anonymous peace of the riverside to take a Sunday afternoon stroll with Wallis. He was concerned by Wallis's appearance. In the intervening weeks after the O'Donnell disappearance, he seemed to have aged and grown unkempt, the sign of a man not properly looking after himself. Not taking pride. Perhaps in emotional difficulty. Brooks waited till they had agreed the operational detail – where Wallis seemed as perceptive and meticulous as always – before gently tackling him.

'David,' he said in his most affectionate tone, 'you look exhausted.'

Wallis tried to raise a grin. 'Working too hard, I expect.'

'My dear chap, you don't need to do that. Don't worry, you'll fly through your master's. I'll see to that.'

'I'm sure you will, Jimmy.' Brooks welcomed the sardonic note, more like the Wallis he knew. 'Actually, I reckon I could make a good lawyer.'

'Waste of your talents. But, of course, if you want a quieter life—'

'Who knows what one wants?' Wallis interrupted. Momentarily, his face carried the gloom of the condemned man. Then, suddenly, it brightened, with the magnetism that could cast a heroic sheen on him. 'For fuck's sake, Jimmy, let's cut the agony-uncle crap and get this thing done.'

Wallis slapped him on the shoulder and marched off. It was the last time the two men breathed on each other.

Brooks read, as he had so often before, the recording that followed that final meeting.

17 April 1994

Saw Jimmy. We struck a deal. I will see this through and help in the concluding operation. But it's on condition that the brother is not to be harmed. They can remove him from the scene. He can disappear for a few months. And, when they've got what they wanted, they allow him to reappear. Jimmy agreed he'll have no power left with the other three gone. He'll be unable to cause trouble. I told Jimmy I won't allow him to rest if this agreement is not kept.

Brooks closed the file, carried it upstairs to his safe, and locked it away. He took off his reading glasses, rubbed his eyes, and crept down the passage to the bedroom. He shuffled in, the usual floorboard emitting its signature creak, lowered himself onto the bed and removed his slippers. He laid his head on the pair of pillows and awaited sleep. Beside him, Dorothy stirred.

'You really loved him, didn't you?' she said.

'He was a beautiful young man,' replied Brooks.

'Well, we may have had our loves, Jimmy, but we've cared for each other.' He stayed silent. 'Haven't we?'

'Yes, dear.' He returned her pat on the arm. 'We survived.'

That night, Anne-Marie read the same diary entry – the last in the extracts she had been given: '. . . the brother,' David had recorded, 'is not to be harmed.' Yet Martin had disappeared, never to reappear. They had killed him – a sacrificial victim for a so-called peace. It meant they had also betrayed David. She fought to repress a welling of atavistic fury at the treachery of the British state, even to one of its own.

CHAPTER 28

Post-election, Saturday, 20 May

The information he had just received from Amy left Carne no choice. The prospect appalled him. He knew it would be decisive for his relationship with Anne-Marie – perhaps even, he sometimes dared to hope, for his future life, too. He texted her that he had some news; she replied that she normally kept Saturday nights sacrosanct but he could come to her flat from 9 p.m.

She greeted him with obvious pleasure, which only increased his fears. She saw through him instantly.

'You look as if you've seen a ghost.'

'Chasing them, more like,' he replied. The smile he attempted faded to a pale dullness.

'Something's happened, hasn't it?' It was an assertion, not a question. 'Something that's not good.'

'I don't know,' he said. 'That's why I need to see you.'

He followed her into the sitting room and she waved him towards the sofa.

'Drink?'

'Better not.'

He pulled the ring box from his pocket, opened it and handed it to her. She held it for a while, then placed it on the glass table. The way she peered down at it left no doubt. She went to the bathroom; he could hear a tap running and imagined her rubbing her face and wiping her eyes. He felt like a criminal intruder on private grief.

After a few minutes, she returned, forcing a smile.

'I shouldn't have taken it to show you,' he said. 'I'm breaking every evidence rule in the book.'

'We made an agreement,' she said. 'Wherever it leads.'

'I haven't forgotten.' He paused. 'I'm hating this.'

'It's OK. Go on.'

The ring has your prints on it.'

'Yes, it would.'

'And there's a lock of hair in the box. With your DNA.'

She narrowed her eyes. 'That's why your girl took those swabs.'

'Yes.' He searched for an excuse. 'We'd have had to do it sometime. No one was closer to him than you.'

'It only means I gave him a ring. He gave me jewellery, too. I showed you.'

'I know,' he said. Her reply told him she was holding back. Whatever the consequences, he had to find out if she had been there at the final moment. He played his card. 'The angle of the ring in the remnants of clothing as it lay beside the skeleton suggests that it was placed there after he'd been taken to the field. Otherwise it wouldn't have lain so flat.'

'What do you want from me?' She had bought his bluff. He had never felt so cheap.

'I want you to go on trusting me. And I want to know what happened. What really happened. I can't force you. But I don't believe we can have freedom with each other unless we share everything.'

She walked over to the screen of glass and stared out. It seemed the longest wait of his life. Finally she turned, walked into her bedroom and reappeared with an overcoat.

'Let's go for a walk in the park.'

Monday, 25 April 1994, the small hours

She dreams the front doorbell is ringing. Or thinks she does. As sleep is dragged from her, she realizes the ringing is repeated and urgent. She checks her bedside clock – just past 1.30 a.m. There's a tap on her bedroom door.

'There's someone wanting you, Maire.' It's Mrs Ryan's voice. She forces herself out of bed and opens the door. Mrs Ryan stands there in a dressing gown, hair netted, expression grim. 'You better get dressed and go with him.' Her tone allows no dissent.

'What's it about, Mrs Ryan?' she asks, her stomach churning.

'You better come down, love, and speak to him yourself.' She sees the sympathy in Mrs Ryan's eyes of someone who has watched others marched to their doom.

At the front door is a man in a woolly hat and denim jacket.

'Who are you? It's the middle of the night.' Her hushed voice seethes at the intrusion.

'I've been sent to bring you,' he says. 'They're holding your friend David. He's asking for you.'

'Whaddya mean, holding David?'

'They got him, you need to come,' he insists.

'It can't be him, it's a mistake. He's gone home.'

'It's not a mistake,' he states flatly.

'Oh, God.' She knows it's for real – some sort of reality that will fracture her. 'Who sent you?' she whispers.

'Joseph. Joseph sent me.' She drops her head and closes her eyes. 'And Martin's been took,' he continues. All she wants is to go back to bed, for it to be a bad dream.

'Took by who?' she asks.

'Brits, of course. Who fucking else?' His question doesn't require an answer. 'You gotta come.'

She reopens her eyes – he stands watching her, motionless, waiting. She has to go. Whatever David's captors want out of her, she must try to help him.

'OK, gimme a minute to grab some clothes.' She returns to her bedroom. It's 1.38 a.m. She assembles a small pile on the bed. From the basin she grabs hairbrush, toothbrush, toothpaste, deodorant. She removes the holiday snap of the McCartneys and Kennedys from the chest of drawers and adds it. Anything to remind them that the man they're holding is with Martin McCartney's sister and they should spare him.

She knows enough about these people to calculate the ghastly process that might linger on. She cannot remember her dates and adds a couple of tampons. She rummages through the chest of drawers and finds the earrings and bracelet he left her. She will wear them – it might help. What else has David given her? There's the birthday card with the sweetness of his message. She retrieves it from under the bedside table.

She hears a brisk hoot from the car below, draws back the curtain and mouths, 'I'm coming.' She steps into her black-leather skirt – she doesn't want to wear jeans – pulls her red sweater over her long hair, slides on ankle boots, grabs her coat, descends the stairs and clicks the front door quietly behind her.

The driver hovers on the pavement. Close up she still does not recognize him, and he does not introduce himself. He beckons her to follow him to a dirty brown Datsun parked across the road. He points to the back door and she opens it to let herself in. He jumps into the driver's seat, turns the rear-view mirror to check her, readjusts it and accelerates through the darkened city. It's nearly 2 a.m. and the street lights are off. There's only the hum of the engine, the driver's curses at red lights and occasional oncoming night buses. Soon the brick-sided streets of urban life give way to open road, monotonous white lines in the middle illuminated every now and then by beams from small-hour headlights.

With the palms of his hands guiding the steering wheel, the driver rolls a cigarette with his fingers. She cannot help a twinge of admiration for his dexterity. He lights it and inhales with a long sigh of relief. The sweet smell wafts into the back and a wave of nausea rises within her. She keeps silent, knowing that any protest will only draw his contempt. She tries to distract herself by watching road signs, calculating distances, how far they've gone, how far they might have to go, what their average speed is, when the next bend in the straight road heading north will come.

'Where are we heading?' she asks.

'You'll know when we get there.' She could have written the answer before she asked the question. Mind games will not dismiss the swirling thoughts. Perhaps it might not turn out so badly after all; perhaps she can talk them out of it, make them see there's no point, that David is harmless. If he's done something stupid, let him melt away if he promises never to come back. Then she remembers the words 'Martin's been took' and knows it can only turn out badly. It dawns on her. Is she to be punished too? Otherwise, why exactly do they need her?

'Did I have a choice?' she asks him.

'No.' She cranes her head to catch his eyes in the mirror. They remain blank, an unreadable threat.

They pass a sign to Dundalk. She remembers the last journey in the coach up this road and back, David pissing in the coach park. What was he doing back in these parts?

'You can at least tell me which side of the border,' she says.

This time he answers. 'They took him into the North.' He pauses. 'Safer on home territory.' His voice is bleak.

They turn west onto a B road, white lines still giving her something to stare at, and then onto lanes, only faint shadows of hedgerows brushing past. Despite the twisting narrowness, he maintains his speed and she rocks from side to side, grabbing armrests to steady herself, a helpless petal in the storm.

'You're driving too fast,' she says.

'We'll get there quicker, won't we?' He draws on the cigarette, the paper crackling and retreating to the edges of his thumb and forefinger. He opens the window to hurl it out – she feels the wind hit her like the slap of a man's hand.

They turn onto a lane, which begins to climb. Steep dips and rises alternate with sharp curves as they corkscrew up a hillside. They gain height, occasional twinkles of light appear below. Finally, they turn into a track, juddering across potholes and rough stones, every limb shaking and cold. Ahead she sees a weak light from a farmhouse. They pass it, take a turning and jerk to a halt by a barn. He throws open his door and opens hers.

'Follow me.'

She gathers the small bag with her hurriedly assembled belongings and follows him inside. She sees men ahead sitting on bare wooden chairs. Two lamps hang from steel beams supporting a sloped corrugated-iron roof. A desolate, low-lit torture chamber, windowless and airless. She sniffs a background smell of cow dung, or is it silage? She's disoriented by the lights and bareness, unable to trust her senses.

One man rises from his chair and comes over to her. Joseph.

'Thanks for coming, Maire,' he begins.

'I was told I had no choice.' Her reply has no fight.

She follows him towards the chairs. Two men sit on them – as with the driver, she does not recognize them – rise and nod to her. One is slim and tall, wearing a dark beard and spectacles; the other squat with curly brown hair. They could be lecturers she can imagine shuffling around the corridors of Trinity.

In the farthest chair, facing the corner, his back to her, a figure slumps, bound to the frame by taut ropes. A thick bandage is wound around his head, below hangs the waterproof nylon jacket, then his jeans-covered legs splayed out in front. There's enough muscle left to hold his head in place. He's alive.

'Wait here,' Joseph orders her. 'We'll turn him round.'

The squat man joins Joseph and they take one side each, lifting him by the armpits, the strapped chair revolving with him. She sees bruises on his cheek and blood seeping from his teeth and mouth. They unpeel the bandage layer by layer, finally revealing a black eye mask, ensuring his total blindness.

'We'll leave that on for the moment,' says the squat man. He raises his voice. 'David.' A low moan comes back. He increases the volume. 'David Vallely!'

Two mumbled, fragmented words are just audible. 'Fuck off.'

'Mind your language, David,' the tall man says with deliberate calmness. 'There's someone here to see you.' Another moan.

Joseph removes the mask. David's eyes flutter and then blink more slowly as he adjusts to the light. She senses him bringing the faces in front of him into focus.

'It's me, David. Maire.'

'Why?' he groans. 'Why you, Maire?' He looks up at Joseph and across to the two men. With an agonized bellow, he cries, 'Why don't you just finish it?'

The tall man lets the desolate cry drift into the night. 'We can't do that, David. Not till you tell us what's been happening. For Maire's sake, you need to speak. That's why we've brought her here. So she can advise you to help us. Then we'll go easy on you.' He pauses, moving closer to David. 'And her.'

'*Don't you touch her!*' His screech is deafening, scaring her.

The squat man allows the cry to fade. 'You owe Maire an explanation, too, David. Look at the trouble you've got her into. You speak to us and she'll be fine.'

'She knows nothing,' he says. 'And I've nothing to say to you.' He allows his head to drop. 'Just do what you want with me,' he whispers.

'What have your friends done with her brother, David?' he asks. 'That's the least you owe her.'

'I don't know.'

'OK, David,' says the tall man, 'let's try again. Who are you?'

'My name is David Vallely,' he says hoarsely, 'doing an MA in law at Trinity College, Dublin.' The squat man jumps at him, smashing a knuckleduster-covered fist into his face and mouth. Maire cringes at the moist crunch of steel on flesh and teeth, and the bloody spurting spume.

David sinks further. There's silence, interrupted by the tall man. 'This is getting us nowhere. We need to finish it.'

The squat man goes over to him, whispers in his ear, then stands beside Maire holding the knuckleduster to her cheek.

David's face raises itself, as if lifted by some external force pulling from above. The sight of the squat man holding his hand by Maire's head seems to rouse him. He mumbles.

'Speak more clearly, David,' barks the tall man.

Maire is surprised at his tone. She's assumed Joseph will be running this macabre exercise. But it's clear by now that the other two men are in charge. The ammunition of her connection to Joseph is valueless.

'They said they wouldn't kill him.'

'Say that again,' says the tall man. 'Clearly now.'

David shouted. '*They said they wouldn't kill him.*'

'You mean not like Sean Black and Brendan O'Donnell.'

'I don't know what you mean,' he whispers. There are tears in his eyes. 'They promised me they wouldn't.' He looks up at Maire. 'Because he's her brother.'

'Did you believe them, David?'

'Yes.' She sees a pathetic, wounded animal, desperate to be put out of his misery. Her sorrow, she realizes at this closing moment, is not about his deceit, but his love.

'Who are they, David?' asks the squat man.

'I don't know them,' comes the hushed reply. 'Just told where to go.'

'Who are you working for, David?' asks the tall man.

'Never gave me his name,' murmurs David. Maire sees he's fading again. She hopes unconsciousness might rescue him. And perhaps her, too, though she suspects their threats are bluff.

'I reckon that's it,' says the tall man. 'We'll get no more. And we hardly need confirmation of Sean and Brendan.'

It comes to her from nowhere – a last throw of the dice. However much he's deceived her, she has to give it a chance. Knowing they're calling the shots, she addresses the two unknown men.

'Have you tried Martin's phone?' she asks.

'Can't do that,' says the squat man. 'The Brits can intercept the signal, trace where it's coming from.'

'Try it,' she pleads. 'Just once, won't take a second. Say he's still alive. Still being interrogated.' She points to David. 'Like him. It'd change everything. You could trade David for him.'

The two men walk a few yards away and have a whispered discussion.

Feeling a numb powerlessness, she approaches David. The tall man notices but lets it go. She takes a tissue from her pocket, soaks it with her saliva and pats his forehead gently with it. Traces of blood seep into it and she raises the tissue to her own forehead and dabs it on her skin. She lowers it again to clean the blood around his mouth but it's too wet. She crumples it, stuffs it in her pocket and takes out a last tissue. She wishes she'd thought to bring a towel.

She kneels beside him and strokes the curl of brown hair falling over his ear. It is dank with sweat.

She nuzzles his ear, then whispers in it.

'What happened, David?'

He tries to shift his strapped back and hands but all he achieves is a faint wobble of the chair. He looks down at his knees.

'My legs won't move.' She inspects his mud-splattered jeans and gently strokes from the top of his thigh down to his ankle. The legs are motionless and he lets out a whimper of pain as her hand moves over his knees. 'They hit me in them.' He breathes heavily, even the attempt at speech exhausting him. 'It's why I couldn't run away.'

'What were you running away from, David?' she asks with a gentle insistence.

'It doesn't matter. Too late now.' Quiet sobs shake his shoulders. 'They said they wouldn't kill him.'

'I know, David, you told us that.' She pauses, trying to work something out. 'Did you ask them not to kill him, David?'

'Yes.' Tears flow down his cheek, mingling with the red traces of blood to form a pale, weak stream dropping onto his collar.

'Did you believe them?'

'Yes.' He raises his eyes to her, pleading for her absolution. A memory of when she herself was once told there would be no killing and believed it flashes before her.

'What went wrong, David? Why did they get you?'

He groans. 'All happened too fast. Don't know. They were shooting.'

'How many of them?'

'Don't know.' She feels him sinking, then trying to turn his head towards the two men.

The squat man walks towards them and she raises herself from her knees.

'OK, Maire,' he says, 'a decision's been made to try what you say. He looks down at David. 'His phone's smashed so we'll use one of ours. It's risky but we'll do it for you – and for Martin. Just in case.'

Maire retreats to join Joseph. 'Who are they?' she asks, nodding towards the two men.

'They're from the leadership, Maire. Best you don't know more.'

'Not your friends, then, Joseph?'

'No. But getting him was too big. The leadership had to be involved.'

'They won't mind losing Martin, will they? One way of dealing with the split.' She's having the germ of an idea.

'Christ, Maire, blood runs thicker than that.'

'You think so, Joseph?' she continues. 'What was it they said, Sean and Brendan gone too?'

'Aye, they just disappeared, we dunno how.'

'So then it'd be just you left, Joseph, wouldn't it?' she says. 'Just the one to go.'

'I dunno what you're suggesting, Maire.'

'I think you do. You move now and spring David, he can help you. Maybe you'll get away with your own life too.'

'Jesus, Maire, you're fucking crazy.' He's almost spitting in her ear.

'Have a think about it, Joseph. Have a think about who's crazy.'

The tall man has produced a mobile phone and punches in a number from a scruffed-up notebook. 'OK, it's ringing,' he announces. Maire imagines the ringtone and counts the number of double bleeps. Five, eight, twelve. No answer, no voice message. Silence. He cancels the call and casts 'I told you so' glances. 'Well, we gave it a try, didn't we? No one could say we didn't make the effort.'

'But the number rang,' says Maire.

'Yes, the number rang.'

'You need to give them more time.'

'I gave them time. I saw you counting.'

'Give it another try. They might have been thinking. Put yourself in their shoes. It's a big decision to answer that call or not.'

Joseph interjects. 'It won't get anywhere, Maire. Sean and Brendan never came back. Be the same with Martin. The leopard doesn't change his spots.' Maire senses Joseph trying to ingratiate himself with the two men. Has her message got through? Is he working out the odds? Any time she can buy might help.

'Try it once more,' she says. 'It's my brother's life we're talking about.'

The three men shrug shoulders and exchange resigned glances. As they reach silent agreement, the phone bursts into life. They stare at it in disbelief.

'For Christ's sake, answer it,' Maire shouts. 'We gotta save Martin.'

The tall man hands it to the squat man. He presses answer and waits. More silence, then he speaks fast, muffling his voice. 'Yes?' The others watch as the squat man listens. He cups the mouthpiece with his hand and looks up. 'He's asking, "Who is this?"'

'Just say, "We got David,"' says the tall man. 'Tell him we might be willing to trade.'

The squat man does as instructed. 'He says he wants to hear from David.'

'What's his accent?' asks the bearded man.

'Dunno. Sort of sounds mid-Ulster but could be faking.'

'A Brit, then?'

'Possibly.' The squat man hesitates. 'Line's not great.'

'Let me have a listen,' says the tall man. He takes the phone. 'We want to hear from Martin.' He passes on the reply. 'He says they need to hear from David first.'

'Let them,' says Maire. 'What's to lose?'

'Them tracing this fucking call, that's what's to lose,' says the squat man. 'Thirty more seconds, max.' He takes the phone over to David and holds it to his ear. 'Speak, David.'

Maire nods at David, encouraging, urging. 'You can save your life, David,' she pleads.

She sees him grasping his waning energy, gathering himself, eyes boring beyond her into an eternity of space. '*They're going to kill me,*' he yells into the mouthpiece. It is a dying wolf's howl, rending the night.

The tall man snatches the phone and listens. 'Line's gone dead.' It's said with stark, lethal simplicity.

'Why, David?' she asks. 'Why?'

'He's dead. And I am too.'

'You said they promised.'

'Yes, he promised.'

It is the ending of a tragedy. There's no audience to applaud, no lights to come on, no bows to take.

David tries to raise a finger at Joseph. 'You,' he rasps, 'the one who gets away.' His voice tails off, leaving a ghostly stillness. It's interrupted by the squeaking of the barn door. The driver enters and quietly announces, 'The man's arrived.'

'OK, we'll leave it with you, the man and Joseph,' says the tall man. 'It's time we headed off. Long past it. OK, Joseph?'

'Sure.'

'And remember, no speaking of this. We'll be making no claims. Might get in the way of the negotiations. Tonight never happened. Got it?'

'I got it,' says Joseph.

'Interesting what your man says, Joseph,' says the tall man. 'It's just you left now, isn't it? Four of you, now just the one. The survivor.'

'I dunno what you're meaning,' replies Joseph. Beads of sweat cluster on the top of his nose and forehead, and a faint colouring in his cheeks betrays a quiet fury.

'We've lost three good men – Martin, Sean, Brendan,' continues the tall man. 'I'm sorry we didn't see eye to eye in recent times. But they were good men. It's time for the movement to be united. Time to move on.'

'Are you threatening me?' Joseph asks roughly.

'For fuck's sake, Joseph,' says the tall man, pointing at David. 'There's your threat. Your Brits.'

'It's good to hear you still think it.'

The tall man narrows his eyes – for the first time, Maire smells his menace. 'You be careful, Joseph.'

There's murder in Joseph's eyes, but he stays silent.

The tall man addresses Maire with what seems more like embarrassment than anything else. 'Sorry, Maire.'

'Yes, sorry, Maire,' agrees the squat man. With undisguised, almost childlike eagerness to avoid her reply, they're out of the barn without a backward glance. A few seconds later, a car engine fires up and a screech of acceleration conveys them into the night.

It spits with rain, drops beating rhythmically like a ticking clock on the aluminium roof, interrupted by sporadic groans of pain wheezing from David. Maire and Joseph watch him in silence, alone with their desolate thoughts. The driver hovers by the door.

'Bastards,' murmurs Joseph.

His remark startles Maire. 'Whaddya mean, Joseph?' she asks, her voice low, both of them in unspoken agreement to stop the driver listening in.

'Maybe you're right.'

Her brow furrows. 'Go on.'

'Maybe I'm a dead man now, too.'

'I wasn't making it up, was I?'

'Martin and me, Sean and Brendan, too, we made our decision. Took our fork in the road. But we lost, didn't we? And I'm the outcast. And I still don't fucking understand how.'

Maire is overwhelmed by a sense of loss, caught between two defeated, broken men. And Martin, too, gone. The three most significant men, the only significant men in her life.

A rush of guilt – that somehow she's been responsible, that it's her fault, that there's some lethal magnetism set deep in her subconscious, that she's some sort of involuntary *femme fatale* – overwhelms her. Her rational mind tries to fight back, telling her that the cataclysm of this dreadful night is not the result of anything she has done to them, but of what they have done to her.

'What actually happened tonight?' she asks.

Before Joseph can reply, the driver interrupts. 'We should leave.'

'A minute,' replies Joseph, his eyes on the slumped David. 'He's hardly going anywhere, is he?' He resumes the murmured conversation with Maire. 'It happened fast.'

'That's all David could say too,' she says. 'There must be more than that.'

'We were in the Black Brimmer. Martin, me, a few others. It was one of the boys' birthday. After Sean and Brendan disappeared, I told Martin we were joined at the hip from now on. We had to protect each other, couldn't afford to let each other out of sight. And we'd always have escorts. With guns. He wasn't keen, said he could look after himself, but I insisted.'

'Martin always hated to depend on anyone.'

'Well, he's been proved wrong, hasn't he? We were leaving, no big drinking or anything.'

'He didn't drink.'

'No, Maire, Martin didn't drink. And don't say not like me. OK?'

'Go on.'

'We were leaving, Martin and me, the other two following. He says he needs to piss. He crosses the road to the hedges, a minute or two passes, he comes out, he's crossing back. A car screeches past, seems to knock him. Two of them leap out. Pile him in. A third man's running towards the car. One of ours fires at him, slows him. Now we're firing at the car but it's bolting. Then it's away, out of sight, gone. What's left is your man screaming in the road. Screaming after them, screaming for his legs. He puts his hand inside his jacket but we're on top of him by then. We get his gun.'

'David had a gun?'

'Yes, he had a gun.'

'OK.' She bows her head in resignation.

'That's it. End of story. End of cause. End of fucking everything.' Joseph points to David. 'End of him.'

'Did you smash his knees too?' Maire asks.

'One of the boys wanted to make sure. Got a bit carried away.'

'You didn't need to do that.'

'He had to be immobilized, Maire.'

Maire glances at David. He's cast in stone, a reclining statue marred by chips and fissures. She is too numbed to know how to feel. Betrayal? Surprise? Confirmation? None of them make sense. As he nears the end of his life, she feels at one remove from this ghastly place in a weightless corner of a universe where the deepest of sorrows collide with the deepest of loves. And then feeling dies and souls disintegrate into dust.

The driver and the newly arrived 'man', a dark scarf covering his nose and mouth, a woolly hat over his eyes and forehead, walk over to David. The man produces a knife and expertly slices through the straps holding David to the chair. As they work loose, his body lists to one side, a sinking vessel in a fathomless ocean. They catch him, push him upright, then half-carry him to the door, his lower legs and feet bouncing like a rag doll's across the floor. She tries not to hear his yelps and trails the dismal procession into the dark. There are two pairs of headlights, the first from the car she arrived in, the second presumably belonging to the man.

Her driver points to the man's car. 'We'll get us all in there. Then we'll come back and I'll take her home.'

'No!' It comes out more stridently than she means. She turns to Joseph. 'I'm coming with you. With him.'

'You can't do that, Maire. It's not . . . it's not appropriate.'

'Fuck's sake, Joseph, what planet are you living on?' Again she's surprised at her vehemence.

The man stays silent – she suspects he never speaks. Understandable if he's the executioner she assumes him to be. It shows what cowards they are not to do it themselves. The driver looks at him – she detects the hint of a nod in response. He turns to Joseph, who sourly shrugs his shoulders.

'If it's OK with you, I suppose it's OK with me,' he says. 'Doesn't make it right, though.'

'I wanna be with him in the car.'

'Can't get five in,' says the driver.

'Then one of you follow in the second car,' she says. They shrug shoulders again; she hides her surprise that they appear to be accepting her authority. All sons of Catholic mothers, brought up to kowtow to the Virgin Mary.

The driver addresses Joseph. 'You follow, she can come with us.' Maire has a moment of sympathy for him in his new isolation.

The man's car is some kind of jeep, tailor-made for impoverished stony farm tracks. They drag David towards the left-side rear door, open it and bundle him onto the back seat. She heads to the right rear door to jump in beside him but, as she grasps the handle, the driver crunches his hand around hers. 'No. You go in the front, the man will take care of him.' She doesn't argue, her brief period of authority is over.

She takes her place in the front passenger seat and lowers the sun blind, hoping it will contain a mirror. It doesn't. She cranes her neck to look around. The 'man' is placing the black mask over David's eyes.

'You don't need to do that,' she says.

The man stays silent. 'Best to take precautions,' the driver replies on his behalf.

They accelerate off, guided only by sidelights, Joseph following close behind.

'I can't see. Let me see.' It is the whimper of an old man, once blinded in battle and seeking revelation before his final breath.

'Shut it,' orders the driver. She hears a thud from the back and David's groan of pain. She guesses the man must have slapped him – and he stays quiet for fear of provoking more. She tries to imagine herself as David, flashes of moonlight shooting through tiny gaps at the side of the mask the only markers of his final destination.

What is he thinking? Or does the pain preclude thought? Is he already beyond life, or thoughts of life? She looks round at the 'man'. 'Let me touch him,' she says. After a second or two, he nods. She lays her hand on his. It is damp, cold, like steel, bereft of emotion or acknowledgement. Fighting off the feelings of betrayal and anger, she strokes the fingers and, as lightly as she can, the tiny hairs on the back of his hand, then moves up the wrist and under his jacket sleeve to the beginning of his forearm. He slowly, hesitatingly revolves his hand so that he can place his middle and forefingers on her wrist. With the smallest of movements he traces a circle the size of a sapphire on her skin. She smiles and does the same back to him. His movement ceases but their skins remain linked and she feels him warming under her.

The jeep lurches right through what she can see is an open field and stops. Joseph behind drives past the turning, then reverses back into it blocking the exit. He stays sitting in his car. The driver opens the back door and, helped by the man, drags David out. She feels his hand tightening around her arm as they pull but it is too weak to gain any traction. She gets out of the car and slams her door.

'Don't fucking do that! You wanna advertise we're here?' says the driver.

'Sorry,' she says, 'didn't mean to.' Though she did, however futile it might be. She runs back to the car behind and bangs on Joseph's window. He sits there, immobile, not acknowledging her. She bangs again, louder. This time he winds down the window, its unoiled squeak the only sound in the night.

'Whaddya gonna do, Joseph?'

'Whaddya mean, what am I gonna do?'

'This is your chance. You can take those two on, 'course you can. I'll help. Then I'll take David. Whatever he's done to me, I'll do that for him. Then you can run.'

'They took my gun. Before you came. It's over, Maire.'

'If you do nothing, you'll be damned.' She delivers the sentence like a black-capped judge.

'We're all damned, Maire. He's dead meat, it's about me now.' He winds the window back up and turns his head to stare blankly at the darkness in front. She lets go a sigh of contempt, kicks his door with her heel and stalks off.

They pull David to a corner of the field some thirty yards from the jeep. The rain is now a steady seeping blanket of mist casting a thin film of moisture on her face and clothes. She is enveloped in dampness, her short-heeled boots casting faint impressions on the grass as she catches up with them. They're beside a shallow grave, crudely dug out of the earth, but deep enough to house a man's body and cover it. Another contributor to this mournful ritual must have been sent ahead to prepare it. David was right: they were never going to spare him.

They prop him up on the edge of the grave, his broken legs dangling inside it. She drops to the ground beside him, putting both arms round him. He murmurs something, his voice muffled by the wounds to his mouth and teeth.

'What did you say, David?' she asks.

'I . . . need . . . absolution.' He forces out the words one by one.

'Do you want me to ask for a priest?' He nods his head and then looks hard into her eyes. 'Maire, it wasn't planned. I just met you.' A tear appears at the corner of an eye. 'And then they made me do it.'

'Do what, David?' she whispers.

'I didn't want it.' His voice ebbs and his head droops.

She stays silent for a few seconds, then says only, 'I loved you, David.' She sees more tears in his eyes.

'I need a priest,' he whispers. There is a pathetic urgency in his plea. 'And Maire . . . I want you to do it.'

She stands up and approaches the driver and the 'man'. 'You heard, him, he needs a priest. You're not going to deny him that, are you?'

'Give me your bottle of water,' the man says. They're the first words she hears him speak. A soft, gentle voice, the south of the island, she thinks, a voice to comply with. She hands him the bottle.

He kneels down beside David. 'Are you Catholic, David?' His eyes flickering open and shut, David nods his head once.

'David, are you sorrowful for your past sins? Do you trust in God and resign yourself to His will?'

'Yes.' It is barely more than a movement of his lips.

The 'man' drips water from the bottle onto David's forehead and slowly rubs it in circles. 'Through this holy unction may the Lord pardon you whatever sins or faults you have committed. May the Lord who frees you from sin save you and raise you up.'

David turns his head to him. 'Thank you.'

The 'man' stands up and the driver turns to Maire. 'Time for you to leave, Maire.'

'Just one more minute,' she says, 'no more, I promise.' She looks from one to the other.

'OK,' says the man. She whispers to him and he hands her an object.

'No tricks,' says the driver. 'I've got one pointing at him. And you.'

She crouches beside him again. 'I bought a ring for you, David,' she whispers. 'I'm gonna put it in your pocket.' He raises his eyes to her and manages to form the trace of a smile. She produces a box from the inside sleeve of her jacket, removes a gold ring, holds it close to his eyes, puts it back in the box and places it deep in his jacket pocket.

Then she puts her arms around him and holds him close for a few seconds. The muffled crack of a single shot echoes like a dog's bark. She stands and walks away. After she's gone some twenty yards or so, there's a second shot. She reaches the car, sits down on the passenger seat, and breathes slowly and deeply.

The sound of an engine firing startles her. She jerks upright and looks around to see the second car, Joseph Kennedy at the wheel, heading out of the field and back down the farm track.

The driver sprints towards her, shouting.

'What the fuck's happened?'

'I dunno.'

'Couldn't you see?'

'Do you think I was looking?'

'For fuck's sake!' He sounds desperate.

'You won't catch him now,' she says. 'Leave it.'

'They'll fucking have me for this.'

'It's too late. Just tell them a story.'

The driver scans the horizon, no more than black shapes and contours lost in the mist. It is silent, no car noise, no lights, no life.

He slowly makes his way back to the grave to throw the final sods of earth on another dead man.

The driver returns her to Dublin. It is a slow, silent journey. The end of life. Emptiness. Utter powerlessness. At the city outskirts, glimmerings of early-morning light peer through the window; she averts her face from them. As they near the house, she asks the driver one question.

'Why did you come for me?'

He doesn't look round. 'They told you. To get him to talk.' He pauses. 'Probably needed to check you were sound, too.' She understands the menace. It doesn't touch her. Nothing again will.

He drops her at the end of the street. 'You get out here.' She walks slowly at first, a dirge-like trudge, then lifts her head and picks up speed. She silently unlocks the front door and climbs the stairs, praying that Mrs Ryan won't emerge.

She looks out at the brightening sky, sits down at her desk, places a book on it and begins to read. She opens a notebook and writes in it. A tear falls onto the page. She wipes it away and arouses herself to anger and purpose.

CHAPTER 29

'That was it,' said Anne-Marie, 'the end of David Vallely. Or should I say Wallis?'

They had walked up and down the riverside as she told her story and were now at rest, leaning against railings, peering down at the moonlit water. 'It must have been horrible,' said Carne. 'Terrifying.' He felt his inability to find words of comfort. And an overwhelming relief that she had told him.

'It's a long time ago. When I think about it, it still feels like yesterday.'

'Have you ever told anyone else?' he asked.

'No. Until tonight, the only people who know are the ones who were there.' She paused. 'That's my shadow. The things I know and the things I don't know.'

'So, the here and now,' said Carne, wanting to re-engage her. 'You never saw Joseph since that night.'

'Yes. That was the last time I saw him. Alive, anyway. The next time it was his body hanging in the garage.'

'He must have reckoned he was next for a bullet in the head. Either British or IRA.'

'He certainly put saving his own skin first.'

Carne tried to picture the scene. 'David didn't make it any easier for him – "the one who got away". Why would he say that?'

'Because Joseph had survived, I guess,' she replied. 'You can't read more into it than that.'

'Maybe.' He stared down, avoiding her eyes, as if ashamed. 'There's one thing, Anne-Marie.'

'If you must.'

'At the very end, it wouldn't matter who actually fired the first shot into his head, would it?'

'What do you mean?'

'I mean he was going to die, anyway. So it would have been a merciful release for that shot to be fired before he was expecting it. When he felt comforted. And not alone.'

'Yes.' She was almost inaudible against the hum of traffic.

'If anyone in that position had the courage to do that,' he continued, I would support them.'

'Yes.'

'But say, just say, Joseph had seen something. Had known who fired the first shot. Who actually killed him. That might give him his threat.'

'That wasn't Joseph's threat,' she countered, then paused. He stayed silent, wondering if she would say more, rubbing his eyes with his hands and keeping the palms on his face, in some sort of supplication. No further words came – there was still something withheld. Perhaps it was merely embarrassing, or awkward. She would reach it in her own time.

'I have a nightmare,' she said. Her tone indicated a change of subject, a move away from Joseph. 'For a year or two afterwards, it recurred quite often. Then it stopped. Since that sighting of the man in the brimmer hat, and now the deaths, it's come back. It will go away in time. But, for now, it's haunting me.'

He felt she was trying to find a way of telling him something. Or, perhaps, of avoiding it. 'What happens?' he asked.

She picked her words carefully, but with a distancing abstraction, as if she were talking about a third person. 'I think what it's about is becoming him. Experiencing his journey, inhabiting his body. His fears, his knowledge about the end he's facing, a blankness in a far-off, isolated place. He doesn't understand why, or how, he's come to be in this place. Some accidental wrong turning has brought him there. It's a case, almost, of mistaken identity. It shouldn't be him, it should be someone else.' She stopped. 'Sorry, it sounds silly, doesn't it, far-fetched?'

'I don't think so,' he replied gently. 'The priest at the funeral – Father Simon – told me something curious. The last time they met, David said he was trapped in a conflict of duty and love. He wanted the priest to give him a resolution. The priest instructed him that it was a choice only he could make. So, perhaps, love had made him the wrong person in the wrong place.'

She slumped. The movement was almost imperceptible, but enough for him to feel it. 'But duty prevailed in the end. Is that what you're saying? Poor, bloody, trapped fool.'

'Not entirely,' said Carne. 'He told you he believed he'd made a deal over your brother. He must have thought that resolved the conflict. He could complete his duty and look forward. Until, at the end, he realized it was a contradiction which eliminated hope.' He fell silent, watching her trying to make sense of the conflicted young man.

'If only he could have spoken of it to me,' she said. 'Actually, now I think of it, he did say something – that he'd solved, what was it, two conflicting propositions? He was talking about his thesis but I guess that was just code. I still don't know if he ever wrote a word of it. The curious thing is that I'd have forgiven all

the deceits if he'd had the courage to say it openly. And I'd have
got him away.'

'Yes, and he'd have known that you'd try to stop him. To save
him from himself. To separate him from his bosses. Even if it
meant exposing him.'

'Possibly, yes.'

'So it took another form of courage to complete the task he'd
set himself.'

'Or others set for him.'

'If he agreed, it makes no difference.'

'If I think back over his behaviour in those final weeks,' she
reflected, 'he must have been torturing himself. He probably knew
it would destroy him. So why go on?'

'Because,' replied Carne, 'he must have still thought he was
doing good. That's what everyone who knew him says. He wanted
to do good.'

'To kill? Or, rather, murder?'

'There was a ceasefire four months later.'

'Ends can never justify means if it means murder,' she declared.
'Or disappearances. Or torture. Or all the other brutalities they've
invented. Isn't that what the history of the human race is about?
And why we have laws?'

'Men's hearts are complex,' he replied. They held each other's
eyes for a second. He had never seen such a beguiling combination
of mind and body.

'Anyway, back to the dream. It changes. He comes into view
and I'm now in my own body, controlled by the captors. Slowly
he turns, his bloodied, broken face looms into the frame. It's
cinematic. A Gothic horror movie. And a disembodied voice
shouts at me to shoot.'

'Do you?'

'I don't know because I wake up.' She raised a hand to his cheek and lips and to shush him. 'That's enough of an answer. And enough questions. You've done your job. You know everything.'

That he could not yet believe. But the weight of his suspicion, aroused by the fingerprint and DNA, had slipped away. 'The oddity is this,' he began. 'I, we, know what happened. But we still don't really know how, or why, it happened. Or what the plan was.'

'Of course we do,' she answered peremptorily. 'He was a British agent captured in a botched operation against the IRA and summarily executed. There's no mystery about that. They were a paranoid organization.' Her firmness and precision had returned; she sounded like a nurse with a confused patient unable to comprehend his treatment.

'It was a botched operation against a wing of the IRA the leadership would have been happily shot of.'

'You mean David was doing the IRA's dirty work for them so they should be nice to him? Forget it, a Brit spy's a Brit spy.'

'It's too neat,' he said.

'You're thinking too hard. Give it a rest. Wait for the daylight to clear your brain.'

Exhaustion, compounded by what felt to him a life-affirming release of tension, overwhelmed him. 'You're right. I need to go home. But trust me. It doesn't add up.'

CHAPTER 30

'There's no Black Brimmer pub either side of the border, boss,' said Billy.

'Could be a burnt-out wreck, Billy? Some crook punting for the insurance?'

'Got a Black Hat, though.'

'Fuck's sake, Billy!'

'Wonder why they changed the name.'

'Economizing on the sign paint, you daft bastard.'

As they turned off the M1 towards Banbridge and Newry, Carne was still reflecting on the conversation with Anne-Marie. Maybe the picture on the surface did indeed go no deeper. Brit operation screws up, Brit agent makes a mistake, falls into IRA bad hands, interrogated, beaten up, executed.

He was not a conspiracy theorist and tried persuading himself to accept it at face value. But Joseph Kennedy did not fit the picture. The one who got away. Maybe nothing wrong with that either. He had got himself on the wrong side of an internal feud, isolated, no choice but a lifetime of hiding. Then the girl he knew from childhood and once loved – with whom he's for ever locked by their shared knowledge of what happened on that terrible night in April 1994 – surfaces in a position of power. He makes contact, wants her help to return from the nether regions to the living world and, as a dying man, spend his last months at peace. Yet that made no sense. He must have wanted to use her for more than that. But what?

'What're you thinking, boss?' asked Billy, turning onto the minor road towards Crossmaglen and the border.

'Probabilities and improbabilities,' replied Carne.

'We could just stick to the facts.'

On their left rose the whale's back of Slieve Gullion, revealing its contours and the crag of its summit, now more like a dolphin's head. The cerulean sky was marked only by stray wisps of white.

'Fancy a climb?' suggested Carne.

'That's a shame, boss, I left my climbing boots behind,' replied Poots.

Carne looked at Poots's tough, black, waterproof shoes.

'Go on,' said Poots, 'I'll mind the car. Can't trust the natives round these parts.'

Carne strode off as grassland gave way to heather, leaving modest single-storey farmsteads as dots below in a patchwork of postage-stamp fields. A landscape returned to its insular peace without the soundtrack of Chinooks and Lynxes, jeeps and crackles of AK-47s. Little more than an hour later he was at the top, alongside the renowned south cairn leading to the passage tomb constructed by Bronze Age man some six thousand years before. At least they once buried the bodies here with proper ceremony.

On this untypical, luminous day he took in a 360-degree sweep – his beloved Mourne Mountains to the east and the sea beyond, the wilds of his adopted island stretching untamed to the west. Somewhere out there lay more bodies. Bodies that James Beresford Brooks said would never be found.

Images of the two that had turned up floated in front of him: the bones and tattered clothing of David Wallis and the sunken, diseased flesh of Joseph Kennedy lying on the mortuary table. Some weird connection made Carne think of the Japanese soldier who had hidden for three decades in the jungle after the war's end, refusing to surrender. He had given up only when his elderly, frail commanding officer had flown the thousands of miles to Luzon to order him.

Was Joseph Kennedy operating solo, or did he have a commander too? Why did he have to be silenced? Assuming he was. And by whom?

Poots was waiting for him. 'Two hours, twenty-one minutes and ten seconds. I was phoning the undertaker.'

'I was delayed thinking of the dead.'

'How're they doing?'

'Better informed than the living.'

The Black Hat lay on the main N53 road leading west out of the border town of Dundalk, the IRA's grim playpen. It was a long, low, white building designed for the Irish peasantry before the advent of McDonald's.

If the Black Brimmer had once been like that, the makeover to the Black Hat was transformative. Neat wooden wagon wheels lined the bottom of the walls by the pavement and coloured lights were ranged beneath the guttering. The paintwork was as smooth and unflawed as a rich man's billiards table. Above the front door, a sign announced the landlords as, simply, Henry and Carl. Inside, along with the mandatory stouts and bitters, were well-stocked wine chillers and a menu, including a dish for vegans.

The barman was in his mid-forties, sporting an infant paunch beneath his pink-striped T-shirt, pale washed jeans, greying hair with a blond wave lining the middle, and a chunky gold ring with inlaid onyx on his right forefinger.

'If that's Carl or Henry, I wonder what Henry or Carl's like,' whispered Poots.

'Don't worry, Billy, they won't fancy you,' Carne reassured him. 'Just remember it's legal now. Both sides of the border.'

'How d'you know I wasn't fancying him?' whispered Poots.

'You're surreal.'

They reached the bar. 'What can I get you two gentlemen?' asked Carl or Henry. The accent was Dublin soft, a touch of the lyrical.

'I'll take a glass of that nice-looking Viognier,' said Poots. Is he winding me up, or them? Carne asked himself.

'An excellent choice, sir. And your young friend?' Carne reddened as Poots ordered him a Bacardi and Coke.

'Place has changed a lot since I was last here,' said Poots.

'Terrible state when Henry and I took it on,' replied Carl, as he had now to be. 'Windows rotted, render blown inside and out, roof letting the heavens in, the clients had fled. We must have been mad.'

'How long ago was that?' asked Carne.

'Nearly ten years now.' He beamed with pleasure at the shining wooden tables and antique prints on the walls. 'We're finally getting there.'

'Any customers from the old days?' wondered Poots idly.

Carl pointed to an old man in a cap, propped at the end of the bar over a scarcely sipped pint of Guinness.

'Larry,' cried Carl, 'these two gentlemen are interested in the old days here. Can I introduce them to you?'

The old man raised his head and exposed a mottled, red face and scrawny chin. Unkempt grey hair hung over his collar. 'You do that, Carl, so I can tell them to fuck the fuck off.'

Carl beamed at them. 'You're in, gentlemen. It's not many who get as friendly a welcome as that.'

Poots walked over to him. 'Do you remember the night they had the ruckus, Larry? When the Brits took McCartney. And the lads took the Brit.'

'What the fuck's that to do with you?'

'My mate here' – he nodded to Carne – 'he was a Brit soldier. Friend of the boy they took. Close friend. You understand what I mean? He'd like to find out what happened to him.'

Thank you, Billy, thought Carne. It might be a gay pub now but it was not a condition of entry.

The old man eased himself up from his seat. At full stretch, he was well over six foot, looking down at Carne through his rheumy eyes.

'By Jesus,' he rasped, 'you were Brit military.'

'Only a squaddie,' replied Carne. He had no choice but to play along with whatever game Billy was setting up. 'Just the poor bloody infantry.'

'By Jesus,' the old man repeated. 'Fucking exploited like the rest of us. By Jesus.' He offered his hand. Carne took it and shook it. Poots cast him a smug glance. 'Don't mind you being one of them,' confided the old man in hushed tones. 'I've known plenty.' He took slow steps to the door, opened it and waved them to follow.

The car park was a large, smoothly tarmacked square. 'Used to be the heads there.' He pointed to the far corner of the rectangle. 'No one used them, smelt like skunk piss.' Carne and Poots exchanged quizzical looks. 'Heads' was a nautical expression for toilets. 'I was on leave. By Jesus, it happened in a flash.'

'What exactly happened?' Carne asked gently.

'Went by like a bolt of lightning and clap of thunder. Group of the boys were here. Celebrating something. Can't remember.'

'A birthday?' suggested Poots.

'Aye, a birthday, don't know who. The boys leave. There's two big'uns giving the orders. The others hangers-on. I'm sort of watching. Bit cut. The two big'uns are talking, unfriendly, gesticulating. One breaks off, crosses the road. Takes a leak. Turns back – a fucking great thing speeds in, lights flashing, horn blaring. They all freeze. They snatch the big'un from the lay-by. They shoot off. A thousand miles an hour. By Jesus, that motor. Never forget that.' The old man's face shone, brought to unexpected vividness by the memory. 'By Jesus, I'll never forget that,' he repeated. He stared down the road in silence, immersed in dreams of exhaust fumes and burning rubber.

Carne hesitated to break into the reverie. 'And after the jeep sped off . . .?'

'Eh?' His eyes had retreated deep inside their sockets.

'What happened then, Larry?' Poots cut in.

'By Jesus, it was bedlam, it was. Guns firing, screams, wails. "They got Martin," the other big'un says. And then a bloke's scarpering down the road. The boys chase him. They're firing. Bring him down. The big'un says, "Any of youse not involved get back inside the pub. That's an order." So we go back. Next I hear is cars taking off.'

He looked up at his two interrogators, his voice exhausted. 'That's it. Now you buy me a fucking drink.'

As they followed the old man back inside the pub, Carne turned to Poots.

'Get any of that, Billy?'

'Don't worry, boss, we'll deconstruct in a minute.'

The old man settled back on his perch, Poots bought drinks and left a hefty tip at the bar. 'Just going to have a mooch around, Carl. OK with you?'

'Of course. And don't you worry,' he said with a stage wink, 'mum's the word.'

Poots paced the car park, pub frontage, road width, lay-by length and width, the bush and field behind it, and called over measurements for a diagram Carne was drawing.

'OK,' said Carne, 'the old man says a large, fast vehicle – some kind of SUV presumably – speeds in, stops and snatches Martin McCartney as he's crossing back over the road after taking a piss. Assuming it's a stake-out, that implies very precise timing. So the spotter, who is Wallis, must be right by the action – there's just about enough cover in the hedgerows. And the snatch car must be close to achieve that precision.'

'Are you assuming the target was McCartney?' asked Poots. 'Or didn't they care whether they got him or Kennedy?'

'I'm not assuming anything,' replied Carne. 'Maybe they'd have got both if they could.'

'When you were up your hill with the buried bodies, I just happened to find a nice wee pub in a village along the road.' Poots had slipped into his storytelling mode. Carne told himself to be patient. 'I become a historian doing some genealogy and know there's a branch of the Kennedy family that comes from round there. Unlike these fruits, the landlord is local, been raised there, came back when the violence was dying down. So I find myself having a chat with him. You know, the weather, crops, shite Irish beer. Then I say, "Isn't this where that big lad, Joseph Kennedy, came from?" Christ, he fair leaps on me. "Best not mention that name round here," he says. "Oh," I say, all innocence, "why's that?" He leans over and whispers in my ear, "They say he was a traitor. Disappeared. Never came back. Family disowned him, excommunicated him. Give you some advice: don't mention that name in these parts."'

'What are you implying, Billy?'

'You and I know the problem, boss. You can never trust stories and rumours. And Kennedy was on the losing side of the argument.'

'Sure. Doesn't stop us shuffling the pieces of the jigsaw.' Carne looked up and down the road. It had been resurfaced and its markings repainted since 1994 but there was no reason for its course and foliage to have changed. They drove up and down it, a mile in each direction. There were enough verges, a couple of field entrances and, in one direction, a lay-by obscured from the Black Hat car park. Plenty of cover for the snatch car to wait out of sight. They stopped at the lay-by.

'So . . .' began Carne.

'So,' continued Poots, 'they're waiting within five hundred yards at the closest, a mile at the outside.'

Carne interrupted. 'And make it to the car park inside twenty seconds if the vehicle's souped up.'

'OK,' agreed Poots, 'we'll work on twenty seconds.'

They returned to the Black Hat and positioned themselves at the lounge bar exit.

'Right,' said Poots. 'The party's leaving the pub. Let's say six or eight of them, Kennedy and McCartney in front. The two big'uns as the old man calls them.'

'Assume they've had a few . . .' said Carne.

'But they're still being careful . . .'

'Unless tonight their guard is down.'

'McCartney says he wants a piss . . .'

'Is that the cause for the argument? Or discussion? Or whatever it is?'

'Too petty. Unless McCartney's so paranoid he wants someone to go over and stand over him while he does his business.'

'Unlikely. Maybe they've been arguing in the pub.'

'Doesn't matter. We'll never know that.'

The two men walked halfway to the middle of the car park.

'Imagine their car's here,' said Carne. 'Could be closer to the road, could be further.'

'Best we can do,' agreed Poots again.

'You play Kennedy and wait here. I'll be McCartney and cross the road for the piss.' Carne waited for traffic to pass and crossed. At that point the hedgerow was set back a good fifteen yards. He walked towards it, his back to Poots, then turned round.

'Most blokes,' he shouted across the road, 'would want to piss nearer the hedgerow than the road. We'll assume that.' He turned back to the hedgerow and, injecting realism, had a piss.

'Count seconds from now!' he yelled. Carne tidied himself below, did up his zip, turned round and, with no traffic to interrupt him, crossed the road into the car park, rejoining Poots.

'About fifteen seconds, boss.'

'That's tight, bloody tight.'

'So, to get the timing right, the spotter's got to be close enough to see precisely when he's ending the piss.'

'It's dark. He can be hiding in the hedgerow. From there his eyeline takes in the pub, the car park, and the toilets beyond.'

'He wouldn't have known about McCartney, coming over to piss.'

'Christ, if he's in the hedgerow, he must be shitting himself.'

'But if Wallis's the spotter . . .'

'Yes . . .'

'And he's done this before . . .'

'So not shitting himself.'

'OK, but what he, and they, are expecting is the party to walk out of the door into the car park, head towards the car, or cars, and McCartney and Kennedy to get into one of them accompanied by a couple of the hangers-on.'

'And then what?'

'Intercept and seize the two of them presumably.'

'Or track their car, maybe?'

'Christ, they were taking some bloody risk, weren't they?' exclaimed Poots.

'Maybe they had no choice,' replied Carne. 'And were up against a deadline.' He took in the 360-degree view from where they stood. 'But the end result is that Wallis's friends in the snatch car make off with McCartney and Wallis is hunted down and taken by Kennedy and friends.'

'Wallis's compatriots seem to make no attempt to rescue him.'

''Cos they're confident he'll get away.'

'He's always done it before.'

'Surely they'd try to pick him up?'

'Maybe they did try. But too much was blowing off. Remember from what Kennedy later tells the girl – Maire – he and McCartney are on the watch-out by now.'

'Which the Brits know.'

'And they know Wallis is a survivor.'

'Not on this night,' Poots concluded grimly.

Carne thought of the skeleton in the field. The clear blue of midday was giving way to dark, rain-filled, late afternoon clouds. 'We've seen enough, let's go.'

A few miles along the main road, they turned right at a cross-roads north of the border town of Crossmaglen. Set back from the road was a memorial to the nine IRA hunger strikers who died in 1982. Nine neat crosses set into polished marble and lovingly precise engravings of their names. It could have been a roll of honour recalling young men anywhere in the world – Thiepval, Whitehall, Mons, the D-Day beaches – fighting for that they saw as their country and a just cause. Yet, to most of the world beyond, these men were convicted terrorists from the dregs of history. Carne was unexpectedly moved at the list of names. Were they ghosts from a dead conflict or lying in wait for its resurgence? Was that what Joseph Kennedy was all about?

The hills that had been so piercingly clear earlier in the day were now swathed in a coat of drizzle. Clarity giving way to confusion.

'If McCartney was the key target, it fell neatly for them,' said Carne. Poots, driving, said nothing. 'Didn't it? The geography, I mean. The layout,' persisted Carne.

'Aye, boss.'

'You wonder what kind of bedlam there'd have been if they'd had to carve through the group to snatch both the big men.'

'Aye,' repeated Poots.

'Gone dumb, Billy?'

'Aye.' Poots was peering through the windscreen wipers and gloom with studied deliberation. An excuse not to talk.

'Though I suppose,' continued Carne, 'they didn't have to go through with it that night. Maybe it wasn't even the first attempt. Just waiting for the right chance. Whenever it came.'

'Aye, you could be right, boss.' Carne gave up. No chance of extracting any blood from the stone beside him.

'Boss,' said Poots.

'You're alive. Thought there was a robot at the wheel.'

'Something's been gnawing at me. It's a bit awkward, like . . .'

'Don't hold back, Billy.'

'Aye, maybe . . .'

'Don't bottle it in.'

Poots pulled in at the side of the road and cut the engine.

'I'm waiting,' said Carne.

'Aye, boss.' He paused. 'It's the girl. Maire. Anne-Marie. Whatever she calls herself.'

'What about her?'

'You like her, boss. Grown fond of her.'

'That's irrelevant.' More silence. 'Say what you mean.'

'It's just that all this has come from her. Hasn't it?'

'What do you mean, Billy?'

'The account of the night we've been working from comes from her. From what she says Kennedy told her happened after they'd fetched her.'

'Yes, that's right. Partly. But we have facts. Wallis was captured, his body found over two decades later. Kennedy disappeared, body found hanged in the here and now. McCartney disappeared, body never found. Same goes for O'Donnell and Black. And we've got the old man's recollection of the ruckus in the car park.'

'That could be folk memory,' said Billy. 'We're in Ireland. Land of legends.'

'Yes. But it's consistent.' This time, Carne hesitated. 'You'd best tell me what you're thinking.'

'It's just that we, you, are taking the girl on trust.'

'You think she's leading me on, is that it? You reckon I've gone soft on her.'

'It's what I said earlier. When I was playing us as the poofters. Appearances. You can't always trust them.'

'I'll bear what you say in mind, Billy,' said Carne coolly.

Just short of Newry, they turned onto the A1 to Belfast. Not a word had been spoken, a rare unease tugging at them. Carne reached for the radio and tuned to Radio 3.

'Do you mind, Billy?' he asked.

'Don't imagine you'd like marching bands, would you, boss?' replied Poots. Carne grinned at him and the tension vanished with the music.

An hour later, they drew into the dull, flat buildings of Castlereagh police station. It was early evening; Poots said that, for once, home and wife beckoned more attractively than office and colleagues. Carne headed into CID headquarters alone. The desk officer intercepted him.

'The boss wants to see you, sir.'

'What about?'

'Didn't say. Only that it was urgent and I should catch you as soon as you were back.'

The boss was Assistant Chief Constable Raymond Walsh – a local man, Catholic, Queen's University first, younger, and in the fast lane. Carne did not actively dislike him, if only because the surface was too smooth to get your teeth into. He knocked on the door.

'Come in.' The voice was soft, the appearance formal. Dust, mark, and dandruff-free uniform – the last an exception within the force – hair trimmed and parted, glasses designer and narrow-framed.

'You asked to see me, sir,' said Carne.

'Yes, thanks for looking in, Jon, I know how busy you are,' replied Walsh. The courtesy was a mask.

'So . . .'

'I'll come to the point. There's been some murmuring . . .'

'Murmuring?'

'Aye, whispers from across the water. Unhappiness with your interventions in the Joseph Kennedy case. It's the Met's case, not ours.'

Carne bristled. 'He's relevant to the Wallis case. Maybe to three other disappearances, too.'

'That was a long time ago.'

'Murder is murder, sir.'

'You're never going to convict anyone.'

'I have witnesses.'

'Well, that may be an issue too, Chief Inspector.' The switch from first name to rank was a signal. They had moved onto formal territory. 'I understand that you have been – how shall I put this? – cultivating one particular witness. Now a prominent person.'

'You mean Ms Gallagher. She is relevant to the inquiry.'

'I'm not doubting that. But this cultivation has been irregular. Meetings at her flat. Chats over glasses of wine. Assurances that may be inappropriate from a professional detective.' Carne felt a dryness in his throat and sweat in his palms. The strip light on the ceiling came in and out of focus, casting an unsteady glow. He tried to calm himself and understand.

'They've been watching, haven't they?' he said. The dryness made him hoarse. 'Listening, too.'

With a ratcheting of dread and his heartbeat pummelling the wall of his chest, the scales fell from his eyes. If they knew the details of his conversations with Anne-Marie, they must know, and have been monitoring, recording, perhaps even filming, everything. Carne chided himself for his innocence and felt an instant shame at his country for its loss.

'I've no idea what folk have been up to,' Walsh replied. 'All I know is that such a message has been conveyed to the Chief Constable and he has delegated the matter to me to discuss with you.'

'Who conveyed the message, sir?' asked Carne.

'I don't know, Jon.' He had returned to informality. 'And, if I did, I'd have been under instructions not to tell you.'

Carne was working it out. 'It tells us they're worried, doesn't it? That they, whoever they may be, have got something to hide?'

'You don't want to go there,' warned Walsh. His tone was friendly but Carne knew it was an instruction, not a suggestion. 'Leave Kennedy to London. And write me a report on the results of your investigation into Wallis. I'll be happy to forward it to the Director of Public Prosecutions here.'

'My investigation is incomplete. You're guaranteeing that nothing will happen. It will just go away.'

'No, it will go where the evidence leads it.'

Carne needed an idea, an inspiration. 'Are you intending to bring disciplinary charges against me, sir?'

'No. As you've indicated, there's no lawfully obtained evidence to substantiate any.'

'In that case,' Carne continued, 'I'd like permission to take five days' leave. With immediate effect.' Through the narrow spectacle frames he could see Walsh's eyes boring in on him, penetrating and inscrutable. The eyes looked down at a piece of paper on the desk, then up again.

'Permission granted, Chief Inspector. That will be all.' There was no smile, no movement of facial muscle, no hint of connivance or collaboration. But the cold man had shown a beating heart within. Carne rose, surprised into silent retreat.

He picked up his car and drove east to Newtonards to Billy Poots's home, buying two cheap and simple pay-as-you-go mobile phones on the way. He tried to keep an eye out for followers but felt his lack of expertise. During his training, they had taught him how to spot a tail, and how to lose it. But that was nearly twenty-five years ago, a quarter of a century; he had never needed to use the knowledge. He had been a pursuer at times. This was the first time he was the pursued.

Outside the Pootses' pleasant, seventies, detached box on a quiet middle-class estate, the hooting of his horn sounded peremptory and displaced. He saw Billy push aside a net curtain and gestured him to come out. He quickly recounted the details of his conversation with Walsh and his forthcoming absence on leave.

'You take care, boss,' said Poots. 'If they, whoever they are, killed Kennedy—'

'I know,' Carne interrupted.

'You could just walk away.'

'I walked away once before. I won't do it again.'

Poots fell briefly silent – there was no point in arguing the different circumstances. 'It was a long time ago, boss. This is about her, too, isn't it?'

'That's enough, Billy. A couple of things you can do for me.'

'Yes, boss.'

'First, see if there's any immediate Kennedy family in Belfast. Parents, sisters, brothers. If there are, talk to them. Second, check out the grave of the McCartney parents. Have a peek at what's written on the gravestone. Third, ask your Special Branch mates for the informer files of the early 1990s.'

'You don't ask much, do you?' said Poots.

'I try not to,' replied Carne. 'Good hunting, Billy.' Carne gave him one of the two new mobiles and the number of the other one that he had kept. He suddenly wondered whether he would ever see his sergeant again and told himself not to be so melodramatic.

Back in the city, he stopped to get cash, then, avoiding the Internet, at a travel agent, where he used some of the cash to book a one-way ticket to London on the first available flight in the morning. He returned to his flat, packed two changes of clothes and a washbag into the largest case he could take as hand luggage. He placed his passport into his wallet. He checked that his debit and credit cards and photo-ID driving licence were all there, hoping he could find a way to use none of them. He remembered his paper driving licence, fetched it from a filing cabinet and slid it inside the sleeve containing his boarding pass. He cancelled the milk delivery. He inspected his wallet again and removed his police ID. He opened up his smart phone and extracted the SIM card. He looked at the phone itself. Instead of returning it to his jacket pocket, he put it on his bedside table. He went to the bathroom and switched the hot-water timer to permanent off. He opened the bedside table drawer and looked at his service revolver. He decided to leave it and take only his camera for a weapon.

And then he lay down on his bed, stared at the ceiling, and thought. He went over his diagram of the geography of the Black Hat, car park, main road, hedgerow, lay-by, corners, other concealed nooks. He calculated walking speeds, running speeds, car speeds, distances and timings. Five hundred yards, given nought-to-sixty acceleration in five seconds and time to screech to a halt. Five seconds to sixty, five seconds at sixty, five seconds down to zero. Fifteen seconds at, say, an average forty miles per hour. Distance two hundred and ninety-three yards. It did not add up. Increase the average speed and shrink the seconds to stop. It still fell short of the five hundred yards he and Poots were working on. Unless they had missed a hiding place. He looked again at the curvature of the road and was sure they had not.

There was something missing. Something he was not factoring in. As the second hand of his bedside clock ticked round and round, and the noises of the night began to subside, he thought on and on about what it could be.

As the morning light crept through gaps in the curtains, he at last reached a destination of sorts. An understanding of the missing factor. And how intricately the operation must have been planned. Above all, if he was right, the amoral genius of the mind that had planned it.

He closed the curtains fully, undressed, and lay down beneath the sheets. He looked at the framed photograph of Alice on the table beside him, turned his eyes away and switched off the light. He could allow himself three hours' sleep before leaving for the airport.

CHAPTER 31

Post-election, Wednesday, 24 May

The early morning airport departure concourse seemed to him teeming with potential tails. No one stood out, though they could have been anyone. The baggage checkers were no less petty than usual, the stewardesses no more friendly, the CCTV cameras pointed in the same directions. He reminded himself not to look at them.

During the flight, he considered the potential history and extent of their surveillance. He assumed, because of Anne-Marie's background, that it had begun with her and spread to include him. They must have had voice-activated recording technology in her apartment, maybe pinhole cameras, too. That was not an overnight job.

How long had they been monitoring her? From when the local party chose her as their candidate? Or when she began to make a mark as a lawyer?

Or from further back? From the night of Wallis's disappearance? The day he first laid eyes on her? The moment they alighted on her as a mark? Perhaps even before that? He imagined how they might see her: first the sister of a top terrorist, then the lover of a British spy who disappeared, finally a suddenly and unexpectedly promoted minister. A woman who might hold secrets, perhaps dangerous ones. A woman who could not be allowed ever to roam free.

He imagined them observing her discovery of Joseph Kennedy's body, her identification of it in the mortuary, and their attention switching to him. Then his meeting with Brooks – yes, he must have known precisely when to expect him. And perhaps, like David Wallis two decades earlier, they had been hiding in those hedgerows opposite the Black Hat watching him and Poots measuring up the distances.

As to who 'they' were, the whole nature of the Wallis and Kennedy cases, not to mention the involvement of Brooks, allowed no alternative. This was not police, or even Special Branch: this was a fully fledged state intelligence operation. It would have begun with MI6 and Brooks in Dublin but, as a domestic operation, must now be MI5. Given their rivalry, he asked himself whether they were in it together. Or was Five clearing up the mess of a rogue element in Six?

A more troubling question reared up at him. If Anne-Marie had spent most of her adult life under their gaze, did they have reason? That way, he had told himself so often, lay madness. She had asked him to trust her; he had agreed. There was no turning back.

He jolted his head to restore sense to a brain in unwelcome overdrive. That sense led him back to one overriding question. If they had got away with removing Kennedy, why were they still so worried? And so active? Was it something that he had discovered? Or that she might do?

He took the train from Gatwick to Victoria, bought a third phone and new SIM card, and checked into an anonymous guesthouse in the Pimlico grid south of the station. The late morning was bringing premature summer heat. He changed into jeans and a T-shirt, put on dark glasses and a blue-and-white cap, and stepped onto Belgrave Avenue. A tourist out to see the sights. To complete the outfit, he walked north to Victoria Street and bought a compact camera to hang round his neck and a selfie stick.

He had no detailed knowledge of her movements but she had mentioned that she usually escaped the office at lunchtime and went to relax among the ducks and trees of St James's Park. He was too early and decided to kill time at Westminster Abbey. Entrance charge £18. He bridled at their cheek and settled for a free wander around College Garden, stretching the time by calculating the angles of the sunlight streaming through the tall plane trees.

A few minutes before one. The Abbey exit led him back into Victoria Street, then first left into Great Smith Street, and across the lights into Marsham Street. Ahead on the right lay the exterior rectangle of the Home Office, its expanses of glass and inner atria. His memory from his time in London was of the three dull concrete towers of the Department of the Environment. He missed their ugliness. It suited the world they stood for.

He reckoned he could afford to stroll once southwards down Marsham Street and once back northwards. Anything beyond could arouse the security cameras' interest. He did the walks. No sighting. At the crossroads with Great Peter Street, the lights were green for east–west traffic. The forced stop allowed him to look back and around. There she was, just joining the pavement from the concourse outside the main Home Office entrance. Beside her was a woman. All he could see in the time he allowed himself to look was that she was young and blonde, and they were smiling and relaxed. An assistant perhaps. Certainly someone junior. He felt relief.

He crossed the road into a Pret a Manger and queued to order a coffee. As he reached the front, they came past, heading north. He smiled ruefully at the assistant, explained that he had forgotten his wallet, exited and followed them. They continued up Great Smith Street and crossed into Storey's Gate. Now confident that they were heading for the park, he could hang back.

A few minutes later, he was within yards of them as they stood at the railings by the lake. He ranged alongside her. Wearing his best tourist smile, he said 'Excuse me, madam, don't I recognize you?' and gave her a tap on the foot. She looked around at him, alarm turning to puzzlement to a flash of recognition. 'Sorry, I think it must be from the television,' he continued. As he said it, he placed a note in her pocket.

As he was leaving, he heard the young assistant say, 'An admirer, Minister?' To which she had replied, 'Rather nice-looking wasn't he?' For the first time in what seemed an age, he felt a spring in his step.

Back in her office, the Minister read the note. 'Meet me 9 p.m. riverside. Same bench.' She looked up to catch Nikki grinning at her.

Carne killed the afternoon seeing a film. He needed to give Poots at least a day to bring some answers. In the early evening back at the guesthouse, he asked to use the house phone to hold off using his new mobile for as long as possible. Despite the extortionate rate that was demanded, he called the mobile he had given him.

'Yes.' Poots's voice.

'Keep it brief, Billy,' he said.

'OK, boss. Number one, no immediate Kennedy family in the neighbourhood. If any are still around, they must have left, for whatever reason. Point two, it reads "In memory of Stephen and Rosa McCartney, who never recovered from losing their beloved children, Martin and Maire".' Carne allowed himself a subdued whistle. 'Point three,' continued Poots, 'yes, there was someone big, 1991–1994. Codename "Salmon". No clue to name, sex, age or which side. Identity kept as tight as a Fenian's arse.'

'You're a genius, Billy,' said Carne, 'Thanks. See you in paradise.' He put down the phone.

There were two and a half further hours to kill. He spent much of it thinking about the ways a parent could lose a child. Death and disappearance. But also separation, for whatever reason. Geography, distance, no money to travel, claustrophobia, escape, going on the run. Saddest of all, the deadening of any need or wish to see each other, whether from apathy or sheer dislike, even hate.

He could not imagine Anne-Marie not loving her family. But as a hater of place, of environment, of a society's straitjacket, yes, that he could see. He could also imagine the parents not daring to breach her reinvented life. Always being guided, or perhaps misguided, by 'what's for the best'.

And now there was 'Salmon', a high-up informer deep within the IRA; but no indication of which wing of that organization he, or she – he must not forget that possibility – inhabited.

At precisely 9 p.m. Anne-Marie and he converged on each other at the park bench. He had added a tracksuit top to the tourist outfit; she arrived on her bike in Lycra pants and a loose sports shirt. As she dismounted and he saw the contours of her body, he felt goose pimples.

'So . . .' she said.

'Let's go by the river, see the sundown,' he replied, raising a
finger to his lips. She followed him and they looked down at the
gleams in the water. Her face shone in the sun's reflection. She
raised her head and turned to him.

'Your flat is bugged and probably being watched, inside and
out, by secret cameras.' He was talking down into the water
and she strained to hear him. 'It's likely we're being watched
now but if we speak to the river, it will be hard, even for the
long distance directional microphones they have, to get what
we're saying.'

'I see,' she said. Her poise, as always, seemed remarkable to him.

'I think I understand what happened,' he continued. 'I can't
prove it. My only remaining move is to put it to the man you
know as Jimmy and see how he reacts. He may not agree to see
me again. But he won't refuse to see you. He can't. And there's no
point in me trying to surprise him, they're watching everything.
So I'm here to ask you to contact him – I have the numbers – and
arrange a meeting at his home in Wiltshire. I'll accompany you. I
want you to be my accomplice, and my protection. Not to mention
my key witness. I'm asking a lot.'

She said nothing, eyes fixed rigidly ahead. He turned to her,
breaking his rule. 'I know you have to trust me.' He looked back
at the water.

'OK.'

'Thank you.' He handed her a piece of paper. 'This contains
his full name, address and contact numbers. Below those is where
I'm staying. You can have a message delivered to me there when
the meeting's fixed.'

A realization suddenly dawned on her. 'Tomorrow's the state
opening.'

'It can wait a day.'

'No, I want to do it now. Give them as little time as possible. I'll attend the formal ceremony and the speech, then I'll leave. Sod them. You said it was a couple of hours so I'll try to set it up for 5 p.m.'

'OK.' He paused. 'If you're sure. The note also contains a different mobile number for emergency use only. All your present phones are bugged. Home, office, private mobile, office mobile.' He cast a 360-degree look around and slipped the third mobile he had bought into her hand. 'If you need to, use this to ring the number on the note.'

'I understand.'

'We should travel separately.' She realized it was an instruction.

'My driver will take me.'

'That's all right. In one sense he's a protection for you. But he'll also be working for them. By which I mean the Security Service.'

'I don't think so,' she said. It was her first note of resistance.

'Yes,' he insisted. 'Trust me.'

'Jesus.' He sensed her shock. 'Five or Six?'

'Five will be running it now. David was working for Six. One final thing. Don't be surprised or frightened by anything I say. I'm testing them, not you. But rebut me where you should. And as fiercely as you want. They'll be recording it, of course. Probably filming it too.'

'OK.' She raised a hand to his shoulder and gripped it fiercely. 'I'll be OK.'

'Good. I'll wait for your message.' They looked hard at each other and he felt an overwhelming desire to hold her by the head and hair. Even before he discarded the thought, she had removed her hand and turned on her heel.

Thursday, 25 May

He rose early and hired a car at Victoria Station. He drove west without waiting for confirmation of the meeting from Anne-Marie. There was nothing else to hang around for, anyway. And, once the meeting was arranged, they would waste no time making their preparations.

He reached Devizes by 9.30 a.m. Still in his tourist gear, he visited the grounds of the local castle, bought a green jacket and cap from the one men's clothes shop in the high street, then awarded himself a coffee break at the seventeenth-century coaching inn bordering the market square. Inside was a picture of rural innocence: ruddy-faced men, broad-shouldered women with tinted grey hair, dogs lying comfortably at their feet. His phone beeped. The message was numerical only: '17.30'. It came from the mobile he had given her.

That left six and a half hours. He gulped the coffee, burning his throat, and drove the few miles down a minor road to the Old Witham turning. The lane into the hamlet was a cul-de-sac. On the other side of the road a wheat field rose gradually to a brow affording a view of the junction and the lane's comings and goings.

He could find cover for himself, less easily for the car. He remembered a pub a mile or so back and dumped it there. He slung the new jacket over his shoulder, gathered the camera and long lens, put on the cap and cut up by hedgerows to reach the brow. And then he waited. Was 'Uncle' Jimmy Brooks going to play it solo – or would he invite some friends?

The first movement came within an hour, Brooks alone in his car turning from the lane into the road. He snapped him. The early afternoon dragged on. Around 3 p.m. a grey SUV turned into the lane. There were two men in it: a surveillance and recording team, perhaps. A minute or two later, Brooks reappeared. Carne was checking his photographs of the SUV and heard the car only just before it turned. He thought he saw a second man in the passenger seat, but missed the shot.

At 4.30 p.m. a black BMW arrived, a man and woman in the front seat. He shot them. The photograph, marginally out of focus, revealed little more than that they were neither very old nor very young. It at least confirmed that a significant welcome party was gathering. He took the digital card out of the camera, transferred the photographs to his phone and emailed them to Poots. It hardly mattered now if they had traced his new phone and therefore him.

With the meeting set for 5.30 p.m., he could not risk waiting longer and walked back to the car. A note had been taped to his windscreen. 'This is not a free car park. Please pay inside.' At least there was no clamp. He thought about it, decided to go in to the pub, apologize and offer payment. He was greeted with unsuspected warmth – perhaps it hardly ever happened – and promised he would be back for a drink later. He hoped they would not mind if he sat in the car for a few minutes as he was visiting his mother but was a little early. They did not.

Travelling from London, the Minister's driver would approach Old Witham only from this one direction. At 5.27 p.m. the ministerial car passed the pub car park. He felt his heart ticking and an overwhelming need to stay close and follow her. Instead, he waited and counted down eight further minutes.

As Hinds slowed to turn into Old Witham lane, Anne-Marie turned to peer through the back window, assuming Carne would be close behind. The two cars following carried straight on – she was alone. Hinds checked the sat nav, picked up speed and drove on around the side of the churchyard and into the car park and front entrance of Rectory Garden Cottage.

Brooks was waiting on the threshold. 'Welcome, Minister.' He was at his most oily and stretched out a hand. She shook it as briefly as courtesy allowed.

'I had hoped our meetings were long over,' she said.

'Yes,' he replied. 'But at least this gives me the chance to congratulate you. I always understood what a talented woman you were. And are.'

Brooks led Anne-Marie past the kitchen, where his wife was chopping vegetables, resisting any temptation to look up and into the drawing room. There a man and woman sat, legs stiffly together, on a sofa. They rose as one.

'Hello, Jemima,' said Anne-Marie. If she felt any surprise, it was well concealed.

'Hello, Minister.' Jemima Sheffield failed to hide her discomfort. There was no handshake.

'And your friend, Jemima?' continued Anne-Marie.

The man stepped forward and thrust out his hand. He was early fifties, grey suit, light-blue shirt, subtly striped beige tie. 'The name is Donald, Minister.'

'Ah, Mr Duck, no doubt,' said Anne-Marie. Jemima Sheffield winced.

Brooks rubbed his hands, the whiskery grin in place. 'Splendid. Teas? Coffees? Dorothy!' he yelled towards the kitchen.

A silver trolley, adorned and gently rattling with china cups, saucers and teapot, was wheeled in. Almost reverentially in the embarrassed hush, Brooks poured the tea, offering milks and lumps of sugar, which were politely declined with small asides

about watching waistlines. Anne-Marie felt she might be in a
genteel murder thriller denouement.

The ring of a doorbell pierced the silence. Anne-Marie detected
tiny frowns of anxiety flashing between Brooks and Donald.
Reality returned and relief swept through her.

CHAPTER 32

Carne had left his car a hundred yards down the lane and walked into the Rectory Garden Cottage drive. Anne-Marie's car was pulled up alongside the black BMW – Brooks's car, presumably, was in the garage. There was no sign of the SUV. It confirmed its occupants were coverts. If they had arrived, installed their equipment, and left, he had missed them turning onto the road. Either the SUV was tucked away somewhere or there was an exit through farm tracks at the end of the cul-de-sac.

He crept towards Anne-Marie's car from an angle to avoid being seen in the rear mirror. Over the final yards, he quickened and snatched open the driver's door. Hinds looked up from his newspaper with a start. 'Who the hell—' he began.

'DCI Carne. Keep your voice down, please.' Carne scanned the interior. 'You know who I am. And the reason for my presence.'

'Yes, sir. And, no, I had not been informed of your attendance.'

Carne hid his surprise – they had not been as thorough as he had imagined. 'But you know what this is about.'

'Only what I need to know.'

Carne moved close to him. 'What she needs, Mr Hinds, is your protection.'

'She has it.'

Hinds gently closed the car door. Carne headed towards the cottage and rang the bell.

Brooks opened the door and, to Carne's satisfaction, registered surprise. 'Mr Carne, I thought you were taking some well-deserved leave. I wasn't aware an invitation had been extended.'

'I'm invited all right, Brooks,' Carne replied roughly, pushing through the door. Brooks slammed it shut, catching up with him just short of the drawing room.

Carne added them up. Brooks, Mrs Brooks in the kitchen, Anne-Marie, the man and woman in the car. No passenger collected by Brooks, no driver and passenger from the SUV. Not two, but three coverts. Brooks motioned him to a chair.

'Thank you for coming, Mr Carne,' said Anne-Marie. She looked around. 'Detective Chief Inspector Carne is investigating the death of David Wallis. He is also involved in the investigation of Joseph Kennedy's death.'

'I understand—' began Donald.

Anne-Marie interrupted. 'I asked for this meeting with Mr Brooks. He decided to invite some colleagues.'

'Former colleagues,' said Brooks coolly.

'Former colleagues,' continued Anne-Marie, addressing Carne, 'from the intelligence services. They have introduced themselves to me as a Mr Donald and Miss Jemima Sheffield. Do continue, Mr Donald.'

'I understand the Metropolitan Police have confirmed Kennedy's death was a clear case of suicide.'

'It is certainly not that,' said Carne.

Brooks intervened. 'Chief Inspector, as this is a private meeting, could I ask if you have any recording equipment on your person?'

'Go ahead,' replied Carne wearily. Brooks expertly frisked him. 'I'm sure you have your own cameras here.'

'Search me too,' said Anne-Marie with a quiet fury.

'There's no need for that, Minister,' said Donald.

'So, Minister,' said Brooks, busying himself with coffee pouring, 'how may I assist you?'

'DCI Carne tells me that you feel bound by the Official Secrets Act but are willing to correct any factual errors arising from his investigation.'

'Yes.'

'In that case I suggest Mr Carne tells us of his findings.'

Carne stood. It was an involuntary movement. Four pairs of eyes were trained on him. 'I am a detective. I collect evidence.' He paused. 'Then I try to come to conclusions.' He paused to take in this bizarrely assembled audience. 'One living person links David Wallis and Joseph Kennedy.' He was staring in Anne-Marie's direction, but beyond her. 'The woman who was once Maire McCartney.'

Anne-Marie looked up at him, unspoken questions in her eyes. 'No one disagrees,' continued Carne, 'that British intelligence, in the form of David Wallis, used Maire McCartney as bait. Could the reverse also have been true? Ms Gallagher herself told me that she had noticed David Wallis, whom she knew as Vallely, and targeted him before they ever exchanged words.'

'Yes, I liked the look of him,' said Anne-Marie. Brooks smiled limpidly, the other two remained motionless.

'Wallis had served in Northern Ireland. He may have been recognized by someone connected to IRA circles when he arrived in Dublin. If Ms Gallagher's brother had asked her to report on him, she may well have agreed.'

'I was not in contact with my brother at that stage. We no longer saw eye to eye.'

'Yes, Ms Gallagher,' said Carne. 'But we only have your word for it.' Anne-Marie stayed silent. Carne had never felt more alone. 'If this scenario is true, it would mean that Maire McCartney could have told her brother or intermediaries in the IRA of Wallis's departure from Dublin in the early morning of Sunday, April the twenty-fourth, 1994. On the night of Wallis's disappearance, some sort of ambush therefore lay in wait for him.'

'Aren't you forgetting one thing?' Brooks asked with a condescending incredulity. Donald shot him a warning glance.

'No, I am not forgetting it, Mr Brooks. To some extent, the plan failed. Although Wallis was captured, his squad managed in return to capture Martin McCartney.'

Donald peered up at him studiously. 'What you're telling us, Mr Carne,' he said, 'is that David Wallis could himself have been unmasked by the IRA and that it was a premeditated IRA operation that led to his death.'

'Yes.'

'And that this is consistent with the legitimate operation to cultivate Miss McCartney.' He turned to Jemima Sheffield. 'Which is properly recorded in the files and the Hawk reports.'

'Yes, sir.' It was her first contribution and showed that she, a seasoned case officer, was far junior to the man beside her.

'It seems plausible to me,' said Donald. 'Brooks?' Carne wondered whether Donald was so senior that Brooks would now defer to him.

'Yes,' said Brooks. Carne had his answer. Brooks had been effectively silenced after his previous step out of line.

Carne sensed Anne-Marie's loathing of Donald. He caught her eye and made the faintest shake of his head. She drew back. He would see his gambit through.

'If Maire McCartney was acting for the IRA,' he said, 'and

instrumental in David Wallis's death, it raises questions about the person we know today as Anne-Marie Gallagher.'

'And what questions would those be?' Donald asked silkily.

'Her brother,' replied Carne, 'was the prime mover in a hardline faction that wanted to pursue a long-term war against the British. After his disappearance, would not his sister have wished to keep that candle alight?'

'Interesting,' said Donald. 'Though our vetting did not throw up these indications.'

'You told the new Prime Minister you don't vet ministers,' interrupted Anne-Marie.

'There are exceptions,' replied Donald smoothly. 'Where the security of the state is at issue. Perhaps Mr Carne should continue.'

'Since Ms Gallagher's appointment as Minister,' resumed Carne, 'there has been the puzzling reappearance of Joseph Kennedy. I have become aware that you know every word of Ms Gallagher's phone call with Kennedy before he died. And his apparent urging of her to take some form of revenge.'

'Yeees.' Donald elongated the word as he calculated the implications. Carne saw it was now his turn to stay quiet. Donald filled the silence. 'Of course, given that your investigation into Wallis's death has thrown up this result, it will naturally be referred to the highest levels.'

'A theory, not a result.'

'Yes, but one that accords with the evidence,' insisted Donald.

'And therein lies the problem, Mr Donald. The picture we have now been able to piece together of what happened that night at the Black Brimmer car park shows that the theory of Maire McCartney as an *agent provocateur* must be wholly false.'

Donald's eyes ignited with menace. 'Then what the fucking

hell have you been doing with this rigmarole, Mr Carne?' His voice was steeped in menace.

'I was demonstrating, Mr Donald,' replied Carne, 'how grateful some people would be for an explanation of David Wallis's death which could lay the blame wholly and solely on the IRA. Even at the cost of an elected minister's reputation and career. We now even have concrete evidence of this due to the recording I'm sure you are making of this meeting.'

'You pointless, putrid, little pedant.'

The mask had slipped. Donald's rage vibrated through the room. Beside him, Jemima Sheffield kept her head down, staring vacantly at a notebook. Carne noted that Brooks was finding it hard to repress a smirk.

'I had wondered,' said Carne, 'whether Mr Brooks would also be grateful for this theory. But I rather think he knows the truth too well to allow himself that luxury.'

The smirk disappeared from Brooks's face. 'Go on, then, Carne,' he said, 'let's hear what you've got.'

Carne took a couple of strides to pick up his china cup. It gave him the chance to exchange glances with Anne-Marie. She gave him the slightest of nods.

'There are facts,' he resumed. 'Operation Hawk. The disappearances of Sean Black, Brendan O'Donnell and Martin McCartney.' He swung round to face Brooks. 'Mr Brooks's confirmation to me that there is no point in looking for their bodies, as they will never be found.'

Donald turned sharply towards Brooks, who had removed his glasses and was studiously wiping them with a white handkerchief. Carne continued. 'The capture of Martin McCartney. A few seconds later, the capture of David Wallis by Joseph Kennedy and his associates.'

Carne paused and took a sip of coffee. Donald gave a long yawn. 'This is all very fascinating, Mr Carne, but leading us nowhere.'

Carne ignored him. 'Kennedy was present at the final scene of Wallis's short life. However, he was not in control of events. This had been assumed by two senior members of the IRA leadership who had been summoned to deal with what was clearly a delicate situation.'

'You're making this up,' interrupted Brooks.'

Before Carne could respond, Anne-Marie spoke. 'He's not. I was there.'

Her five short words fell on the room like a sonic boom, spreading and subsiding to leave a stunned silence.

'No, no that surely cannot be,' said Brooks, his voice resigned and flat.

'I was there,' she repeated.

A spasm of alarm was detectable in Donald. Their shock was unrehearsed. Neither Brooks nor his intelligence colleagues, both past and present, had known. Carne blessed whatever sixth sense it was that had led Anne-Marie to leave the flat he now knew to have been bugged and tell him her story by the riverside. Their surveillance at that stage could only have been electronic.

'A driver came to my flat,' Anne-Marie continued. 'I was given no choice, I had to go with him. They were in a barn. David strapped to a chair. Two men interrogating him. Before you ask, no, I didn't know them. I tried to comfort him. Then they took him into a field and shot him. That was it.'

'Did David tell you anything?' asked Brooks.

'That is between him and me.'

Her reply brought a further silence. Carne broke it gently.

'Perhaps that question can be put differently. Did David tell you anything that might help us determine the circumstances of his abduction?'

She took a deep breath, thinking, perhaps calculating. 'He pointed the finger at Joseph and said, "The one that got away." Joseph was standing apart. It was as if he'd been ostracized.'

'What happened later that night to Joseph?' asked Carne.

'He drove off, scarpered, ran.' Her eyes were lifeless, the memory unwelcome. Telling the whole story to Carne had been enough. 'He was scared.'

'From this eyewitness account,' Carne resumed, 'we know that Joseph Kennedy escaped the scene of the crime. He did not resurface for more than twenty years, when he made contact with Ms Gallagher, resulting in their one telephone conversation. Within forty-eight hours of that call, he was dead. A murder, dressed up to look like suicide.'

'You have no evidence for that,' said Donald.

'That's untrue,' said Anne-Marie. Again, her intervention electrified the room. 'The phone conversation I had with Joseph is proof positive that he was not going to kill himself.'

'We only have your version of that conversation, Ms Gallagher,' retorted Donald. Again, Anne-Marie bit her tongue.

'Perhaps Miss Sheffield can help us here,' suggested Carne. 'I presume that phone conversation was recorded.' Her moment of panic was transparent; he even felt a wave of sympathy for her. 'Indeed, you yourself were close by.' She looked at Donald for help, receiving no more than a shrug of the shoulders.

'Thank you, Miss Sheffield.' Carne paused, content with her lack of denial.

'There is also the fact that the so-called suicide letter was not there when I discovered Joseph's body,' said Anne-Marie.

Her intervention went uncontested; Carne allowed time for it to be digested. 'My colleague and I visited the Black Brimmer and its car park. Today it's a gastropub called the Black Hat, but the layout is essentially the same.'

Carne passed round his diagram of the pub, car park, road, and cover and waiting places provided by hedgerows, corners and the lay-by. He went through his calculations of speeds and distances. 'The window of opportunity for a snatch vehicle to arrive at the scene and capture Martin McCartney during his return from the hedgerow to the car park is simply too tight. It does not stack up. This was a highly skilled operation, run by professionals. They would not have run that risk.'

'You're losing me again, Carne. All this stuff with a calculator. Never bothered with that in my day,' said Brooks.

'I'm surprised to hear that, Mr Brooks,' replied Carne. 'And also because it's obvious, isn't it? An operation like this could only work if, in addition to David Wallis, there was a second person that night working with the abductors. Wallis was there to keep watch and give the initial cue to the snatch car. But someone else had to provide whatever distraction might be needed to allow the snatch car to complete its task. An informer working with the British.' Carne paused, scanning the eyes trained on him. 'A file held in the Special Branch vaults of what was then the Royal Ulster Constabulary shows that, at the period, an informer, codename Salmon, existed in the highest echelons of the IRA.'

'That file does not exist, Mr Carne,' murmured Brooks.

'But you have just called it "that file", Mr Brooks,' replied Carne. Donald glared at Brooks. 'There was one man who ran off that night because he feared the IRA leadership had uncovered him. Who David Wallis, in his dying moments, realized was the betrayer.'

'It couldn't be Joseph,' said Anne-Marie. 'He was too committed.'

'Once he had turned,' continued Carne, 'or been turned, he needed to appear more committed than ever. Let's follow his life through. He escapes from the IRA that night and enters a nether world. There's been no preparation for his informer's afterlife and he finds himself fending for himself. Over the years, as he establishes a new identity, Joseph Kennedy has time to think.

'He comes to realize that a trick has been played on him. After that night, he is an embarrassment to British intelligence, an informer who's served his purpose. As he's been involved in the disappearances of Black and O'Donnell as well as the capture of McCartney, he knows altogether too much. And he begins to see that what his British handlers have done is chuck him like a bone to the IRA wolves. We'll never know exactly what Wallis meant by "the one who got away". But the IRA leadership is capable of working it out for themselves. Joseph Kennedy isn't the hardliner after all, he's turned traitor. And is now as good as dead.

'But one silver lining begins to appear in Joseph's cloud – the ascent of his childhood friend, Maire McCartney, now Anne-Marie Gallagher. He's tracked her progress over the years and is the only person who knows of her involvement. Indeed he may be the only person who fully recognizes her as having once been Maire McCartney.

'The night she's elected a Member of Parliament, an opportunity he could never have imagined opens up. And then she's made a minister. He's a dying man, he has nothing to lose. And what a story he has to tell! The murder by the British state of three unarmed, unconvicted men, his one-time comrades in the Gang of Four. His tool, his mouthpiece, will be the Minister. And, if she doesn't comply, he will, to put it crudely, blackmail her.'

'How will he do that,' asked Brooks.

'He will threaten to reveal her as the person who shot dead the long-disappeared British soldier and MI6 agent, David Wallis.'

'There's no evidence I did,' protested Anne-Marie. All eyes were on her. 'Nor, of course, did I.'

'That doesn't matter to Joseph,' said Carne. 'What happened that night is your word against his. It's enough. Joseph's telephone conversation with you would have set the wires burning. What happened then we shall probably never know. But Kennedy had to be silenced. Was it passed on to Mr Brooks to resolve as a private enterprise? Or was it a state responsibility? Did MI5 believe it had a duty to clear up the mess left behind by MI6, its distrusted rival? Perhaps Mr Donald, or Miss Sheffield, may know the answer.'

Donald stifled a yawn and looked at his watch. 'Well,' he said, standing up and rubbing his hands, 'thank you, Chief Inspector Carne, this has been a most interesting afternoon. But time is up and I hope you will accept my apologies if Miss Sheffield and I now leave. I shall report to my superiors in Whitehall that, however intriguing your speculations, you have unearthed no evidence which need cause us to revisit the case of David Wallis. Nor indeed further investigate the sad suicide of Joseph Kennedy. Come, Jemima.'

She jumped to her feet, followed Donald through the room as he briskly shook hands, and marched towards the front door, followed by Brooks.

As Donald was about to shut it, he said, 'Do please thank Mrs Brooks for the delicious tea. Lovely china.' With those parting words, they left the house, made for their BMW with almost indecent haste and accelerated away, showering gravel over one of Dorothy Brooks's flowerbeds.

Brooks rejoined Carne and Anne-Marie in the sitting room. 'My apologies for the reptilians our service now harbours. A drink, perhaps?'

'I'm not going to let it go, Jimmy,' said Anne-Marie.

'You have to,' he replied. 'For your own good. For your career. It's the past.'

'The state can't go around killing people. Not then, not now.'

Brooks turned to Carne. 'You're welcome to stay in this room or to leave. But you've done your performing today. And it was a good performance. Congratulations.'

He walked over to Anne-Marie. 'Maire, there's someone you need to meet. Would you follow me?' He shot Carne a warning glance. 'Not you.'

She looked to Carne for guidance. He nodded to her. Brooks was already out of the room, she jumped and followed him down a hallway. The house was longer than she had imagined from the outside, labyrinthine and deceptive. Just like its owner. At the end of a second passageway, they climbed a narrow staircase. At the top, they turned back on themselves and into a small sitting room overlooking a vegetable garden.

A man with his back to them was watching television, a documentary on the first battle of Ypres, a century ago. Wisps of fair hair stretched back over his balding head, spectacles hanging forward from his ears. He rose and turned.

She stopped with a stunned jerk, as if she'd walked into a brick wall. Or seen a ghost. He was older, plumper, balder, but little else had changed.

'My God,' she whispered. 'Oh, my God. But they killed you.'

'Hello, Maire,' he said quietly, as if he was addressing a lost child.

'Hello, Martin,' she replied. And then she began to shake.

CHAPTER 33

Her shock was so violent that Martin found himself moving forward to put his arms round her and steady her. Unlike his sister, he knew this moment was coming. He had wondered what would happen, how she would cope, whether she would even recognize him. But he had not anticipated that the impact would be so severe. She must never have questioned that he was dead, killed on that same night as David Wallis.

Slowly the shaking and tears ceased. She broke away from him and searched for a handkerchief in her handbag. Brooks handed her one and she wiped her eyes.

'Sorry,' she said.

'It's OK, Maire, you're OK.'

She looked at him through bloodshot eyes and tried to force a smile. 'You were dead, Martin. It was one of the things I knew. Why didn't you tell me? There'd have been ways.'

'I couldn't, Maire.'

'What do you mean?'

'You'd better know everything.' He turned to Brooks. 'Jimmy, for fuck's sake, get some drinks in here.' The familiarity with which her brother addressed him alerted Anne-Marie to further shocks.

'It began when you were arrested,' said Martin.

'What do you mean, it began with my arrest?' asked Anne-Marie.

'It's a long story. You'd best prepare yourself.' Martin rubbed his eyes beneath his spectacles, then took them off and wiped the glass. Dark circles beneath the irises revealed themselves; she was not sure whether it was his own ill-preparedness for the pain of remembering or just the passing of the years.

'The police took me in. They usually did when something big went off. Killing Halliburton – Brit Special Branch – was big all right. They weren't interested in fitting me up for it. Knew they'd got nothing on me. They only wanted to tell me they'd got you. I couldn't believe it, couldn't believe my kid sister had got involved like that. With her brains, her looks, that's never what we wanted for her.'

He was addressing her in the third person, looking away. She wanted to see into his eyes but he would not, or could not, engage. 'I'm sorry,' she whispered, 'not for me, but for you.'

He rounded on her with an agonized despair. 'How could you have done it, Maire? You of all people.' She felt a childlike fearfulness, seized by memories of the big brother she had been in such awe of.

'I told you at the time, Martin, I thought you wanted it. That you would approve. I'd never have got sucked in otherwise.' She pleaded with him. 'I believed Joseph. He lied to me.'

She caught Brooks in the corner of her eye, standing at the edge of the room. He noticed and left, closing the door softly behind him. Martin calmed and put his spectacles back on. 'Joseph. It always comes back to Joseph, doesn't it?'

'What do you mean?' she asked.

'Let me tell you what happened first. The police started hinting at a deal. If I helped them, maybe they'd help you. I didn't trust them. They were still sectarian, leaked like sieves. And they were local, part of the community. But, a couple of times before when I'd been pulled in, I'd met this Brit called Jimmy. He was obviously MI5 or 6. He'd left me a number to call if I ever had something to say. It's weird. The Brits were the real enemy, on the other side of the line. But you can deal with the enemy, it's clear where you both stand.'

Brooks rejoined them. 'We're not being recorded, Maire, I was just checking none of our friends had lingered. This is a private meeting. Let's say we're keeping it a family secret.' He eased into an armchair beside them.

'Anyway,' continued Martin, 'I told them I'd think about it but I needed time – which they agreed. No hassle, no more interrogating. Maybe they saw something weakening in me. I phoned the number.' He nodded towards Brooks. 'He said he was somewhere else but he'd come right over. We met the next day at a service station just by the airport. I asked him what the deal would be. You tell her, Jimmy.'

'I offered your brother a job,' said Brooks, looking at her through narrowing eyes. 'We needed inside information more than ever. We knew there were whispers in the air, talk of the political strategy taking over, more ballot than bullet. Tiny tremors, but you could feel them. But the IRA was showing signs of splits. We needed to figure out the potential peacemakers and the hardliners. Martin's role was to play the most intractable of the extremists, so that we'd know every move they were trying to make.'

'And the price,' interrupted Maire, 'was that I'd be allowed to go.'

'Yes. More than that. The record of your arrest was expunged, your file destroyed. Your interrogators were told there had been an error. It never happened. There could be no stain.'

'I see.'

A silence fell. Finally, Brooks broke it. 'There were benefits for Martin, too. An assurance of a new life.'

She was staring at her brother, shaking her head. 'You needn't have done it, Martin. I was grown up, eighteen. I knew what I was doing. I deserved the consequences.'

'Maire, you were still a child. To me, anyway. And it wasn't just you. I couldn't forgive Joseph, either.'

She was alert, remembering something. 'Now that I think of it, he never said you *did* approve, he only said you *would* approve. There's a difference.'

'There's no difference. It compounds the deceit.'

'But when you spoke to me . . . after what happened . . .' She was digging into her memory. 'What was it you said? "I won't piss on Joseph. He's important to the movement."'

'I know I said that, Maire. I was acting my new role. I had to deceive everyone. You included.'

'You turned, became an informer. The most shameful thing an IRA man could be.'

'Aye,' said Martin.

'For me.' He did not reply.

An atavistic, visceral, long-forgotten urge gripped her like the coil of snake, suffocating her. She turned to Brooks. 'You turned him into a grass.' Her voice was hoarse with the fury of historical remembrance.

'Good men and women do what they think is right at the time,' replied Brooks gently. 'In my view your brother is a good man who acted honourably in near-impossible circumstances.'

'So Joseph was never an informer,' she said.

'No,' confirmed Brooks.

'Well, that's something, isn't it?' Her unstaunched anger implied a biblical judgement on her brother. 'You'd better tell me the rest. Like why would David Wallis be using me to spy on my brother when he was already on your side?' She paused, her face paled with scorn. 'Unless there's a happy ending, and you let my brother off grassing because you didn't trust him any more.'

'You've made your point, Maire,' said Martin. He was drooping in his seat, crushed, a light within extinguished. A few minutes ago, she had been the guilty party; now, she was shifting that guilt to him. His voice enfeebled, he responded with devastating words. 'Did you not change sides too?'

As suddenly as she had felt the rage, she was overcome by shame. The shame that had allowed her, even for a moment, to succumb to ancestral prejudice. To be irrational. She went over and put her arms round his neck. 'I'm sorry, Martin, I'm so, so sorry.'

They sat quietly, stunned by the mutual confessions and frailties they had induced from each other.

She broke the silence. 'Surely you could have made contact. Let me know you were alive.'

'If you'd been carrying that knowledge, it could have killed you. It was better I'd died. For Ma and Da, too. It was too big a secret to carry. Too much disgrace on the family if it ever got out.' He paused. 'Better for me too.'

Brooks, like a party host attempting to move beyond his guests' shared distress, resumed his story. 'Deploying David Wallis, or Vallely as we called him, was my idea.' He turned from brother to sister. 'The IRA leadership had begun to suspect there was a mole right at the heart of the organization. And they were right. "Salmon" did indeed exist. We knew from Martin himself and other rumours that he was under their microscope. Kennedy in particular was behaving oddly towards him. Maybe he was genuinely suspicious, maybe it was a power play to usurp Martin as leader of the hardliners.'

'He was always ambitious,' said Anne-Marie, her calm restored. 'We needed to protect Martin,' continued Brooks. 'I had, and please forgive the word, an inspiration. I'd kept an eye on you after the Halliburton incident and knew you were in Dublin. I also knew David Wallis was kicking his heels, itching for a new adventure. Why not put the two of you together and let the rumour river flow? If whispers started circulating that a British agent was using Martin McCartney's sister as a means of getting intelligence on him, what surer guarantee could there be that Martin was not an informer?'

Anne-Marie slowly shook her head. 'Twisted minds, evil schemes.'

'You can think that,' said Brooks. 'But it offered Martin an element of safety and, eventually, his new life . . .'

'A life that was a living death.'

'. . . as well as helping towards peace.'

'That's no excuse for what you did to me.'

'Is it not? In the same way that Martin had helped you, were you now not helping him? Even if you didn't know it?'

'You can find so many reasons, can't you?' She sighed. 'What about David? What you did to him.'

'David wanted it,' protested Brooks. 'Soldiering had gone sour on him. It gave him a new purpose. A new way to serve his country.'

'He ended up with a bullet in his head in a field.'

'Yes. Sadly there were factors I did not foresee.' Brooks rose from his seat, stretched and walked over to a drinks cabinet. He waved the Scotch bottle at Martin, who nodded his head and held out his glass. He topped it up, refilled his own and, pacing up and down the room, continued his narrative.

'For a while, it was the perfect operation. I didn't consult Martin in advance because I suspected he would never go along with it. He never stopped loving and caring about you.' Brooks smiled fondly at Martin. 'Wallis, of course, never knew that his real purpose – at the outset, anyway – was to protect Martin. It was knowledge he didn't need and would have made his part too difficult to play. But, after David succeeded in persuading you to take him to Belfast, Martin did have to know. That visit was the crowning coup. Martin, the leader who alerted his comrades that David might be connected to the hated British military machine.'

'And you'd laid the seed with David telling me his father was a soldier,' said Anne-Marie.

For once, Brooks seemed almost embarrassed. 'Yes. I'm afraid I had. But,' he resumed, regaining his bonhomie, 'the potential bonus was that Joseph's failure to remember it could possibly release a drip of suspicion against him. And there was a further advantage.' He paused for effect.

'Get on with it,' said Anne-Marie. 'You're not on stage.'

'We didn't know which way you would jump. The beauty was that it did not matter. If you went against David and reported the military connection, that would further reinforce Martin's position. In retrospect, that might have been the better outcome. The operation would have served its purpose and I would have had to pull David out.'

'You could have done that, anyway.'

'Yes, perhaps. But, given the delicate state of the peace feelers and the IRA split, it was too tempting to leave him in Dublin.' He paused. 'Mind if I smoke?' Without awaiting a reply, he removed a silver case from an inside breast pocket. He was about to take one for himself but, halted by a sudden memory, offered it to Anne-Marie. 'I seem to remember one occasion—'

'And the last,' she interrupted, waving him away.

He withdrew the case, took out a cigarette for himself and lit it. 'There was also a further factor,' Brooks resumed. 'David was enjoying himself. If I'd tried to order him to leave, he would have ignored me. You were the greater siren.'

'Not just me,' she said. 'He seemed to be interested in his studies. Even a bit obsessed at times.'

'Yes, though I was never entirely sure I believed that,' he replied, 'particularly as he complained that I was not allowing him to undertake further intelligence forays against the Gang of Four. He could never know that I was getting everything I needed from Martin.' Brooks sipped his drink, puffed from his cigarette and collected his thoughts. 'But it was worth keeping Wallis in place for any endgame.'

'You mean the disappearances of your so-called Gang of Four,' said Anne-Marie.'

'So you say,' replied Brooks.

'It gets worse and worse.'

'The simple fact,' continued Brooks, 'was that Black, O'Donnell and Kennedy above all were obstacles in the way of peace. Threats to the security and stability of the state.'

'It doesn't matter – you were embarking on state murder.'

'That will remain for ever unproved. All we know is that two of those men disappeared.'

An understanding was dawning on Anne-Marie. For the moment, she kept it to herself, allowing Brooks to continue.

'By spring 1994 there was only Joseph Kennedy left and Martin McCartney to be extricated. But there was a difficulty. DCI Carne saw it but he was looking through the wrong end of the lens.

Rather than Martin insisting on being joined to Joseph's hip because he suspected him of being the mole, it was Joseph who was chaining himself to Martin. After Black and O'Donnell's disappearances, his suspicions of Martin resurfaced. Somehow we had to rescue Martin while also eliminating Joseph as a threat. So, yes, on that night at the Black Brimmer, we did indeed have two agents working for us. David Wallis concealed in the hedgerow, watching out and giving us the signal to move, and Martin McCartney.

'As arranged, Martin managed to break off to cross the road to relieve himself in the hedgerow. When he began zipping up his trousers, Wallis – he was a remarkable operator to be able to lie so close without being observed – transmitted the signal. However, Martin then delayed for fifteen seconds before moving out slowly. At the precise moment he reached the middle of the road, the SUV stopped by him, bundled him inside, giving the appearance of an abduction, and made off.'

'What about David?' she asked. 'Why did the SUV not stop to pick him up when he was by the road trying to stop it? That must have been the plan he'd been given?'

'Yes,' said Brooks. 'Tragically, that was the element that went wrong. By then Kennedy and his friends had started firing. It was too dangerous to stop. The SUV had to accelerate away. There was every reason to assume that Wallis was too good an operator to get caught and would manage his escape to a safe hiding place.'

'But he didn't, did he?'

'No. Unfortunately, the SUV appears to have clipped his leg, slowing him down. His captors were able to make ground towards him and further slow him by firing at his legs. This accounts for the mark on his femur.' He paused. 'And that's it.

Everything. As to what transpired later, it rather seems you know more than we do.'

His performance over, Brooks subsided into his armchair. There was a prolonged silence, his words stifling the room.

'It's plausible,' said Anne-Marie. 'Congratulations.'

'I beg your pardon.' Brooks said it as if she had committed some sort of social *faux-pas*.

'I said congratulations. It's clever.'

'What do you mean, Maire?' asked Martin. 'It all happened like Jimmy says. Not that I'm proud of it, running away like that. But it's the way it was.'

'It's all right, Martin,' said Anne-Marie, 'they'd never have told you this part of it.'

'You're speaking in riddles, Maire,' said Brooks.

'The car bumping into David, failing to stop for him. It doesn't ring true. A few minutes ago, while you were spinning your story, I realized why you were lying.'

'Spinning? I'm afraid you're losing me totally now,' said Brooks.

'Oh, I doubt that. I suspect Joseph Kennedy eventually realized it too. He must have seen close up what happened but didn't immediately understand its meaning or importance. He simply assumed Wallis's capture was an accident of war, something that went wrong. But as he constantly revisited it, the truth finally hit him. What happened to David that night was not something that went wrong, but something that went right.'

CHAPTER 34

She expected Brooks to interrupt or object. Instead he stayed silent, his eyes betraying a war weariness.

'Joseph worked it out,' she continued 'The only explanation that made sense of the SUV's course and speed was that British intelligence made a deliberate decision to feed one of its agents to the enemy. They did it in the certain knowledge that this would lead to his death. Chief Inspector Carne got it the wrong way round. It wasn't Joseph Kennedy who was thrown to the IRA wolves, but David Wallis.'

Brooks took the handkerchief from his breast pocket, unfolded it, wiped his lips, refolded the handkerchief and restored it to the pocket. 'Why in a million years would we do a thing like that to a brave young man like David?'

'Because he had the proof, didn't he?' Brooks stayed silent. 'He was part of the assassination squad, or whatever you care to call it, wasn't he?' she continued. Again there was no reply. 'As you yourself were, too, no doubt.'

'I admired him,' said Brooks softly. 'Perhaps like you, I even loved him. Differently, of course, but just as sincerely, I hope. He was a magnetic, and magnificent, young man.'

'Yes, why is it we so often end up destroying those we love? You feared that you were losing him. His conscience was making him go soft. Turning him into a maverick agent. One who might expose the whole, dirty operation and ruin you in the process. Perhaps he even wanted revenge on you personally for what you had done to him.'

Brooks, for once, looked bereft, quivering. Theatrically, he affected to wipe a tear from his eye. 'At every point, I gave him the opportunities to do what he wanted. What *he* wanted,' he repeated, 'not I.'

'But he turned out to be not just magnetic but a good man,' said Anne-Marie. 'A better man than you ever understood. That was your problem.'

'No, the problem was you.'

'Me!'

'Yes, he made the ultimate mistake. The boy fell in love. And with the wrong sort of person. In the battle between duty and love, man's enemy since the dawn of history, he allowed himself to go soft.'

Brooks stubbed out his cigarette, rose heavily from his chair, walked over to a filing cabinet, knelt to open it and drew out a file. Still with his back to them, he stood erect, straightened his tie, stroked his moustache, and turned round to hand her a sheet of paper, its edges tinged by the pale brown of age.

'It's the transcript of his final recording. He made it two days before he was captured. I kept it back from the file. You will understand why. I offer it to you, and you only, as an explanation.'

21 April 1994

Jimmy says this is the last one. Will it be? Once you enter the cesspit, there's always one more stinking piece of dung to be rid of. So, Jimmy, this is from me to you.

You say my conscience can be clean because of our agreement that her brother is to be taken alive. You say you still win because his capture will mean their failure. Even that by living he is seen to have lost – so win–win for you. Do I believe you? Am I sure his life will be spared? Or are you just playing another of your games? Once I believed in a simple world. Right was right, wrong was wrong. It didn't matter how right was achieved. As long as it was.

Now softness has penetrated me. I know what it feels like. It's the chill Irish damp from their misty hills. Did you understand when you invented your operation what the consequences might be? Or did you think my heart was so hardened that it could no longer feel? Perhaps you thought she was just some slut. Nothing more than an inanimate tool. There to be exploited. Yet you must have seen her. You described her to me. Not very nicely as I remember. So you knew she is lovely. And that she's breakable. There can be no victory. If you allow the brother to live, he becomes the convenient hate figure. The so-called peacemakers can unite to condemn him. The cynicism of the calculators.

Perhaps then it is better that he should die. Better that you and I carry the guilt of our actions. Better she can be left to grieve. I will do what you call my 'duty' this one last time. Then I will retire. Perhaps I'll become a country lawyer with a loving wife and respectful children. My God, the sickness of the joke makes me want to retch. When we meet again, it will be in hell. The Devil willing.

She read it once, then again and, finally, a third time. He stretched out his hand, she hesitated.

'I'm sorry,' he said, 'I must have it back.'

'Yes, of course. It does you no favours.'

'No, Maire, it does *him* no favours. It shows he was going rogue.'

She returned it. 'If he'd told me, I could have stopped him.'

'No,' said Brooks sharply. 'He would have finished the job. Whatever the inner torture – whatever mad thing he might have done had he survived – he could not duck out. It would have been cowardice.'

'It would have been bravery.'

'The sighting of doom does not stop a soldier marching towards it.'

'And you knew that because you had organized his doom.'

'What would you have done? Imagine you were the Minister then, in charge of safeguarding your country. What comes first? The peaceful future of your nation? Or one man's life? When he first joined the army, David knew the deal. He assumed he would die on a distant battlefield. Instead he died out of uniform nearer home. But he was still serving the same state.'

'The state that killed him.'

'That is your supposition.'

Brooks stood up to make a show of addressing her formally. 'Let us stick with the facts. Black and O'Donnell disappeared, there is no proof they are dead, let alone murdered. Joseph Kennedy was branded an informer by his own side, drummed out of his country by them, and finally died a lonely death from cancer. David Wallis was an unfortunate casualty of an otherwise successful operation. Martin McCartney was extricated from danger and is owed a debt of gratitude by the British, and Irish, people.' He paused to peer down at her like a bishop dispensing a blessing. 'And Martin's sister, now Anne-Marie Gallagher, became a successful lawyer and has a glittering political career in front of her.' Brooks smiled at the brother and sister in front of him.

She did not return it. 'You can get away with the past, but not the present. Joseph Kennedy was murdered. I am the witness who can prove it.'

'Let me tell you something about Joseph Kennedy,' said Brooks, steel in his voice. 'Joseph Kennedy was a dangerous man, a fanatic. You don't think he and his lot have given up, do you? Why did he make contact with you?'

'Because he wanted the truth to come out.'

'For God's sake,' Brooks almost shouted, 'he wanted to get his claws into you. Just like 1991. To pump you up, activate you. He'd done it once, he could do it again. That was what his so-called truth was all about. Just another way of damaging the nation he hated. And you would be his instrument. He'd have probably ended up giving you a gun to shoot the Prime Minister.'

'You're being absurd.'

'No, Maire. Don't you get it? Joseph Kennedy was killed to protect you, for God's sake.' He hesitated, the gambler deciding whether or not to go all in. 'Let me tell you something else. Ever since that night, you've been under constant MI5 surveillance. Your whole life has been lived under a microscope.'

'You're trying to frighten me.'

'And the reason is Joseph Kennedy. Who would be the one person he'd try to contact if he ever saw an opportunity to make trouble? Maire McCartney, of course. You were the potential pot of gold at the end of the rainbow. How he must have celebrated when he saw you infiltrating, to use his words, the British state.'

'I don't believe you.'

'And in return that British state has protected you, nurtured you, established you as Anne-Marie Gallagher, a brilliant woman of humble origin and impeccable background, not a blemish on her record.'

'Are you threatening me now, Jimmy?' She made it sound like a gentle enquiry after his health.

'I would never threaten you. I just want to look after you. And you to look after yourself.'

They had both shot their bolts, there was nothing left to say. Martin broke the silence. 'What are you going to do, Maire?'

'One thing I'd like to do is see you again, Martin.'

'I can't, Maire,' he replied softly.

'Where are you living? What are you doing?'

'I can't tell you that either.' He forced a smile and hugged her. 'It was the choice I made. I always knew when it was all over, if I made it through alive, I could never be me again. That's the sacrifice. Friends, comrades, family, you give them all up.'

'Are you happy?'

'I'm happy to see you succeed.'

They stood up and she went over and hugged him hard, then pulled away, held his face between her two hands and kissed his forehead. She nodded cursorily at Brooks. He took the hint and left the room.

'What do you want of me, Martin?' she whispered.

'It's your destiny, not mine,' he said. 'Remember what I once said. It never goes away. What you're born to. It's always there.'

She broke away and headed for the door. Brooks was waiting for her in the hallway.

'Don't go just yet. Come for a walk in the garden.'

She narrowed her eyes. 'Is this another of your tricks, Jimmy?'

'No. I have a proposition. Given what you seem determined to do, you owe it to David and yourself to allow me to lay it before you.'

Half an hour later, after a walk around the flowerbeds and among the gravestones of Old Witham Church, Anne-Marie and Brooks reappeared in the driveway. Carne and Hinds were sitting on the bonnet of her ministerial car.

'I'll go back with him, Keith, sorry to keep you,' she said and walked towards Carne's car.

'Early start tomorrow, Minister, 7 a.m. I'll be there,' Hinds said to her retreating back. She did not look round.

They drove down the lane, through the town and onto the main road in silence. A few miles out Carne pulled into a lay-by.

'Did it work OK?' he asked.

'I think so,' she replied. 'I switched it on in the toilet.' She unbuckled her trouser belt. 'Look away.' She slid down the top of her trousers, removed the belt and the pouch strapped to her crotch and handed it over to him. He took a small silver recorder from inside, wound it back and played a few sentences from the conversation. Then she told him, uncensored, everything of the conversations in the house.

'I should have thought of Martin,' said Carne. 'Too fixated on Joseph.'

'How could you have?' She examined his profile, flickering from the shafts of evening sun breaking through the roadside trees. 'I never gave you the evidence you needed. Not all of it, anyway.'

'No.'

'That terrible thing I did was too much.'

'Yes.' He said it dully, conveying no meaning. She had reached the end. The something she had withheld for so long was not a mere embarrassment or awkwardness: it was truly dreadful. A shame that must have blighted her adult life – but one she had been strong enough to cope with. Battered further by the later misfortunes for which she was blameless, she must have forced herself to banish self-pity and forge an underlying ruthlessness. She was a complexity that he had never before come near to experiencing.

She knew he was thinking of how, even once and in different times, she could commit such an act. 'I didn't believe they were going to kill him. Joseph promised me.' She was almost pleading.

'It always comes back to Joseph,' he said.

'Yes, that's just what Martin said. I felt disgust at what I'd done. Not guilt so much, more a recurring nausea. And, you being a policeman, I've sometimes wanted to bury myself.' She breathed deeply. 'I would understand if you can no longer be my friend.'

Hearing her words, that instinct he had come to feel so forcefully reared up at him. He must not lose her friendship; he must not lose her. 'It was a long time ago,' he said at last.

'We can say that about everything, can't we?'

'Except the murder of Joseph.'

'Yes, the circle closes with Joseph.'

She wanted to stroke his cheek with her hand but realized it was too much. He seemed to concentrate with a new ferocity on the road ahead.

'What now?' she asked.

'Go back, I guess.' He sounded rueful. 'All avenues closed except the road leading to home.'

'You could return to London.'

'And rejoin the Met? I can't.' He hesitated.

'Why not?' She frowned.

'Not now.' He sounded almost brusque. 'Anyway, you could come home, too. Do the reverse escape.'

'I wouldn't mind seeing the place again. But a day or two's enough. Then I'd be going mad.'

He was silent for a few seconds. 'I'll take you up on the day or two,' he said softly. 'Be your guide.'

His eye was caught by flashing in his rear mirror. 'Hold on.'

A grey SUV was on his tail, headlights flashing on and off. Instinctively he knew it was the car that had turned into Witham Lane a few hours earlier with the covert backups. He accelerated. It speeded up with him. He slowed, and it followed again. To make sure, he put his foot down. They were on a short roller-coaster of road cutting through Savernake Forest, which evened out into a series of sharp bends. Sixty, seventy, eighty miles an hour, the SUV kept pace. He was thankful she was at his side, as they must know. For once, she was his protection. He slowed, the SUV still tucked in behind him. Finally he pulled over onto the verge and stopped. The SUV accelerated, lowering black blinds over its nearside windows as it passed them.

He sat rigid, checking other vehicles as they approached from behind.

'That's their idea of a warning,' he said.

She lowered her voice. 'My conversation in the garden with Jimmy is on that tape too. Guard it well.'

CHAPTER 35

Post-election, Thursday, 1 June

They rose in a horseshoe. She recognized four of them: the Prime Minister; Steve Whalley, who she had not been told would be there; Rob McNeil, likewise; Sir George Jupp, her Permanent Secretary; and a fifth.

A Gang of Five. How different from the 'Gang of Four' gathered in her Belfast home so long ago. The stench was just as toxic.

Lionel Buller's eyes moved along the gathered faces. 'You may not have met Sir Ted.' The fifth man, tall and bald with a thin nose bearing small oval spectacles, stretched forward a clawlike hand. She recognized Sir Edward Latimer from his appearance before Parliament's Intelligence and Security Committee. She would have taken him for the repressed headmaster of a failing boarding school. 'As you may know,' continued Buller, 'Sir Ted spent most of his career with the Special Intelligence Service before being asked by my predecessor to take up the reins at the Security Service. So he is particularly well placed to bring an intelligence services' perspective to your concerns.'

Buller gestured Anne-Marie towards the empty chair. Seats had been arranged around a small circular table to avoid any suggestion of taking sides. On it were placed five bound documents: the report Anne-Marie had sent the Prime Minister on the circumstances surrounding the murders of Sean Black, Brendan O'Donnell and Joseph Kennedy, and the activities and death of David Wallis. It included the infiltration of her and her family by Wallis, a.k.a. Vallely, her change of name after Wallis's disappearance, MI5's monitoring of her, and her discovery of Joseph Kennedy's body. It made no reference to other events in her life. Or of her brother.

'Anne-Marie,' began the Prime Minister, 'may I first say how enormously grateful I am to you for this.' There were nods and approving murmurs around the tables.

'Yes, indeed.'

'I couldn't agree more, Prime Minister.'

Only Whalley stayed silent, a smirk playing around his lips. She told herself not to be provoked.

'It is a most commendable report,' continued Buller, 'and I'm grateful to you for drawing these matters to my attention. At this stage, I have discussed it only with those in this room. I've included Rob because of his and his family's relationship with David Wallis. Sir Ted, your thoughts.'

The tall man's small piggy eyes flashed through the spectacles, a vivid awakening from the half-dead. He picked up the document. 'As you say, Prime Minister, it is an excellent report, which I view with the utmost seriousness. Indeed, I have already launched a trenchant internal inquiry into any possible misconduct by individuals in 1993 and 1994.'

'It is toward the actions of the state,' interrupted Anne-Maire,' not individuals, that my report directs itself. Actions both past and present.'

'Yes, yes,' said Buller, conveying his displeasure. Not a man improved by power, she thought. 'But even today the Irish peace is fragile. We have regular reports of weapons finds, foiled bombings, sectarian shootings. We are still reconciling ourselves to the past.'

'I'm interested in state killing today,' said Anne-Marie. 'The murder of Joseph Kennedy.'

Latimer raised an eyebrow to Buller. 'If I may, Prime Minister?' A glacial smoothness infused his response. 'That, Minister, is a matter for the Metropolitan Police. I am told there is no possible connection with the Security Service.'

'That is not true,' retorted Anne-Marie. 'The Security Service kept a constant watch on me precisely in order to intercept any potential contact from Kennedy.'

'That is an operational matter, Minister,' said Latimer. 'I repeat that my service had no connection with the death of Kennedy. We do not go around killing people these days. Or, indeed, in past days.' He put down his copy of the report and closed his hands together. 'That, Prime Minister, is all I will say. Indeed it is all I am able to say.'

'There needs to be a public inquiry,' said Anne-Marie. 'We all know what happens to internal inquiries.'

'Yes, Anne-Marie, we've all read your document,' said Buller icily. She felt isolated and wanted to escape; to unleash a volley of accusation; to propel the sounds of slammed doors through the complacency of Whitehall.

'Sir George?' asked Buller.

'My department *per se*,' replied the Permanent Secretary, 'is not connected with the matters in this report. My duty is to my Minister. I do plead with her to allow the appropriate investigations to be made by the relevant agencies. As Sir Ted has said, we do not, and never have, condoned state murder in this country. If the case can be proved, the authorities will act.'

'The death of Joseph Kennedy has already been covered up,' said Anne-Marie.

'Minister, I've spoken personally to the Commissioner about this. I understand that your eyewitness statement was taken into full account but the forensics did not show foul play. Nor was there a trace of evidence pointing to any individual suspect.'

'Of course not. We don't pay MI5 to leave a trail of guilt.' She addressed her remark to Latimer. He emitted the mildest of snorts.

'This is not just a matter of state,' said Buller. 'There is also the personal side. David Wallis's family. We should take their wishes into consideration. Rob?'

'Let it rest, Anne-Marie,' said McNeil. 'Let him rest.'

'I was there when David was dying. There is no rest.'

Buller made a show of looking at his watch. 'Time moves on and we have covered the ground. Anne-Marie, I will read your report again and decide whether a public inquiry is warranted.'

'If you decide against it, Prime Minister, you will be undermining the principles of human rights, individual justice and state accountability that this government stands for and our party fought the election for.' She spoke the words with quiet deliberation, rose from her chair and nodded to the five men in turn. 'Thank you for your time.' As she left the room, she sensed long masculine sighs of relief rippling between the grey suits behind the closing door.

The call came within two hours, the messenger McNeil. 'Anne-Marie, I'm sorry, it's not what you wanted. The PM's asked me to say that he's given it deep thought but doesn't consider it in the national interest to have a public inquiry. Not to mention the cost, of course. He also wants you to know that he holds you in the highest regard and views you as a vital member of his administration, both now and in the future.'

'We've let David down,' she said. 'You've shown yourself to be a weak man, Rob, something David knew, too. And why he used you.'

'Anne-Marie, that's—'

'You said you wanted to know the truth about your friend's death. I found it for you. You should have supported me.'

'It wouldn't have made a difference. I don't count.'

'Then it would have cost you nothing to back me.' She put the phone down, then regretted that she had not said goodbye. It was not Rob she was fighting.

That evening, she texted Carne. 'Can I take up your offer?'

The reply came instantly: 'Collect you from the airport Saturday morning?'

She answered, 'Yes x'.

Saturday, 3 June, to Sunday, 4 June

It was drizzling when her plane landed.

'It's just how I always remember it,' she said as he led her to his car. Once inside, she peeled back her hood and he helped her off with her coat. She pecked him on the cheek. 'Thank you for doing this.'

She shook her hair and watched the rain crawling down the windscreen. He found himself drawn to her more powerfully than ever, however much he tried not to be.

'Where to?' he asked.

'The field first, I think.'

An hour and a half later, he turned into the lane that twisted up the mountainside. It was less than four weeks since that first summons to a skeleton, but now, miraculously, the clouds were lifting and the rain easing. The curtain rising for her entrance.

He retraced the route of dips and rises until it evened out into the gradual climb to the now decayed barn and fields above. The gate was closed and he parked just beyond.

'I remembered boots,' she said. They were the first words spoken for a while, both silenced by the invasion of memory, his of a corpse, hers of a young man about to die. The grass, now lit by breaking sunlight, was sleek from rain but firm underfoot. She seemed to him to float across it.

They arrived at a rectangle of fresh earth covering where he had lain. At its head stood a small wooden cross, just two lengths of wood, joined by a single nail. Carne wondered if Amy had planted it.

'It was the middle of the night,' she said. 'It could have been anywhere. But I'm glad to see it in the light.' She looked down at the earth and cross, breathed deeply, raised her head and imbibed the clean air of the clearing sky and the shades of green stretching below into the distance of her homeland. Clumps of late spring heather still sprinkled the field. She broke off a handful of blue flowers and scattered their petals over the earth.

Carne had told her about her parents' gravestone and she asked him to pass by it on the return to Belfast. He pulled up outside the cemetery and, pointing her in its direction, waited by the gates. She stopped a couple of hundred yards away, a slim outline balanced delicately in the breeze over the stones of mortality and loneliness. She stood many minutes longer than it would have taken to read the inscription.

When she returned, he opened the passenger door for her, closed it gently, walked round the back of the car to let himself in and set off. She said nothing, as if struck mute. Nor did she cry or sigh. Her expression was blank, unreadable, immobile.

'You know what the gravestone says?'

'Yes,' he replied.

'They thought they'd lost me.'

'I know.'

'They didn't. I often thought of them. But I had no choice. I couldn't come back.'

'No.'

'I hoped they'd understand.'

'I'm sure they did. More than you think.'

'I did love them. In my way.'

'And what I think the gravestone really shows,' he said, 'is how much they loved you.'

She was looking away from him, through the window towards the cemetery. He could see a single tear dropping down one side of her cheek. She wiped it away. There were no more.

That evening, after a day of memories and long silences, they stayed in and ate at his flat. He ordered pizzas and found himself watching as she licked traces of cheese and tomato off her small hands and fingers. She caught him in the act and had a *déjà vu*.

'You're staring at me like David used to,' she said with a certain prickliness.

He swivelled his eyes away. 'I can't not,' he said. 'You're too – what's the word? – alluring.' She shook her head and smiled. She thought of returning the compliment but decided not to.

They found themselves talking about their early lives, words flowing easily like crisscrossing streams. Childhood, family, youthful ambitions, music – she had noticed his piano, a pile of sheet music on the floor beside it – embarking on their careers. They allowed themselves to touch on past affairs.

'I'm not a monk,' he said.

She gave him a quick smile. 'And I'm not a nun.'

'But it never means anything.' She stayed silent – enough had been said. With relief, she suddenly remembered his unexplained remark in the car.

'So why did you really come back here?' she asked. He sighed and closed his eyes, his shoulders dropping. 'Only if you want to.'

'I'd like to tell you. Otherwise, like I couldn't fully know you, you can't fully know me.' He gathered himself to delve into past loss, whatever it might be. 'I was a young detective constable in south London,' he continued, 'around '93, '94'

'Just when David was in Dublin.'

'Yes, I guess so. To cut it short, I made the mistake of discovering that the detective chief inspector at the head of my small food chain was corrupt. I knew he was friendly with one of the kings of our manor, as they saw themselves. That could have been permissible if he was interested in turning him. But I saw him accepting cash in an envelope. A white one, as it happens. Couldn't have been anything else. I was naïve, I suppose, and came to realize it was common knowledge. But no one cared. Or maybe they were too sensible to care. Being the fool, I then made a second mistake. I confronted him and told him I was going to report him. Which I did. To the divisional commander.'

He stood up, walked over to the piano and looked at the framed photograph placed on it. He had lapsed into silence. 'Your wife?' Anne-Marie suggested.

Her prompt reawakened him. 'Yes. Alice. It wasn't just the *omertà* from top to bottom that was shocking. It was the denials, the vanishing of records, the finger pointed at me as the wrongdoer, not him. And then came the threats.' He turned to the photograph. 'Not me, her. Taps on car windows, knocks on doors, encounters in the dark. They even killed her cat. Pathetic, trying to be jumped-up Mafioso. Instead of fighting it, I gave in. Withdrew the allegation. I knew there'd be no career for me there. Alice would have always wanted to come back here, so we did it right then. At least they gave me a good reference for the force here. But I was a coward.'

'That's ridiculous,' Anne-Marie protested. 'You had to put her first.'

'Well, since she died,' he said, 'at least I've had nothing to lose. I'm beholden to none of them.' He shot her a look. 'Except now to you.'

'That's ridiculous too. You owe me nothing.'

'No, I do. Meeting you, coming to know you, however strange the circumstances, has changed me. The melancholia has lifted. I want to smile. And I don't want ever to be beaten again.'

She rose and joined him by the piano. 'Play me something.'

'I'd be embarrassed,' he said. 'I'm hardly Rubinstein.'

'You can't let that beat you.'

'You always have an answer, don't you?'

He took a slim book of music from the pile on the floor. She saw the cover: 'Liszt. Consolations'. She stood over his shoulder moving her eyes from his fingers to his ear and cheek, watching the fluttering of his eyelashes as he became lost in concentration. She knew little of classical piano and had not heard the piece but understood why he had chosen its flowing cadences to console for their loss.

As he came to the end, and his fingers gained pace climbing the octaves, he faltered but found a way through to the finish.

'That was lovely,' she said, 'really lovely.' She looked at her watch. 'Now I need to sleep.'

He had moved out of his bedroom to make way for her. On her pillow he had placed a miniature box of dark chocolates, remembering her preference from that night at her flat. When she saw it, she chuckled, embraced him and said a firm 'Goodnight.' The feel of her breasts against his chest electrified him.

At 4 a.m. she woke abruptly, assaulted by waking seconds of uncertainty about her whereabouts and the aftershock of the returning dream. But this time it ended differently. She finally broke and unleashed tears streamed down her cheeks. She heard a tap on the door – he crept in and sat on the bed beside her.

'I heard you,' he said. 'Do you want to talk?'

She stopped shaking and he handed her tissues to dry her eyes and face. 'Damn!' she whispered.

'No, tears are the release.'

She sat upright, legs crossed, looking at him but through him. 'It was the dream again. It began the same way, the blindfold in the car, flashes of light. Then, when I saw his profile, this time he turned all the way round. In his arms he was holding a newly born baby. I went over and crouched beside him. He handed me the baby.' She stopped to give her eyes another wipe. 'I took it and it flopped in my arms, cold to the touch. It was dead.'

'You poor girl.' He offered her his arms. She sank into them briefly, then eased herself away.

'I was carrying his child.'

'God above!'

'I'd confirmed it a few days before. I was three months in. There was no doubt. Finals were in two weeks, I had to decide straightaway. I phoned the number on the card Jimmy had left me and he gave me the money to sort it.'

'I am so sorry.'

'Abortion was illegal in Ireland. I didn't have time to travel. There was someone in Dublin who did it for students. I bled and bled. She damaged my uterus.'

'She?'

'Yes, she. At least she was willing to help. I could have had another operation to fix myself but I didn't care at the time.' She looked away from him. 'It's never been relevant since.'

'You haven't wanted children?'

'I made the decision then that I would never trust any man enough to have them with.'

'It's not too late to allow that now.'

She found no words of response. In another place, at another time – perhaps it would have needed another world – she could have imagined herself with this man. She turned away and curled up – a wounded animal. He watched her for a minute or two before raising himself from the bed. With a jerk she turned back and sat up.

'Jon, I'm so grateful to you.'

'How could I not have wanted to help you, to be with you?'

She stood up, her silk nightdress falling just below her thighs, and took both his hands. 'If you want to, we can make love.' Her voice was soft and clear.

'As a thank-you?' As soon as the words came out, he wished they hadn't.

'No. No, of course not.' Her protest was too instant and too strong.

'Of course I want to,' he said. 'But not now. Not like this.'

'I just wanted you to know.'

'I understand. Maybe when it's all over.'

She smiled. 'Yes. Maybe. When it's all over.'

She had booked her return flight for the early Sunday afternoon. They rose late, neither displaying any urge to attend church in this still-God-fearing island. It was more a shared relief than a celebration. Instead, they strolled under the vaulting oaks of the botanical gardens, the June sun streaming through the branches. There was no reference to what had been said in the night.

On the way to the airport, they discussed her parting conversation with Brooks in the garden. They listened to some of the tape and he felt a cold shudder.

'If you tell the whole story and expose them too, you risk everything. Your career, your reputation. Not to mention the enemies you'll make.'

'Do I have a choice?' she asked.

CHAPTER 36

Post-election, Monday, 5 June

'Good weekend, Minister?' Hinds asked, breezy as always. He had arrived, as usual, at 8.10 a.m. She wondered what he knew, whether they were still listening in and passing it all on. If so, he was giving nothing away.

In the private office Alan, Nikki and Dan looked up and smiled. 'Good morning, Minister,' they chirped in unison. They had seen how distracted she had been and wanted her tuned back to her work and to them.

'You're nice and supportive people,' she said, 'I want you to know that. But there's now a letter I must write and you must deliver without delay to Number 10.' She dictated:

'Dear Prime Minister. As you are aware, I have found myself caught in what has become clear to me is a conflict between promises I made to my constituents and what you and others deem to be the overriding interest of the state. I have decided that, as there seems no resolution in sight to this conflict, I should resign from your government. I will give a full account to the House of Commons but, in advance of that, I would like to express my gratitude for the honour you showed me in inviting me to join your administration and your personal kindness. Yours sincerely Anne-Marie Gallagher.'

'You can't do this, Minister,' protested Alan.

'Please, Minister, think again,' joined in Dan and Nikki.

'I have no choice,' she told them. How many more times would she have to use that word? 'I can't tell you why now. You'll find out soon enough.'

Rob McNeil lifted the phone as soon as the letter arrived in the Prime Minster's office.

'Don't do this, Anne-Marie,' he said.

'I decide what I do and don't do, Rob,' she replied. She needed to sound at her most implacable, to convince him, and anyone else, that their interventions would be shot down.

'But why?' he asked. 'It's not worth it. It will end your career. Ruin your life.'

'My life went a long while ago.'

'Do you honestly think David would approve of what you're doing?'

'It would be as little his business as yours. Though now that you ask, the answer from the man I knew at the end would have been yes.' She paused. 'Except that he might have dispensed a different form of justice.'

'Is there nothing I can say, or suggest, to persuade you to reconsider?' She could detect the defeat in his voice. Oddly, it provoked a tiny wavering. She crushed it.

'No, Rob.'

'Or Lionel himself.'

'Lionel least of all.'

'OK, I wish you well. But don't be surprised if Lionel delays in replying his acceptance. Indeed, don't bet on him accepting it just like that.'

She ordered Dalrymple to contact the office of the Speaker of the House of Commons to make time the next day for a personal statement. The reply came instantly. The Speaker, never unwilling to embarrass the Prime Minister, would give her fifteen minutes at noon.

Before she left the building, Steve Whalley popped his head around her door asking for a quick word.

'I'm sorry, Anne-Marie,' he said quietly as they stood close together in the corridor. 'Mind you, I always knew it would end in tears. I told Lionel that.' She had nothing to say to him. 'I've some advice for you, kid. Keep your mouth shut, leave the bodies undisturbed, you can come back. He'll give you a second chance.'

She smelt the menace as he turned on his heel and retreated down the corridor. She felt nothing. Nothing at all. No fear, no celebration. She smiled and returned to her office.

News of her letter of resignation broke in the early afternoon. Speculation for the reasons was limited, so genuine was the surprise. Carne was in the CID office with Billy Poots, writing up the results of their investigation into David Wallis's death.

'Did you know, boss?' asked Poots.

'I'd hoped she wouldn't,' replied Carne.

'Well, that's the end of her,' said the sergeant gruffly.

'Billy?'

'Yes, boss?'

'I need your help.'

They left the office a few minutes after the 3 p.m. news bulletin.

Carne said that, for the same reasons as before, he would use a travel agent to book the next available flight. He told Poots to dress casually, avoiding bright colours, and take a small bag with the bare essentials for one, maximum two, nights. They should have their police IDs but would be unarmed.

They disembarked at Gatwick shortly after 8 p.m., reached Victoria station by 9 p.m., and Vauxhall tube station twenty minutes later. They had made it before sunset. Carne was sure that nothing could happen before darkness came and thanked heavens that summer hours had allowed them to make it in time.

They walked along the river from the Tube station, reaching the apartment block as the sun set over west London. They found a bush to relieve themselves, knowing that, once they were inside, their vigil could last through the night. Carne could see from Poots's sceptical eyes that his sergeant thought he was being an idiot but, after all the times they had spent together, was happy to tolerate him. He hoped his foreboding was indeed far-fetched and the night would pass uneventfully. Even after everything he had learnt in the past few weeks, would they really dare to act again? In the law-abiding state he had believed he lived in, it should have been unthinkable, but some instinct told him not to risk leaving her unshielded.

At full darkness, they walked to the apartment block entrance and he punched the entry code, which he knew from previous visits. He was a familiar enough visitor for the commissionaire to do no more than raise his head, nod and say 'Good evening'. They entered the lift, pressed Floor 11, exited, and, Carne pointing silently, took up their positions in the two recesses he had earmarked in the curving corridor. He had decided not to tell her or warn her. He did not want to alarm her and she had work to do. Their preparations would be the same, whether or not she knew of their presence.

That night, working alone in her flat on her speech, Anne-Marie felt a curious combination of inner peace and righteous anger. As she had risked before, she would risk again.

Tapping lightly on the keyboard, she went over and over that last conversation with Brooks in his garden.

'You're determined to expose them, aren't you?' he had begun.

'Why are you asking?' she replied, walking alongside him beside a flowering violet hydrangea.

'And name names,' he continued, ignoring her question.

'Of course. Where I can.'

'Including me, dare I ask?'

'Can't see why not,' she said lightly.

He stopped, the flowers and branches overhanging, took a 360-degree sweep of the garden, and moved close to her.

'If you keep my name out of it,' he spoke softly, 'I will help. I'm just a minnow.'

'I'm listening.'

'I didn't tell you this. And you've never heard of me. Agree?'

'Agree.'

'I told you that the Hawk operation, both Phases One and Two, were discussed by me with a then rising star of my service.'

'You did.'

'That man was Edward Latimer, now Sir Edward.'

She felt her pulse racing. 'I see.'

'At that time he was MI6.'

'Go on.'

'Latimer also commissioned the dispatching of Kennedy shortly after he made contact with you in that phone call.'

'Who did it?' she demanded sharply.

'That I cannot tell you.'

She thought of her Achilles' heel. 'OK. Just tell me who put the newspaper cutting in his pocket.'

He stole another glance around. 'That was me. After they'd done it. I was trying to warn you not to pursue it.'

'Who else knows about that?'

'I've told you. No one. It was erased. It never happened. I kept that promise.'

'OK.' She made to turn and head back to the drive. He grabbed her arm.

'There's more.'

She halted. 'I'm still listening.'

'A senior government minister and also a shadow minister were informed of Hawk and agreed to it.'

'How do you know?'

'Doesn't matter how I know. It required approval.'

'Both phases?'

He stared at her angrily. 'They're not stupid. It didn't have to be spelt out.'

'So not documented.'

'It doesn't matter. Anything you say in Parliament is privileged. You don't need written proof.'

'I do know that.'

'Apologies.' He took a deep breath. 'The then government minister is long dead.' He gave her the name. 'The then shadow minister is very much alive and kicking.' He bestowed a beneficent smile on her.

'For fuck's sake, Jimmy.'

'Whalley.'

'Whalley!' Her calm, clear voice jumped an uncharacteristic octave.

'Yup,' replied Brooks with satisfied glee. 'And there's more. He's our Joe.'

'What the hell are you talking about?'

'Five recruited him in the mid-seventies.'

'What? Why would he do a thing like that?'

'Easy,' replied Brooks. 'Money. We were desperate for inform-ants from inside the unions. They were ruining the country in our view. We identified candidates we thought might be weak links. He was an ambitious young trade union official. Bit our hand off. Greed, sheer greed.'

'There must have been more than that.'

'We promised we'd do everything to support him up the greasy pole. But he had to play our game. That's why we got his approval for the 1994 operation. It's worked out well for him, hasn't it? We've been with him all the way to the very top of the Home Office. The man with ultimate responsibility for the very organiza-tion that recruited him. There's an irony for you.'

'What about the killing of Joseph? Did Whalley know?'

'What do you think, Maire?' he replied. 'You're the one with Parliamentary privilege, not me.' With that, he turned nimbly and led her back to her car.

Shortly before midnight, she took a break. As was her habit when summer finally arrived, she opened the door onto her small balcony overhanging the river below. She could just see the minute hand of Big Ben on its hesitant march to the Roman XII and hear the hushed sounds of the city floating above the water.

Her eye was caught by a man a hundred yards or so up the towpath who seemed to be watching her. He raised a hand, waved, then suddenly turned and walked off, disappearing into the shadows. She caught the unmistakable outline of a dark brimmer hat. For a moment it spooked her. Then she understood something and it made her smile. Her own Big Brother.

She returned to her desk, anticipating her final chauffeur-driven ride to the Gothic horror of the Palace of Westminster. On the way, she would cast her eye on the fawn ugliness of MI6 and its occupants, look up at its windows and cast her contempt.

She assembled her roll call of ignominy. The murder of Joseph Kennedy by the state. The same state that carried out disappearances and murders two decades before in the name of peace. Operation Hawk, the product of the same perverted minds. The final betrayal and discarding of the state's own agent, David Wallis. The personal responsibility of the politician and the official now in charge of the nation's Security Service.

And she would not stop there, ascending to the very top and a Prime Minister who, despite his much trumpeted belief in the sanctity of an individual's human rights, did not have the courage to inspect the poisoned entrails of the nation state he claimed to preside over.

She worked on into the small hours, so consumed by her story, so exhilarated by the devastation she was preparing that the hum of the city and the creaks and groans of the building she lived in became a wall of silence, and the only sound she heard was the time bomb clicking on her keyboard.

All she needed to do was light the fuse.

Carne and Poots waited. Though it was hardly an everyday occurrence, they were both trained in stake-outs. If necessary, they could go through the night. They knew that most stake-outs lead to nothing. It was a job, like any other. They were professionals.

They could faintly hear Big Ben strike the quarters of hours and the hours themselves: eleven, twelve, one, two, three . . . three-fifteen . . . three-thirty . . .

The lift stirred into motion. Alerted, Carne tensed. From his vantage point he could see the lift light rising fast through the floor numbers: two, five, eight, nine, ten, now slowing, eleven. Butterflies buzzing in his stomach, he knew it was going to stop. Eleven. It passed and stopped at twelve. He turned towards the stairs, listening out for descending footsteps. The only muffled sound was a door above clicking softly shut.

It was not in London but another part of the country that two hooded figures in skin-tight black clothing, knives in hand, approached a front door. One of them removed objects from his pouch. Standard lock picker's tools: thin metal rods, torque wrench. In a few seconds they were easing the door open and creeping silently into a hallway and up a flight of stairs. At the top they separated. Both were familiar with the geography of this house.

One headed into a bedroom, and made silently towards the shape of a single person lying on one side, softly snoring with a peaceful regularity. With extreme speed, the head was turned and the knife sliced across the sleeper's throat. The snoring ceased.

The second figure in black headed towards a room at the end of a corridor where the back of a broad-shouldered man, lit by a single Anglepoise lamp, was crouched over a computer. The figure tiptoed towards the man, grabbed his head from behind and brought the knife to his throat. The man reacted with surprising agility for someone of his age, screamed at his assailant and a brief struggle ensued before he was overpowered and his throat slit.

The two black-clad figures then used a safecracker key to ease open the safe in the study, removing cash, valuables and a stash of documents. They returned to the bedroom, took whatever jewellery they could find easily and quickly, descended the stairs, silently closed and locked the front door and retreated into the night.

What they did not know was that the man's safe was wired to a local police station. But it mattered little as, by the time the station's fatigued duty officer managed to mount a response, their black clothing had been disposed of and they were many miles away.

CHAPTER 37

Post-election, Tuesday, 6 June, 8.30 a.m.

She rises later than usual. It is an early summer day of particularly English brilliance, the sun already high, the sky an unbroken sheet of piercing blue, a light breeze fanning the city. Perhaps she will do some circuits round the park to calm her for the fifteen minutes delivering the speech that will define the rest of her life.

9.15 a.m. Her front doorbell rings. Not the entrance to the apartment block, but the door itself. She feels a tremor of fear, tells herself to catch on. Still in her bathrobe, she opens the door.

It is Carne – worn and unshaven. A smack more of surprise than alarm hits her.

'Jon! What are you doing here?' She regrets her sharpness. 'Sorry, I guess it's the nerves. Where have you been hiding?' She is half-joking.

'In the landing outside the lift,' he replies. He is not. 'I needed to know you were all right.'

'Sure you're not going paranoid?'

'I wish.'

She smiles curtly. 'Come in just for a minute. But then I've got to get ready.'

'OK, thanks.' He enters – there is an unfamiliar awkwardness between them. 'I feel a fool now.'

'Me too. I can't imagine there's ever been a maiden speech that's a resignation speech too.'

She smiles – the tension eases. But she does not offer him coffee or a chair and he knows her well enough to get the message. 'I'll leave you in peace,' he says.

'Thanks,' she replies softly. 'I could do with the time.' She walks over, pecks him on the cheek and sees his regret as he turns back to the door.

Just as he is closing it, he halts. 'I'll still be watching over you.'

'Just this day to get through,' she says.

10 a.m. After briskly showering, she switches on Sky News. She doesn't want to be caught on the hop by last-minute chicanery from Number 10. She sees a reporter standing in front of a house that looks vaguely familiar. A banner headline on the lower third of screen says 'WILTSHIRE DOUBLE MURDER'. She pays closer attention, gasps and turns up the volume.

The reporter describes how, in the small hours, local police are alerted by an alarm triggered by a safe inside a house in the village of Old Witham. Initially, as most such incidents in this peaceful part of the country are caused by faulty equipment, they phone the house telephone number but there is no answer. Within forty minutes a patrol arrives at the scene. The house is locked. After repeated knocking and ringing with no response or sign of activity inside, police officers force open a window and gain entrance. Upstairs they find the dead bodies of an elderly couple, James Beresford Brooks and his wife Dorothy. Locals say they have lived in the village for many years and are highly respected – Mr Brooks is a long-serving churchwarden and pillar of the community, Mrs Brooks a keen amateur gardener and organizer of Old Witham's entry into the annual competition for England's best-kept village.

The reporter speaks of a village in disbelief. Police sources say that this appalling tragedy has all the hallmarks of a burglary gone wrong. Cash and jewellery are missing both from the safe and from Mrs Brooks's jewellery box in the bedroom.

It is an extreme shock. She tries to work it out. She recalls the conversation in the garden and Jimmy's constant glancing around. They must have eavesdropped and recorded it – he was neither as smart nor as careful as he liked to boast. Or grew careless with age. They have punished with utter ruthlessness his threat to trigger the public washing of his organization's dirty linen, both past and present. Perhaps they view his killing as the execution of a soldier who has deserted to the enemy, his wife collateral damage. And it is risk-free: Jimmy is a faceless man from a dark world, and few will mourn him.

Her phone bleeps – a text from Carne telling her to look at the news and offering to be with her. It ends with a single word: 'Paranoia?'

She replies. 'I'm working it out. OK for now. Will get you a place in the gallery. A-M x'. She feels temporarily safe. They have cleaned their stables and no one has come for her.

Hinds insists on driving her to the House of Commons. 'You're still a minister, Minister,' he tells her, 'till you're not. And I'm still your driver. Till you've sacked me.' She feels reassured with him – realizing by now that he is in the know and, she believes, on her side.

11.30 a.m. The car arrives. The sun is directly above, casting a halo. On what? Her triumph? Her disaster? She has come too far to treat those two imposters just the same.

As they approach Vauxhall Cross, Hinds engages her in the mirror and speaks. 'Minister?'

'Yes, Keith.'

'I've been asked to pass on a message.'

'Oh?' She displays polite but only mild curiosity. 'Who from?'

'They just want me to say it's from people who wish you well and want to be your friends.'

'Ever more mysterious.' She tries to stay light and bright.

'Yes, Minister.' The car stops at lights and he turns round, intent etched in every crevice of his face. 'This is the message.' She watches him summon up exact words: '"There is no one now who can ever harm you. They have all gone. There is nothing known or to know. We will help and look after you without limit."'

'Who are these people, Keith?'

They cross Vauxhall Bridge. As the lights go green and they turn onto the Embankment towards Westminster, he swiftly jerks his head ninety degrees to the right to face MI6 across the water. The monstrous palace of games.

She makes no phone call, she sends no text. She has twelve minutes. She takes a detour via the Central Lobby and stops in front of the fourth plinth, the statue of Margaret Thatcher. She has a frisson of unfinished business.

Noon. The Speaker of the House of Commons reminds the crowded chamber that resignation speeches are traditionally heard in silence and without interruption. It is thirty-two days since that night of her election to Parliament and the words that sent shockwaves through Whitehall and the nation beyond.

She rises from her seat, not from the front benches but from the back, the same feather-light, enticing figure with the pure voice of flowing clarity. Her face fresh-looking, her eyes sparkling, she betrays no hint of the hardworking night and the weeks of menace and sorrow that have preceded it.

Lionel Buller, Steve Whalley and other senior ministers sit on the front bench with their backs to her. In the gallery above, her eye is caught by Rob McNeil. Alongside him, Alan Dalrymple and Jemima Sheffield, talking with a discomforting familiarity. Carne has been allocated a seat just behind. She glances at him, immobile in that apparent melancholy he can display.

She begins by asking the House's patience as she outlines the story that has led to her letter of resignation. She describes her parents, and her and her brother's working-class, Catholic childhoods, which ran in parallel with the Troubles that led her brother to join the IRA.

She tells of the entrance of David Vallely into her life, her relationship with him, his disappearance, the visit by a mysterious Englishman who helped her create a new life in England and advised her to change her name.

Then, after a pause during which her audience detects her steeling herself, she winds the clock forward two decades. 'Four days after the election – one day after my right honourable friend, the Prime Minister, invited me to join his government – these events in my past came back to haunt me. The body of the man I knew as David Vallely was discovered buried in an Irish field. It turned out that Vallely was an alias and his real name was David Wallis. He was a former British soldier, recruited by MI6 for undercover work. Wallis's mission was to inveigle his way into my life as a way of gaining intelligence on my brother, Martin McCartney, who was believed to be the leader of a faction inside the IRA determined to oppose a ceasefire and carry on their armed struggle. A few months later, around the time David Wallis went missing, my brother also disappeared from Ireland. I have had no contact with him since.'

The chamber is hushed, gripped, entranced, even, by the dramatic story revealed by this lightly framed woman. So far she has proceeded on script – now is the pivotal moment. She leafs through the typed words in the coming pages – the touchpaper for her bombshell. State murder both then and now. Steve Whalley, the new Home Secretary, Sir Edward Latimer, the new head of MI5, key conspirators complicit in the Hawk disappearances and the Kennedy killing. A cover-up rising all the way to the new Prime Minister himself. An image of the Brooks's dead bodies flashes in front of her.

The chamber is expectant. One, two, three seconds pass. Insider or outcast. Self-sacrifice or self-advancement. Too many seconds have passed – she must speak. One thought from two decades before leaps at her. It crowds out everything around her – the faces on the benches, the spectators in the gallery, the cameras and microphones, the lights. They have used me – I must now use them. She turns over the remaining pages and stares at the blank backs of paper. She thinks of those words of Martin 'Destiny . . . what you're born into . . . always there.' She decides.

'Over the past weeks I have come to realize that my failure to inform the Prime Minister of these circumstances in my past, however innocent a victim I was, and also to inform him that I changed my name at that time, however legal that was, might cause me to become an embarrassment to him. When I accepted his invitation to join his government, this seemed of little account. But our media will not allow the past to be past – and one may reasonably ask: why should they?

'It became apparent to me that my innocent involvement in these events of 1993 and 1994, and my response to them, could make me the subject of media scrutiny that would stand in the way of the vital work this administration needs to do. I want to make two things clear. Firstly, I bear no ill will towards our intelligence services for the operation they mounted which involved me. It was both understandable and, in my view, legitimate at that time. Secondly, it is for the reason I have stated, and that reason only, that I tendered my right honourable friend my resignation.'

She looks up at the gallery. Rob McNeil colours with astonishment. Alan Dalrymple and Jemima Sheffield exchange a brief smile. Behind them, a glimpse of Carne.

Her words are received initially in silence, followed by growls of 'hear, hear'. Lionel Buller catches the Speaker's eye and rises to his feet. 'We have just heard,' begins the Prime Minister, 'a remarkable and courageous speech. I am sure that the whole House and the whole country beyond will, like me, be overwhelmed with admiration for my honourable friend's courage, honesty and the unselfish offer she has made to me.'

The cries of 'hear hear' grow louder and order papers are waved. Buller continues. 'My honourable friend is aware that I have not yet replied to her letter. Now that I understand more fully her underlying reasons, I would like to assure her that her resignation is not necessary and that I will not accept it. I very much hope that, after the most generous reception by this House, she will now feel able to withdraw it and continue her important work in this government.'

Anne-Marie rises again to her feet and says simply, 'I am deeply grateful to the Prime Minister.' Buller waves her towards him and she descends five rows to the front bench. As she passes Steve Whalley, she pauses and, with a smile, whispers, 'I know, Steve. I know who you are.' She enjoys his flicker of fear. The Prime

Minister motions her to sit beside him as the House resumes its business.

Her political career is secured, the shadows gone, the ghosts banished. She thinks of David and Joseph. Both dead. Her brother Martin, as good as dead. And now Brooks, too. 'Uncle Jimmy Vallely'. And Dorothy. Perhaps she also knew too much. Hinds's words clamour in her ears. 'There is no one left who can harm you. No one who knows. They've all gone.'

But there is one person left who does know. Who knows everything – because she told him everything. The man who put his trust in her and helped her wrest back her life and overcome her past. The last man standing, dead or alive. She looks up at the gallery and sees him gazing blankly ahead. She catches his eye.

Carne slowly shakes his head, not in accusation but in bewilderment. Something must have happened. She seemed so set on her course. He had come to believe there might truly be a future – the two of them standing together against the demons the speech she had intended would unleash. A togetherness beyond anything they had achieved so far. But she's changed the script. Why? Into whose hands has she committed herself? Has she been offered something impossible to resist? Is she a captive? But then he understands he never came close to the recesses of her mind and heart. Or soul – if she has one. She will be forever opaque – that complexity that can never be untangled.

Is he casualty, victim or fool? Or all three combined? Not that it matters now. He breathes hard, tries to bite on feeling or regret. Can it really be over? The end of the story? Must it be? He is afraid for her. In that fear lies his only solace: that she will need him again. He turns to leave the gallery. For himself, he is unafraid because, without her, what is there to live for?

She casts a look of panic at his disappearing back. A premonition seizes her. Has she now condemned this man to death too? This good man. A man she had even begun to feel for – feelings she had thought lost for ever. Has she used him – just as David used her? Has she betrayed him? Has she deprived herself of a renewed life?

It is too late. She has made her choice.

She looks out over the pink, grinning faces sweating under the chamber's lights, their bovine cheering, their outdated waving of order papers. She thinks again of those she knew who are dead or disappeared.

The noise in the chamber calms and its occupants subside onto its benches. She flicks a glance at the Prime Minister beside her and the pillars of his government beyond. They have no inkling that she has found the way to keep her options open. She will await her moment. To embrace them can be to subvert them.

Yes. Atonement is needed. She will ensure it comes. And she will decide how.

She remembers her brother's words of long ago: 'You're the ballot, not the bullet.' It is no longer true. She is both. She is a woman of state.

Acknowledgements

My thanks to those whose expertise, insight, support, inspiration and calm surroundings made such a difference; Julian Alexander, Andrew Allberry, Sue Carney of Ethos Forensics, Hugh Dent, Gavin Esler, Joanna Frank, Lucy Gilmour, Paul Greengrass, Val Hudson, Brian Lapping, Lucinda McNeile, Lisa Milton, Sophie Nelson, Juliet and Charles Nicholson, Babs Oduwole, Ana and Graham Ross, Dominic Streatfeild, Robert Young and the friends in Ireland I never forget.

ONE PLACE. MANY STORIES

Bold, innovative and
empowering publishing.

FOLLOW US ON:

@HQStories